UNCERTAIN DESIRES

Rennie raised her face toward Jarret's, rubbing against him as she moved. Her lips grazed his mouth.

She had his complete attention now. His eyes opened wide then closed again, surrendering as her mouth moved over his. His hands cupped either side of her face and stilled her. His voice was husky, whiskey laid over velvet. "Is this what you really want?"

She didn't know what she wanted, but she understood that he did. She was willing to let him teach her. "It must be," she said. "I ache when I'm not touching you."

His resolve collapsed with her softly spoken admission. "Do it, then," he whispered against her mouth. "Touch me."

Her mouth moved over his, nibbling at his lower lip, sweeping her tongue on the sensitive underside of his upper. He tried to catch her lip in his teeth, but she dodged him, spreading hungry, tormenting kisses across his brow and temples.

Jarret's hand closed around her wrist, stopping her as her fingers edged just below his jeans. He hauled her upward so that he could have her mouth again. She gave it to him obligingly, engaging his tongue and lips in sweet battle.

Jarret buried his face in her neck. "Do you want me to stop?" he asked.

He felt, rather than heard, her denial.

Books by Jo Goodman

Published by Zebra Books

JO GOODMAN

ROGUE'S MISTRESS

ZEBRA BOOKS
KENSINGTON PUBLISHING CORP.
http://www.kensingtonbooks.com

ZEBRA BOOKS are published by

Kensington Publishing Corp.
850 Third Avenue
New York, NY 10022

All Kensington titles, imprints and distributed lines are available at special quantity discounts for bulk purchases for sales
promotion, premiums, fund-raising, educational or institutional
use.

Special book excerpts or customized printings can also be created to fit specific needs. For details, write or phone the office of the Kensington Special Sales Manager: Kensington
Publishing Corp., 850 Third Avenue, New York, NY 10022.
Attn. Special Sales Department. Phone: 1-800-221-2647.

Zebra and the Z logo Reg. U.S. Pat. & TM Off.

First Printing: 1993
10   9   8   7   6   5   4

Printed in the United States of America

For Lisa, Renee, Aimee, Gwen, Tom, Clarence, Georgie, Karen, and Karen. They can all bear witness to the potential danger of lemon balls and the effectiveness of the Heimlich Maneuver.

Prologue

Most days Jarret Sullivan appreciated the happy uncertainties of life. This particular afternoon was showing a decided bent for caprice. How else could his presence in Manhattan, let alone in the Worth Building, be explained? He was about to enter the inner sanctum of one of the most powerful men in the country. He, Jarret Sullivan, son of an Irish laborer and a Kansas City schoolteacher, was only a door away from meeting John MacKenzie Worth.

"Not the usual riffraff," he said under his breath.

"What?" Ethan Stone asked, his voice impatient.

"Nothing." Jarret was sensitive to his friend's mood. He couldn't recall a time when he'd seen Ethan coiled so tightly. Taking off his hat, Jarret slapped it against his thigh. Dust motes, gathered on the long rail journey from St. Louis to New York, scattered in the air and collected in a pencil-thin sunbeam. Jarret slipped the black felt hat back on his head and raised the brim a notch with his forefinger. His boots tapped lightly on the polished wooden floors as he and Ethan crossed the hallway. Dim gaslights flickered in their wake. Jarret's hand drifted absently along the outside of his coat to the gun at his hip.

"You won't be needing that," Ethan said, catching sight

7

of Jarret's movement out of the corner of his eye. "There's not going to be any violence."

"So you say." Still, he let his hand fall. Jarret knew Ethan was coming to Jay Mac Worth with the best of intentions; he didn't know if that carried weight with Jay Mac. Jarret didn't think much of Ethan's strategy. Facing down the father of the woman he had abducted and seduced, well, it wasn't a plan that recommended itself to Jarret. He had counseled Ethan against it and gotten nowhere. In the end the best Jarret could do was volunteer to cover his friend's back. Ethan said he wasn't anticipating violence, but Jarret realized John MacKenzie Worth had his own reputation to consider. He could very well think it a father's prerogative to shoot the U.S. marshal who had put his daughter, indeed, his entire family, in life-threatening danger.

Jarret didn't envy Jay Mac's position either. He knew some would say the railroad tycoon deserved whatever he got, and they would say it was because Jay Mac had trampled the Lord's commandments most of his life. Jarret thought it was because the man had five daughters. Where was the peace of mind in that?

Ethan was concerned with only one daughter: Mary Michael. The safety of the other four was Jarret's job. He began clicking off on his fingers. "Mary Francis. Mary Margaret. Mary Schyler. Mary . . . Mary . . ."

"Renee," Ethan said. "Mary Renee. Michael says she's called Rennie."

"Rennie," Jarret repeated. He thought about it a moment, then shrugged. "I'll just holler Mary when I want one, and they'll all come running."

One corner of Ethan's mouth lifted in a tautly amused grin. "If you think any one of them will come, let alone on a run, well, ah hell, Jarret, find out for yourself—the way I did."

Jarret laughed lowly. The sun lines at the corners of his eyes deepened. His smile faded only as he felt Ethan's tension return. He looked away from Ethan and noticed for the first time where they were.

The letters on the frosted glass were glossy black and outlined in gold. John MacKenzie Worth. That was all. Nowhere did it say Owner, Northeast Rail Lines. It would have been a waste of black paint and gold leaf. Just about everyone in the country knew of Jay Mac. His rails moved a nation. Jarret Sullivan found himself uncomfortably impressed. Damn, he thought, what had his friendship with Ethan Stone brought him to now?

Ethan's hand twisted the glass door knob, and they filed in.

Jay Mac's secretary looked up. The jerk of his head was as stiff as his blackened mustache. "How can I help you . . . gentlemen?"

Jarret's smile returned, this time derisively. It was clear the secretary didn't think much of their wrinkled dusters and sweat-banded hats. Officious little toady. He let Ethan handle him. He also let the toady get a glimpse of his Remington.

John MacKenzie Worth swiveled in his large leather armchair as the door to his office opened. The deep burgundy leather held the aroma of cigar smoke. It was the way he liked it, even before he'd given them up seven months earlier. He'd bargained with God for the safe return of his daughter Mary Michael, and God had been kind.

"Your two o'clock appointment is here," Wilson said. "He's brought someone with him."

"Show them in, Wilson." He looked beyond the secretary's shoulder and saw two men approaching the office's threshold. "Never mind. They've found their own way." He stood up, came around his desk, and dismissed Wilson while holding out a hand to his visitors.

They both looked bone weary, stiff from days and nights of train travel to which neither was accustomed. They did

9

not have the appearance of men who tolerated confinement, much less enjoyed it.

Jarret stood back while Jay Mac extended his hand to Ethan. In the short time it had taken them to cross the office, Jarret had been aware of the rail man's regard. He had studied them long and hard, with the impassive expression that Jarret relished facing across a poker table.

Jay Mac was several inches shorter than Ethan, but it was something Jarret noticed only as Worth was turning away. The father of all those Marys had an aura of authority and power that lent him a stature that didn't physically exist. He had a thick head of dark blond hair, turning to ash at the temples. No surprise there, Jarret thought. All those daughters. The miracle was that he wasn't completely gray. Or bald.

Jarret found himself grinning again. It drew Jay Mac's attention.

"This is Jarret Sullivan," Ethan said as Worth's implacable green eyes drifted to the man at his side. "I've asked him to help. We go back a few years together, since the Express days."

Now Jarret felt the force of Jay Mac's stare. What was the man thinking? Was he being measured against Ethan or against any man? Listen, he wanted to say, I've got no designs on any of your daughters. None. Instead, he remained silent and let Jay Mac size him up.

Jarret Sullivan was just over six feet, putting him on a plane with Ethan. There was only a superficial resemblance between the two men. Jarret was slightly broader in the shoulders, but leaner overall. Long-limbed, he held himself loosely, so that he appeared lithe rather than powerful. There was a sense of calm surrounding him, a lazy watchfulness that made him seem more relaxed than he actually was. A faint lift of one corner of his mouth signaled Jarret's sometimes cynical, sometimes genuine, amusement of what went on around him. He was never as removed from events as his remote, dark blue eyes seemed to indicate.

The deep sapphire eyes were a startling feature in a face that was tanned and weathered by the sun. The sharply cut jaw and patrician nose gave him the arrogant air of a blue-blood. The beard stubble on his chin and jaw made him look dangerous. His hair was dark blond, too long at the nape for New York fashion, but somehow suited to him.

"Sullivan?" asked Jay Mac, finishing his assessment. "That's an Irish name, isn't it?"

Jarret had little patience for Jay Mac's scrutiny, but in deference to Ethan he made an attempt to answer politely. He couldn't resist a credible Irish brogue. "County Wexford on my da's side."

Jay Mac chuckled. He indicated the chairs in front of his desk and asked Ethan and Jarret to be seated. He stood, leaning back on the edge of his desk, and lifted the black lacquered box of cigars beside him. Raising the lid, he offered them to his guests. "I gave them up myself," he said. "But I wouldn't mind smelling one burning. I don't think that would be going back on my promise."

Jarret accepted one after Ethan passed. He heard his friend ask, "Promise?"

Jay Mac closed the lid, clipped and lit Jarret's cigar before he answered. "I made a bargain to stop smoking if God returned my daughter safely." He vicariously enjoyed Jarret's second-hand smoke. After a moment he straightened, sighed, and went around the desk to his chair. He sat down and gave Ethan Stone his full attention. "I got your telegram five days ago," he said. "It seemed to me God was going back on His word. I never said as much to Moira or Mary Francis. They'd be sorely disappointed to hear me talk that way, but it's what I've been thinking."

To a casual observer Jarret seemed removed from the conversation, even uninterested, intent perhaps on nothing more than the flavor and aroma of his cigar. The casual observer would have been wrong. Jarret's hearing was fixed on

11

the names he had just heard, filing the information away. Mary Francis was Jay Mac's oldest daughter, a nun with the Little Sisters of the Poor in Queens. Moira Dennehy was Worth's mistress and, according to Ethan, had been for more than twenty-five years. Moira was also the mother of Jay Mac's five daughters. Five *illegitimate* daughters all named Mary. Jarret managed to temper his amusement by exhaling a blue-gray ring of smoke.

"Tell me, Mr. Stone," Jay Mac was saying, "how much danger is my daughter really in?"

Jarret felt Ethan's glance, but he gave it no attention. He remained comfortably stretched in his chair, his long legs crossed at the ankles, and continued to give every evidence that he was enjoying his cigar. Ethan, he knew, couldn't affect such calm. There was tension in every line of his body.

"If I didn't think that Houston and Detra would come looking for her, I wouldn't have wired you or come here myself," he said. "She will need protection. I don't believe for a minute that Houston and Dee will slip away quietly and live the rest of their lives in anonymity. If you'd seen the look Houston gave your daughter as he was being sentenced, you wouldn't believe it either."

Jarret's hooded glance became still and watchful as Jay Mac picked up a letter opener and tapped the flat of it lightly against his palm. Jarret recognized the agitation and anger in the gesture. An irate father might just plunge it into the heart of the man who hurt his daughter. Ethan's tin star wasn't much protection. Jay Mac probably bought federal marshals the way other men bought a shirt.

"I didn't want her testifying at their trials," he said sharply. "That should have been your job alone."

"She would have been subpoenaed," Ethan told him. "She was a witness to almost everything."

"I have you to thank for that, don't I?" He slapped the letter opener a little harder against his skin. "And if you don't think I could have kept her from testifying, you're seriously underestimating my influence."

"You couldn't have bought me, Mr. Worth."

Jarret had to give his friend credit for standing up to Jay Mac. The fact that Worth was right didn't make it easy for Ethan. Mary Michael had witnessed robbery and murder and ended up in the thick of everything because of Ethan Stone.

"I don't want your money," Ethan said.

Jarret wondered if he could have said that. He relaxed slightly as John MacKenzie Worth backed down and looked away. The letter opener was tossed on the desk. It skittered across the surface and spun like a compass needle before it fell still.

"I was just blowing off steam," he said.

Ethan nodded once, accepting the near-apology. "You never tried any bribery at all, did you?"

"My daughter knows me too well. She warned me not to do it. Warned me, not asked me. Michael would cut off her right hand before she asked me to do anything for her. She insisted on testifying; said it was her privilege and her right. Stopping her would have meant losing her, Mr. Stone, and that's the one thing I won't have. Michael and I don't always see things the same, but God knows, I love her."

Jarret glanced at Ethan and knew Ethan felt the full weight of those words, the entire responsibility. Ethan Stone had crossed half a country to put things right with Mary Michael. Jarret Sullivan had come for the money.

Picking up an ashtray, Jarret knocked a little ash off the glowing tip of his cigar. He began to explain the situation to Jay Mac, since Ethan's hurried telegram had been short on details. "Detra Kelly had the help of a guard at the woman's prison. Apparently she seduced him." His lazy grin deepened. "I don't think it hurt that she also promised a sizable share of the robbery money that's never been recovered."

"I didn't hear about her escape until she aided Houston in

13

his," Ethan said. "That was ten days ago. Michael testified against other members of the gang, but they were either injured or killed in their escape attempt. Houston himself may be wounded, but his lover managed to get him away. They've eluded every search party sent after them."

"Ethan and I split from the main posse and tracked them as far as St. Louis," Jarret said. "I lost them then. The trail went cold." The knowledge still rankled. He was good at what he did, but he still had to prove it to Dee and Houston. Having one or both in hand before he left New York was the only way to do it.

"Houston and Dee could already be in the city," Ethan said, "and I doubt we'll find them first. Have you acted on the suggestions in the telegram?"

"Moved my family out?" Jay Mac asked. Incredulity was clear in the expression. "Mr. Stone, I couldn't have moved Moira and my daughters out of New York this week with anything less than the 7th cavalry." He put on his spectacles, took his watch out of his pocket, and glanced at the time. "Ninety minutes from now my daughter is getting married. They've been planning and carrying on for months. The news of Nate Houston's escape made them pause for all of a second. They went right back to choosing flowers for the church and arguing about the menu for the reception. Took their cue from Michael, they did, and when she wasn't concerned, they weren't concerned. Or at least pretended not to be."

Jarret watched Ethan out of the corner of his eye. His friend was pale. At the mention of the wedding it seemed that the blood drained from his face. When Jay Mac offered them both a drink Ethan accepted, then knocked it back as if it were water. Jarret sipped his own, his amusement rooted in the fact that Ethan was so deeply in love that he wasn't thinking clearly. Jarret's attention shifted to John MacKenzie Worth. The old codger was crafty. "Ethan told me you have five daughters," he said. "Now which one would it be that's tying the knot?"

Jay Mac's level gaze slipped away from Ethan and fell innocently on Jarret. "Didn't I say? I thought I mentioned it was Mary Renee."

Ethan's immediate relief was quickly overshadowed by anger at being manipulated. "You wanted me to think it was Michael."

Jay Mac shrugged, putting away the liquor. He carried his own glass back to his desk and sat on the edge. "I needed to know what you felt for my daughter," he said without apology. He glanced at Jarret. "I think he loves her. What do you think?"

"The very same, sir." Jarret's voice was polite and grave. He felt Ethan's glare, and he gave it no weight. "Is Michael expecting us?"

"I didn't tell her," Jay Mac said. "I was afraid the news would send her packing."

Jarret doubted Ethan was pleased by that news. It couldn't have been heartening to know that Michael would do anything to avoid Ethan, yet had no sensible fear of the criminals who were after her.

"Jarret and I discussed a plan on the way here," Ethan said. "We think Michael should go on with her routine, apparently just as she has. That will draw out Houston and Dee. In deference to the rest of your family's safety, however, I think they should leave the city for a while."

Jay Mac was silent. He took another sip of his drink. "I can't say that I like the idea of Michael being used as felon bait, and that's exactly what you're both proposing. On the other hand, I don't have any hope of convincing her to leave her job at the *Chronicle* for even a day, let alone the weeks or months that it might take you to flush out Houston. Mary Francis will be quite safe at the convent. Maggie and Skye and their mother will go to my summer home in the Hudson Valley."

Jarret had been mentally clicking off the girls and their whereabouts. Someone was unaccounted for.

Ethan said, "And Rennie will be honeymooning with her new husband."

Rennie, Jarret thought. Why did he have so much trouble remembering Rennie? And why was Jay Mac hesitating in confirming Ethan's assumption?

"Rennie poses something of a problem," Jay Mac said carefully. "I'm not so sure she'll agree to leave the city once she finds out you're here."

Jarret dismissed the notion. A wreath of blue-gray smoke hovered in the air in front of him. He exhaled, blowing it away. "Surely her husband will have some say in that." It was a statement, not a question.

"Hollis Banks?" Jay Mac's snort was clearly derisive. "He wouldn't have the nerve to gainsay Rennie. He'll do what she says."

Ethan said it, but Jarret was thinking it. "Don't you have any daughters who do what they're told?"

"Not a one." Although he threw up his hands, he didn't sound especially disappointed. "Moira's raised them with a mind of their own, I'm afraid."

Jarret doubted that was entirely truthful. He suspected Jay Mac's influence. "What's to be done, then?"

Jay Mac finished his drink. "I was rather hoping this business with Houston would have a silver lining. I thought it might put Rennie's wedding on hold." He pushed his spectacles up the bridge of his nose and looked at his watch again. "Just a little over an hour now. I wish to God she weren't marrying that milksop."

Jarret grinned, making an obvious show of enjoying his cigar. "I take it you'd strike another bargain with God if you had a vice to give up."

Jay Mac blinked at the younger man's impudence. Then he gave a short bark of laughter. "You're exactly right, Mr. Sullivan, exactly right."

Ethan stood. Rennie's wedding wasn't his problem. "Jarret will stay with Michael's mother and sisters in the valley.

If you're quite certain·Mary Francis will be safe, there's no need for additional protection there. If you don't trust Rennie's future husband to do right by her, then I suggest you hire someone. I'll be with Michael."

Jarret put his shot glass on the edge of the desk and followed Ethan's lead. "I suppose we'll meet them all at the wedding, then. We're not really dressed for it though." Neither was Jay Mac, he realized. "Should we follow you there?"

Dead silence followed Jarret's question. Jarret only understood he had inadvertently broached a subject that was meant to be avoided.

Jay Mac went around his desk, drew out a paper and pen from the middle drawer and quickly wrote out directions. The rapid movement of his hand across the page made the slight trembling of his fingers almost invisible. When he spoke his voice was carefully modulated. Only the dark green eyes hinted at the intensity of his pain. "I won't be attending the wedding," he said. "Or giving Rennie away. One of the prices a father pays for siring bastard daughters, I'm afraid." His smile was filled with self-mockery. "Perhaps that's the silver lining. I don't have to see her make the worst mistake of her life."

He blew on the paper, drying the ink, folded it into quarters, and passed it across to Ethan. "The wedding's at St. Gregory's here in Manhattan. I'm leaving with Moira and the girls in the morning for the summer house. I've hired protection of my own. We won't be needing Mr. Sullivan."

Jarret nodded. It suited him anyway. He wanted to be in the city when Houston and Dee showed themselves. "Then I'll stay close to you, Ethan."

Jay Mac shook his head. "I'd feel a lot better if you stayed close to Rennie."

All vestige of amusement faded from Jarret's face. He crushed his cigar in the ashtray. "On her honeymoon?"

17

"Since I doubt she'll agree to leave now, she'll need as much protection as Michael."

Jarret and Ethan spoke at the same time. "Why?"

Jay Mac's head tilted to one side, and his sandy brows drew together. His forehead was ridged, his expression puzzled. "You really don't know, do you? Michael never told you about Rennie."

Jarret looked at Ethan, waiting for his reply. What the hell was going on?

"I'm not certain what you mean," Ethan said.

This time when Jay Mac Worth threw up his hands he was clearly frustrated. "That's just like her," he said, more to himself than his guests. "And Rennie would have done the same thing. They've been playing these sort of games with people since they were children. One would think that now, at twenty-four, they wouldn't take so much delight in it, but obviously some things never change. God only knows when she would have thought to tell you."

"Tell me what?" Ethan asked, impatient.

"Tell him what?" Jarret asked, intrigued.

"Michael and Rennie . . . they're identical twins."

Ethan's mouth had opened a fraction. Now it snapped shut.

Jarret whistled softly. "Twins. Imagine that." His black brows rose a little as the full implication set in. "Houston and Dee might stumble on the wrong sister."

Jay Mac's gaze shifted from one man to the other. "Precisely. And that fool Hollis Banks can't protect her. I'm not sure anyone can"—he looked significantly at Jarret now—"if Rennie decides to draw attention to herself to save Michael. And that, gentlemen, is just the sort of maggot Rennie's gotten into her head." He pushed away from his desk and stood. He took off his spectacles, folded them, and put them in his breast pocket. "I'd be willing to pay ten thousand dollars to stop that wedding."

"I don't want your money, Mr. Worth," Ethan repeated.

He held out his hand to Jay Mac, shook it, and turned to go.

Jarret Sullivan followed suit, but on the point of leaving he turned back to Jay Mac. There was the suggestion of dry amusement in the line of his mouth. "About that ten thousand dollars," he said. "I could be very interested."

Chapter One

The bride was not blushing. The hint of color in her cheeks was the result of sheer exasperation. Her dark emerald eyes were bright, not with anticipation, but with impatience. Her full mouth was set in a flat line that was both serious and forbidding. Narrow shoulders were braced stiffly, her slender figure at attention. Even her wildly curling hair had been tamed, the vibrant auburn color smoothed over her scalp and twisted into plaits at the back of her head. She had the look of a woman prepared to do battle, not walk down the aisle.

Everyone was hovering. Rennie closed her eyes and gratefully accepted the peace darkness momentarily afforded. She tried to think of something other than the vows she would soon be exchanging. It was impossible. She could only imagine herself in the main chapel, in front of dozens of guests, saying the words the priest prompted.

And she would say them, she thought. There was no backing out, even if she wanted to. She didn't want to. Hollis Banks was the perfect life partner. Partner. Not husband. Her choice of words did not surprise her. Her marriage was a business arrangement, and she could admit it to herself, though pride and good sense kept her from admitting it to anyone else.

Rennie opened her eyes. They were still hovering. This time it made her smile.

Skye Dennehy was on her knees in front of her sister, making last minute adjustments to the hem of Rennie's gown. Her small oval face was flushed, and tendrils of flame red hair were curling away from the smooth chignon at the back of her head. She mumbled around a mouthful of pins, and no one paid her the least attention.

Maggie fiddled with the bouquet, arranging and rearranging the orange blossoms to display them to their best advantage. Her small, delicate features were taut, her mouth screwed comically to one side as she concentrated on her work.

Mary Francis, her beautiful face framed in the cornet of her habit, fussed with Rennie's hair, tucking hairpins back in place and adjusting the veil. She hummed lightly while she worked, carrying the same tune the organist played in the main chapel, and inadvertently reminding everyone there wasn't much time left.

The mother of the bride smoothed the satin sleeves of Rennie's gown. Moira's hands shook slightly as she worked, her brow creased with concern. Her dark red hair was covered by a lace scarf. From time to time she glanced worriedly at Rennie.

"A wake is more fun than this," Michael said. She was on her knees beside Skye, threading a needle.

"Michael," her mother admonished.

"Well, it is," she said, unrepentant. She gave the needle and thread to Skye and carefully plucked the pins from her sister's mouth. "Looking at all of us, one would think the Irish only know how to have fun at funerals. All this last minute fussing because Rennie tripped on the steps and ripped out her hem, soiled her gown, and tossed the bouquet before she was supposed to. If I were a bit more superstitious, I'd say this wedding wasn't meant to happen."

Rennie glanced down at her sister, her mouth twisting in

disgust. "I'll thank you to keep those kind of thoughts to yourself. I know you mean well, but I've heard all I care to hear from you on the subject of my marriage to Hollis Banks."

Now that Skye's mouth was free of pins, she took up Michael's cause. Her young face was earnest. "It's not that we don't like Hollis. Well, it's not exactly that we like him either."

"Schyler," Moira said, shaking her head in despair. Where had her daughters learned to speak their mind so bluntly? It was Jay Mac's influence, she thought, and he wasn't here to see what he had wrought. "She didn't mean it quite that way, Rennie."

"Yes, I did," said Skye. "Hollis is all right, I suppose, but he's not the sort of man I imagined you'd marry." Rennie was strong-minded, independent, and plain-speaking. Skye doubted Hollis appreciated any of those qualities. He probably suffered them.

Rennie snorted delicately. "I can only guess at what you conjured in that head of yours. Hollis suits me just fine. He's kind and gentle and smart and—"

"He's after your money," Mary Francis said with serene confidence.

Moira gasped at her eldest daughter's pronouncement.

"Actually," Maggie said, shaking the bouquet at Rennie, "he's after Jay Mac's money and thinks you're just the Dennehy who can get it for him. Skye's too young, I'm not pretty enough, Mary Francis is a nun, and Michael's seven months pregnant."

Moira fanned herself. She wished she were a woman given to fainting spells because she would have liked to have had one right then. As it was, her daughters completely ignored her.

"This is a fine time to be telling me what you think," Rennie snapped.

Michael stabbed the collected pins into the pincushion.

"We've been telling you all along. You didn't want to hear."

"You should be supporting me now. You should be happy for me, wishing me well." Rennie started to shake everyone off, feeling as if she were being pulled in five different directions. She was only peripherally aware that she had caused them to back away, shame-faced and sorry for their lack of sensitivity. In spite of the activity all around her, something else had caught Rennie's attention.

Two men stood on the threshold of the side chapel, hat in hand, looking distinctly uncomfortable in their dust-covered and travel-wrinkled clothes. Their gunbelts were jarringly out of place. One of the men shifted his weight from one foot to the other, hesitant, as if he were gathering courage. The other leaned negligently against the door frame, amused and watchful.

Rennie's back straightened. She raised her chin as her eyes darted from one man to the other. Without even realizing it she took a protective step toward Michael. "Is there something we can do for you?" she asked.

Her voice was cool, Jarret thought, and sharp, like the stinging spray of white water. There was an aggressive tilt to her chin he did not care for and a feral look in her eye that could only bode trouble. Jarret's smile hinted at deeper amusement. Poor Hollis Banks. Jarret began to believe that the intended groom would be grateful for his interference.

The stranger's ill-concealed humor was unwelcome and annoying. Rennie's gaze shifted to the other man and watched as his own eyes wandered past her mother's worried countenance, past Mary's questioning gaze, past Maggie's nervous fingers plucking the bouquet, past young Skye's fiery hair, and finally came to rest on Michael's profile. In that moment Rennie knew who he was.

"My name's Ethan Stone," he said quietly. "I've come for Michael."

Like hell, Rennie thought. Gathering the folds of her

24

white satin gown to one side, she squeezed through the circle of her family and approached Ethan, not sparing a glance for the man at his side. She stopped just in front of him and addressed him in a voice that was still bitter, cold, and remote. "Marshal Stone?" she asked. "The man who abducted my sister?"

Jarret's eyes were on Rennie. Everyone else was looking at Ethan. "Yes," Ethan said, standing his ground. "The man who abducted your sister."

Rennie's response was delivered without hesitation. Her hand swung in a wide arc. A mere inch from Ethan's face the sweep of her hand was halted. Not by Ethan, but by Jarret. He pulled her to one side, twisted her arms behind her back, and yanked her flush against his body. She was stunned into absolute stillness. So was everyone else.

For all of five seconds.

Michael put her hand on Schyler's forearm and raised herself up, turning fully in Ethan's direction. Hands on her hips, the material of her pale blue overblouse was stretched taut across her belly. There was no ignoring the advanced state of her pregnancy. Rennie knew her twin felt cornered as Ethan's eyes dropped from Michael's face to her abdomen. Michael came out fighting, stiffening her shoulders and raising her chin as Rennie had done earlier.

Michael faced Ethan squarely. "Tell that man to put my sister down."

Jarret didn't wait for Ethan's directive. Belatedly he realized that he was actually dangling Rennie a few inches off the floor. "Name's Jarret Sullivan, Miss Dennehy," he said politely. He lowered Rennie slowly but didn't let her go. Stepping farther into the room, he kicked the door closed behind him. Over the top of Rennie's head his dark blue eyes rested on Michael's abdomen. He glanced at Ethan. His friend had been struck dumb.

"He didn't know," Jarret said under his breath.

Rennie's whisper was harsh. "Of course he didn't know."

25

She tried to pull out of Jarret's grasp, but he merely held her tighter.

Mary Francis found a chair for her mother. Moira looked as if she might faint after all. Mary slipped off the white silk Chinese fan that dangled from her mother's wrist and waved it in front of Moira. She watched Ethan consideringly, gauging his reaction to Michael's pregnancy. Mary had wanted Michael to inform Ethan of her condition months ago, and Michael had refused. Ethan didn't love her, she said. Mary Francis only thought Michael was wrong then. She *knew* Michael was wrong now.

Maggie's nervous fingers were destroying Rennie's bouquet. Looking down at what she was doing, she sighed, took aim, and pitched the flowers at Ethan. They missed their mark and bounced harmlessly off Jarret's shoulder. His low laughter incensed Rennie.

"Maggie!" she cried, renewing her struggles. "Those are my flowers!" She felt the vibration of Jarret's silent laughter this time. His breath was warm against her ear. Rennie twisted her head and glared at him. He ignored her.

Skye leaped to her feet, picked up the abused bouquet and waved it threateningly at Ethan. "Well, someone needs to do something . . . say something." She looked pointedly at Ethan.

Jarret shook his head. John MacKenzie Worth's daughters were as fierce as lionesses. He wouldn't have wagered much on Ethan's chances of surviving. But then his friend seemed nearly oblivious to everything going on. He only had eyes for Michael. "He's a goner," he said to himself.

Rennie snarled.

"Is there somewhere we can talk?" Ethan was asking Michael. He looked around and added significantly. "Privately."

"I don't want to talk to you," Michael said firmly. "Now or later. Private or not. I know why you're here, and it has nothing to do with me or my baby. This is about Houston and Dee escaping. Well, you'll just have to find them on your own, Marshal Stone, because I'm not interested in helping you!"

"Michael!" Five voices, almost identical in pitch and degree of horror chorused her name.

Jarret whispered in Rennie's ear, "Turning traitor on your sister?"

Rennie had an urge to bite him. Her dark green eyes flashed. "You don't know a thing about it," she whispered back.

Michael's eyes snapped at Ethan in a similar fashion. "How did you find us?" she demanded.

"I've already talked to your father today."

"And he sent you here?"

"Yes, he sent me, but he didn't tell me what I might expect. He left it to me to find out for myself. How could you, Michael? Why didn't you tell me?"

Her face flushed. "I am not having this conversation in front of my family!"

"Then, tell me where we can talk alone."

"I don't want to be alone with you!"

"Then, we'll discuss it now!"

"Ethan! We're in the middle of my sister's wedding!"

Schyler's head had been turning back and forth between the combatants. She looked at Ethan now, awaiting his retort, and was disappointed when Jarret answered.

"That reminds me," he said. He let Rennie go, slipped out the door, and closed it without another word.

Rennie watched him go, open-mouthed. "Well, I like that," she said sarcastically. She straightened her gown and rearranged her veil. "Who *is* that man?"

"I've never seen him before," Michael said. "But if Ethan claims him as a friend, you'd do well to stay away."

Rennie was thinking much the same thing. She had never been touched with such disregard for her person. She may as well have been baggage. Jarret Sullivan's hold had been impersonal, careless, and rough. There would be bruises where he had gripped her wrists and a film of dust on her wedding gown where he had trapped her against him. Rennie impatiently brushed herself off.

"He's my deputy," Ethan said to Rennie, ignoring Michael's slur. "And when your mother and sisters go to the valley tomorrow, he'll be staying with you."

Rennie blinked widely. "Staying with me? Not likely. Hollis and I will be staying at his parents' home, and your deputy isn't welcome."

Michael looked at her sister, dismayed. "Rennie, what about your honeymoon? You don't mean not to go?"

"Of course I mean not to go," she said firmly. "I'm not leaving you alone here while those criminals are free. I may even be able to help. There's no reason you should put yourself or the baby in danger, not when I can take your place."

"I won't have it." Michael punctuated her statement by stamping her foot. "You're not going to do anything of the sort."

"Oh, dear," Moira whispered.

Mary Francis sought the calming influence of her rosary beads.

Maggie and Schyler exchanged knowing glances.

Ethan wished he could pull out his gun, fire off a few rounds, and be done with the arguing. How could Jarret have deserted him now? "You," he said sharply, pointing to Rennie, "not another word. I'm here to take care of your sister, and that's what I plan to do. I've discussed it with Jay Mac and it's settled. Jarret will be looking after you, and there will be absolutely no heroics on your part."

Rennie's mouth opened and closed. She could think of a hundred names to call him and not one that could be said in church.

Michael stared at Ethan, her mouth slightly parted in surprise. "You can't speak to my sister that way," she said.

"It seems he just did," Mary Francis said practically. She

28

stepped away from Moira and turned on Michael. "And he's making some sense. You've not taken anything having to do with those criminals seriously. I, for one, am comforted that Mr. Stone is at least willing to look to your best interests. You've ignored Papa's warnings, and you've been thinking of no one but yourself since you learned of the escape."

Rennie watched Michael's face flush at Mary's words. Mary Francis was serenely soft-spoken; yet she was capable of delivering a tongue-lashing that left one smarting for days. Though she agreed with everything Mary was saying, she still felt sorry for her twin.

"Mary," Michael said imploringly, "how can you say that? I've been anything but selfish. I've tried not to interfere in Rennie's wedding plans or make my problems any part of your lives."

"That's just it," Mary said. "We're family and you're treating us all as if we're strangers. Do you think any of us is really unconcerned? Look at Mama. Do you think she's not worried about you? And Rennie? Rennie's prepared to take on the world on your behalf. Do you think she's underestimating the danger to you?"

The room was silent. Michael stared at Mary, blinking back tears. She looked helplessly at her mother, then at Rennie. Maggie looked away guiltily and Skye plucked the bouquet.

"Oh, I'm sorry," she said, tears trickling past the corners of her eyes. She shook her head as if she could not believe what she had done. "I'm so sorry."

Rennie started to go toward her sister, but it was Ethan who reached her first. Rennie stopped and watched, her heart in her throat as she saw Ethan hesitate, his dark lashes lowered, hiding the longing, the universal vulnerability, as he risked rejection. His deep whiskey voice was a mere whisper as he said Michael's name. What would her sister do?

Michael turned and stepped into Ethan's arms.

Skye slipped Ethan a handkerchief. He brushed at Michael's tears and kissed her forehead. Her hard belly pressed against his middle, and he felt his child kick. His breath caught and he waited, wanting to feel it again.

Something of what he felt, the enormity of the responsibility, the wonderment of the moment, showed on his face. Moira and Mary nodded approvingly. Schyler grinned. Maggie sighed wistfully.

Only Rennie frowned. It was borne home to her that she would never share a moment like that with Hollis Banks. She couldn't imagine Hollis being so deeply or spontaneously touched. Suddenly she ached inside.

Ethan was talking now, something about taking Michael home, that he loved her and wanted to protect her, but Rennie only listened with half an ear. The hollowness she felt made Ethan's words echo strangely in her head. She came out of her trance when she heard her name.

"I can't leave," Michael was saying. "Rennie's wedding."

Rennie noticed that Marshal Stone was looking distinctly uncomfortable. His hands fell away from Michael, and the sun lines at the corners of his blue-gray eyes deepened as he winced. He glanced at Rennie briefly and looked away.

"About the wedding," he said slowly. He'd have rather faced a herd of stampeding buffalo, a blizzard in the Sierras, or Nathaniel Houston with his gun drawn, than have to explain what Jarret was most likely doing. "You see, I had a conversation with Jay Mac today," he began again, "and he expressed some doubts about the impending marriage."

Rennie's hand flew to her mouth. She looked wildly at her twin and saw her own fear mirrored there.

"Ethan," Michael said, "what's going on? What have you done?"

"I haven't done anything," he said. "I've been here, haven't I?" He saw them all nod, Michael and Rennie a little more reluctantly than the others. "But Jarret, well, I think he's gone off to strike a deal with Hollis Banks. I doubt there's going to be a wedding."

At Jarret's request the organist had stopped playing the wedding prelude. "Thank you," Jarret said politely. His hand fell away from his gun, and his duster draped the weapon again. "Now, if you'll just point out the groom."

A shaking finger obliged, indicating the man in earnest conversation with three ushers.

"Thanks again," Jarret said. He tipped his hat and started down the steps from the choir loft at the rear of the chapel. His unusually light tread on the stairs was the only thing that could be heard in the silent chapel. Even Hollis Banks had stopped talking as Jarret approached. Guests turned in the pews and watched Jarret's progress down the long center aisle toward the groom. Their heads swiveled as he passed, their eyes darting to one another in question.

Hollis Banks drew away from his friends. He took a step toward Jarret and stopped and waited.

Jarret Sullivan had formed a picture of Rennie's intended. Hollis Banks looked nothing like that picture. Hollis was as tall as Jarret, husky, but not heavy. He had powerful shoulders, a broad face, and a wide chest. His dark brown hair was clipped in the latest style, parted in the middle, and slicked back with Elgin's Hair Tonic. His mustache was neatly waxed, and his side whiskers followed his strong jawline. He was wearing a black morning coat, dove gray trousers, and shoes almost as shiny as his hair. His mouth was set tightly. His dark eyes were hard. He did not seem the sort of man one would describe as a milksop.

What had Jay Mac been thinking? Jarret wondered. But he knew. John MacKenzie Worth wanted this wedding stopped, and he was not above lying to get his way. The corner of Jarret's mouth curved in a self-mocking smile. Ten thousand dollars had seemed like a lot of money in Jay Mac's office. He should have held out for more. He bet Jay Mac would have paid it.

"Hollis Banks?" Jarret said, stopping less than two feet in front of the man.

Banks nodded curtly. His shoulders were set squarely, his feet planted firmly. His narrowed eyes held both curiosity and disdain. They darted over Jarret, taking in the wrinkled and dusty clothes, the tear in the jeans at the knee, the worn boots and sweat-banded hat. The outline of the gun was unmistakable under the duster.

Jarret was unmoved by the censure he saw on Banks' broad features. He nudged his hat upward with a forefinger. "Sorry about the interruption. Is there somewhere we can talk privately?"

Banks' eyes widened slightly, his surprise evident. "You *do* understand you're interrupting a wedding?"

Jarret looked around as if he'd taken no account of his surroundings before. The congregation was sitting on the edge of the pews, their ears cocked toward the altar rail, as they hoped to hear some portion of the conversation. There were vases of orange blossoms and baby's breath decorating the windowsills. The ushers behind Hollis were dressed similarly to the groom, their crisp breast-pocket handkerchiefs folded in a triangle. The priest was facing the guests; the altar boy had just finished lighting the candles. He turned back to Hollis. "By God, you're right. Except for the absent bride, it has all the earmarks of a wedding," he said.

A ruddy flush started at Hollis's neck and passed over his face. "I do not suffer fools gladly," he said tightly. "State your business and leave."

"Here?"

Hollis hesitated. "Oh, very well." He glanced at the ushers behind him. "Give us three minutes." He turned and headed for a door off to the right of the chapel.

Jarret grinned at the ushers. "I gather I'm expected to follow." He fell in step behind Hollis.

When they were alone in the small room where the altar boys put on their robes and the priest made last minute notations on his sermon, Banks turned sharply on Jarret. "Your name and your business?"

Jarret was slow to respond, glancing around the room as if time were of no account. Eventually his gaze settled on Banks, and he offered with quiet purpose, "Jarret Sullivan. I've just come from a meeting with Jay Mac. I'm prepared to offer you one thousand dollars to leave Rennie at the altar."

For a moment Hollis Banks was struck dumb. His mouth parted slightly, his eyes widened, and no hint of comprehension touched his features. Then he laughed. He had a big, booming, hearty laugh. His eyes crinkled, and tears appeared at the corners. His shoulders shook. It was loud, infectious laughter, and outside the room Jarret could hear the titterings of the guests as they caught the sound of Hollis's genuine enjoyment.

"Pardon me," Hollis said. He took the sharply folded handkerchief from his breast pocket and dabbed at his eyes. "All of a thousand dollars, eh? That doesn't sound like Jay Mac. Are you certain you met him?"

Jarret drew his Remington and pointed it at Hollis's chest. There was no longer any evidence of a smile or any indication that Jarret had found anything amusing—ever. "There's this as well," he said calmly.

One of Hollis's dark brows arched. "Jay Mac told you to kill me?"

"Let's say he didn't tell me not to."

"I see." Hollis eyed the gun consideringly. "I wonder who he has in mind to take my place."

"Can't say. Rennie's pretty enough, I guess. She'll find another stallion to corral."

"I wasn't referring to being Mary Renee's husband. I meant with Northeast Lines. I'm Jay Mac's vice president of operations."

Nothing showed on Jarret's face, but he was damning John MacKenzie Worth. He shrugged.

"Does Mary Renee know what you're doing?"

"I've already spoken to her, yes. She's in the side chapel with her sisters and mother."

Hollis Banks looked at the Remington again. He'd never had a gun pointed at him, but his estimation of Jarret Sullivan was that the man was prepared to use it. "Nate Houston," he said slowly.

This time Jarret's surprise showed. He blinked. "What?"

"Nate Houston," Banks repeated. "That's who you are."

There was something not quite right with Banks' assertion beyond the fact that the vice president of operations was dead wrong. Rennie's fiancé had the proper look of a suddenly frightened man. A bead of perspiration had appeared on Hollis's forehead, and his eyes darted nervously between Jarret's face and the gun, something they hadn't done before. Yet something didn't ring true, and since Jarret couldn't put his finger on it he played along. "How do you figure that?"

"It wasn't all that difficult. You could only be Marshal Stone or Nathaniel Houston. Jay Mac's been warned that Houston escaped and might come here. That would bring Stone on his trail."

"That so?"

Banks nodded, his eyes dropping uneasily to the Remington again. "I imagine the marshal would only be interested in Michael, especially since she's carrying his child. And Mr. Worth would never offer a thousand dollars to stop Rennie's wedding."

"Actually, that's my offer." Jarret's smile came slowly, and it hinted at something intimate, something Hollis Banks would understand. "I've taken a fancy to Mary Renee."

"Which makes it reasonable to assume you're Nate Houston. How else would a man like you have come by the thousand dollars?"

Jarret raised his gun slightly at Banks' condescending assertion. "It's hard to say, Mr. Banks. After all, this is a world where a man like you could become Jay Mac's son-in-law."

Hollis didn't answer immediately. The mask of fear slipped, and the look he gave Jarret was long and thoughtful. "Careful planning," he said at last.

The answer was just about what Jarret had expected. It appeared more and more as if the impending marriage was no love match. "Reconsidering taking the money? Or is a bullet more to your liking?" Holding the gun steady, Jarret reached into his back pocket and pulled out a clip of twelve hundred-dollar bills. It was all the money he had in the world, most of it won during the long poker game on the rail ride east. He hoped Jay Mac meant what he said about the ten thousand.

Pinching the money between his thumb and forefinger, Jarret held it out for Hollis to take. At the same time he slowly drew back the hammer on his Remington. "There's not much time," he said. "Your friends will be coming in after you. Will they find you on the floor or a richer man?"

Banks raised his hand carefully, palm out. It wavered between the gun and the money, then went for the money. "Rennie will never believe this happened, Mr. Houston. She trusts me."

"But I don't." Jarret dropped the money just as Hollis's fingers would have closed around it. Hollis reacted predictably, bending as he tried to grasp the bills. He didn't see the descent of the Remington as Jarret brought it down on the base of his skull. Grunting softly, Hollis collapsed, the money on the floor beside him just outside his grasp. Jarret prodded him gingerly with the toe of his dusty boot. There was no movement.

With some reluctance Jarret left his money where it was, tucked his Remington away, and took the side door exit so that he wouldn't have to face the congregation. Estimating he had less than a minute before Hollis's friends found the unconscious groom, Jarret hurried along the outside of the church and entered again from the front.

He ran headlong into Rennie as he stepped into the side

35

chapel. Jarret's arm swung around her waist, steadying and securing her in the same motion. Glancing around, he saw that Ethan and Mary Michael were gone. "He's taken her to the hotel then?" he asked.

Moira, Mary Francis, Mary Margaret, and Mary Schyler all nodded. Mary Renee balled up her fist and hit him in the stomach. "Of course he's taken her," she snapped, struggling to be free of Jarret's iron grip. "You don't see Michael, do you?"

"A simple 'yes' would have sufficed."

His calm and his faint smile were infuriating. He hadn't even winced at her punch, but then, she thought, his belly was as hard as his head. She would probably have bruised knuckles, and he hadn't felt the least pain. "Will you kindly let me go?" she asked stiffly.

Jarret ignored her and looked at the others. "Actually, it's time we all left. There's not going to be a wedding . . . at least not today."

Mary Francis's smile was serene as she touched her rosary. "Thank God for that."

Rennie sucked in her breath, and Jarret's arm naturally settled more tightly around her. "Mary! How can you say that?" She raised her eyes to Jarret and demanded sharply, "Will you please remove your arm? I'm going to—"

Moira rushed forward as Rennie slumped in Jarret's embrace.

"She's fine, ma'am," Jarret assured her. "Just fainted. Does she do that often?"

From across the room Maggie whispered dryly to Skye, "Only when she's held in a vise."

Skye smothered a giggle behind her hand.

Jarret slipped his free arm under Rennie's knees and lifted her. "She's not pregnant, is she?"

Mary Francis stepped forward to support her mother. "I think you forget yourself, Mr. Sullivan. We're grateful for your help as well as for your interference, but that doesn't give you leave to ask such personal questions."

He felt himself flushing under the soft rebuke. "Beggin' your pardon, Sister."

This time Skye's quiet laughter was joined by Maggie. Having been on the receiving end of Mary Francis's admonishments more than a few times themselves, they felt a faint tug of empathy for Jarret Sullivan.

"We have to be going," Jarret said. "There's a carriage waiting out front that will accommodate all of us. I don't expect things will remain quiet for long." He was referring to Hollis Banks unconscious in the chapel, but he could have spoken the same words of Rennie. He felt her stirring in his arms. "Quickly. We should leave now."

Moira shook her head. "I can't leave. What will our guests think? I must stay behind and make our apologies."

"I'll do that," Mary quickly promised her mother, giving her a gentle nudge toward the door. "You go with Mr. Sullivan. Skye. Maggie. You, too. I'll speak to everyone." She stepped back and pointed in the direction of the door. "Hurry. Before Rennie starts fussing."

Before Moira could voice another protest, Maggie and Skye ushered their mother into the hallway and out the large oak doors. Jarret turned to follow but stopped when he felt a light hand on his shoulder.

"She's not pregnant," Mary Francis said. "But you should treat her gently nonetheless. My sister is all snap and spit when she needs to be but here—" Mary touched her own heart—"she's tender."

Jarret frowned, not certain he understood. "I've signed on to protect her, Sister, not provoke her."

"I'm not sure you can help it," she said softly, smiling her beautiful, enigmatic smile.

Rennie was shifted in Jarret's arms as he shrugged. "Hollis was out cold in that little room at the front of the church. Except for an aching head he'll be all right."

"He fought you for Rennie?" she asked, puzzled by the possibility.

"No, I dropped him when he accepted the thousand dollars I offered to call off the wedding."

"Oh, dear." It was quite an effort not to laugh. "Rennie won't think much of Hollis for that."

"Hollis says she won't believe it."

Mary's smooth brows came together as she realized Hollis Banks was probably right. She didn't confirm it for Jarret. "You'd better go, Mr. Sullivan. They'll be waiting for you in the carriage." She escorted him to the main doors of the chapel and opened them. "God bless you," she whispered as he passed in front of her.

He grinned. "I'd be a fool not to think I need it." He hurried down the stone steps, Mary's light laughter in the air around him.

The house at the intersection of Broadway and 50th Street was only slightly smaller than the palatial French country home on which it was modeled. If Moira Dennehy had had her way, she would still be living in the cramped and cozy apartments on Houston Street where she had raised her daughters; but Jay Mac had his own ideas how his mistress should live, and when New York's elite started moving uptown, Jay Mac moved the Dennehys right along. A relatively quiet scandal resulted as neighbors whispered Jay Mac had no right, and the newspapers hinted that he had overstepped the bounds of good taste. His own home, after all, was only a few blocks away, just west of Central Park, and much was made of this fact. It didn't matter to John MacKenzie Worth, and, if the truth had been fully known, it mattered not a whit more to his wife.

Jarret waited in the carriage until the driver had helped Moira, Maggie, and Skye alight. Though he was quite conscious of Rennie's anger, he smiled encouragingly in her direction. "Will you need help, ma'am?"

All the replies that came quickly to Rennie's mind seemed so trite that she held her tongue. She doubted she could shock him by telling him what he could to with his help. It was far more likely that he would be amused, and if he laughed at her again, Rennie thought she might just go crazy with anger. "I can manage," she said coolly.

Jarret watched her consideringly for a moment longer. A pale wash of color flushed her cheeks, followed by a flash of something lively in her green eyes. She was making an admirable effort to hold herself in check, and Jarret thought he had better exercise the same restraint. There was nothing to be gained by baiting her further. He moved his long legs so that they were no longer blocking her exit, grinning behind Rennie's back as she practically leaped from her seat to take the driver's extended hand.

Rennie went straight to the front door, but her mother and sisters waited politely for Jarret. He tipped his hat slightly as he spoke to Moira. "If you don't mind, ma'am, I'd like to scout around the house, get a feel for it, so to speak."

Moira's eyes darted between her daughters, then settled gravely on Jarret. The threat to her family seemed very real again. "You must do what you think is best, Mr. Sullivan."

Rennie paused in opening the door to her home and glanced back over her shoulder. "Certainly, Mr. Sullivan," she said, her tone too sweet to be respectful, "you must do what you think is best. Tramp all over Mother's flower beds, jiggle the locks, pry at the windows, and please, *please,* make a nuisance of yourself." She stepped in the house and slammed the door behind her.

Jarret held up his hand, stopping Moira's apology. "I'll be careful of your flower beds, ma'am." He tugged his hat lower over his brow and began walking the perimeter of the house.

The mansion had the look of a fortress, with its large blocks of smooth gray stone, a wrought-iron railing bordering the property, and prickly rose bushes edging the foundation. But it also had twenty windows and four doors on the ground floor, and none of them were particularly secure. The lock on the delivery entrance was so loose that a single hard twist was all Jarret required to get inside.

It was when he stepped into the hallway that he bumped into Rennie—on her way out. "I thought you'd be in your room sulking," he said.

"And I thought you'd still be skulking," she snapped.

He grinned. "Obviously I'm done. Lucky for you. I might have missed your exit if I'd been on the other side of the house." His eyes were drawn to the open collar of her coat. "You've changed your gown."

"I thought I'd save my wedding gown for my wedding."

"Makes sense." Jarret leaned back against the door jamb, blocking Rennie's access to the delivery area and the freedom beyond. His thumbs were hooked in the pockets of his duster. "You were thinking of going somewhere?" A thought occurred to him. "The privy, perhaps."

Rennie rolled her eyes. "The privy is *indoors*, Mr. Sullivan."

"Imagine that."

"Oh, dear God," she said, sighing. "That Jay Mac could have saddled me with you."

"You read my mind."

Moira appeared at the other end of the long hallway. "Rennie, what are you doing there? Sure and it's wanting to worry me sick that you're not in your room right now."

Rennie was immediately contrite. "Mother, you know that's not true, but you can't expect that I'm just going to go along with Jay Mac's plans. Papa had no right to interfere."

"Perhaps not," Moira said. "But it's done for now. Let it be."

Turning on her heel, Rennie walked briskly toward her mother, the hem of her hunter green gown swirling about her legs. Her shoes tapped lightly on the carpet runner. "I want to see Hollis," she said, lowering her voice.

Moira shook her head. "I want your promise that you'll stay here. How can Mr. Sullivan protect you otherwise? Now join your sisters upstairs and help them pack for tomorrow while I see to Mr. Sullivan's comfort."

Rennie's mouth curved sardonically. "Then we'd better move the privy outside."

"Rennie! Mr. Sullivan is—"

"Standing right behind you," Jarret said softly.

Embarrassed, and angry for being embarrassed, Rennie darted Jarret a scathing look. "I don't appreciate you sneaking up on me."

"I merely followed you," he said, unrepentant.

"And I find myself growing increasingly weary of that edge of humor in your voice. I see nothing at all amusing."

"That's because there's no mirror handy."

Moira clapped her hands and effectively silenced both combatants. "That's enough, both of you. Rennie, you're being unconscionably rude. As I was trying to say, Mr. Sullivan is our guest. When your sisters and I leave he will be *your* guest, and I expect you to treat him as such." She raised her gently lined face to Jarret. "You have my permission to lock her in her room if that's what it takes—"

"Mother!"

"But I suggest you cease teasing her," Moira said. "Rennie is not known for her sense of humor."

"Mother!"

Jarret nodded. "Your point is taken," he said solemnly. "I apologize, Miss Dennehy."

Rennie opened her mouth to accept, albeit with little grace, when she realized he was apologizing to her mother, not to her. A muscle twitched in her cheek as her teeth ground together. "If you'll excuse me," she said tightly.

Moira and Jarret watched Rennie's stiff retreat up the stairs. "You're incorrigible, Mr. Sullivan," Moira said, but she was smiling now. "Sure and it's a time of it you'll have with that one."

"Can't say that I'm looking forward to it, ma'am."

Her response was soft. "Liar."

Before Jarret could convince himself that he'd heard correctly, he was being ushered through a succession of parlors, corridors, and stairways as Moira made him familiar with her home. In contrast to the fortresslike exterior, the inside was welcoming and warm. The sitting rooms were filled with overstuffed furniture, fringed pillows, figurines, and photographs. In the dining room the large walnut table was covered by a splendid Irish linen tablecloth. A portrait of the five Marys as children graced the wall above the sideboard. Walnut wainscoting trimmed the walls and unified the rooms in a single design. Blue and gold wallpaper carried color down the long hallways and brightened the staircases. Moira took Jarret into the kitchen and introduced him to the cook, Mrs. Cavanaugh, who was preparing him a meal, and let him explore the pantries as well as the wine and fruit cellars.

They took the mansion's rear staircase to the upper floor and weaved in and out of the bedrooms, sitting rooms, dressing and bathing rooms, until Moira showed Jarret to the room where he'd be staying.

He shook his head. "It's not close enough to your daughter's room. I'm afraid it won't do. I already have to contend with locks that don't lock and more windows than I want to think about. I'll just bed down in the hallway outside Miss Dennehy's door. The truth is, ma'am, that right about now I'm so tuckered that I—"

Moira was instantly contrite. "Forgive me, Mr. Sullivan—"

"Jarret."

She smiled. "Jarret. Of course you're tired. I've been foolish to forget. Let me show you another room where you can sleep. Do you have any bags?"

Jarret dutifully followed Moira down the hall. "My bags are with Ethan, wherever he is now."

"That's fine. I'll send Mr. Cavanaugh to get them at the St. Mark." Moira opened the door to a bedchamber on the northeast corner of the house. "This will give you a view of the street, and it's not far from Rennie's room."

Jarret glanced around the room, trying not to look overly eager to use the bed. He parted the dark blue drapes and surveyed the avenue below, first Broadway, then 50th. Satisfied with the location, he turned to Moira and thanked her for her graciousness in trying times.

She colored prettily and slipped a lock of dark red hair behind her ear. "Sure and you're welcome," she said warmly. "I'll see that you have everything for a bath, fresh linens and such, and we'll send Mrs. Cavanaugh's meal to you straight away."

When she was gone Jarret opened the door to the connecting room and found the dressing area and, beyond that, confirmation that the privy was indeed indoors. He didn't wait for fresh linens—the ones he found in the storage cupboard seemed fine to him—and stripped to the buff when the tub filled.

The water was cool, but it didn't matter. Jarret welcomed the chance to get rid of the grit that clung to him like a second skin. He scrubbed enthusiastically, sluicing water over his face and shoulders. His tuneless humming stopped when he heard a sound from the other room.

Because her hands were busy with the tray of food, Rennie nudged open the door to Jarret's bedroom with the toe of her shoe. Maggie followed behind with warm towels, and Skye entered last carrying Jarret's carpetbag of belongings.

"Well," Rennie drawled, as she looked around, "this is fine protection. I certainly hope Michael is receiving better from the marshal. I'm of a mind to go to the St. Mark and see to it myself."

Skye dropped Jarret's bag on the chair by the fireplace. "Oh, stop it, Rennie. Mr. Sullivan is probably in the bathing room. You're not going to the St. Mark—"

"Or anyplace else," Maggie said. Her mouth flattened as she surveyed her older sister. "I find myself losing all patience with you. Mr. Sullivan is hardly the villain you've made him out to be."

Setting down the tray of covered dishes, Rennie rounded on both sisters. "Have you forgotten this was my *wedding* day? I certainly haven't. To my way of thinking, Mr. Sullivan has much to answer for."

Skye's cheeks brightened to a shade only a little less volatile than her hair. "Papa is the one who needs to hear this. He's the one who interfered."

"Papa didn't lay Hollis out on the floor of the chapel."

Maggie hugged the towels she carried protectively. "I don't think it was all that dramatic, and what Skye says is true. If Papa hadn't put forth the notion, Mr. Sullivan would have hardly acted as he did."

"And," Skye said, "it seems to me that you're more angry than hurt or disappointed." At Rennie's start of surprise, Skye added, "It's something to think about, isn't it?"

Feeling betrayed, Rennie's dark green eyes darted from one sister to the other, and the hurt that Skye had noted was missing earlier was now there for both of them to see. "There's no talking to either one of you," she said softly.

"Rennie," Maggie implored. "We didn't mean—"

"Just put the towels down," Rennie said. "I'll see that Mr. Sullivan gets everything." She turned her back on her sisters, effectively dismissing them. She felt their hesitation, could imagine them exchanging pained glances, but she would not relent. Did they really think she was without any feeling? When the door shut, and she was alone, some of the steel went out of Rennie's spine. Her shoulders slumped, and her knees wobbled. She placed one hand on the edge of the bedside table to steady herself.

44

That was how Jarret found her, looking oddly vulnerable with her eyes closed and the slender weight of her braced against the table. He stood in the doorway, a towel hitched around his waist, watching her silent struggle for a moment; then knowing that she wouldn't thank him for the intrusion, he quietly backed into the dressing room.

"Is someone there?" he called.

His voice jerked Rennie to the present. "It's Rennie, Mr. Sullivan. I've brought your dinner."

"Right now I'm more interested in some clean clothes."

"Oh." Rennie imagined Jarret's wicked grin at her flustered response. She drew in a steadying breath. "Of course. I didn't think."

"I'm decently covered."

Now she was certain he was laughing at her. Gathering the loose threads of her composure, Rennie managed to answer coolly. "Stay where you are and I'll take your word for it. Your bag's in here on the chair, and Mother's sent warm towels, too. Someone will collect your tray later. Good evening, Mr. Sullivan."

"Good evening, Miss Dennehy." He doubted she heard him. The door was opening and closing as he was speaking.

Chuckling to himself, Jarret left the dressing room. He ignored the dusty carpetbag of fresh clothes and helped himself to one of the warm towels, rubbing it briskly against his dark blond hair. He also exchanged the damp towel around his waist for a dry one, then sat on the edge of the bed and investigated the dishes Moira Dennehy's cook had prepared.

He would have eaten sawdust and drank hot candle wax. It made him all the more grateful that neither of these items was placed before him. Mrs. Cavanaugh had given him thick slices of roast beef, a mountain of mashed potatoes with a deep reservoir of gravy, and tender baby carrots. The dinner rolls were hot to the touch and shiny with melted butter. The coffee was just the way he liked: steaming, black, and lots of it.

Jarret ate everything, sopping up the gravy with his roll, finishing the pot of coffee with the last bite of black cherry pie. Replete, feeling the meal settle heavily in his stomach, Jarret pushed the tray away and lay back on the bed. He cradled his head in his hands and stared at the ceiling, wondering if he dared close his eyes. Outside his window he could hear the rhythmic clatter of carriages and horses, the excited chatter of neighbors on their way to the theater. He knew better than to close his eyes. He pinched the bridge of his nose with his thumb and forefinger, then rubbed his lids. Jarret did not remember falling asleep. In moments he was.

Rennie pushed the door open when there was no response to her knock. There was no light in the room, and she paused on the threshold until her eyes adjusted. When she could finally see she wondered if that was necessarily a good thing.

Yes, he was decently covered. But only just. Rennie became impatient with herself as she felt her cheeks grow hot. She considered herself rather a worldly woman, yet here she was in her own home sporting a face like a brush fire. All because of Jarret Sullivan. It was not a situation that endeared the man to Rennie. Setting her shoulders stiffly and cocking her head to the side, she stared defiantly at her unwanted guest.

His form was not unpleasing, she thought. With a hint of the objectiveness in which she prided herself, Rennie admitted that quite the opposite was true. His hair was still damp, darker at the edges where it framed his face, and streaked with sunshine at the crown of his head. In repose his features did not look so sharply cut; the hardness that lay just beyond his amused, lazy smile was absent. But then, Rennie realized with some regret, so was the smile.

Her eyes rested briefly on his mouth, then followed the strong line of his jaw to where a droplet of water lay in the

46

hollow of his throat. His chest rose and fell in an even cadence. She made out the curve of his rib cage and the slope of his hard belly. An arrow of dark hair disappeared beneath the ridge of his loosely tied towel, and lower, the material split intriguingly along his right thigh. As Rennie stared, the split opened farther. She blinked widely, hardly believing the towel was slowly rising.

Jarret snapped to attention, sitting straight up and drawing his knees to his chest. He hid the heavy fullness of his groin, but the ache remained. His brows arched in question a moment before he found his voice. "You've seen enough?"

Rennie held her ground and answered boldly, "More than I cared to, actually."

"Really?" The smile was back, this time edged with derision. "You were staring pretty hard for someone who had taken her fill." Jarret felt a measure of satisfaction as Rennie's face flamed and her icy shield of arrogance began to melt.

"You're a vile, boorish man, Mr. Sullivan."

"That so?" He was genuinely amused now. "Most people just call me a son of a bitch."

She hated the fact that he was laughing at her. She hated the fact that in spite of his near nakedness, he had somehow gotten the upper hand. She wished she *had* called him a son of a bitch, for surely that's what he was.

"There was something you wanted?" he asked. "Or am I to assume you moseyed on in here simply to look at me?"

Rennie's chin came up a notch, and the butter-wouldn't-melt expression returned. "You may as well learn now, Mr. Sullivan, that I've never *moseyed* anywhere in my life. I don't amble, sashay, saunter, or stroll."

"Damn the torpedoes. Is that it, Miss Dennehy? Full speed ahead?"

Rennie's mouth pursed impatiently. "I walk. Sometimes I run. Always with a destination in mind. Not only do I know where I'm going, I know why I'm going there. I've never been inclined to mosey, and it's not a trait that I particularly respect in others."

"You may get where you're goin', but you're missin' the trip."

"Please spare me the good ol' boy homilies. I've been managing just fine on my—"

Jarret held up his hand. "Whoa! You may not walk in circles, but you sure do talk in them. You're making my head ache."

She smiled sweetly as he began to massage his temples. "If my presence here is as welcome to you as a hangover from a three-day drunk, then, Mr. Sullivan, I feel I've accomplished my life's work." For a moment she thought she had gone too far. He stared at her, his features void of any discernible expression; then without warning deep, rumbling laughter shook his shoulders and made his striking eyes crinkle at the corners.

"Your life's work, eh?" He shook his head, still chuckling, and turned on the bed so that his legs dangled over the side. "I'm getting up now, Miss Dennehy, and I'm going to get dressed. I feel a warning's in order since you appear rooted to the floor."

Rennie was indeed rooted. The arrow of hair on his belly drew her eyes as he stood, and the outline of his groin in the towel held her attention. The words came rushing out hoarsely. "We've been invited to a wedding," she said. "My sister's marrying your friend within the hour." Turning on her heel, Rennie fled.

"Wait a minute!" Jarret called after her as she disappeared into the hallway. By the time he reached the door, Rennie had already vanished into one of the neighboring rooms.

Jarret dressed quickly and sought out Moira. He found her in the front parlor using the beveled mirror above the fireplace to adjust the brooch on her shawl. Her concentration was such that his first words frightened her.

"I'm sorry," he said as Moira lifted her index finger to her mouth. "Did you hurt yourself?" He approached and drew out her hand, examining the injured finger.

"A scratch," she said. A pinpoint of blood clung stubbornly to the tip. She accepted the handkerchief Jarret offered her as well as his assistance in fastening the brooch. She noticed his large hands were not at all clumsy when it came to delicate tasks.

From the doorway Rennie took note of the same thing. Over Jarret's shoulder Moira caught her daughter's bemused expression; then she caught her daughter's eye. Moira was not surprised when Rennie's immediate response was to throw up her guard and pretend she had never been observed in a moment of vulnerability. Rennie liked to believe her thoughts were impenetrable. Perhaps that was the case in the board room, Moira thought, but not here, not with her family.

Jarret smoothed the shawl over Moira's slender shoulders; then his hands fell to his side. "Your daughter told me Mary Michael and Ethan are marrying tonight. Can that be true?"

Before Moira could answer, Rennie interrupted from the threshold. "I'm not in the habit of lying, Mr. Sullivan."

Moira leveled Rennie with a stern look and a no-nonsense tone. "I don't think that's what Jarret meant, Mary Renee." She turned her attention back to Jarret. "Apparently it's quite true," she said. "I confess I was surprised myself when the messenger arrived with the invitation. Michael's timing leaves something to be desired."

"Better now," Rennie said, quickly rising to her twin's defense, "than after you've all left for the summerhouse."

"Yes," Moira said, sighing. "You're right, of course. It's only that I can't see the sense of rushing now."

"She's seven months pregnant, Mother."

"That's just it. Rushing would have been in order seven months ago." Moira went to the sideboard and poured herself a small glass of sherry. "I can't help but wonder if that man's marrying her because of the baby."

Now it was Jarret who spoke up in defense of his friend. "Ethan's about the bravest man I know, save for where your daughter's concerned. That baby may have given him the courage to ask Michael for her hand, but don't think for a minute he's not stupid in love with her."

Rennie smirked. "Stupid in love," she said, offering Jarret a sherry. "What an apt expression."

Moira watched her daughter and Jarret over the rim of her glass. "No possibility of that happening to either of you," she said solemnly.

Neither of them heard the faint sarcasm in Moira's tone or caught the mocking gleam in her eye. They answered in unison. "No possibility."

As far as Moira was concerned, their chorus meant they were already working together.

Chapter Two

Everyone was gathered in the judge's darkly paneled chambers. Jarret appreciated anew the power and influence of even the illegitimate side of John MacKenzie Worth's family. Judge Halsey was a long-time friend of Jay Mac's as well as Mary Michael's godfather. He seemed to be taking circumstances quite in stride, as if it was not at all unusual to perform a wedding in his private chambers shortly before midnight.

In the hush before the ceremony was ready to begin, Jarret asked Rennie, "Who's *your* godfather?"

Rennie offered him a smug glance. "You should be anxious. He is at least as well-connected as the judge."

Standing in front of them, Skye overheard the exchange and whispered to Jarret over her shoulder. "Don't worry, Mr. Sullivan, it's not the pope. Papa's a Presbyterian."

Rennie wrinkled her nose at her sister as soon as Skye turned around. It would serve Jarret Sullivan right if he *did* think it was the pope.

Jarret managed to temper his smile. Rennie may as well have telegraphed her thoughts, she was that easy to understand. He watched her out of the corner of his eye, and as her features softened and her hands grew still, he realized the judge was speaking.

Of all the things Jarret had anticipated happening on his trip to New York, he had not been able to foresee standing in as best man at his friend's wedding. He listened as Ethan and Mary Michael exchanged vows and heard the solemn purpose and promise in Ethan's voice, the loving commitment in Michael's. At the final pronouncement they could only stare at one another, neither moving, as if they'd forgotten everyone else serving witness.

Judge Halsey broke the expectant silence. "Well, go on, son, this is the time to kiss her."

Ethan grinned. Bending his head, he touched his mouth to Michael's. Her lips were soft and pliant beneath his; her mouth tasted faintly of peppermint. Her beautiful smile was full of promise when he drew back.

Jarret's gaze shifted from Ethan and Michael to the father of the bride. That very afternoon he had witnessed John MacKenzie Worth's stoic acceptance and deep regret at not being able to be present at Rennie's public wedding, but here, in the privacy of his old friend's sanctuary, there was a place for him with another of his daughters. Jarret could see the powerful man was powerfully moved.

Jay Mac pressed a handkerchief into Moira's hand even as he fought to temper his own emotion. She gave him a sideways look, a watery smile, and squeezed his hand. Mary Francis saw the affectionate exchange between her parents, and her own heart swelled with love. No one who saw Jay Mac and Moira together could doubt the depth of the commitment they shared. Mary Francis poked Maggie in the side with her elbow just as Moira leaned into Jay Mac and his hand came around her waist.

Maggie's smile mirrored her sister's as her eyes drifted from the wedded couple to her unwedded parents. She turned to Skye and saw that her younger sister had already observed the same thing. Simultaneously they glanced over their shoulders to look at Rennie. She seemed to have forgotten Jarret Sullivan's hovering presence for the moment because her mouth was curved in a gently wistful smile.

Jarret also observed Rennie's rare and beautiful smile and suspected, like her sisters, that he was no longer on Rennie's mind. He watched as Michael turned away from Ethan and sought out the dear, precious faces of her family. In a moment they were surrounding her, smothering her with hugs and good wishes. Jarret heard Ethan's low laughter and was surprised at the twinge of envy he felt as his friend was similarly taken into the fold.

"It's the right thing you've done," Moira whispered in Michael's ear. She drew back, took the measure of her daughter's glowing happiness, and nodded. "Sure and you know it, don't you?"

"I know it, Mama." Michael glanced at Ethan. "He's the one."

Jarret intercepted Ethan's modest grin and laughed himself. He stepped out of the way as Mary Francis came forward to kiss her sister's cheek.

"I suppose he knows you're willful and stubborn and can't possibly honor that vow you made to obey."

Must be a family trait, Jarret thought, seeking out Rennie for a moment. She was eying the door, looking as if she was contemplating escape. Jarret caught her eye and gently admonished her with a shake of his head.

Rennie managed to catch herself before she stuck her tongue out at him. The thought that he had nearly reduced her to such childish behavior gave her pause. Gathering her composure, she turned her attention back to Mary Francis and Michael.

Mary Francis had just finished enumerating Michael's independent qualities. She was staring hard at the groom. "You know all of that, don't you?"

"I know it," he said solemnly. "I don't love her in spite of that. I love her because of it."

Rennie tried to imagine Hollis saying something like that and couldn't. Except for the slight heave of her shoulders, the faint rustle of her dress, her sigh was inaudible. She noticed that Mary Francis seemed to be satisfied by Ethan's response. Her sister's features were calm, her beautiful face serene. She was touching the crucifix that rested against her wide, white collar.

"Good, because I'll break your kneecaps if you ever hurt my sister."

"Mary Francis!" Moira admonished, shocked. She cast a significant look at Jay Mac as if to hold him responsible for his daughter's outrageous threat. Jay Mac held up his hands innocently, but his eyes were amused.

Rennie drew Michael aside as the rest of the family spoke to Ethan. She searched the face that was so much like her own and found every nuance of expression that made it different. Michael's dark green eyes were radiant, illuminated by some deep happiness within her. There was a becoming blush of color on her cheeks, and the normally elusive dimples on either side of her wide mouth were fully evident.

It was Rennie's mouth that had flattened seriously, her eyes that were dark and worried. "Say the word and I'll take your place," she said.

Michael laughed, pretending to misunderstand. "With Ethan? Really, Rennie, don't you think he'd know?" She looked down at her abdomen, then back at her sister. "We're not so much alike right now."

Rennie took her twin's wrists and gave her a little shake. "Don't you dare make light of me. I'm thinking of you and the baby."

Michael's beatific smile disappeared. "I love you for that. There's no one else like you."

"That's quite a compliment," she said quietly, "coming from my twin."

Michael hugged her. "I mean it," she whispered back. "There is no one else like you. I don't want you to do anything that would place you in danger. I couldn't live with that, Rennie." She stepped back and searched her sister's face. Rennie was making a good show of being calm, but Michael knew better than anyone the strength of the anger that was being suppressed. "I'm sorry about your wedding." And lest Rennie misunderstand, Michael added, "Not sorry that you're not marrying Hollis, only sorry that it wasn't your decision. You believe that, don't you?"

"You know I do." She jerked her thumb over her shoulder to indicate Jarret Sullivan's shadowy presence by the door. "I wish Mary Francis would threaten his kneecaps."

Michael laughed. "And what about Jay Mac?"

Rennie's emerald eyes shifted from Michael's face to where her father stood deep in conversation with Ethan and Judge Halsey. She shook her head slowly, her expression torn between admiration and anger. "I'm not one to back down from a challenge," she said. "I'll think of some way to outmaneuver him for the trick he's played me."

Michael almost felt sorry for her father. "Good for you, Rennie." She squeezed her sister's hands, offering encouragement. "But don't marry Hollis Banks to spite Papa. You'd only be spiting yourself."

Rennie opened her mouth to reply, but Michael was not letting her get the last word in. Before Rennie could say anything, her twin was moving away, rejoining Ethan, Judge Halsey, and Jay Mac.

"She's right, you know," Jarret said.

Rennie jerked in response to the unexpected voice at her ear. Her look was sour and her voice was tart. "If you're going to live in my pockets until Nate Houston is caught, then I suggest you do so quietly and with as little interference as possible. I'll thank you to remember you're no real part of my life, and therefore your opinion is quite unwelcome."

"You know, ma'am," he drawled, "that's an awfully high horse you're ridin' now. A lady could get hurt fallin' from an animal like that." After delivering his set down, Jarret sauntered away.

Rennie was stranded in the middle of the room. Her mother was talking to Mary Francis. Jay Mac was laughing over something amusing the judge had just said. Michael was encircled by her husband's arms. Skye and Maggie had been quick to include Jarret in their animated conversation. Rennie had never felt so isolated or so heartsick. For a moment she actually hated all of them; then it passed and she was left hating herself. While Jarret was occupied, Rennie slipped out the door.

She made it down the courthouse steps before her elbow was seized in a bruising grip.

"Don't you have regard for anyone but yourself?" Jarret asked.

Rennie tried to shake him off. Her efforts only increased the pressure of his hold. Her chin came up challengingly. "What do you know about it?"

"I know that the moment your family realized you were gone they were sick with fear."

"Oh, you mean they actually missed me?"

Jarret's fingers eased around her arm. "Feeling a little sorry for yourself, is that it?"

Shrugging him off and turning away, Rennie hugged herself. "Feeling a whole lot sorry for myself. That's why I left. I'm not fit company."

Her honest self-assessment surprised Jarret. He fell in step beside her as she began walking away from the courthouse. "We should take the carriage," he said. "It's safer."

"I want to walk."

"All right." He handed her the shawl she had left behind and watched her throw it carelessly around her shoulders. "The carriage is warmer."

She ignored him.

Burying his hands in his duster's pockets, Jarret shrugged. He knew she was cold, knew she was nearly shaking with it, and yet she seemed to accept the brisk night air as if it were a deserving punishment. Under the street lamps the delicate lines of her profile were starkly etched, and the expression in her eyes was somehow both empty and filled with hurt.

It had seemed a whimsical thing to do, Jarret thought, to stop Rennie's wedding when Jay Mac made his outrageous offer. Now he wondered how many other women of his acquaintance would have acted with as much spirit and aplomb. He couldn't think of one. Hardly realizing his own intention until it was done, Jarret stepped a little closer to Rennie to protect her from the buffeting wind.

"Your sisters would like you to journey with them to the summerhouse," he said.

Rennie shook her head. "They're only hoping that if I go with them, I'll elect to stay. It will simply be another disappointment when I return to the city."

"You won't consider changing your mind?"

"I want to be close to Michael and as far away from Jay Mac as I can be right now. That shouldn't be so difficult for anyone to understand—even you."

"I thought perhaps my presence here would tip the scales in favor of the valley."

She stopped in the circle of light from a street lamp. The gaslight bleached the color from her face and turned her hunter green gown black and her emerald eyes gray. "Your presence here has little meaning to me now and even less when my mother and sisters leave."

Looking down at her, Jarret was struck again by her resolve and the gravity of her tone. He was also struck by how very kissable her mouth looked. It was the more unsettling of his observations. He lifted the collar of his duster and turned away. "Let's go." When she hesitated Jarret slipped his arm beneath hers and gave her a nudge.

Rennie almost brushed him off, then thought better of it. She would concede this small skirmish to Jarret, but she would win the war.

Jarret was largely unfamiliar with the city, but he knew how to mark a trail. On his ride to the courthouse he had looked for landmarks that would help him find the Dennehy home again without assistance. Now, as Rennie took him past the St. Mark Hotel and Union Square, he knew he was not being led astray.

Broadway was a busy thoroughfare even after midnight. The traffic on the street and sidewalks forced Jarret to remain hypervigilant for any sighting of Nathaniel Houston or Detra Kelly. His eyes marked the features of every hack driver, flower vendor, and weaving drunk. His ears registered the noise as individual sounds. A milk wagon rattled down the street. A spritely pair of beautifully matched grays whinnied in unison. A fruit seller cursed his wife, and a whip snapped smartly behind him to his left.

"Do you really think they'll just appear on Broadway?"

It took Jarret a moment to realize that Rennie was addressing him. "What?"

She sighed. "Do you really think Nate Houston and his consort are simply going to appear in the middle of the street in the middle of the night?"

"Stranger things have happened."

"I'd be hard pressed to think of one. Isn't it taking coincidence a little too far?"

Without looking down at her, Jarret answered. The tension that kept him alert for more hours than he cared to think about was finally transferred sharply to his voice.

"It wouldn't be coincidence at all, Miss Dennehy. Nathaniel Houston knows what he wants, and she's here in New York. It would be far stranger if the man never showed up."

Rennie shivered, and this time it wasn't from the cold. Stepping around Jarret on the sidewalk, she raised her hand and hailed a hansom cab. She pulled the shawl more tightly around her shoulders as she sat down. "You shouldn't be here with me," she said, staring out the window of the hack as he joined her. "You should be tracking that killer down."

Jarret leaned back in the leather seat, propped his feet on the bench across from him, and folded his arms comfortably against his chest. He closed his eyes. "It would be infinitely more difficult for me to find him than for him to find your sister."

"It's a waiting game."

He nodded. "Exactly."

She itched to slap him. "Then, you should be with my sister."

"You know how to make that happen."

"I'm not leaving."

Jarret opened his dark blue eyes and leveled Rennie with a hard, implacable stare. "Neither am I."

The remainder of the journey was passed in silence. When they reached the house Rennie alighted without waiting for Jarret. He yanked her back as she would have used her key in the door.

"What do you think you're doing?" she demanded.

Jarret's eyes darted across the dark face of the house. Where was the cook and her husband? "Didn't you knock?"

"No, I didn't. It would hardly do—"

Jarret rapped on the door.

"—any good," she said. "They live on the upper floor

59

of the carriage house. That's the house around—"

"I know where it is," Jarret said shortly. He took the key from her hand. "Wait here while I make certain everything's as it should be."

Rennie was on the point of snapping at him, when she saw the gun. The outline of the Remington was a powerful silencer.

Jarret saw her reaction to the weapon. "I know you find it easier to be fearful for your sister than for yourself, but it's time for you to understand the danger to you is real." He saw her nod slowly. "Wait right here."

The house was very nearly impossible to search thoroughly. Jarret started on the ground floor, weaving in and out of the rooms with the stealth of a shadow. The thick carpet runner on the grand staircase absorbed his footfalls as he climbed to the second floor. When he was satisfied that every room was empty he went back down to get Rennie. A soft thud in the front parlor drew his attention.

Rennie lifted the hem of her gown and raised her knee. Standing on one leg, she held her injured foot and massaged two stubbed toes. She swore softly, grimacing with pain; then even that faded to nothingness as she realized she was no longer alone. Her heart stopped, then resumed beating with such a slam to her chest that she thought she would faint. When she looked up she found herself nose to nose with Jarret's Remington.

Fear made her furious and foolish. She slapped Jarret's hand away from her face and swore hotly. "Damn you! How dare you scare me like that!" She pushed him hard in the chest. When he didn't budge she pushed him again, this time hard enough to rock him on his heels. "If you can't get the hell out of my life, Mr. Sullivan, then have the decency to get the hell out of my way."

He grabbed her by the back of the neck as she brushed past him. His fingers tangled in the thick coil of hair at her nape. The pressure of his hand warned her that if she moved he would scalp her. He waited until she stilled before he holstered his gun. His voice was soft and restrained, and menacing because it was both those things. "I've never hit a woman in my life, Miss Dennehy, but if a man had pushed me the way you just did, I'd have given serious consideration to laying him out. I'm warning you now, the next time I'll give you the same consideration." He paused, waiting for his words to register. When he felt her stiff and reluctant acknowledgment, he continued. "As for scaring you, well, it works both ways. I told you to wait at the front door." In the darkness he found her hand and drew it inside his duster to feel the butt of the Remington. "I'm carrying the gun. You might want to remember that the next time you see fit to scare me."

Rennie knew then that she had come close to being shot in her own front parlor. "I'm sorry," she said lowly. "I should have listened to you."

Jarret didn't expect her to remain contrite for long, especially if he didn't let her go. Yet the urge to hold her was there. Strands of silky auburn hair were threaded through his fingers. Her skin was warm and soft beneath his hand. Her breath smelled faintly of wintergreen. That he was even contemplating what it might be like to kiss her worried him. His fingers dropped away from her neck and came up to rub the bridge of his nose.

"God, I'm more tired than I thought." He shook his head to clear it as his hand fell to his side. "There for a moment . . ."

"Yes?"

Jarret caught himself. "Nothing."

Rennie waited. When it seemed that he was not inclined to say any more, she offered him a cup of coffee. "It may

61

be a while before Mama and my sisters return. I intend to wait up for them."

"I'll take the coffee, then." He lighted the table lamps while Rennie went to the kitchen, and paced the length of the room from the fireplace to the large arched window. The catnap he had taken earlier hadn't been nearly enough.

From the doorway Rennie watched him. His deep blue eyes were shaded, not by his usual lazy watchfulness, but by sheer fatigue. His duster had been tossed over the back of a rocking chair, and tension was now a visible line down his back. Beneath his crisp white shirt the muscles in his shoulders were bunched. He alternately rubbed the bridge of his nose and the back of his neck.

Rennie set down the serving tray. "You could sit down, you know."

"I've tried that," he said wearily.

Belatedly she noticed the indentations in the cushions of the armchairs and the sofa. "Too comfortable?" she asked.

"Exactly."

"You don't have to stay up. I don't intend leaving the house tonight."

"You'll understand if I don't trust you quite yet."

She shrugged. "Suit yourself. How do you take your coffee?"

"Black."

Rennie poured a cup and handed it to him.

"Thank you."

"You're welcome."

They stared at each other for a long moment, then laughed uneasily, a little startled by their lapse into civility.

Rennie recovered by going to the window and drawing back the drapes. Jarret recovered by growling at her to get away. She stayed right where she was until he tugged the drapes from her hand and let them close.

"You made a splendid target," he told her. "You were clearly visible to anyone from the street. This damn fortress you call a home needs a stone wall around it, not an iron fence."

Over the rim of her coffee cup, Rennie rolled her eyes. "What did you do to Hollis to stop my wedding?" she asked.

"Who says I did anything to him?"

"I do. Hollis is my fiancé. I think I know him well enough to know he wouldn't have simply stepped aside."

"He didn't step aside. He practically rolled over." Jarret watched Rennie's face drain of color. "I'm sorry. That was a rotten thing to say."

"Yes, it was," she said quietly. "Was it true?"

He was saved from having to reply by the arrival of Moira, Jay Mac, and Rennie's sisters.

"I told you he would find her, Mama," Maggie said. "I'll wager she didn't get as far as the street before he pulled her up short. Am I right, Rennie?"

"Very nearly," Rennie said. "Mama, I'm sorry I worried you. I simply had to get out of there."

Moira came forward and hugged her daughter, giving her a kiss on the cheek. "I know you felt you had to, but it was very frightening for the rest of us." She turned to Jarret. "I thank God you were there."

Rennie managed not to choke on her coffee. "Where's Mary Francis?"

"We took her back to the convent," Skye said. "Papa wants to leave for the summerhouse tonight."

Jarret watched Rennie look squarely at her father for the first time since he entered the room. There was no animosity in her glance, merely a challenge. "Is that so?" she asked him. "Are you anxious to leave the city for some reason? Running scared from Nate Houston perhaps?"

Jarret couldn't imagine many people were privileged to talk to Jay Mac in that tone. Rennie's father didn't blink.

John MacKenzie Worth raised a finger and pointed at his daughter. "Don't you provoke me, Rennie. You know well enough that I'm more scared of you than I am of any thieving murderer."

"With good reason," she said. "You have a lot to answer for."

"Hollis Banks doesn't deserve you," Jay Mac said. "He's good enough to be a vice president at Northeast, but he's not the sort of man I had picked out for you."

"Thank you very much, Papa, but I'll do my own choosing." She paused a beat and gave a him significant look. "And you still have a lot to answer for."

"He'll answer on Judgment Day just like the rest of us, Mary Renee. You've no right to be so critical of your father."

That brought a rich burst of laughter from Maggie and Skye. They had listened to Moira harangue Jay Mac on Rennie's behalf the entire way home. Skye grabbed Maggie's hand. "C'mon, Mag. Let's get our trunks. Maybe Jarret will help us take them out to the carriage." The girls disappeared into the hallway and up the stairs. Jarret took advantage of the opportunity they afforded him and excused himself.

"It's not settled between us, Papa," Rennie said when she was alone with her parents. "You had no right to do what you did."

"If Hollis Banks wants my money, then he can damn well work for it like the rest of my employees. And if you want a place in my business, you can do the same. He doesn't need to marry you and you sure as hell don't need to marry him."

Rennie opened her mouth and was cut off by her

64

mother. "That's enough. Both of you. I won't have it. Not now, not when we're going to be separated. If you want to engage in a constructive argument, Jay Mac, then try to convince your daughter to come with us to the valley while I finish packing." Having said her piece, Moira swept grandly from the room.

Jay Mac watched her go, then turned back to Rennie. He stroked his side whiskers. "Well, Rennie? It wouldn't be the first time your mother's right. Can we agree to a truce?"

She didn't hesitate. "Truce."

"What about the other? Will you join us at the summerhouse?"

Again, she didn't hesitate. "No."

He nodded, expecting as much. "Tell your mother I put forth an eloquent argument and you inherited all her Irish stubbornness."

"Irish stubbornness? I thought it was the Worth intractability."

Jay Mac was sufficiently put in his place to grin sheepishly. "Well, whatever you call it, you came by it honestly and that's a fact."

"The coffee's hot," Rennie said, smiling. "Would you like some?"

"I'll get a cup."

While he was gone Rennie started a fire. They shared a few quiet minutes on the sofa together before Skye bounded in and announced they were ready to leave. She bounced out again, her flame red hair like a beacon of light, to supervise the loading of the carriage.

Jay Mac stood. "I suppose I should help Jarret with the trunks. That man's done enough for one day."

"He certainly has."

Studying his daughter, Jay Mac ran his fingers through his thick, dark blond hair. "Don't blame him overmuch,

Rennie. I offered him what must have seemed like a king's ransom to do what he did." A fee, he reminded himself, that he still owed the deputy.

"I have no respect for a man seduced by money," she said. "He didn't have to do what he did."

Jay Mac hesitated, his mouth set seriously in his broad face. "I hope you heard what you just said." Then mimicking Moira's lilting brogue, he added. "Sure, and I hope you did."

Rennie allowed Jarret to draw her back inside the house as the carriage carrying her family turned the corner on Broadway. "Will they be all right?" she asked.

Jarret's hand idly smoothed his trouser pocket. He felt the outline of Jay Mac's personal draft for ten thousand dollars accompanied by a twinge of regret. "They'll be fine. Your father seems confident of the men he's hired. That satisfies me."

"And Mary Francis?"

"Houston isn't stupid. Even if he knows about Mary Francis, I seriously doubt he'd attempt anything at the convent. He'd have to be desperate and frustrated to do that."

"Michael?"

"Do you want reassurance or the truth?"

She stared at him unblinkingly. "The truth."

"Ethan Stone will give up his life protecting your sister."

Rennie nodded, realizing she had to be satisfied with that. Jarret could offer no certainties. "I'm going to bed now," she said. "Will you see to the lamps, or shall I?"

"I'll do it." He stepped aside and let her pass. Watching her climb the staircase, her head bowed wearily, Jarret realized that once again she hadn't asked anything about herself.

Jarret turned in his sleep. The bed creaked. He lay very still, alert now, listening. Was it his own movement he'd heard or perhaps something else? The sound came again: a faint shuffle, the brush of the sole of a shoe against the carpet. Rennie apparently didn't understand that picking up her feet would have been quieter than sliding stealthily along the hallway runner.

Sitting up, Jarret pulled on a pair of jeans. The bed creaked again when he stood, but it was the last sound he made as he padded barefoot to the door. Jarret allowed himself to entertain the slim possibility that it was an intruder moving along the hallway. He opened the door only a crack at first. He was in time to glimpse Rennie taking the corner to the rear staircase. Pausing long enough to get his bearings, Jarret took the main steps to the first floor, ran down the hall, and was waiting for Rennie when she reached the servants' entrance near the kitchen.

Arms folded across his naked chest, leaning negligently against the door jamb with a smug smile on his face, Rennie thought he looked too cocky by half. Hot candle wax dripped on her fingers as her hand shook with anger. Jarret reached out and took the candle from her. The fact that he could hold it steady simply fueled Rennie's fury. Her anger, in turn, made her speechless.

Jarret skimmed her attire. She was wearing a navy blue gown, walking shoes, and carrying a small beaded bag around her wrist; hardly what she'd be wearing to make hot milk in the kitchen.

Although there was no excuse she could offer, Jarret waited to hear what Rennie had to say. He was prepared for a diatribe. It was only when she said nothing that he understood how deep her hurt and anger went. His smug smile faded as he straightened and used his free hand to indicate the kitchen. "Let's get the candle wax off your fingers."

Rennie followed him to the sink and surprised herself by allowing him to care for her hand. After he ran cold water over her fingers the burns only tingled. She withdrew her hand from his. "It isn't fair," she said quietly. "I shouldn't be a prisoner in my own home." Without waiting for a response, Rennie turned and mounted the steps to her room.

Jarret followed. When Rennie opened the door to her bedroom, he put his arm out and blocked her entrance. "Your mother suggested I lock you in if I had to."

Rennie blinked. Her face flushed hotly. "My mother was teasing. She knows very well there aren't any keys for these doors anymore."

"I was afraid you'd tell me something like that." He sighed, resigned to what would have to be and not liking it much. "Let me see the inside of your room," he said tiredly.

"Oh, by all means." She curtsied and waved him inside with an exaggerated flourish. "Please, feel free to treat my home as your own. Go anywhere you like."

Jarret chose not to bite. He used his candle to light the oil lamp on the nightstand. When he could see he looked around slowly. His interest wasn't in the furnishings, or the items contributing to the personal clutter on the highboy and the vanity, or even in the fact that Rennie had apparently packed a small bag of clothes for herself, then left it behind in her excitement to leave. What Jarret cared about was the other means that Rennie could use for escape.

"Where does that door lead?" he asked, pointing to the door situated to the left of the fireplace.

"You'd believe me if I told you?" she said.

"Never mind. I'll see for myself." He opened the door and glanced around. As he expected it was a dressing room. Unfortunately it connected to a bathing room and another bedroom beyond that. "That's a problem," he said to himself.

"Don't mumble," she told him.

He merely gave her a sharp look. She brazened it out and stared right back. Jarret rolled his eyes and shook his head. "What about these doors?" he asked, pulling on the brass handles of the French doors on the outside wall. The double doors jiggled but didn't budge.

Rennie sat down on her bed. "What about them?"

"They're not opening."

"That's because there's a latch at the top and bottom. You may want to consider thinking before you resort to brute force."

"You may want to consider changing your tone."

"Or what?" Rennie asked, challenging him.

Jarret pretended he didn't hear. He unlatched the doors, opened them and stepped out onto the balcony. He could hardly credit his own stupidity as the doors were slammed behind him and the latches dropped into place. Jarret pounded on the door frame with the flat of his hand. "Rennie! Open up!"

There was no response.

"Rennie! I mean it! Open these doors!" He waited a beat, peering through the windowpanes into the bedroom. He couldn't see her anywhere. Jarret put his shoulder to the door and tried to force it. The latches held. He considered breaking individual panes to reach the locks and door handle, but it would have taken too long.

Jarret leaned over the edge of the balcony. It was everything he was afraid it might be when he was considering Rennie's possible routes out of the house. Now it was a welcome sight.

Beneath Rennie's balcony was nothing but a straight twenty-foot drop to the ground. To the side and a few feet down, however, was the overhang for the delivery entrance. Once there, it was simply a matter of shimmying down one of the supporting columns.

Jarret made the leap easily, landing with a fair amount of agility and grace on the overhang. His bare feet held his footing on the shingles better than if he had been wearing boots. Using the gutter for a grip on the overhang, Jarret heaved himself over the side and hugged a support column with his legs. In a few seconds his feet were touching the damp grass.

He had no clear idea whether Rennie would leave by the front, back, or side of the house. He made a choice quickly and hoped he was right. Her destination was easy enough to figure, but knowing that she was going to see Hollis Banks, and knowing where Mr. Banks lived, were two entirely different things.

Jarret sprinted around the back of the house, sliding on the wet lawn as he rounded the corner, and kept going until he reached the side opposite Rennie's room. Enough light from street lamps reached the side yard for Jarret to pick up her trail almost immediately. He followed her steps in the crushed and matted grass straight to the side gate. The gate still swung loosely on its hinges, so he knew he wasn't far behind. He picked up her trail again on the other side of the neighbor's flagstone walk where Rennie tramped through their lawn. Over stone walls, through gardens and hedges, even over a little foot bridge built to accent a neighbor's pond, Jarret traced the path of Rennie's escape.

In the alleys behind the brownstone mansions, cats jumped out of the way as the chase quickened. In the stables at the rear, horses snorted and shifted nervously in their stalls. One stray dog alerted his chained friends, and the resulting cacophony had sleepy servants stumbling outside to scold them all and shoo the stray. The neighborhood was waking up, and dawn had yet to make its presence felt.

Rennie raised her skirts and clambered over the fence between the Marshalls' and the Stewarts'. Her gown caught in the decorative but dangerous iron spikes. She pulled hard, ripping her dress, but not enough to free herself. It was where Jarret found her.

He leaned against the fence, catching his breath, grateful for the chance to do so. When Rennie yanked on her gown again he merely reached through the fence, grabbed a handful of material and held on. Running had made his voice husky. "Don't try my patience any more than you already have," he said.

Rennie gulped for breath herself. "Are you threatening me?"

"Yes." Jarret was pleased to find that shut her up. He climbed the fence and dropped down lightly beside her. "I'm unhooking you, and then we're going right back to the house. There will be no running attempts on the way because I'll carry you if I have to. If you're so all fire anxious to see that Banks fellow, then I'll arrange it tomorrow. I don't believe it's escaped your notice, though, that he hasn't exactly been beating down the door to see you."

"Don't talk about him! You have no right!"

Jarret shrugged. He freed her gown, expecting no thanks and getting none. "Let's go. I'm tired even if you're not."

The voice that came out of the darkness was deep and clear and demanding. "What the hell is going on here?"

Jarret stepped protectively in front of Rennie. He dropped his hand casually to his holster only to realize he wasn't wearing one. At least he knew the man wasn't Nathaniel Houston. There would have been no time to con-

71

sider going for his gun.

"Michael? Is that you?" The speaker moved from the deep shadows of the back porch to the lawn. He lowered the Colt .45 he was carrying as he neared the couple.

Rennie stepped out from behind Jarret. "It's Mary Renee, Mr. Marshall. Michael's sister."

Logan Marshall slipped his gun into the waistband of his trousers. The tails of his nightshirt were bunched there as well. "Rennie? My God, it's been a while, hasn't it? You and your sister are still a matched pair." His eyes dropped to her flat abdomen. "Well, perhaps not so much at the moment." He caught her embarrassed glance again. "Is this something you want to tell me about or should I pretend I'm having a very strange dream?"

Rennie peered sideways at Jarret. He didn't even have the grace to look abashed. He was standing in Logan Marshall's yard wearing nothing but a pair of faded jeans and looking for all the world as if he had every right to be there. Rennie's deep green eyes were imploring. "I think we'd all do better to say we've been dreaming."

Jarret smirked.

Logan caught Jarret's derisive smile, then looked at Rennie again. "Are you all right?"

She nodded. "Yes. I'm fine. I may have acted a bit precipitously tonight."

Logan raked his copper-threaded hair with his fingers. He knew Rennie's explanation wasn't meant for him but as an apology to the man at her side. He didn't think the stranger believed it. "Everything is all right at your house?"

"Yes. In fact we're going back now."

Logan glanced at the fence behind her. A swatch of white material from her underskirt fluttered on one of the spikes like a small flag of surrender. "Rennie, are you certain I don't need to send for the police? I know about

72

Nate Houston's escape. The *Chronicle* received a telegram from Ethan Stone a few days ago. He wanted it kept out of the paper until Jay Mac told your sister personally. That's all been taken care of, hasn't it?"

Belatedly Jarret recognized Logan Marshall as the publisher and co-owner of one of New York's foremost newspapers, as well as Michael Dennehy's employer. He had expected the force behind the *Chronicle* to be older, not of an equal age to him and Ethan, and certainly not so physically formidable. Marshall was tall enough to return Jarret's stare and possessed of both the muscular strength and sharp agility to take him on in Rennie's defense.

Jarret was aware of Logan's wary regard as well. The publisher was taking measure of the man who'd been vaulting fences in pursuit of Rennie Dennehy. Jarret began to feel a bit uncomfortable under Logan's scrutiny. Didn't Rennie have any common neighbors? Was everyone a Marshall or an Astor?

Rennie realized that at three o'clock in the morning she owed Logan Marshall a little more explanation than good manners had him requesting. "This is Mr. Jarret Sullivan, Mr. Marshall."

Jarret couldn't think of anything else to do save hold out his hand. "Ethan Stone's deputy," he said.

Logan shook the offered hand. "The bounty hunter?"

Jarret nodded, aware of Rennie's start of surprise beside him. "Sometimes that. Right now a federal deputy."

Releasing his hand, Logan frowned slightly. "Rennie, I thought Michael told me you were marrying Hollis Banks today . . . yesterday . . ." He rubbed his temple a moment. "God, it's the middle of tomorrow already."

"Michael got married instead," she said.

"To Hollis Banks?" He *was* having a bad dream.

"No, to Ethan Stone. We just came from the wedding."

"More or less," Jarret muttered, looking down at his attire.

Logan held up both hands. "Never mind. I'm sure this all makes sense to you, but I'm going back to bed. I'll think of something to tell Katy." He nodded to both of them. "Good night. Oh, and you can use the gate. No sense risking impalement a second time in one night."

Rennie's smile was weak. When he was gone she looked down at the ground and prayed to be swallowed whole by some freakish shift in the earth's mantle. Wisps of hair fluttered across her forehead as she heaved a sigh. "That may be the single most humiliating encounter of my life," she said.

"That's only because the night's still young." Jarret locked his arm around Rennie's and forced her to match his quick stride. Her protests about being dragged and yanked and pulled like saltwater taffy were given no response. Inside the house he marched her directly upstairs, past her bedchamber and into his.

Rennie pointed behind her. "Wait! You've missed my room."

"No, I didn't. For tonight at least, this *is* your room." He pointed to the oval braided rug in front of the fireplace. "And *that's* your bed."

She tried to pull away from him. "I'm not sleeping on the floor!"

He held her fast. "Suit yourself. But know this, Miss Dennehy, I've spent the better part of three days sitting in the cramped confines of a rail car, and before that a few days sitting in a saddle, neither of which were particularly conducive to sleeping. Except for a few hours here and there, I haven't had a full night's shut-eye in over a week. *I'm* taking the bed. You've got the floor. And I don't give a good damn whether you sleep or not."

Jarret let Rennie's arm go only to hunker down and take

a fistful of her underskirt. Before she knew what he was about he tore a strip that took the entire hem.

She was too startled to scream. "What do you think you're doing?" Rennie backed away from the hint of feral pleasure in Jarret's eyes as he straightened. She nervously pushed aside a strand of dark red hair that had fallen across her cheek, and her eyes darted toward the door. She held out her arms to ward him off as he approached. "What are you going to do with that?"

Jarret didn't answer. He simply moved forward, holding the strip of cloth taut between his hands, and waited. Rennie backed right into the heavy armchair behind her and plopped down with a faint "oof." Her eyes widened with surprise, and she clumsily tried to pull herself out again. Her tattered underskirt and gown tangled in her legs and confoundered her efforts. Jarret grabbed her flailing hands in one of his and quickly tied her wrists together. It was not much different than roping a calf, but Jarret refrained from making the comparison.

When he had her trussed to his satisfaction, he slid the braided rug across the floor until it rested next to the bed. Pulling Rennie by her tether, deaf to her entreaties, he managed to tie the open end of the leash to one of the foot legs of the bed. Rennie had little choice but to fall on her knees or be bent awkwardly and painfully at the waist.

Jarret tossed a blanket at her and deliberated about a pillow. Finally he gave her his. "Guess it don't matter much," he said, deliberately goading her by affecting a lazy drawl. "I'm used to sleepin' without one most nights. Sure was a treat, though."

Her emerald eyes glittered as she glared at him. "Go to hell, Mr. Sullivan."

"Jarret. Seein' that we're sharing a room and all, it makes sense to call me Jarret."

She kicked at him. It was a useless gesture that resulted

in Rennie banging the crown of her own head against the bed frame. Tears sprang to her eyes, partly out of pain, partly from the sheer frustration of not being able to rub the tender spot herself.

Jarret patted her lightly on the head and leaped onto the bed as she tried to bite him. Laughing, he stretched out on the bed, turned back the oil lamp, and rolled on his side, slipping one arm under his head.

"Good night, Rennie."

"I haven't given you leave to use my Christian name."

In the darkness Jarret smiled. He pulled a blanket over his shoulders and rubbed his cold feet against the sheets. "Good night, Miss Dennehy."

Rennie seethed. When anger alone could not sustain wakefulness, she tossed and turned as much as her bonds would permit. She tore at the knots with her fingernails for the better part of an hour before she admitted that she couldn't loosen them. Through it all Jarret slept peacefully, occasionally emitting a soft snore as if to remind her he was still there.

Against her will, against all reason, Rennie found herself struggling harder to stay awake than to get away. She heard the grandfather clock in the entrance hall strike four, then the half-hour. It was the last thing she remembered.

Jarret stood over Rennie. His hair curled damply at the nape. He wiped a bead of water from his chin with the towel that was draped around his neck. He picked up a chambray shirt at the foot of the bed and slipped it on. Rennie didn't stir.

She had found, it seemed, the only position that could have offered her a modicum of comfort. She was curled on her side, knees drawn close to her chest. Her face rested precariously close to the bed post, and her hands were actually wrapped around it. Even in profile he could see the shadows beneath her lashes and knew her rest had been much less satisfactory than his.

He grimaced when he saw the abrasions on her wrists. Her navy blue gown was twisted around her, the sleeve torn at the elbow. The length of her calves was visible where she had kicked off the blanket. Her stockings had a few snags and tears in them, and her ankle boots were caked with mud at the heel and toe.

During the night, or during the fight—Jarret wasn't sure when—most of her hair had been loosed from its pins. There was a tangle of auburn waves and dark copper strands across her pale cheek. A bit of greenery near her ear gave evidence of one of the many hedges she had barreled through. If the truth were told, she looked rather worse for the wear.

But that was only if he didn't take her mouth into account, and that was something Jarret couldn't quite keep himself from doing. In sleep, Rennie's lips were faintly damp, slightly parted, and enticingly full. He found himself very intrigued by the shape of her mouth, with its vaguely pouting lower lip and sensual curve for the upper one. Mary Renee's mouth could make a man forget he was courting trouble just considering kissing her.

Jarret reached for his valise and rooted through it until he found his buck knife. He unsheathed it and knelt beside Rennie to cut her bonds. He was leaning over her, the knife poised next to her hands, mere inches away from her face, when Rennie woke.

Jarret was close enough to feel Rennie's chest heave as she gulped in air. He managed to get a hand over her mouth before her scream reached a glass-shattering pitch. Her struggles forced him to toss aside the knife before he hurt her with it.

He spoke to her gently. "I want to let you go. There's no reason to scream. I'm not going to hurt you."

She couldn't breathe. His hand covered her mouth and nose, and the pressure cut off her air. She shook her head and struggled harder, trying to get him to dislodge his hand. Her eyes were wide and panicked. She clawed at the bed post, and the knots were pulled more tightly on her wrists.

Mrs. Cavanaugh knocked on the door to Jarret's room. "Mr. Sullivan, are you in there? I'm looking for Rennie. I can't find"—she opened the door a crack and poked her head in—"her anywhere."

Jarret's hand slipped from Rennie's mouth as the cook screamed. He sat back on his haunches, shaking his head and gazing heavenward. Rennie sucked in great draughts of air and began tearing a strip into him that would have put a sailor to shame.

Jarret picked up his knife, tossed it on the bed, and stood. He left Rennie where she was and walked directly past the hysterical Mrs. Cavanaugh. "Less bawling than this in a Chicago stockyard," he muttered disgustedly.

Chapter Three

Mrs. Cavanaugh rushed in the room as soon as Jarret exited. "Has he hurt you?" She dropped to her knees beside Rennie and stroked her hair. "What was he doing? Has he lost his mind?" She crossed herself. "Saints! That your mother could have just gone off and left you. Sure and I'll never understand. I'm getting the mister right now and sending him for the constabulary. I'm not leaving you alone with Mr. Sullivan anymore."

Rennie summoned patience. It was clear to her now that Jarret never intended her any harm, not that what he had done was in any way forgivable, but he hadn't had murder as his motive. "Could you release me, Mrs. Cavanaugh?" she asked, indicating her bound wrists.

The cook's hand fell away from Rennie's hair. "What? Oh! Of course!" Her capable fingers, strengthened by years of kneading dough and peeling potatoes, immediately took up the task. "Sure and I can't imagine what I was thinkin', going on while you're trussed like my best Christmas goose."

Rennie smiled weakly at the comparison. "The knife he left behind would be better suited to the task," she said.

Mrs. Cavanaugh glanced at the buck knife, then at the series of knots again. Her narrow face was set in disapproval. "I've got a meat cleaver that would do the job with more finesse."

Rennie was helpless to do anything but wait. She was uncomfortably aware of certain body functions that required attending. The thought that she might have to relieve herself right where she lay was another reason to contemplate Jarret Sullivan's slow, tortured death.

"Here, and I'll have it in a moment," Mrs. Cavanaugh said, picking at the last knot. "The man's a brute."

Rennie concurred. "A monster."

"A madman."

"A cretin."

Mrs. Cavanaugh nodded. "Handsome, though, wouldn't you say?"

Rennie's hands were suddenly free. She used the bedpost to pull herself upright and let the cook gingerly massage her wrists. "What have his looks to do with anything?" she demanded. "His behavior's been reprehensible."

"Oh, yes," the cook said quickly. "There's no excuse, of course. I was just saying, though, that he's rather a fine figure of a man. It's neither here nor there, just an observation." Ignoring Rennie's sour look, Mrs. Cavanaugh helped her to her feet. "I'll see about the police now. Your mother told me the man was sworn to protect you. I'm thinkin' she'd want him out now."

"She certainly would," Rennie said feelingly. "She'd want him in jail."

Mrs. Cavanaugh escorted Rennie to her own room, helped her draw a bath, then went downstairs to search for her husband. It occurred to her that in twenty-four years of knowing Mary Renee no situation was ever as straightforward as it seemed. Making a sudden decision, she left Mr. Cavanaugh to his pruning in the side yard and sought out Mr. Sullivan instead.

* * *

The lure of bread baking and bacon frying drew Rennie to the kitchen. Mrs. Cavanaugh stood in front of the large iron stove, scrambling eggs and eying the perfectly round pancakes bubbling and browning on the grill.

"It all smells wonderful," Rennie said. She crossed the kitchen to stand at the cook's side and put one arm around Mrs. Cavanaugh's slender shoulders. "Can I help you with something?"

"There's coffee brewing. You might see if it's ready."

Rennie smiled, not at all surprised that she was given such a simple task. Mrs. Cavanaugh was invariably suspicious of Rennie's help in the kitchen. "You know, Mrs. Cavanaugh, I've really got to learn to cook someday."

"Not in *my* kitchen."

Looking down at the cook's pristine apron, Rennie sighed. In spite of Mrs. Cavanaugh's activity of the last hour, her apron was spotless, the table was clear, the sink was empty, and the floor was clean. Rennie, on the other hand, made a mess filling salt shakers.

"In fact," the cook was saying, "you'd better step away from the stove before you get burned." She'd no sooner spoke than a bubble of grease exploded on the skillet and splashed the back of Rennie's hand. "There! See that! Go on with you. Put it under cold water, then have a seat at the table. I can't cook and be watchin' for what mischief happens here when you're around."

Laughing, Rennie did as she was told. "Has Mr. Cavanaugh gone for the police?"

"Everything's been taken care of."

That surprised Rennie. She hadn't heard any sort of commotion upstairs. It seemed unlikely that Jarret would vacate the house without some manner of protest. "He didn't draw his gun, did he?"

Mrs. Cavanaugh shook her head. She flipped a pancake with a flick of her wrist, then went back to stirring the eggs.

"I half expected that he might."

"Well, he didn't."

Rennie became aware of an edge of impatience in the cook's voice. She saw now that Mrs. Cavanaugh's movements were rather stiff and tightly controlled. She seemed to be attacking the food, spearing the bacon and catapulting the pancakes. She set out a tray, added two plates, and stacked pancakes on one and arranged the bacon and eggs on the other. The cook placed a mug on the tray, filled it with hot, black coffee, surveyed her handiwork, and hefted it off the counter.

Rennie's eyes widened at the heap of food. She held up both hands, shaking her head. "I couldn't possibly eat that much."

"I don't expect you could," Mrs. Cavanaugh said briskly. "That's why there's tea in the pot and two warm muffins in the oven. This is for Mr. Sullivan."

Rennie had no difficulty reading the cook's emphatic nod and smile. Both clearly said, "So there." Dumbfounded, she watched Mrs. Cavanaugh march out of the kitchen.

Jarret slid the *Chronicle* aside when Mrs. Cavanaugh entered the dining room. His reaction was similar to Rennie's when he saw the portions prepared for him. "I think you've overestimated my appetite just a bit," he told her.

"Sure and go on with you," she said, setting down the tray. "Can't imagine a man like you not needin' something after the night you had."

Jarret opened his napkin and laid it across his lap. Under Mrs. Cavanaugh's watchful eye he tucked into the food she set before him.

"Exactly what sort of night was it?" Rennie asked from the doorway. Her cheeks were flushed hotly, and her hands were balled into fists at her side. "What have you told Mrs. Cavanaugh?"

Jarret rose briefly, indicated the chair at the corner to his right, and continued eating. Glancing worriedly between Jarret and Rennie, Mrs. Cavanaugh eased herself out of the room. Rennie thrust white-knuckled fists into the pockets of her dove gray day dress.

"She was going to send her husband for the police," Rennie said. Her voice did not sound completely her own. It was brittle with the strength of her anger. She was hardly aware that her feelings were oddly misplaced, not directed at Mrs. Cavanaugh at all, but at Jarret.

"Perhaps she has," Jarret said carelessly. His eyes wandered to the folded newspaper beside his plate. He began to read a crisply told account of a murder in the Bowery.

Rennie approached the table. "Stop that. You know very well you're only pretending to read to avoid my questions."

Preoccupied, it was a moment before Jarret looked up. "I'm sorry. You were saying . . ."

"You're doing this on purpose," she said, her eyes accusing. "No one can be this aggravating except by design."

Jarret considered that. "Really? I find it works as a general guiding principle."

Rennie kicked out the chair beside him and sat down heavily. Her hands came out of her pockets and gripped the gracefully curved armrests. There was some small part of her that recognized she was not fighting him as much as she was fighting the urge to laugh. Conflicting emotion did not set well with Rennie. She liked having things clearly delineated, ordered and catalogued. Amusement and anger did not belong in the same file.

"What did you tell Mrs. Cavanaugh?" she asked again.

"The truth." Jarret offered her a strip of crisp bacon. "Get yourself a plate and join me."

Rennie took the bacon but shook her head at his suggestion. "What sort of truth?" she asked.

"Are there different sorts? That's a rather ponderous, philosophical question, isn't it?" He raised his mug of coffee, held it between his palms, and gave a good account of himself as a man in deep contemplation.

Rennie quelled the urge to tip hot coffee all over his chest. "I'm losing patience with you, Mr. Sullivan."

He nodded. "Then, we're on equal footing." He sipped his coffee, placed the mug down, and speared some eggs. "I told Mrs. Cavanaugh exactly what happened here last night, no more, no less. Interestingly enough, shortly after three this morning she and her husband were awakened by dogs barking all over the neighborhood. Her experience only reinforced what I was telling her. She understands perfectly why I was forced to . . . to . . ." He paused. A glimmer of a smile came and went across his face. "To truss you like a Christmas goose, I believe is what she said."

Rennie snapped off a piece of bacon with her teeth and glared hard at Jarret. "You must have enjoyed hearing that."

"It was an interesting point. I had likened the experience to calf roping, you see, so I appreciated hearing Mrs. Cavanaugh's perspective."

She was thankful she had already swallowed because surely she would have choked. "I want to see Hollis today," she said in flat, no-nonsense accents. "Can that be arranged?"

"I said I would do it, didn't I?"

"I hardly know you well enough to say if you're a man of your word."

84

All vestige of humor left him. The brilliant sapphire eyes darkened and grew cold. The lines of his face became more defined, the set of his features gravely serious. The only movement was a faint working of his jaw. "I think you're lying, Miss Dennehy. The one thing you know for sure about me is I'm a man of my word." He looked at her for a moment longer, spearing her with his glance; then he said quietly, "Now, if you'll excuse me."

When he didn't move, but began to eat again, Rennie realized *she* had been dismissed. Her mouth parted, closed. She was too stunned to respond. Jerking upright, she pushed her chair away from the table and sought the refuge of her own room.

Rennie couldn't concentrate on the book she had chosen to read. Her thoughts invariably swung back to Jarret's comment in the dining room. His tone had almost been threatening, as if he dared her to take exception to what he said. Alone in her room, curled like a young child in the large, comfortable armchair, Rennie felt now that she hadn't accepted the challenge inherent in Jarret's voice, but run away from it.

How was she supposed to know he was the sort of man who could be counted on to keep promises? Based on what facts? He'd never made any commitment to her. The man was a bounty hunter. If that didn't indicate someone with a mile-wide streak of independence and no conscience, she didn't know what did. So what if he was temporarily a federal deputy? He probably hadn't even taken an oath. He wasn't bound by any promises that she could see.

He owed her sister the benefit of his protection, not . . .

Rennie closed the book slowly. In less than twenty-four hours of making her acquaintance, Jarret Sullivan had stopped her wedding, dogged her footsteps from the courthouse to her home, chased her across three Manhattan blocks in the middle of the night, and tied her to his bed.

Putting down the book, Rennie stood. She smoothed the folds of her gown over her hips, secured an errant tendril of hair behind her ear, and went back downstairs to make her peace with Jarret.

He was in the front parlor, slouched in a wide chair, one leg resting negligently over the arm, the other hooked across a footstool. When he saw Rennie he straightened, stood.

She motioned him to sit down again. "You looked as if you were deep in thought," she said. "I didn't mean to disturb you."

Since he'd been thinking of her and the bent of his thoughts had been disturbing, it seemed to Jarret that it didn't matter what her intention was. He ran his fingers through the crown of his dark blond hair as he sat down. "Mr. Cavanaugh has already been sent 'round to fetch your fiancé."

Rennie's slender hand traced the curved back of the sofa as she passed behind it. "I didn't come here about that, but thank you. I appreciate the opportunity to speak to Hollis." She rounded the corner of the sofa, hesitated, then sat down. When she looked at Jarret she realized he was not watching her expectantly as she might have hoped, but suspiciously. She felt a flash of irritation. "Actually, I came to release you from your promise."

One of his brows lifted. "Oh?"

"Yes," she went on hurriedly. "Your promise to protect me. That's it, isn't it? Why I'm supposed to know you're a man of your word, I mean. You've sworn to protect me, and you have . . . you are." She waited, thinking he might say something. His handsome features remained impassive. "It's admirable, really. I should have seen that earlier. Instead I've been caught up in the interference of it all.

86

I've been thinking that we should talk about this calmly and entertain the notion of compromise. To that end, I'm prepared to release you from your promise."

"I see."

She smiled encouragingly. "You do? Well, that's a start."

He shook his head. "No. It's an end. It's not a promise I made to you, Miss Dennehy, but one I made first to Ethan, then your father, then your sister. It's a sworn duty I took when I was made Ethan's deputy. I'm not going anywhere."

"But I don't want you around here!"

"I know," he said quietly. "Have you asked yourself why?"

She stiffened as she heard the challenge return to his voice, gentle this time, probing. "I . . . you . . ."

"Yes?"

Rennie stood, agitated now. On the surface his words were quite clear, easily understood, yet there was an undercurrent between them that hinted of something not so simply defined. Her eyes widened slightly, caught and held by his as he rose from the chair and approached her. Rennie suddenly found it difficult to breathe. Her heart was beating too loudly; her fingers twisted the fabric of her gown. She wanted to take a step back. Instead, she held her ground.

When Jarret's face was above her, his chest just a hard heartbeat from hers, he stopped. "I could tell you why you don't like it," he said lowly. "But you wouldn't believe me. I could show you, but the promise I made, the one you think you don't understand, won't let me."

Rennie's shake of her head was barely perceptible. Her eyes never left his. Her voice was a whisper. "You're speaking in riddles."

"I don't think so." His head lowered a fraction. He was

87

close enough to feel Rennie's breath catch. For the briefest moment his eyes dropped to her mouth.

Then he abruptly stepped away. "You have company, Miss Dennehy," he said pleasantly, as if the husky menace in his voice had never been. "Your fiancé's come calling."

Rennie felt as if she'd been tumbling down a deep, dark well, only to be snatched up by the same person who had pushed her over the ledge. "You *are* a son of a bitch, Mr. Sullivan."

Jarret's slight smile was his only acknowledgment.

Brushing past him, Rennie gathered the pieces of her shattered self-confidence and went to meet Hollis in the entrance hall. How was it Jarret had heard his arrival when she hadn't heard anything above the slamming of her own heart?

Hollis was giving Mr. Cavanaugh his coat. The older man slipped away as Rennie extended her arms to her fiancé.

"Rennie!" Drawing her in his embrace, Hollis held her tightly. "God, I was glad to hear from you! I read the papers this morning . . . I didn't know what to think. I was certain there'd be some mention of Nate Houston and our aborted wedding."

Rennie drew back; her feathered brows were fiercely knit. "You read the paper to see if our wedding fiasco was mentioned?" she asked, appalled. "It's after ten! Didn't it occur to you to come here on your own? To see if I was all right, to find out for yourself what was going on?"

Hollis's hands rested on Rennie's shoulders. His palms slid down her arms until he cupped her wrists. He gave her a small, patronizing shake. "Rennie, Rennie. What's happened? You're acting completely out of character." He tried to lead her into the parlor, but she pulled out of his light grasp. He saw her wince and looked down at her wrists. The bruising just below the cuffs of her gown was clearly visible. "Did I just do that?" he asked.

Tears sprang immediately to Rennie's widely spaced emerald eyes. Hollis's figure shimmered in front of her. That he could demonstrate such concern and fear of his own strength moved Rennie deeply. After a moment she allowed herself to be enfolded against his wide chest and powerful shoulders. This bear of a man, with his husky frame and broad, appealing face, could be fierce and threatening when he was challenged, but he would never hurt her.

Hollis patted her lightly on the back of the head, satisfied that his world had been righted again. He urged her gently into the parlor, eased her onto the sofa, and poured her a small glass of sherry.

"It's too early for that," she said, when he handed the glass to her.

"Nonsense. It will calm your nerves."

He sat down beside her, aware that Rennie's misty eyes were darting around the room. "Are you looking for something?" he asked.

Rennie laughed weakly, mostly out of relief that Jarret Sullivan wasn't lurking somewhere in the parlor. "No, it's nothing. May I borrow your handkerchief?"

It was a source of some annoyance to Hollis that Rennie never seemed to have her own. Under the circumstances he thought it better not to hint at it again. "Certainly," he said, passing it along. She wiped her eyes and tucked it under the cuff of her sleeve. Hollis knew he would never see it again. "Tell me what's going on. Mr. Cavanaugh said only that you wanted to see me. I couldn't even get him to tell me how you were."

"I'm fine, Hollis." She sipped her sherry. "Perhaps a little confused. More than a little actually. I don't know what happened yesterday. Why did you agree to call off the wedding?"

Hollis looked properly affronted. His brows, the same dark chocolate shade as his eyes, rose imperiously. "Who told you I agreed? It took the point of a gun to make me see that Houston meant to stop the ceremony." He lifted Rennie's hand to the back of his head. The lump was still very much in evidence. "I suppose I'm fortunate that's all he did to me. The man had murder on his mind."

"He clubbed you with his gun?" she asked.

"You don't think our wedding could have been called off for less, do you?"

"I didn't know what to think. No one told me anything. I fainted at the church. Twice. I know, I can hardly believe it myself."

"You shouldn't have had to face Nate Houston without me," Hollis said.

Rennie frowned. "That's the third time you mentioned Houston. He's not here. At least not that anyone knows for certain. It was Mr. Sullivan who knocked you out. Papa paid him ten thousand dollars to stop our marriage."

"Ten thousand!" Hollis's face flushed with ruddy color. "What do you mean the man wasn't Nate Houston. That's who he said he was."

Rennie sighed. Quite a lot was becoming clear to her. Jarret had intimidated Hollis, a man who was not easily threatened, not by wearing a gun, but by wearing the reputation of another man. She finished her drink and placed the glass on a doily on the end table. "His name is Mr. Jarret Sullivan. He's a deputy to Ethan Stone. You know, the marshal who saved Michael's life?"

"Who fathered Michael's baby," he said.

Rennie chose to ignore his self-righteous and rather priggish tone. "Mr. Sullivan traveled east with Marshal Stone to find Houston and Dee Kelly. His plans were altered slightly when Papa informed him Michael had a twin. He got the job of protecting me by default."

"That should be my job."

"My sentiments exactly. And it would have been if not for Jay Mac's interference."

Hollis shook his head. "I don't understand your father. He receives my work very well, values my judgment and my contributions, treats me as he might a son. Why in the world wouldn't he want me to marry his daughter?"

"He's got it into his mind that you're not right for me," Rennie said. She was not going to insult Hollis with an accusation that he was after her money. "And you know Jay Mac. He's not likely to change his mind any time soon. We can wait him out or plunge ahead on our own." She looked at Hollis expectantly.

"Plunge ahead," he said without hesitation. His response coaxed forward one of Rennie's rare and beautiful smiles. It softened her taut and anxious features. It also disappeared at his next words. "In due time."

"What do you mean?"

"Rennie, be serious. From what I can tell your family's not even around."

"Michael and Mary Francis are still in town. Papa's taken everyone else to the country."

"And that's how you want to marry? Behind his back, as if we were undertaking a crime?"

"No, but . . ."

"Then there's my parents to think of. You know I'd have been here before if it weren't for them. Mother's taken to her bed with a migraine and Father's nearly apoplectic. They were very embarrassed by yesterday's uproar, to say nothing of frightened."

Rennie bowed her head, humiliatingly aware of the extent of her own selfishness. "I'm sorry, Hollis, it's just that I . . ."

"I know," he said earnestly. "I want to be married, too.

91

My feelings for you haven't changed. You believe that, don't you?"

She searched his face. There was no denying he was an attractive man, but Rennie was looking for something beyond the handsome cut of his features. She wanted steadiness and reliability. It didn't matter that he didn't stop her heart. She wasn't marrying for love, and she suspected that Hollis wasn't either. "I believe you," she said softly.

He leaned forward and kissed her cheek. Rennie turned so that his lips touched hers. She closed her eyes as Hollis accepted her mouth. He increased the pressure in slow increments, easing his lips over hers. One of his hands slid to the small of her back, supporting her as her arms came around his neck. Her mouth opened under his. She felt his mustache and side whiskers abrade her skin. It was not unpleasant.

"Forgive me."

Rennie thought at first it was Hollis who was apologizing. Then her mind registered the tone and nuance of that voice. Although Hollis pulled away immediately, Rennie was purposely slow to let her arms fall from his neck. She glanced over her shoulder to the open doorway. "Hollis, this is Mr. Sullivan. Don't let his lazy smile bemuse you. That he's here at this moment proves he has the timing of a Swiss watch."

Jarret sauntered into the room and held out his hand to Hollis. "Mr. Banks. Good to see you again. You look none the worse for your encounter with Nate Houston."

Hollis saw no humor in the observation. He remained seated and ignored Jarret's hand. "You should have told me who you were."

Jarret's brows raised slightly. "I thought I did. In fact, it seemed to me . . ." He trailed off as Rennie's eyes became more anxious. What was fair? he wondered. Should he give Rennie every detail of his conversation with her fiancé, or should he allow Hollis to shade the encounter with his own particular version of the truth? Hollis had wanted to believe Jarret was Nate Houston to make his surrender less distasteful to Rennie.

"Yes?" Rennie asked, prompting him to continue.

"Nothing."

She relaxed slightly. "I've already told Hollis that Jay Mac offered you a great deal of money to do what you did."

Hollis nodded. Out of his vest pocket he took a slim cigar, offered it to Jarret, and when it wasn't accepted, clipped and lighted it for himself. He inhaled deeply and blew out a leisurely cloud of smoke above his head. "It's understandable that a man like yourself could be influenced by that kind of money."

Jarret merely stared at Hollis, his mouth flat, his eyes knowing. What about you, he wanted to ask. A mere twelve hundred bought you off.

Rennie found an ashtray for Hollis and brought it to him. She rang Mrs. Cavanaugh for tea and told the cook there would be three for lunch. "Was it really necessary to hit Hollis?" she asked when she returned to the sofa.

"Yes," Jarret said without compunction. "I thought so." He looked at Hollis. "No worse for your experience, are you?"

"I wouldn't say that, Mr. Sullivan," Hollis answered. He placed one hand over Rennie's and patted it gently and with a certain air of ownership. "Mary Renee would be my bride today."

Instead, Jarret wanted to say, she slept with me last night. Something of his thoughts must have reached Rennie because he saw her blanch. "Apparently the inevitable's merely been postponed," he said politely.

"So you were listening at the door," Rennie said, accusing.

"Not at all," he said. "Anyone looking at the two of you would draw the same conclusion. A couple as much in love would hardly let a thing like Papa's objections get in the way."

He's lying through his teeth, Rennie wanted to tell Hollis. Don't believe anything. She leveled her most insincere smile at Jarret.

"As for me," Jarret went on, "I was paid to stop one wedding, not a succession of them."

Hollis nodded. "Then, we have no reason to anticipate further interference from you."

"That's a fact," he drawled. At that moment Mrs. Cavanaugh arrived with tea. Jarret used the distraction to grin wickedly at Rennie. In turn, she looked as if she might like to spill hot tea in his lap.

Hollis stubbed out his cigar. "Tell me, Mr. Sullivan, how long can we expect this business with Nathaniel Houston might last?"

"There's no telling. A few days, a week, the better part of a month."

"A month!" Rennie said.

Jarret shrugged. "It's possible. Can't flush out the varmint if you don't know where his hole is."

Hollis raised his cup. "Is it really necessary for you to stay here while we're waiting for this . . . ummm . . . varmint?" He sipped his tea. "I mean, it's not quite seemly, is it?"

"No one knows he's here, Hollis," Rennie said. She worried her lower lip on the lie as she remembered the confrontation with Logan Marshall. Studiously avoiding Jarret, she added, "Except for Mr. and Mrs. Cavanaugh."

"Yes, but they stay in the carriage house."

"What are you saying?" she asked, bristling. "That there may be some impropriety during Mr. Sullivan's residency?"

"No, of course not," Hollis said quickly. "No, I don't think that. Never." He patted her hand again. "But you must be aware that not everyone will understand the circumstances of his presence here. I'm thinking of your reputation."

And yours, Jarret thought. Hollis did not want it passing through upper-crust circles that his fiancée had taken up with another man.

"I told you, Hollis," Rennie said, "no one knows he's here."

"Rennie," Hollis said patiently, "he interrupted our wedding ceremony. Our guests saw him walk through the church. He struck with his gun and disappeared. Mary Francis was offering her apologies to the crowd when I was revived, but her explanation was not very forthcoming. We are, quite frankly, the talk of the town."

"I think it's more to the point," Jarret said, "that not many people know Rennie's still here. I believe her sister let it be thought that Rennie was leaving town. As long as she stays in the house, then there's no reason for anyone to suspect otherwise. When Nate Houston is captured you two can have a grand reconciliation in front of a throng if you choose. Until then, her safety depends on her seclusion." He paused. "And her reputation relies on our discretion."

Hollis addressed Rennie. "You understand that I would feel better if you were with me. I'm quite capable of protecting you myself."

"I know," she said.

"You're satisfied with this arrangement, then?" he asked.

"Hardly. If it weren't for Michael still being in the city, I'd join the rest of my family. But it's not really a choice for me, Hollis. I need to be here. Even if there's nothing I can do for her, at least I'll know I didn't turn my back. She would do the same for me."

Hollis realized he had to be satisfied with that. It didn't set well with him. "Then, I'm to go on at the office as if all is well?"

"All *is* well. I didn't stand you up." Rennie finished her tea. "I really don't care to discuss this in front of Mr. Sullivan any longer." She looked pointedly at Jarret, but he merely sipped his tea and smiled politely. "We'll speak of it again privately."

Mrs. Cavanaugh interrupted a few minutes later, and Rennie, desperate to think of safe topics of conversation, was grateful for the diversion. Lunch went smoothly. Between the soup, salad, and shepherd's pie, Rennie engaged Hollis in business chatter, all but excluding Jarret. Out of the corner of her eye she noticed he seemed more amused by her machinations than offended.

"You could have let me speak to him alone again," she said after Hollis left. "You knew I wanted to."

"Oh, then you *were* aware I was eating lunch with you?"

One corner of Rennie's mouth lifted in disgust. "How could I not be? You were slurping your soup so loudly I'm surprised the neighbors didn't complain."

He grinned. "Noticed that, did you?"

She simply glared at him. As far as she could tell, Jarret Sullivan was without conscience.

He escorted her from the entrance hall back to the parlor. "Actually, Rennie, I could see that nothing good was going to come out of a private conversation with Hollis."

Rennie didn't bother to reprimand him for his familiarity again. "What do you mean?"

"You were going to try to convince him to elope, weren't you?"

She took the offensive. "Where do you get these ideas?"

It didn't matter to Jarret if she admitted it or not, he was satisfied he had reached the proper conclusion. "I don't think Hollis would have agreed. He seems to want the sanction of your entire family. After all, where's the benefit if he gains Jay Mac's daughter but loses Northeast Rail? And you need him in his present position, don't you?"

"What is that supposed to mean?"

"Haven't I got the gist of it?" Jarret's fingers threaded through his hair as he considered what he had heard. "From your luncheon conversation it seems that most of what you like about Hollis has to do with his current level of influence in your father's company."

"As usual, you don't know what you're talking about."

"Don't I?" He walked over to the window and drew back the drapes. He scanned the street for unusual traffic, a wagon or pedestrian that did not fit the neighborhood mold. Everything appeared to be as it should. He turned back to Rennie. "It's a relief in a way if I'm wrong. Eloping would have meant being on my guard again, not just for Nate Houston, but for you as well." He gave her a small nod and a pleasant smile. "If you'll excuse me, I have some doors and windows to secure. Mr. Cavanaugh's going to help."

Unsettled, Rennie slowly sat down. The man was very nearly able to read her mind. But he didn't understand everything. He needled her about marrying Hollis Banks because she was ambitious. Rennie could only imagine what he would do if he suspected her other reasons.

Her gaze fell on the half-smoked cigar Hollis had left in the lead glass ashtray. Michael used to smoke cigarettes quite a bit, but Rennie had never acquired a taste for them. She picked up the cigar and rolled it between her thumb and forefinger. Smoking had been Michael's way of thumbing her nose at society's conventions. That, and taking a position with the *Chronicle* as its first woman reporter. Rennie had never had any desire to write. She wanted to run a railroad.

Holding the slim cigar up to her lips, Rennie struck a match with her free hand. She puffed gently, rolled the taste of the smoke around her mouth, then exhaled. It wasn't so bad.

She leaned back on the sofa and propped her legs on the coffee table in front of her, crossing her feet at the ankles. This time when she drew in the smoke, she took it all the way into her lungs. The subsequent coughing spasm shattered her mood.

Passing in the hallway, Jarret paused outside the parlor. He shook his head, not quite believing what he was seeing, but not terribly shocked by it. Grinning, he hefted the hammer in his right hand and continued on his way upstairs.

They ate dinner in the kitchen. Rennie insisted because she didn't want Mrs. Cavanaugh catering to them. She also promised that she and Jarret would manage the cleanup and let the cook and her husband retire to the carriage house early.

"More bread?" Rennie asked, passing Jarret the tray. "Mrs. Cavanaugh makes her own jam. She never buys it from the fruit sellers. I could get you some."

Jarret shook his head. "No, butter's fine." He tried to imagine what she wanted.

"Did you get everything done that you wanted to today?"

"The house is more secure, if that's what you mean. There was a bent gutter and a few loose shingles that I fixed as well." It seemed a fair thing to do since his jaunt across the porch roof had brought about their damage. "I helped Mr. Cavanaugh with some general maintenance."

"That was kind of you."

"Not particularly. I was bored."

She nodded. "I know what you mean. I'm anxious to get back to my work. Michael's probably feeling the same way."

"I doubt it. She's on her honeymoon, remember?"

Rennie's eyes dropped to her plate. She pushed peas around with her fork until she felt the heat retreat from her face. "I'd like to have some papers from the office."

Jarret refused to be drawn along the lines of her wishful thinking. "What exactly is it that you do for Northeast Rail?"

"I work for the director of new projects."

Jarret interpreted. "You're his secretary."

She heard disparagement in his tone and said with a mixture of defensiveness and pride, "I have a lot more responsibility than that. I've been working for Northeast in one capacity or another since I was fourteen."

"That's commendable."

"What were you doing at fourteen?"

Jarret finished buttering his bread. He was careful not to respond to the challenge in her question and answered matter-of-factly. "I was with the Express."

"The Pony Express?" She was impressed in spite of her desire not to be.

"Hmmm. That's where I met Ethan. My parents owned one of the way stations outside Salina, Kansas. For the short time the Express was operating, they kept fresh stock for the riders. I joined up with the outfit a few months before it all ended."

"You must hate the railroads."

"Hate them? No."

"But rails ended the Express."

"It was a business. Oh, I know what people in the East thought about it; for a while I entertained some of the same notions. But that was romantic twaddle, perpetuated by reporters who hadn't been west of Pittsburgh. The

99

work was dangerous and dirty, not nearly as exciting as it was exhausting. My parents knew that; that's why they let me try out. They weren't nearly as surprised when I made the cut as I was."

"They sound very wise, letting you discover some things for yourself."

"I think they were attempting to find the lesser of two evils. They could let me go, or I was going to run away." His grin was filled with self-mockery, and he adopted a confidential tone. "I hadn't come into my common sense yet."

Rennie laughed lightly. "Oh? And do you in fact know when that event happened?"

A shadow crossed his face. "I do."

Rennie realized he was looking through her now, not at her, and what she had intended to be a teasing question had taken on other significance for him as he recalled his past. "You don't have to tell me," she said.

"What?" He shook himself out of his reverie. "No, it's all right. I buried both my parents in sixty-seven."

"I'm sorry."

She didn't say it as a matter of rote politeness, Jarret thought. Rennie said it as if she meant it. Her widely spaced eyes were troubled, her feathered brows delicately knit. Her mouth was flattened, lips pressed together in a manner meant to keep something in. Jarret had the oddest feeling that she was swallowing his pain. "It was a long time ago."

Nine years didn't seem so long in some ways, yet when Rennie considered the extent to which Jarret still hurt, it was an eternity. His smiles, his mostly unflappable nature, his mocking and teasing, all of it was meant to maintain a distance. She studied him with new interest. "Was it illness?" she asked.

Jarret shook his head. "They were in Hays on cattle

business. The town was barely a town in those days, more of a meeting place for traders and the like. There were lots of soldiers there because of the fort, and cattlemen came through with their herds. Money flowed pretty freely, and it attracted people who didn't necessarily want to work for it. My parents were killed making a deposit at the bank."

It was as awful as Rennie had expected, yet she was certain the deaths of Mr. and Mrs. Sullivan weren't the end of the story, or even that the story had an end. She wanted to know and couldn't bring herself to ask the right questions. "Tell me about your parents," she said instead. "What sort of people were they?"

Jarret helped himself to another serving of chicken and coleslaw. He was grateful for the opportunity to speak of his parents' lives, not their deaths. "My father was an immigrant. He came to Boston in forty and labored his way west. His intended destination was California. He used to remark that if it hadn't been for running afoul of my mother in Kansas City, he'd have been at Sutter's Fort when gold was struck."

Rennie chuckled softly. "It doesn't sound as if he regretted it too much."

"He didn't."

"You mentioned cattle. Was that your mother's family business?"

He shook his head, swallowing. "No, she didn't have any family to speak of. She was raised in an orphanage here in New York, educated at a local college to become a teacher and give back something to the asylum. Instead she went west and took a position in St. Louis, and later Kansas City. Father met her as she was chasing a truant student down the street. He grabbed the boy by the scruff of the neck and held him until Mother got there. I'm not quite sure what happened then, but it seems the boy was let go and Mother wasn't."

"It was love at first sight."

"Appears that way."

"Do you believe in it?" she asked, intrigued.

"I suspect I might," he drawled, "when it happens to me."

Rennie noticed he said *when* it happens; she would have said *if* it happens. "They settled in Salina?" she asked.

"Eventually. Mother stopped teaching. She had to. The board of education said it was no profession for a married woman."

Rennie grimaced. It was so typical of an attitude that it didn't bear responding. "She taught you, though."

He nodded. "I never went to school a day in my life. But until I went to work for the Express, I never felt as if I left it."

Rennie wasn't surprised he'd been tutored by his mother, only that she had provided the sum total of his formal education. When it suited him he feigned that he had no upbringing at all, but it wouldn't have struck Rennie amiss if he was able to quote Shakespeare.

"My parents were partners," he said. "They worked together on everything. First it was a little mercantile enterprise that when belly up in a few months. Then they tried farming and Father hated it. Mother had some savings from her teaching that Father hadn't let her spend. She finally convinced him they should give ranching a try. It's what they loved. They did pretty well with it, too."

He was proud of his heritage, she thought, proud of the values that were set for him, the work ethic that was lived, the love that was never in doubt. "Do you think you'll ranch some day?" she asked.

"I think on it from time to time."

It was the way he said it that made Rennie realize the subject was closed, as if the future was simply not open to discussion. What sort of man didn't entertain a dream? she wondered.

Jarret finished his meal as Rennie began clearing the table. "I've put a new lock on your door," he said.

She paused, cocking her head to one side, not certain at all that she'd heard correctly. "How's that again?"

"There's a new lock on your door."

For the better part of thirty minutes, Rennie realized, she had lulled herself into believing that Jarret Sullivan wasn't her keeper. They had shared dinner, conversation, a little laughter. Tension had faded, the silences were easy, the companionship pleasant. They might have been two people renewing an old friendship or acquaintances looking to find their common ground.

It had been a sham. She knew that now. Rennie had no one to blame save herself.

"To what purpose?" she asked.

Jarret stood, took the plates from her shaking hands, and carried them over to the sink. He began scraping. "I didn't think you'd want to sleep on the floor tonight."

"I don't." She followed him over to the sink. "What does one have to do with the other?"

"Without that lock I'm afraid you'd have little choice." He began pumping water into the wash basin. "After last night's escapade you don't seriously believe I'd trust you again?"

Rennie dropped soap flakes into the water and moved her hand rapidly back and forth to force suds to the surface. She began tossing silverware in, narrowly missing Jarret's hands. She smiled with sweet insincerity as he made a point of jumping out of the way. "I suppose that visiting my sister this evening is out of the question."

"That would be a correct supposition."

"And retrieving papers from my office?"

"Also out of the question."

103

"Reading in my room?"

"Certainly."

"How about getting stinking drunk?"

He laughed shortly. "That I'd like to see."

"Believe me, Mr. Sullivan, I wouldn't be doing it for your amusement."

Jarret picked up a towel and began drying dishes.

Rennie had never seen a man help with the dishes. Mr. Cavanaugh never assisted his wife. Jay Mac would have never considered it. She doubted Hollis would know what to do with a dish towel if she submitted a plan for it. Jarret's help was so incongruous with her expectations that the sight of him nearly made Rennie forget how irritated she was.

"You're going to lock me in?" she asked.

"Hmm-mm."

"What if there's a fire?"

Trust her to bring up the very thing that worried him. "There won't be." He slid a plate into the cupboard and picked up some of the silverware. "Listen, if it bothers you that much, you can have the bed and I'll just take the floor."

"Put out a guest like that?" she asked. "I wouldn't think of it."

They finished the remainder of their task in silence. When they were done Jarret excused himself and retired to the library, checking on Rennie's whereabouts periodically. For her part Rennie stayed in the kitchen, working at the scarred table, the site of so much affectionate fussing with her sisters as she was growing up. She had a map of Colorado in front of her and the plans for an upgraded trunk line from Denver to Queen's Point. Northeast Rail was slowly outgrowing its name as it moved with the new directions of the country. It was good to be part of it and frustrating that she couldn't do more.

At ten o'clock she closed her books, folded the maps, and pulled all the stray and misplaced pencils out of her hair. She stretched, rolling her neck three hundred sixty degrees as she worked out the kinks. Taking several deep breaths, calming her nerves in the face of her anxiety, Rennie got up from the table and made a pot of coffee. At twenty minutes past the hour she was serving it to Jarret.

"Aren't you going to have any?" he asked, taking the cup she offered.

"Of course." She raised her cup in a mocking little salute, swallowed a mouthful, then placed it back on the tray. "Reading?" she asked, watching Jarret sip his drink. Rennie bent and picked up the book that was lying beside his chair. "John Stuart Mill. *On the Subjection of Women*." She looked at him oddly. "One of your favorites?"

He shook his head. "I thought it might be one of yours. It was well thumbed."

"Actually I like Mill, and I like what he has to say about women; but if it's well thumbed it's because Mary Francis or Michael committed it to memory." She took the book back to the shelves and slid it into place. "Here's his *Essay on Liberty*. Have you read that?"

"Several times."

Rennie turned back from the wall of books. "I'm sorry, you were done with the book, weren't you? You looked as if you were when I came in."

"I was." He pointed to her cup on the tray. "Your coffee's getting cold. I'm already done with mine."

"Would you like more? I suppose I should have brought in the pot."

"It's all right. Finish yours first."

Rennie sat on the high-backed chair opposite him. She had fond memories of sitting in just such a manner with

Jay Mac. He drank Irish coffee and she sipped hot cocoa. They would both have whipped cream mustaches, and Jay Mac would speak of the railroad while she absorbed every word. Sometimes, regardless of her best intentions, she would fall asleep still curled in her chair, and he would carry her to bed.

Jarret caught Rennie's empty cup just as it would have clattered to the floor. He took the saucer from her other hand and carefully replaced the cup, setting both aside. Her lashes curved in a dark fan against her pale skin. The burnished colors of her hair were subdued in the library's dim light. Without knowing that he was going to do it, Jarret's fingers slid across her temple and into her hair. She didn't stir.

"The next time you put something in my drink, Mary Renee, you should make certain I don't switch cups."

Bending at the waist, Jarret slipped his arms under Rennie's still form and lifted her against his chest. With as little jostling as possible he carried her to her room and put her to bed.

Chapter Four

Rennie yawned. She stretched lazily, snuggling back into the thick comforter even as she tried to throw off the dregs of sleep. It was late; she knew that by the slant of sunlight filling her room, but she didn't want to get up. Her toes curled. She turned on her side. She saw Jarret Sullivan.

He was still asleep, folded uncomfortably in the armchair. His head was tilted at an awkward angle against the back, and he was sitting on one of his legs. The afghan that was supposed to be covering him was lying uselessly on the floor while his arms crossed his chest protectively for warmth. There was a shadow of beard along his jaw and heavy weariness in the slumped, contorted lines of his body.

Rennie was without sympathy. She rose silently from her bed and walloped him across the face and chest with her pillow.

Jarret's reflexes were surprisingly quick for a man who had been waked from a hard and heavy sleep. Before Rennie could dance away her wrist was caught, and she was yanked off the floor and onto Jarret's lap. He tossed the pillow on the floor and growled huskily, "What burr's got under your saddle this morning?"

Rennie merely gave him a tart, knowing look.

He had to smile. She was sprawled awkwardly across his lap, her gown hitched around her knees and twisted at the waist. The bodice stretched tautly across her breasts so that a deep, satisfying breath was out of the question. Her thick, curly chestnut mane of hair was the worse for sleep, curved in an unnatural wave near her temple and spilling across one cheek in a ratty tangle.

"By God, you could stop a man's heart first thing in the morning," he told her.

The blush had already begun to color her cheeks before she realized he hadn't meant it as a compliment. Rennie pushed at his chest and he let her go. She slipped to the floor with the ungainly support of her arms and legs. Tossing back her head and raising her chin, she said, "It would be a service to women everywhere if I were to stop your heart."

Jarret rubbed his coarse beard and pretended to think about that. "You could be right. It'd keep me from breakin' theirs."

Rennie was of a mind to slam him with the pillow again. The look he leveled at her, as if he knew her intention, stopped her. She picked up the afghan instead and pulled it around her shoulders. "How did you know about the coffee last night?" she asked.

"So you do admit it?"

She shrugged. "It seems silly not to. Did you suspect right away?"

"When you brought in two cups and no pot, it made me wonder. When I tasted it I had a pretty good idea what you'd done. It was a little too bitter, even compared to the usual brew you make."

"There's nothing wrong with the coffee I make," she said sharply, taking offense.

One corner of Jarret's mouth curled in a baffled smile. He shook his head slowly, perplexed. "A month of Sundays wouldn't serve for figurin' you out. You have no remorse about trying to poison me, yet you get all prickly when I tell you your coffee's too strong."

"One has nothing to do with the other. If I'd known you felt that way about my coffee, I'd have given you the powder in something else. I hadn't meant for it to taste bad. And it was only a sleeping draught that Mama sometimes takes, not poison, as you know very well. Anyway, you had no compunction about turning the tables on me."

She was actually taking him to task! "Lady, when it comes to pure, wrongheaded stubbornness, you could teach new tricks to a jack"—he caught himself—"to a mule."

Her innocent smile also conveyed a certain hint of smugness. "You were saying . . ." she prompted.

What had he been saying? he wondered. She definitely had a way of side-tracking his train of thought. "I switched the cups when you put the book away and let you drink what was intended for me. End of story. You fell asleep almost immediately."

"I didn't think the coffee was too strong," she said, feigning hurt.

Jarret leaned over the side of the chair, picked up the pillow and flung it at her head. Laughing, Rennie dodged the missile.

She had a husky, hearty laugh, he thought, infectious in nature, not the trilling, musical, and sometimes forced laughter he often associated with the women he knew. He watched her straighten, hugging the pillow to her midriff, and was caught by the becoming wash of color in her face and the spirited challenge in her eyes. The corners of her mouth lifted in a wide, beautiful smile.

She stopped his heart.

Jarret drew his stiff leg out from under him and leaned forward. He was frowning now, and when he spoke his voice was edged with threat. "Don't flirt with me," he said. "You won't like the consequences."

Rennie's eyes widened, but the light in them was smothered. Her face drained of color and her features froze. "Go to hell, Mr. Sullivan," she said quietly, with dignity.

Jarret stood. He almost groaned as blood rushed to his leg, sweeping his skin with prickling sensation. He hobbled a little uncertainly out the door, and once it closed behind him, he leaned against it. The ache in his leg was nothing compared to the ache in his groin. He thought of Rennie's smile. It had been a narrow escape.

Rennie and Jarret skirted one another for three more days. She was always aware of his presence in the house even though she never spent more than a few minutes with him in any one room. She carried her own meals to her room and ate alone while he shared his meals with the Cavanaughs. He read in the library, helped Mr. Cavanaugh in the garden, or cleaned his gun under the cook's watchful eye in the kitchen. Rennie made a point to work in the solitary confinement of the parlor and discovered that avoiding him was nearly as difficult and unsettling as being in his company.

When Jarret appeared in the doorway of the parlor Rennie was so certain she imagined his presence that she didn't respond right away. It was the incongruity of him cradling a large stack of papers and files in his arms that made her realize his form was no apparition. He walked in and dropped the stack beside her on the sofa. The papers slipped sideways, fanning out like a toppled deck of cards.

Rennie recognized the files immediately. "Wait," she said, calling him back as he turned and started to go. "How did you—"

"I asked Mr. Cavanaugh to go 'round to the Worth

building and fetch things you might need." He started to go again.

Rennie stood. She started to reach for him, realized what she was about to do, and dropped her hand quickly to her side.

Jarret saw the aborted gesture out of the corner of his eye. He stopped, turned.

I . . . well . . ." Her eyes revealed anxiousness, and her fingers curled in the folds of her plain hunter green gown. "Thank you."

"You're welcome."

They stared at one another for several long seconds, the silence uncomfortable. The stacks of files began to slide again, this time off the sofa. Simultaneously they made a grab for them, nearly knocking heads.

Rennie laughed uneasily, straightening the pile. "It appears he cleaned out my desk and a few other desks besides."

"I told him to get everything. There was only the night watchman to help him locate your office, so I hope you really got what's important."

"I'm sure it's all here. Sam Whitney would have directed Mr. Cavanaugh properly. He's seen me working late on more than one occasion." She hesitated. "I take it there's been no word on Houston or Kelly."

"None. But I felt it was safe to send Cavanaugh last night. He wasn't followed."

"I didn't mean anything by it," she said almost apologetically. "I wasn't questioning your judgment."

Jarret shrugged as if it didn't matter. "You should. It's your life that's in danger."

Rennie sat down, shaking her head. "No, it's Mary Michael's. God, I wish it *were* me. The waiting's interminable. I can't imagine how she's coping with it."

Jarret propped his hip against the arm of the sofa, half-

111

sitting, half-standing in a manner that was not so relaxed as it was indecisive. "Your sister's not gone back to the *Chronicle* yet. I know that much."

"You've been to see her?"

He shook his head. "No."

"But how—"

"I briefly renewed my acquaintance with Logan Marshall. He told me. They're sending work for her to the hotel. I thought if Ethan had surrendered that much, it wouldn't hurt me to do the same."

"Thank God for Ethan," she said feelingly.

"Not many husbands would let their wives work. Your sister's very fortunate to have found someone like him."

Rennie preferred to reserve judgment. "You'll understand if I think it's the other way around."

Jarret's brief smile was indifferent. "Suit yourself." He glanced down at the papers splayed across the coffee table and the maps littering the floor. "What are you doing?"

Rennie couldn't tell if he was genuinely interested or interested because he was bored. The Cavanaughs were used to keeping to themselves; they couldn't have provided much company in the last few days. He had probably sought out Logan Marshall just to hear the sound of another human voice. She wondered if he'd met Logan's wife Katy? The former actress was without question one of New York's most beautiful and celebrated women. He probably regretted he was not sworn to protect her.

"Where does your mind go?" Jarret asked, watching her drift away in front of his eyes. Her furrowed brow and flattened, serious mouth were something to behold.

Rennie registered his voice, looked at him blankly for a moment, then came out of her reverie. "I'm working on some possible routes for a trunk line," she said, answering the only question she really remembered hearing. She began gently patting the papers and maps on the coffee

112

table with the flat of her hands. Under one ridge she found her spectacles and slipped them on. "Here, I'll show you."

Jarret was fascinated. First by the spectacles that crept slowly down the bridge of her nose until they rested on the tip, then by the intensity of feeling in her expressive eyes as she explained her plans. She mapped out the lay of the land to him and spoke of gradient curves, fixed arched bridges, rail joints, spring washers, switch points, and splice bars. She rummaged for a pencil, found one under a map, and sketched a trestle that would span a narrow tributary of the South Platte River. She showed him where crews would have to work day and night for weeks to tunnel through rock. She explained about hauling in the proper ballast to support the ties and spikes on the winding mountain trails, about the switch signals and slide chairs that would be necessary to allow for freight trains to be side-tracked while lighter passenger cars climbed the steep passes in the Rockies. When the line was completed Northeast Rail would have a lucrative track from largely untapped silver mining country to the heart of Denver.

Rennie absentmindedly slid her pencil into the coil of hair at her nape. She looked at Jarret expectantly over the rims of her spectacles. She was aware that he had long since abandoned his sitting-standing position and was hunkered beside the coffee table, giving every impression that he was engrossed. He was also looking at her oddly, as if he didn't quite know what to make of what he'd heard. Self-conscious, Rennie slipped off her spectacles and carefully folded the ear stems. She remembered her habit with pencils and plucked it out as well. "Well? What do you think?"

Except for the slight furrow of Jarret's dark brows, his face was expressionless. "You're an engineer," he said.

His voice was so flat, so matter-of-fact, that she

couldn't tell if he was astonished or accusing. "Well, yes," she said, bewildered. "I thought you knew that."

"Know?" He stood. "How would I know that? I asked you what you did several days ago, and you mentioned working for the director of new projects. I said you were a secretary, and you didn't argue."

"I told you I had more responsibilities than scheduling appointments." She began organizing the scattered papers. "The truth is, I don't get to do a lot of engineering. Mr. Tompkins—he's the director—doesn't let me."

"Then, he's a fool."

Rennie's fingers stilled over the maps. She looked up at Jarret, some of her own doubts surfacing in her eyes. "You really think so?"

"I really think so."

She didn't question the lightening she felt in her chest, the easing of a pressure that had been there so long she had become used to its existence. It seemed perfectly in keeping with the natural order of things to accept Jarret's opinion as fact. "Jay Mac wouldn't like to hear that. He has the greatest trust for Mr. Tompkins."

"And not so much for you?" He shifted the files on the sofa so that there was enough room for him to sit down.

"Perhaps it's not so much a matter of trust as it is confidence. Mr. Tompkins has been working for my father for years, and he has a veritable battalion of engineers at his disposal. That kind of experience and expertise inspires confidence."

"In this case it may be misplaced."

"I'm not sure I know what you mean."

Jarret took from Rennie the topographical map she was folding. He spread it out on the table and pointed to where she had penciled in the path of the trunk line. There were other smudges on the pages that also indicated where tracks might be laid, but they were not set down in her sure, deft hand. "You've set your track along this mountain pass, here at Queen's Point. The grade appears to be a little steeper there; it would have to be leveled out in just the way you described. Surely that's a lot more work and expense than taking this slowly rising, but more circuitous route proposed by your colleagues. So why did you choose it?"

"I don't think their route will support the trestles and tunnels they've proposed. This map indicates — at least to me it does — that this river valley changes shape with alarming frequency, as if the sediment keeps shifting, creating temporary ridges and gorges."

"And how did you arrive at that?"

"I looked at a succession of maps completed by different surveyors in the last fifteen years. The early ones are especially crude, but I believe there's enough evidence to suggest my conclusion."

"But no one else saw it?"

"They saw it," she said, "because I pointed it out, but there are alternative explanations that satisfied Mr. Tompkins that the correct route's been chosen."

"The cheaper route."

"That, too. It has to be a consideration."

"Yet you're still pursuing something else. Why?"

"I think they're wrong. I want to put it before Mr. Tompkins again and try to convince him."

Jarret looked away from the map and studied Rennie's face. "Not Jay Mac?"

She shook her head. "It's not the proper order of things. I have to get Mr. Tompkins's approval first."

"I see." Jarret pointed to the valley again. "The reason this valley appears to shift over time is because that's exactly what it does. Gully washers rip through here every other spring or so. That kind of water power moves most everything in its path. No rhyme or reason for it. Just

115

nature. Supposing the trestle and track were laid in a dry year, the work would be gone in the next thaw."

"You know this for a fact?"

"Me and every other person who's traveled up and around Queen's Point. It's not exactly a secret." His smile was derisive. "Except, I suppose, from rail men like your father with more money than sense. If he'd sent out a competent group of men to survey the land properly, ask the locals, he'd know all this."

Rennie bristled at Jarret's indictment of her father. "Fifteen years ago no one was thinking of a line in this wilderness. Placer gold had just been discovered in the Rockies, and there were rumblings of war here. Plenty of track needed to be laid this side of the Mississippi and north of the Mason-Dixon line. Not all of these maps were completed by Northeast employees," she said. "But the most recent two were, and Hollis Banks was part of the surveying team."

Jarret absently rubbed the bridge of his nose as he considered that information. "You've told him about your conclusions?" he asked.

"I've told him. He says I'm wrong."

Jarret snorted. "The man's either stupid or a liar. I've made up my mind on the matter. What's your conclusion?"

"I don't think I like where this is leading."

He held up his hands, indicating surrender. "I didn't come here to pick a fight with you. I'm just telling you you're right about Queen's Point. Now, you can take satisfaction from that and realize Banks is either foolin' you or a fool himself, or you can believe he's right, in which case you've been working on this trunk line problem for the sheer hell of it."

The truth was that Rennie had thought all along that Hollis and the surveyors had made some incorrect judgments, but it seemed negligent to her rather than purposeful. Jarret, with his contemptuous smile, appeared to be hinting at just the opposite. "There may have been some inattention to detail," she said slowly, considering the ramifications of what she was saying, "but to suggest that there's been deliberate deception . . ."

Jarret shrugged, refusing to be drawn in again. "You know him better than I do."

Rennie was silent a moment, thinking. Suddenly she nodded emphatically. "That's right. I do. Surveying has never been Hollis's forte, nor of special interest to him. He was merely accompanying the team, not supervising their efforts. He's neither stupid nor a liar, but perhaps in this case he was a little careless or a tad too trusting of others."

Jarret realized it was all the admission she was prepared to make. A larger revelation would have left her unbalanced and uncertain. She was still intending, after all, to marry the man. He nodded, accepting it.

"Thank you for telling me about the floods. I'll insist on the changes."

She would insist, he thought, but there was no telling if anyone would listen. "Anything less than your route would be a disaster, financially and in every other way."

Rennie was on the point of thanking him again when Mrs. Cavanaugh came to the door and announced dinner. "Sure and the two of you are talkin' again," the cook said, beaming. "Wasn't natural t'other way. Well, come on with you. I'm not servin' meals in here."

Rennie and Jarret exchanged amused and conspiratorial glances. Jarret extended his hand to Rennie and drew her to her feet. She accepted his arm and allowed him to escort her to the dining room.

That evening, when she bid him good night, it was sheer force of will that kept him from kissing her breathless.

He lay awake a long time thinking about it. The attraction he felt toward her didn't make any kind of normal sense. She was snippety most times, down right caustic others. In spite of her best intentions she was easily riled, rising so quickly to his bait that Jarret felt a vague sense of guilt for targeting her as often as he did. On the one hand she was enormously intelligent, and on the other she was curiously naive. It was as if she didn't know quite what to make of herself, uncomfortable with her femininity and, for all her modern thinking, just as uncomfortable demanding equal footing with men.

She dressed plainly, though not with the severity that Ethan had described of Michael. In spite of current fashion, Rennie's gowns were rarely embellished with ribbon or lace. Except for tiny pearls on her earlobes, she wore no jewelry. She was self-conscious of her reading spectacles, embarrassed by her habit of hiding pencils in her hair, and more than a little uncertain of her looks. For some reason which escaped Jarret entirely, Rennie Dennehy seemed to think she was nondescript. It was not so much that she did anything in particular to hide her beauty, but that she did nothing to accentuate it. It was as if she simply did not recognize it.

Her hair, which easily could have been the focus of some vanity, was kept simply coiled at the back of her head. Untamed and curly, sometimes it stayed in its anchoring pins and sometimes it didn't. It appeared to be a matter of complete indifference on Rennie's part. In repose her features were very nearly serene, even angelic. Awake, Rennie was constantly animated. Her nose crinkled, her eyes rolled, her mouth flattened. She worried the inside of her lip when she was thinking; she flushed when a wayward thought crossed her mind. Her fists clenched when she was angry; her fingers tapped when she was nervous. Composure was a state she had to force upon her-

118

self. As a poker player she would invariably lose her shirt.

Jarret tortured himself with the thought of breaking out the cards. He had a good idea what she was hiding beneath the unbecoming gowns she wore. Her slender shoulders supported breasts that were just fractionally too full for her frame. Her narrow back had the most beguiling curve as it tapered at her waist and rounded gently at her hips. She was no more than average height, but most of it was leg. Jarret had tussled with her enough to have glimpsed pale skin and delicate bones. Her strength was feisty in nature, not physical. She made him think of a banty rooster rather than a lioness.

Not that she would have appreciated either comparison. And not that any of his thinking made the slightest bit of difference. It was just that returning to Colorado would have been a lot easier if he had never heard her laugh. Easier still if she'd never smiled.

Rennie came downstairs late the next morning. Jarret had already finished eating and was stepping inside the front door as she reached the first-floor landing. She had the impression he had just finished talking to someone, and when she peered through one of the long, narrow windows on either side of the door, she caught a fleeting glimpse of a woman getting into a carriage. Rennie got herself a cup of coffee from the kitchen and cornered Jarret in the library. He was standing at the window, staring out onto the side street.

"A tryst?" she asked lightly. She was surprised to see that he actually jumped. He really hadn't heard her enter. "Oh, dear, your thoughts *are* a thousand miles away. This doesn't bode well for my protection."

"Sit down, Rennie."

There was no humor in his voice. None. Rennie sat as if pushed. "What's happened?" Then, because she couldn't help herself, "It's Michael, isn't it? Something's happened to Michael."

Jarret turned away from the window. "It's not Michael. That was Susan Turner. You know her?"

Rennie nodded. She was worrying her lower lip. Her skin was devoid of color. "Dr. Turner's wife. Scott's taking care of Michael for the baby." It was suddenly difficult to breathe, and every one of her fears showed clearly in her eyes. "Oh, God," she said almost soundlessly.

Jarret shook his head quickly as he realized the tenor of her thoughts. "It's not the baby, Rennie. Michael and the baby are fine. It's Ethan. He's very sick."

"Ethan's sick?" She frowned. "How can that be? Is it serious?"

"Susan says her husband doesn't know, but he's not encouraging. He's prescribed some medicine, and they're going to see if it helps. It looks like the influenza, she says, but Turner thinks it's something more serious than that."

"But he doesn't say?"

"He doesn't know."

A little color returned to Rennie's face. She folded both hands around her cup of coffee and raised it to her lips. "This means you'll be leaving," she said.

"No. Not yet."

"You have to go to Michael. If Ethan can't protect her, then you have to."

"When Ethan wants me, I'll go. He only asked Dr. Turner to get me the message that he's ill. He's not asking for help."

"But—"

"But nothing," Jarret snapped. His hand sliced the air for emphasis. "You may find this difficult to understand, but there are some of us who do what we're told. I respect Ethan's judgment. If he doesn't want me there, then I'm not going." Yet, he thought.

"Then, let me go. I could help Michael nurse him. She doesn't need the extra work now."

"Susan says Michael's not in any danger . . . from the illness. Your sister's quite able to care for Ethan, and nothing's changed as far as you're concerned."

"I'm not spending another minute here." She set her cup on an end table and stood.

"Don't you dare try leaving this house."

"Or what?"

Jarret took a step forward. "I'm not of a mind to fence with you, Rennie. Do it and find out."

It was meant as a warning. Rennie heard it as a challenge. Ignoring him, she walked out of the room and went straight for the coat closet. She found a light wrap and put it around her shoulders. "Mr. Cavanaugh!" she called. When the cook's husband appeared she asked him to ready a carriage for her. It infuriated her when the man looked to Jarret for permission.

"Then, I'll walk," Rennie said.

Mrs. Cavanaugh came up behind her husband. Her eyes darted anxiously between Jarret and Rennie. "What's the row about this time?"

"She's set herself on leavin'," said Mr. Cavanaugh. "Sure and she wanted me to get the carriage for her."

The cook shook her head and dried her damp hands on her apron. "You're not going to do it, are you?"

Mr. Cavanaugh scratched his salt-and-pepper beard. "Do I look like such a fool, wife?"

Rennie knew their discussion was for her benefit and she could expect no help from that quarter. She glared at Jarret accusingly, blaming him for the rift in loyalties. She didn't even know if the Cavanaughs would be reliable witnesses anymore.

Jarret didn't move past the threshold of the parlor. He had no intention of blocking her path or lifting a finger to

121

stop her until she was ready to walk out the door. He was going to give her every opportunity to change her mind.

"I need to see my sister," she said. Her voice actually trembled. Her eyes glittered with unshed tears. "You don't know what it's like to be separated from her. When she was gone for months out West, there were people who thought she was dead. I knew she wasn't. I *knew*. But it hasn't been the same since she's been back. She's drifting away from me."

"She has Ethan," said Jarret. "She's carrying a baby."

"It doesn't matter. I want her to have both, but this is about *my* need. Michael will understand, even if you don't."

Jarret said nothing. He simply waited.

His silence encouraged Rennie to think he had changed his mind. In retrospect she knew she had only believed what served her purpose. She walked past him and opened the front door. Her feet never touched the stoop.

Jarret grabbed her from behind and hauled her back inside, kicking the door closed with the heel of his boot. She fought with him. Her wrap fell from her shoulders. Her hair fell out of its anchoring pins. She felt a shoulder seam in her dress give way. Rennie's frenzied, frantic movements made Jarret's grip precarious. He managed to hold on, but only just.

Mrs. Cavanaugh's hand drying became more of a hand wringing. "I've never seen her like this. She's not usin' the sense God gave her."

"He needs to turn her over his knee and that's a fact," said Mr. Cavanaugh.

Their comments only made Rennie angrier and Jarret's job more difficult. Since the Cavanaughs showed no sign of leaving the hallway, Jarret knew he had to. Hefting Rennie in his arms, he pitched her over his shoulder, secured her legs against his chest, and let her flail away at his back. The staircase in front of him loomed as large as Pike's Peak. He began to climb.

Rennie stopped struggling as soon as she realized what he was about. "Don't you dare drop me," she said breathlessly.

"Don't give me any ideas."

"Put me down and I'll walk up the stairs myself."

Jarret's breath was coming a little short as he reached the halfway mark. "Now, why don't I believe you?"

Rennie raised her head. Through the curtain of her curly, tangled hair she could see the distraught faces of the Cavanaughs in the hallway below. "Traitors." There wasn't any menace in her voice. She dropped her head as they retreated to the kitchen. "You've lost your audience," she told Jarret.

He merely grunted.

At the door to Rennie's room Jarret paused long enough to catch his breath. Once inside, he unceremoniously dropped Rennie on the bed. He sat down on the edge, grabbing her by the ankle when she would have rolled away. "You need a bridle," he said, hauling her closer.

Sprawled as she was across the bed, her gown rucked up to her knees, her body being pulled inexorably closer to Jarret's, the assumption that crossed her mind was a natural one. She became absolutely *wild* at the thought of being spanked.

"Rennie! For God's sake!" Jarret dodged her right fist as she came at him, but he lost his breath when she hammered him in the midriff with her left. "What the hell's wrong with you?" She tried to sink her teeth into the back of his hand as he caught her wrists. Jarret had to use one of his legs to trap her lower body.

They rolled once, then again. Jarret held her wrists on either side of her head and eased himself off dead center

123

so that she wasn't taking his full weight. She was breathing hard, sucking in large draughts of air. His head momentarily rested against her shoulder while he caught his breath. Both her legs were secured under one of his. Her movements now were not so much struggles as they were spasms of complete fatigue.

Jarret raised his head. A fringe of dark blond hair fell over his brow. "What was that about?" he asked huskily. "Did you think I was going for my gun? I don't even wear it around you anymore."

She turned her head away from him, her eyes closed. "I thought you were going to hit me."

"Hit you?"

Color suffused her cheeks. She opened her eyes but couldn't look at him. "Spank me."

"I see," Jarret said lowly. He began to understand her reaction. It would have been humiliating for her. "I have no desire to rob you of your pride, Rennie. That's not my way. I'd be more inclined to cuff you on the chin." He saw the faintest smile touch her mouth. Her eyes welled with tears. "But it's a nice chin and I'll let it go for now."

She looked at him. "I punched you."

He nodded. "Several times."

"I've never done that before to anyone. I've never even wanted to."

His sapphire eyes were patently skeptical.

"Well, maybe once or twice I've wanted to." Her eyes drifted to his mouth. She realized how terribly close he was; how his body was pressing against the length of hers. His hands were closed over her wrists loosely, the position of his leg more intimate than anchoring. There was something in his darkening eyes now that lent her a different sort of breathlessness.

She raised her head the merest fraction and touched her mouth to his.

124

Jarret's mouth followed her down. His lips nudged hers, tasting her sweetness, her tentative touch, as a hint of honey. Her mouth was warm and pliant, exploring. She slipped her hands out from under his grip and looped her arms around his neck. Jarret groaned as she opened her mouth under his. Her response to the entry of his tongue was hesitant, surprised at first, then curious, and finally eager. She mimicked his exploration, the foray along the ridge of her teeth, the teasing of her sensitive upper lip. He was made to feel those things in turn, and when the gentle thrusting gave way to something with more carnal intent, it was Jarret who drew back.

He rolled away and sat up. His fingers threaded through his hair. His sigh was audible. "I think I better go."

Rennie pushed herself upright. She leaned against the headboard and hugged a pillow to her chest. Her expression was watchful, her eyes wary. "I made you break your promise, didn't I?" she said quietly.

He shrugged. "You kissed me first. Did you release me or did I break?"

"Is it so important to you?"

"I've never mistaken business for anything but business. Nathaniel Houston is my business. Dee Kelly is my business." He turned his head to look at her. *"You're* my business."

"What if I don't want to be?" she asked boldly. "What if I want to be —"

"My pleasure?"

Her face flamed, but she didn't look away. "Yes," she said. "Your pleasure."

He shook his head and said coldly, "You don't have enough experience."

Rennie recoiled as if struck.

Jarret explained. "You wouldn't know how to walk

125

away at the end, and it's not like I can pay you. Your heart would get all tangled in your expectations. You don't really want to be my pleasure anyway. You want me to make my business teaching you about it. I thought I might like that, but now I don't think so. If I gentle a filly, it's because I mean to ride her. I'm not breaking you in for Hollis Banks."

His crudity shocked her. Wounded, she raised her hand, not to slap him, but to stifle a sob. "Get out," she whispered.

Jarret stood. He walked to the door, took the key out of his pocket, and turned, showing it to her. "Just so you know, Rennie, in spite of what I just said, I'm locking this door as much to keep me out as keep you in."

Rennie watched him step into the hallway. She heard the key turn in the new lock he had installed on the outside of the door, then saw it being pushed under the door. He couldn't get in any more than she could get out. She leaped off the bed and ran to the door, pounding on it. "Who do you think you are anyway?" she yelled. "I wouldn't have you as a gift! You don't have enough money to pay me, you bastard! Do you hear me? You don't know anything about what I want! Not a thing!" She didn't know if he was standing on the other side of the door or not. It didn't matter. She raged until she was exhausted, and then she simply melted against the door, collapsing in the pool of her gown and her tears.

Downstairs, when the fury and thunder ceased, Jarret turned to Mrs. Cavanaugh. "She'll probably sleep for a little while," he said. "She hasn't even had breakfast yet. Perhaps you could take her something later."

The cook nodded. "It's no problem."

"She has the only key to the room. You'll have to get it from her to get in, and you'll need it back when you go. I

126

can't keep chasing her down, Mrs. Cavanaugh. She has to be locked in. Can you do that?"

"I've never seen the like before," she said, raising her eyes heavenward.

"Can you do it?" Jarret asked again.

"If you think it's for the best."

"I do."

"Then, I can do it."

Rennie spent four days in her bedchamber. It didn't matter that her suite of rooms was bigger than the apartment her sister enjoyed at the St. Mark; Rennie felt caged. Mrs. Cavanaugh came and went, bringing food, fresh linens, and taking the trays. She always locked the door, sliding the key back before she left, and short of doing the cook harm, Rennie couldn't think of any means of stopping her or escaping. Rennie made halfhearted attempts to work on the Queen's Point project, but it was increasingly difficult to concentrate.

In truth, she didn't feel like doing much of anything. It was a chore to comb her hair or wash. She didn't bother making her bed or keeping things neat. The room was littered with books from the library and office work, none of which held her attention. The items on her vanity were scattered haphazardly. Oils and perfumes were left unattended. Fingerprints dotted a dusting of face powder.

Dressing was of no particular interest. Rennie abandoned her corset and wore only a chemise and underskirt, sometimes not bothering with her silk wrapper at all. She either sat for hours in a straight-backed chair by the window, watching the traffic on Broadway, never attracting attention to herself, or napped intermittently. She drifted from her bedchamber to the connecting rooms like a wraith, her face nearly expressionless, her mind almost devoid of conscious thought.

"I'm worried about her," Mrs. Cavanaugh said to Jarret. "It's not natural, I'm telling you. She occupies those rooms as though she's haunting them. She doesn't say more than a few words to me comin' or goin'. The mister sees the same thing when he takes up a tray. And she's not even shamed by her state of dress."

Jarret was worried, too, but he didn't have any answers. Mrs. Cavanaugh had made similar complaints the day before. He couldn't let Rennie go on as she was. "Has she asked to see Hollis?"

"Not a word about him."

"I'll let her out as soon as it's safe. I haven't heard anything in days. I don't know what's happening at the St. Mark any more than the rest of you." He sat down heavily in one of the kitchen chairs. Mrs. Cavanaugh pushed a mug of hot coffee toward him. "Maybe I should go over there."

"Wouldn't Marshal Stone send for you?"

Jarret had been asking himself the same question. What if Ethan was too sick to ask for assistance? Would Michael call on him for help or would she want him to protect her sister? He was used to taking the initiative, not waiting for direction. He was as uncomfortable as Rennie when it came to being holed up in the house. The only difference between them was the size of the hole. "Perhaps we should send your husband to bring Dr. Turner here. He can look after Rennie, and I can hear first hand what's happening to Ethan." Jarret raised his mug and smiled at the cook. It sounded like a plan with merit.

It was late that same evening when Jarret knocked at Rennie's room. The key was pushed under the door a few seconds later. By the time Jarret entered, Rennie was once again sitting on the marble apron of the fireplace, drying her hair near the small fire she'd laid there. She gave no indication that she was surprised by his appearance in her room. Her fingers wove in and out of her auburn hair, separating copper strands so that they curled individually in the orange light behind her.

"I've brought you some dinner," he said, raising the tray in front of him. "Mrs. Cavanaugh rewarmed your meal before she went to the carriage house. She said you didn't eat anything earlier." In fact, he'd been told she hadn't eaten all day. It was a damned Irish rebellion, that's what it was. She was going to starve herself. "Is that right?" he asked.

Rennie didn't answer.

"Where do you want me to put it?"

She didn't acknowledge his presence either by looking at him or responding.

Jarret approached and set the tray beside her on the apron. Her naked white shoulders reflected the flames at her back. Color caressed her skin while her fingers continued to sift languidly through her hair. The plain white underskirt she was wearing revealed bare feet and calves and bones that were somehow more prominent than they'd been a week ago. Her wrapper lay discarded over the back of the armchair. Jarret picked it up and tossed it at her. She made no move to catch it, and when part of the sleeve fell into the fire she let it burn.

Jarret yanked it out, took it to the adjoining bathing room and doused the smoldering sleeve in cold water. He laid it across the straight-backed chair to dry when he returned. "Your lunatic act doesn't inspire any sympathy," he said, sitting down in the armchair. He stretched his legs toward the fire and folded his hands on his lap. The heat was welcome; there was a damp chill in the night air that had already pervaded the room. "You may have fooled Mrs. Cavanaugh with your antics, but now that I see them

129

myself, I'm not impressed."

"You may think as you like, Mr. Sullivan. You always do."

He was encouraged more by her second sentence than her first. The dull flatness of her voice was worrisome, but the little gibe showed signs of a certain liveliness. "I was going to send for Dr. Turner today," he said. "But a little over an hour ago his wife came 'round again. She'll have the doctor visit you tomorrow if I think it's necessary. I told her I'd let her know."

Rennie's fingers stilled in her hair. "Is there news of Ethan? Michael?"

"Your sister was ill the other night, but she's completely recovered now. Apparently she was struck down by the same thing that leveled Ethan."

It was impossible to quell her interest. "Oh?"

Jarret leaned his head against the curved back of the chair. He studied the array of photographs on the mantel. Most were formal portraits of the entire family, including Jay Mac. Some showed Rennie with her sisters, a few were of Rennie and Michael together. There was only one of Rennie alone. The quality of the most recent photographs was especially good. In contrast to Rennie's solemn expression, her fair skin was luminescent, her eyes radiant.

He pointed to it. "Was that taken to commemorate any special occasion?"

She followed the direction of his eyes and hand. "My engagement to Hollis. Jenny Marshall took it."

"Logan's wife? I thought her name was Katy."

"His sister-in-law. Christian's wife."

"Christian Marshall the painter?"

"I think he'd prefer the term artist," she said dryly, "but, yes, the very same."

"He's another of your neighbors?" Jarret realized he could cover a hundred square miles west of the Mississippi and never meet anyone with a pedigree. They rubbed shoulders with each other in Manhattan. He and Rennie really did come from different worlds. "Did we tramp through his yard the other night?"

Rennie tilted her head to one side and gently rubbed the damp, curling ends of her hair with a towel. "I'm not discussing this with you any longer."

Jarret realized he was too long at playing his hand. He was losing her. "Ethan was being poisoned," he said. "It may have been meant for Michael. No one's really sure. She only ingested a little of it. That's when she got sick, taking it in her tea. Afterward she complained to Dr. Turner that she was craving a cigarette. That's what tipped him off."

Agitated that he would not come straight to the point or fill in all the details at once, Rennie's feathery brows came together. "Tipped him how?"

"The poison was nicotine, in doses large enough to cause Ethan's cramping and retching. Michael got some in her tea. Enough to make her ill but with no long-range effects except for the desire to start smoking again."

"That's what," Rennie said. "Now tell me who."

"It appears as if we've been concentrating too hard on coming face-to-face with Houston, and haven't given enough thought to Detra. It's been rumored for years that Dee Kelly used drugs to kill her first husband. Her father owned a medicine shop in St. Louis. She grew up around powders and poisons."

"She's been caught, then? The danger's past?"

He shook his head. "No. Nothing's certain. She's probably working as an employee at the hotel. That's the only way she could be managing to poison the food that goes to their suite. Dr. and Mrs. Turner are going to dine at the St. Mark tomorrow. If Dee's there, they'll be able to identify her now that they have a description."

"And have her arrested."

"No. Only identify her. If we show our cards too early, we'll miss Houston. She can lead us to him, but only if she doesn't know we're watching. She'd never give him up willingly."

"How did she locate Michael?"

"From the newspaper. Someone gave out her address at the St. Mark before the order was given to the contrary."

Rennie came to her feet. Suddenly she regretted she hadn't put on the wrapper. She took an afghan from the foot of her bed and wrapped it around her shoulders. "You'll be going, then," she said. "There's no danger here. Houston and Kelly found the right targets after all."

"They may have found the right targets, but I don't trust you not to get in the way. Neither does your sister. She wasn't even certain that I should be telling you any of this."

"I don't believe you. Michael wouldn't want this kept from me."

Jarret sighed. "Your sister is far more aware of the danger than you are. She spent weeks as Houston and Dee's prisoner. They tried to kill her and Ethan once before and very nearly succeeded. This isn't an adventure where any of us know the outcome. Detra hasn't been positively identified, and there's still the matter of finding Houston. I'm afraid that nothing's really changed as far as you're concerned, though you may want to consider cleaning this room and wearing more clothes than a two-dollar whore."

He came to his feet, glanced around her bedchamber, and shook his head in disgust. "It's a sty, Rennie."

For once she didn't try staring him down. It would have been a pathetic gesture given the fact she was crying. She turned away and stared out the French doors as she had on so many other occasions recently. Her vision was too blurred to see anything on the street below or Jarret's reflection in the glass in front of her. She gave a little start as his arms circled her, but she didn't try to move away.

His chin rested in the crown of her hair. It was silky against his skin, fragrant with the lingering scent of lavender soap. "Nothing's been going your way since you met me."

She closed her eyes, trying to stem the flow of tears, and shook her head slowly in agreement.

"I don't expect that's going to change any time soon," he said.

Rennie brushed impatiently at her eyes as she was turned in his arms. The afghan slipped to the floor. She thought he might kiss her, but it was only his breath that stirred the hair at the temples, not his mouth. He held her in just that manner for a long time, absorbing her shudders, stilling her trembling, and when she was quiet he put her to bed and sat with her until she fell asleep. She never missed the photograph he took on his way out.

Four days later Nathaniel Houston was dead, killed not by Ethan or Jarret, but by Rennie's sister.

Chapter Five

Rennie sat with Ethan in the parlor of Michael's suite of rooms at the St. Mark. Their attempts at conversation were awkward. The only thing they had in common was their concern for the woman giving birth in the adjoining room.

Rennie's eyes periodically strayed to the bloodstains on the carpet. Three hours ago Nate Houston had been killed in the chair where she was sitting now. A porter from the hotel had delivered Ethan's hastily scrawled, nearly illegible, message to Jarret and Rennie. For once Rennie was glad for Jarret's terse commands and unflappable nature. Her own thoughts were like a shower of shooting stars, coming to her so fast and furious that grasping a coherent one was beyond her. She depended on Jarret's cool control for direction.

But that was then. Her head had been clear since Jarret had removed Houston's body from the suite and gone after Dee Kelly. That had left Rennie to see to her sister and Ethan. Dr. Turner was with Michael now; that left her with the marshal. She would have rather been with Michael.

"It's too early for the baby," Ethan said. His voice was drawn, haunted.

Rennie wanted to accuse, not comfort, but she also needed to reassure herself. "She was only a few days shy of carrying eight months," she said. "I know a number of women who have given birth at eight months, even seven months. Everything was fine for them and the baby."

Ethan wasn't convinced. Too many times a full-term child was delivered seven months after the wedding. By that same reckoning Michael was giving birth to a child she had only carried two weeks.

Rennie read the drift of his thoughts. "All right," she said. "Some of the women were altering dates to avoid moral judgments, but that wasn't always the case." Rennie turned white then as Michael screamed. She saw that Ethan's hands were shaking. She served him a whiskey from the sideboard and took a sherry for herself.

"Why did you have to leave her alone?" she blurted out. "Mr. Sullivan wouldn't let me out of the house, sometimes not out of my room, for the last two weeks. And *you* just go off by yourself, leave Michael here, even after you knew the danger was imminent."

The pads of Ethan's fingers turned white against his tumbler. His head was bent as he studied the bloodstained carpet at his feet.

"I'm sorry," she said quietly, sighing. "I promised myself I wouldn't do that."

"It's all right." He glanced up and gave her a jerky little self-mocking grin as he raised his glass. "You're not asking me anything I haven't asked myself."

"I don't think I was asking anything," she said. "Not really. I was blaming."

He took a large swallow of his drink and felt it burn the whole way down. "So was I."

Rennie sat down again, this time next to Ethan on the loveseat. "Michael will be so disappointed in us," she said. "She loves us both, and she won't find any pleasure in us not being friends. I know that whatever you did tonight, you had your reasons. You relied on your best judgment."

"You know that?" he asked bitterly. "You can't know that. You don't know me at all. I almost got Michael killed

135

tonight. She begged to come with me, but I thought it was too dangerous. I should have listened to her."

Rennie recognized that Ethan Stone was a man who needed to talk, to purge himself of the events of the evening. In the next room Michael's moan rose to an anguished wail. Rennie could hear Dr. Turner's steady, comforting encouragement, the words indistinguishable from one another, but reassuring in their tone and cadence. "I really don't know what happened this evening," she said. "Mr. Sullivan wasn't very forthcoming."

Ethan was able to shrug off a little tension at Rennie's remark. He permitted himself a small, genuine smile. "Jarret rarely is."

"Well, I don't want to talk about him."

Ethan flinched as Michael's keening cry drifted in from the other room. He began speaking in part because it would cover the sound of his wife's pain, and in part because he needed Rennie to understand. "I decided I was recovered enough to follow Dee this evening when she left work. The Turners had identified her working in the dining room a few days ago."

Rennie nodded. "Jarret told me that was the plan."

"I needed to see where Dee was going to determine if she was working alone or with Houston. There wasn't enough time to send anyone from the hotel to get Jarret, so I decided to do it myself. It never entered my mind that Houston might come here without Detra. I would have never left Michael alone if I'd thought that."

"I believe you," Rennie said. And she did. She wasn't merely mouthing the words because they sounded right or because she thought Ethan needed to hear them. In the end it only mattered what Ethan believed himself.

Ethan shook his head slightly, clearing it. He drained his tumbler but held on to it. "I wasn't gone long at all. I followed Detra into the Bowery, saw the clapboarded dwelling where she was living, and stayed long enough to ask a few questions of the neighbors. They were suspicious, but I was able to learn that she was living with someone . . . a man. One drunk let slip that the man had some kind of leg injury. As soon as I heard that, I knew I had Houston, too. I left immediately and came back here."

He stood, went to the sideboard, and splashed his tumbler with whiskey. "Michael was ten minutes into her labor, and Houston dead just as long."

Rennie hugged herself. It was chilling to imagine her sister alone with Nate Houston, but impossible to imagine that Michael had killed the outlaw.

"He came here to confront Michael," Ethan continued. "He meant to kill her and her child if she refused to leave with him."

"He wanted her?" Rennie asked. The thought raised more gooseflesh. "But what about Detra?"

"Houston always wanted your sister. He was fascinated by her, repelled and attracted. He couldn't help himself from coming here." Ethan sipped his drink. "Because of his injured leg Houston was using a walking stick. It had a spring-action knife concealed in the tip, just the sort of thing Houston would have prized. Michael didn't know it was there; he hadn't threatened her with it."

"Then how . . . ?"

"He riled her," Ethan said as if he still couldn't believe it. "Do you and your sister share the same temper?"

"Actually, we each have one of our own," Rennie said, straight-faced.

Ethan found his first reason to laugh. He looked at Rennie appreciatively. "Then, you know how it could have happened," he said. "She got so damned mad at Houston's demands and the threat to her baby that she picked up his walking stick and poked him with it to emphasize her angry speech. Her action released the dagger. She didn't even know she'd wounded him until she saw the blood. Her first stab was the fatal one."

Rennie's anxiety finally had an outlet in laughter. She imagined Houston's surprise at being hoist by his own petard, and suddenly it was very, very funny. She raised her hand to her mouth, trying to smother her laughter. Tears sprang to her eyes as her dark humor would not be suppressed. "I'm sorry," she said, shaking her head. "I don't know what's wrong with me. There's nothing at all fun —" she swallowed some sherry and tried not to choke on it — "funny about it. Oh, God, that Michael could have . . . He must have been so . . . so *shocked* . . ." Rennie gasped a little as laughter caught in her throat and became a wrenching sob. Suddenly she was weeping.

Ethan put down his drink and became the comforter. His arms circled her, and he let her lean against him. She was the same size and shape as Michael; yet there were differences, and he felt them deeply, felt the need strongly to be holding Michael in just the same manner.

"Don't you have the wrong sister?" Jarret asked, stepping into the suite. He raised the brim of his hat with his forefinger and regarded the entwined couple with lazy interest.

"Don't you ever knock?" Ethan asked.

Rennie stepped back and dried her eyes with the handkerchief Ethan slipped her. She sniffed. "He thinks he can come and go as he pleases."

Jarret grinned. He shut the door behind him and tossed his coat and hat in a chair by the entrance. He winced as he heard Michael's cry from the bedroom. "She hasn't delivered yet?" he asked.

Ethan shook his head. "Dr. Turner says it could take most of the night."

"She's doing all right, though?"

"The last word was that she's doing fine."

Jarret's eyes darted between Ethan and Rennie. "Then why the long faces? Houston's dead. Dee's safely in jail. And in a few hours one of you is going to be a father and the other an aunt. I take it you do know who is who."

Ethan got a drink for his deputy. "Here. I think you'd better have this. You're wound too tight. What happened when you got to Dee's?"

Rennie watched Jarret take the drink, but saw that he had too much energy to sit. She had never seen him like this. He was always so controlled, so contained, that she often felt as if she were running in place beside him. Now he paced the floor, methodically to be sure, but it was Rennie's first indication that he was still operating in the aftermath of an adrenaline rush. Ethan, she noticed, was regarding Jarret with friendly sympathy, proving he understood perfectly what his deputy was going through.

"She didn't hear me," Jarret was saying, "until I was in her bedroom. She was sitting with her back to me, and she called Houston's name, assuming he was the one coming in. She was furious with him for leaving the flat. You know Dee. Her voice was as arched as her back."

"She probably wished it were Houston when she saw you," said Ethan.

Jarret nodded, raising his glass in a gesture of agreement. "I didn't think she could get angrier. I was wrong. She came after me with a pair of scissors. I'm lucky to still have both ears."

Rennie's eyes widened. She noticed for the first time the scratch extending below Jarret's hairline and into his shirt collar. "What did you do?"

"When I couldn't restrain her I didn't have any choice. I knocked her out."

"I thought you didn't strike women," Rennie said sweetly.

"I've always reserved the right to make an exception," he returned dryly, giving her a significant look.

Ethan got his friend's attention. "Did you have any trouble taking her in?"

"None, except I couldn't find any beat cops patrolling the area."

"They don't like to go into the Bowery at night," said Rennie. "It's dangerous."

Jarret raised his eyebrows. "And you've led me to believe the city's so civilized." He looked at Ethan. "Dee woke up at the station. She managed to get a gun from the desk sergeant and used it to keep everyone at bay. I didn't think we were going to get it off of her. There were some moments when I wasn't sure if she was going to use it on us or herself. It wasn't until I convinced her that Houston was really dead that she gave up . . . just sort of caved in." He finished his drink. "I stayed while all the papers were being completed and did my best to make certain they understood how dangerous Detra is."

"Do you think they believed you?" Ethan asked.

"Who knows? Her stunt with the gun underscored my warnings, but Detra's clever. She knows how to make herself seem harmless." He rubbed his neck tiredly, wincing when he touched the scratch.

"You're bleeding," Rennie said as he removed his hand.

Surprised, Jarret looked at his palm. A smear of blood ran diagonally across the heart of it. He let Rennie take him by the wrist and lead him to the loveseat. He also noticed that Ethan was watching Rennie's fussing with great interest. Over the top of Rennie's bent head Jarret scowled at his friend.

Rennie was quite aware of the interplay between Jarret and Ethan. She ignored Ethan's chuckle and dipped her handkerchief into Jarret's drink.

"Hey!" he said. "That was perfectly good whiskey."

"Now it's a perfectly good astringent." She sat beside him and began cleaning the scratch with the damp linen. "This scratch goes into your scalp," she said. "You *are* fortunate to have an ear."

Her fingers were gentle as she brushed aside his hair to examine Dee's handiwork. Jarret had a difficult time hiding his pleasure from Ethan. He flinched when she touched the alcohol to a deeper cut. "Be careful. That hurts."

140

"My sister's having a baby in the next room," she said. *"That* hurts."

"She has a point," Ethan said.

As if on cue Michael screamed with the pain she'd been swallowing for a long time. Rennie saw both men pale. "It won't be much longer," she told Ethan. "That sounds like Michael's last hurrah."

Ethan felt as if the wind had been knocked out of him. He sat down heavily and drummed his fingers against the curved arm of the chair. He was oblivious to everything but the sounds coming from the bedchamber.

"How do you know it won't be long?" Jarret whispered to Rennie.

"I just know," she said. She applied more alcohol to Jarret's wound, following the scratch from his scalp to where it disappeared beneath his shirt. "I've always known about Michael." She hesitated, uncertain if she wanted to tell him, uncertain if he would believe her or understand. "Sometimes I can feel her pain."

Jarret's head turned to the side, and he studied Rennie's strained and solemn features. He remembered her frantic, mad attempts to leave the house, driven, or pulled, by something outside herself. He had thought then that it had only been about seeing Hollis; he realized now that it hadn't been. She had wanted, *needed,* to see her sister.

Uncomfortable with his scrutiny, Rennie pulled her eyes away from Jarret's and bent her head to examine his wound. "You should take off your shirt," she said. "I think she gouged your shoulder, didn't she?"

"I don't know what she did. Everything happened so fast. But I'm not taking off my shirt."

Rennie shrugged. She opened the first few buttons of his cambric shirt and slipped her hand beneath his collar. "How in the world did she get her scissors under here? You'd think she'd have ripped your shirt." She found the deeper wound with her alcohol-soaked handkerchief.

"Dammit, woman!" Jarret swore, pulling away from her. "Your healin' hurts worse than her pokin'."

Disgusted, Rennie threw the handkerchief at him. "Do it yourself then, or have Dr. Turner look at it. You may need a few stitches."

"What I need is another drink," he said, staring at his nearly empty glass. "Ethan? You want another?"

"What?" Ethan came slowly out of his reverie and saw Jarret's raised glass. "Oh. No, I'm fine. I have to save something for the celebration."

Jarret grunted softly, realizing he should probably do the same. He set the tumbler aside, dropped his sodden handkerchief inside, and settled back on the loveseat. Now that he was allowing himself to feel, he realized his shoulder ached. Where Rennie had managed to douse it with whiskey, it burned all the way to the bone. There was virtually no blood, so he knew that Dee had somehow missed an artery; but it was as deep a puncture wound as any he'd ever had, perhaps a little deeper. The pain had been so great when Detra sunk the scissors in that he had almost lost his hold. For a moment he'd lost all sensation in his hand—his gun hand. He wiggled his fingers now, testing them.

Out of the corner of her eye Rennie saw the movement. "I wish you'd let me look at it."

"Maybe later," he said.

By his tone Rennie knew he was only putting her off. "It could become infected." The look that Jarret shot in her direction warned her it should be her last word on the subject. She was not intimidated. Rennie opened her mouth to say something else, but the cry from the other room distracted her. This time it was not Michael.

Several long minutes passed before the door to the bedroom opened.

Ethan shot to his feet in the same moment that Dr. Turner appeared in the doorway. He looked anxiously past Turner's shoulder, trying to see into the bedroom. "Michael?" he asked. "Is she all right?"

The doctor pushed aside the fringe of damp blond hair on his forehead. "You have a fine, healthy daughter, Ethan."

There was no change in Ethan's expression. "Is Michael all right?"

"Your wife's fine," the doctor reassured gently.

Ethan let out the breath he didn't know he was holding. Tension seeped out of him. "I can see her?" he asked.

"You'd better," Michael called.

Scott Turner smiled and stepped out of the doorway. "You heard her."

Ethan practically tripped over his own feet in his haste to reach his wife. Rennie and Dr. Turner exchanged indulgent smiles. Jarret shook his head, his dark sapphire eyes full of restrained good humor.

"Rennie?" Dr. Turner asked. "Don't you want to go in?"

"In a minute. I want to give them some time alone." She pointed to Jarret. "He was wounded tonight by that she-devil. Perhaps you could take a look."

Scott had started to roll down his sleeves. Now he pushed them back up to his elbows. "Since I'm here." He looked at Jarret expectantly and realized for the first time how reluctant the patient was. "Rennie, your sister was saying that she'd like a cup of camomile tea. Why don't you see if you can get some from the hotel kitchen?"

"I could ring for it," she said.

"It would be quicker if you got it yourself."

"Oh." Rennie finally took the doctor's hint. "Of course. I'll get it now."

Watching her go, Jarret shook his head. "You should have just asked her straight out to leave. She'd have understood that quicker."

Scott Turner smiled. "I was thinking of your pride. Now let me see your shoulder."

Jarret blinked in surprise. "How did you know it was my shoulder?"

143

"I don't have to be a doctor to see that you're favoring it right now. Let's have a look." He watched Jarret struggle to use both hands to unbutton his shirt, give up with his right, and continue clumsily with only his left. "That's good enough," he said when the shirt was half undone. He pushed it off Jarret's right shoulder. Knowing that his patient was watching him keenly for reaction, Scott was careful not to give one.

The puncture wound was little more than an inch on the surface, and on close examination, not as cleanly made as Scott would have hoped. "Detra Kelly did this?" he asked without inflection.

Jarret nodded. "With a pair of scissors."

"Were they clean? Rust? Anything like that?"

Jarret's low chuckle ended in a wince. "I didn't get a good look."

"No, I suppose you didn't." Scott went to the bedroom and got his satchel. "Your wound wasn't made in a clean, stabbing motion," he said, pulling a stopper out of a bottle of alcohol. "What happened?"

"She got the scissors under my shirt collar and plunged them in my shoulder."

"Then she couldn't get them out."

Jarret sucked in his breath as Scott applied the alcohol with a clean cotton cloth. "That's what I remember."

"Did she twist them?"

"I don't know. It seemed that way. It felt like she was cuttin' off my shoulder."

"Can you move your fingers?"

Jarret did. "Appears so. They tingle a little. My whole arm does as a matter of fact."

"Squeeze my hand." He held it out to Jarret. It was taken in a firm grip. "Harder." When the grip did not increase significantly Scott Turner's solid, cleanly cut features turned grave.

"What is it?" Jarret asked. "What did that bitch do to me?"

144

Turner sat back and regarded Jarret carefully. "Everything my wife's told me about you, Mr. Sullivan, leads me to believe you'd like your news like your whiskey: straight. The truth is, I don't know the full extent of the damage. She may have injured a nerve; that's why you have the tingling. She didn't sever it or you'd feel nothing. Your shoulder's stiff right now, and you don't have all your strength in your hand; but that could improve."

"Or not."

The doctor nodded. "Or not. There's no way of telling right now. You should know more in a few days." He began bandaging Jarret's shoulder. "Come by Jennings Memorial Hospital early in the week and I'll look at it again."

"I'll be gone by then. Now that Dee's in jail and Houston's dead there's nothing to keep me in New York." His eyes strayed to the door. "Don't tell Rennie about my shoulder. Not that she'd care," he said quickly, "but she'd feel obligated to fuss, and I don't need that."

Scott Turner knew there was more to it than that, but he agreed. "You're going to be tempted to use your arm just to test how it's healing," he said, tying off the bandage. "Don't give into temptation. Let it rest. Straining it may exacerbate the damage. Is that clear, Mr. Sullivan?"

Jarret was reluctant to give his word. He wiggled his fingers again. He wanted to wrap his fingers around the handle of his gun and see if he could still pull the trigger. What if he couldn't hold the gun at all?

"If you have some problem with that," Scott was saying, "then I think I better tell Rennie right now. Her fussing may save your arm."

"No, don't say anything to her. I'll nurse it like a baby."

Dr. Turner allowed himself to be convinced. He helped Jarret slip his shirt over the shoulder again and buttoned it for him. "Don't be so proud you can't ask her for help," he said.

Jarret didn't reply because Rennie walked back in the

room. "Everything's fine," he told her in response to her questioning glance. He watched Rennie's eyes swing to the doctor for confirmation. She was not satisfied until Scott Turner gave his approval.

"Good," Rennie said, setting down the tray. "I have tea enough for everyone. Would you like some, Mr. Sullivan?"

"I'll get my own whiskey, thanks."

"Scott?"

The doctor held up his hands. "Nothing for me. I have to be leaving. I'll see Michael once more before I go." He closed his satchel, stood, and excused himself.

Jarret got up to get his drink. He could feel Rennie's eyes boring into his back. He tried to hold his shoulder naturally and not appear too clumsy as he poured his drink with his left hand.

"What did Dr. Turner really say?" she asked.

"Just what he told you. I'm fit as a fiddle."

"Odd, I don't recall hearing that."

Jarret ignored her, taking a swallow of his drink instead. Dr. Turner came out of the bedroom a few minutes later, cutting through the charged silence that separated Jarret and Rennie.

"She'll have that tea now," Scott said to Rennie, smiling. "And I'll be going."

Rennie helped him with his coat and retrieved his medicine bag. "Thank you for everything," she said. "You and Susan have done so much. I know I speak for Jay Mac and Mama, too. We all thank you."

It was the heartfelt emotion in Rennie's large eyes that touched Scott. "You're very welcome," he said solemnly. He glanced at Jarret. "Take care of the shoulder." Then he was gone.

Rennie shut the door, picked up the tea tray, and went into the bedroom. She hadn't once looked in Jarret's direction, but he felt her disapproval. The doctor's parting shot about

146

the shoulder had been enough to convince Rennie he was lying about the state of his health.

Ethan was sitting on the edge of the bed next to Michael when Rennie entered. He started to rise, but she shook her head. "Stay right where you are. You look too comfortable to move—all three of you."

Michael's smile was beatific. She raised her cheek as Rennie leaned over the bed and kissed her. "I'm so glad you're here."

Rennie squeezed her hand. Her eyes dropped to the baby that was curled against her sister's breast. The tiny face was red and wrinkled and perfectly content. "Have you named her?"

"Madison," Michael said, glancing at Ethan. Love seemed to spill out of her eyes.

Rennie's heart swelled for her sister's happiness. "Isn't that the name of the town where—"

"Where she was conceived," Michael said.

"Then I suppose she's fortunate you didn't name her after the saloon where it happened." Rennie and Michael laughed as Ethan's cheeks reddened at their plain speaking.

Ethan cleared his throat. "I'd be damned before I'd name my daughter after Kelly's Saloon." He looked at the door. "How's Jarret doing?"

Rennie poured a cup of tea for Michael, adding plenty of milk and a dollop of honey. "He's pretending everything's fine, of course. He even elicited Scott's cooperation in his lies."

Michael frowned. "Jarret was hurt? What happened?"

Rennie gave her sister the only version she knew. "That's what Mr. Sullivan says. What really happened is anyone's guess, and frankly, it's his business, none of mine. If Detra Kelly had lopped off his head, it would have been a cause for celebration as far as I'm concerned."

"Rennie!" Michael said, her eyes widening. "Ethan has assured me that Jarret is a very good person, every inch the gentleman."

Ethan coughed lightly. "I don't think I said it quite like that."

Michael ignored her husband. "You're not still blaming him for stopping the wedding, are you?"

Rennie's hand smoothed the downy cap of her niece's hair. "I don't want to talk about him," she said. "Tell me about you. Are you all right?"

Michael did not want to be swayed from the topic of Jarret Sullivan and Rennie's aborted wedding, but she recognized the flat, mutinous line of her sister's mouth and realized there would be no swaying her. "I'm wonderful," she said. "Happy . . . and tired. More happy than tired at the moment."

"You look," she paused, searching for the word, "radiant."

"Do I?" Michael asked, more pleased than embarrassed.

"Yes, you do. Doesn't she, Ethan?" When Rennie glanced at Ethan to get his support she saw Michael's husband was too overcome with emotion to speak. Rennie felt her own throat closing, clogged by the rising lump of tears as Ethan could only nod. His fingers sifted through Michael's damp auburn hair, and Michael turned her face toward him so that she was caressed by the cup of his hand. The baby stirred gently against her mother's breast.

Rennie slipped out of the room.

Jarret never questioned her anxiousness to leave. He was happy to be gone from the St. Mark as well. His shoulder ached abominably, and the jostling of the carriage didn't help. He was grateful for Rennie's silence if not for her scrutiny. When they reached the house he alighted first, then, out of habit, offered his right arm to Rennie as she climbed down. The movement alone caused him to grit his teeth and some of the color to leave his face, but his wounded pride stung more as Rennie reached for his good arm and offered

148

herself as support.

He didn't know which of them was more surprised when he accepted it.

"Did Scott give you anything for the pain?" she asked when they reached his room.

Jarret shook his head. "I didn't ask for anything."

Rennie's look told him what she thought of that. "Mama may have something around here that would help. I could—"

"I'll let you know." He opened the door to his room and stepped inside. In the hallway, Rennie hesitated. "Yes?" he asked.

"Will you . . . umm . . . need some help?" she asked uncertainly.

"Help?"

"Umm . . . with your clothes? Getting into your night-shirt. That sort of thing."

"I don't wear a nightshirt." The comment did not send her running as he hoped it would. It did, however, put a hint of pink in her cheeks and caused her lips to part fractionally. To keep from reaching for her, his fingers pressed against the door and the jamb. The pressure in his right hand sent pain searing to his shoulder.

"I think you need help," she said, her eyes darting over his face.

Jarret let out his breath slowly and said gruffly, "The kind of help I need, you can't give me." He put enough sexual nuance into his rebuff that Rennie could not mistake his meaning. He watched her turn and walk away, her back as stiff as her pride. Jarret closed the door, leaned against it, and wished himself on the next train out of New York.

Dressing the following morning was awkward and slow, but Jarret felt a full measure of accomplishment when he succeeded. He resisted the urge to work his gun hand any

149

more than necessary. His shoulder was still stiff, but it seemed to ease as he allowed himself to move more naturally.

Breakfast was laid out for him on the dining room table, a farewell feast, he imagined. Rennie must have told Mrs. Cavanaugh that he would be leaving soon. He wondered if he could purchase train fare today. Then he wondered if Rennie had already purchased a ticket for him. It would be just what he deserved for the slap in the face he'd served her last night.

Mary Renee Dennehy was a proper, respectable woman, and he had no right talking to her the way he had. His mother would have been shamed by his manners; his father would have taken a switch to his backside. Jarret vowed he would apologize.

Mrs. Cavanaugh came in with fresh coffee. She was talking to herself under her breath.

Used to the cook's breathless mutterings, Jarret smiled indulgently and fingered the morning paper. "Has Rennie come down this morning?" he asked.

"Finished her breakfast an hour ago."

"Then, she's gone to work," he said. "I suppose you know about Houston and Kelly. It's safe for her now."

"Sure and I know all about last night's piece of work." Her eyes strayed to his shoulder, and she saw the swath of bandages through his shirt. "But Rennie's not gone to the Worth Building this morning. She's taken herself off to the station."

The station? Then, she *was* buying him a ticket west. He chuckled to himself.

"You approve, then?" Mrs. Cavanaugh demanded tartly.

"Approve? I don't think that's my place one way or the other. Truthfully, I suspected she might do it. I haven't precisely endeared myself to her."

"What does that have to do with anything?" She pushed a plate of biscuits toward him. "Here, have one of these. I

150

made them fresh this morning."

Jarret obediently took a biscuit and drizzled it with honey.

"It doesn't matter if she likes you or not, does it? Or the other way around, come to think of it. My understanding is that you agreed to protect her."

Jarret bit into a warm biscuit. It was almost unnecessary to chew. It simply dissolved on his tongue. "I did protect her," he said. "But the danger's behind us. Rennie can go anywhere she pleases, and if it pleases her to go to the station, then . . ." Forgetting his injury, he shrugged. The movement was halting and painful. He sucked in his breath, let it out slowly, and forced a smile. "Then she can go."

"I thought you'd object."

Jarret frowned. "Object? If she wants to buy me a ticket home, then I think I should be grateful."

"Buy you a ticket?" Mrs. Cavanaugh waved her coffeepot as she spoke. Dull red color crept along her neckline above her starched collar. "What sort of ticket is it that someone buys at the police station?"

Jarret stilled. "Police station? I thought she was going to the train station."

"Where did you come by a fool notion like that?" Mrs. Cavanaugh asked. "Mary Renee's gone to the station at Jones Street, right next to the Bowery. The same station that's harborin' Dee Kelly, I'm thinkin'." Jarret was on his feet and heading toward the entrance hall. Mrs. Cavanaugh dogged his steps. "So you don't approve," she said with satisfaction.

"Of course I don't approve." He rummaged through the coat closet and found his duster. Ignoring the pain, he shoved his injured arm into the sleeve and shrugged into the coat. "How long ago did she leave?"

"Just before you came down."

"Then, I might be able to catch her before she gets there."

"Mr. Cavanaugh has a horse ready for you in the stables."

Jarret found he could still grin. "You were counting on me."

The cook blushed at the good-natured scolding in his eyes. "Sure and you had me goin' there for a moment."

Rennie marched up the stone steps of the Jones Street Station. She carried a covered basket under one arm and a Bible under the other. Two beat cops on their way out held the great doors open for her. Behind Rennie they exchanged appreciative glances, both for the comely figure and the mouth-watering aroma of fresh biscuits.

Crossing the scuffed wooden floor to the high mahogany front desk, Rennie set her Bible in front of the sergeant and gave him a frank, expectant gaze.

"Ma'am?" Sergeant Morrison's square jaw was outlined by his side whiskers, his mouth nearly hidden by the full mustache. His eyes were kind. He looked down at the Bible. "You're from the church?"

"I'm here to see Mrs. Kelly," she prevaricated.

"Mrs. Kelly? Now, how would you be knowin' about Mrs. Kelly?"

"I read the papers, Sergeant. The *Chronicle* reported the story in their late morning edition."

Sergeant Morrison sighed. "Might have known they'd get the story. Kelly being mixed up with one of their reporters and all." He swiveled in his chair and picked up a ring of keys pegged on the wall behind him. "I don't think there's much hope of savin' her soul, ma'am," he said, handing Rennie her Bible. "She's been like a she-cat since that bounty hunter brought her in here last night. You'll have to stay on this side of the bars. There's no goin' in the cell with her."

"I understand, Sergeant."

He opened the door to the row of cells secluded from the public rooms and ushered Rennie in. "Those biscuits sure smell good, ma'am. Wouldn't mind havin' one myself."

Smiling, Rennie lifted the blue-and-white-checked cover and handed him a biscuit. "I should have brought enough for all the inmates," she said.

"None but Mrs. Kelly this morning. Let the drunks go last night when she was raising hell — if you'll pardon the expression."

The officer led her down the hallway to the last cell. He pulled out his nightstick and struck the bars with it several times. The woman lying on the cot didn't stir. "It's a visitor you have, Mrs. Kelly."

There was no reply.

"She heard me, ma'am, but that's about all the response you'll get from her."

Rennie nodded. "It's all right, Sergeant. You can leave us. I'm not afraid of Mrs. Kelly."

The sergeant was already turning to go as Dee Kelly sat up. The sound of the voice on the other side of the bars drew her attention as nothing the officer said could have. Struck dumb by what she saw, she stared at the woman beyond her reach.

Rennie had never given any thought to Detra Kelly's looks. On the few occasions Michael had spoken of Dee, Rennie had never inquired. In part it was the reason she had come to Jones Street. She had to see for herself the kind of woman who would try to poison her sister and take scissors to a deputy marshal.

Detra Kelly was petite, diminutive in the manner of some dainty figurine. Her curves were lush, though, and in the sea green gown she wore, they were shown in taut relief. When she stood and approached the bars Rennie could see that walking was hardly the correct term for what Dee Kelly did. She swayed and enticed with every step she took. It was a performance that was not lost on Rennie. She could not imagine how Michael had spent any time in this woman's company and remained in command of her wits.

Detra's hair was as black as the jet beads dangling from her ears. There was something sensual inherent in the untidiness of her chignon. Curls tumbled across her neck and swept her shoulder. Only her eyes hinted at the coldness within the woman. They were twin chips of blue ice.

Rennie held her ground as she was examined at length by those coldly remote eyes.

"So you've come," Dee said, her voice softly melodious. "I'm not surprised. Not really. I've lost Houston, but then you've lost your baby." She glanced at the Bible and smiled without humor. "Perhaps it's been an eye for an eye after all."

"I'm not who you think I am," Rennie said calmly. "So you may feel cheated."

Detra frowned. Her fingers slid around the bars on either side of her waist. She stared harder at Rennie. "Who *are* you?"

"Mary Renee Dennehy," she said. "Michael's my sister." She saw Dee grip the bars more tightly, almost as if her legs had given out from under her. "Michael gave birth to a beautiful baby girl last night. *Do* you feel cheated?"

Quick as lightning Dee's hand struck out through the bars. She managed to knock the Bible from Rennie's hand. Her fingers curled like talons, groping for Rennie even as she jumped out of the way.

Rennie uncovered the basket she clutched under her arm. The biscuits and jam jars were discarded on the floor. The nickel-plated derringer was not. She let the basket drop and raised the small handgun. She saw then that Dee Kelly's cold eyes were capable of registering fear.

"My sister and I are very close, Mrs. Kelly, but she would never think of doing this. I've not thought of much else since I learned you were taken alive."

Detra opened her mouth to scream.

Rennie pulled back the hammer on her pistol.

Both women jumped as Jarret's voice thundered in the

154

narrow passage. "For God's sake, Rennie, put that thing down!"

Detra screamed.

Rennie swore.

Jarret had to use his injured arm to block the sergeant from barreling down the hallway after Rennie. "It's all right, Sergeant," he said, catching his breath. "I'll handle it."

Sergeant Morrison hesitated, his eyes darting back and forth between the two women. "She didn't say she was the reporter's sister," he said. "I wouldn't have let her in if I'd known that." He backed off slowly, retreating as far as the door.

"Rennie," Jarret said quietly. "Put down the gun. There's nothing to be gained by killing Dee."

Backed against the wall, Rennie held her stance. The derringer was aimed at Dee's heart.

"Get her away from me, Sullivan!" Dee yelled. "You want your reward, don't you?"

"Forget it, Dee. I got it last night, and you were good to me dead or alive. I don't give a damn what happens to you." He turned his attention back to Rennie. "You're not thinking, Rennie. If you kill Dee, you'll take her place in the cell. Jay Mac himself won't be able to get you out."

Rennie lowered the gun, pivoted on one foot, and stared at Jarret, her mouth flattened in disgust. "You have completely spoiled my concentration," she said. She glanced at Dee, and her smile was rich with insincerity. "I'm sorry, Mrs. Kelly, did I frighten you?" She opened the chamber of the derringer and showed it was empty. "Then it was worth the time making your acquaintance."

Ignoring Dee's outraged cry at the trick she was played, ignoring the biscuits, basket, and Bible, Rennie swept her skirts to one side and blithely walked down the hallway past Jarret's stormy countenance, past the sergeant's slack-jaw and bulging eyes, and past the two beat cops as they reentered the building.

Jarret caught up with her as she was crossing Jones Street in search of a hack. "I rode here on one of your horses."

Rennie kept walking. Her heart was hammering with the residual rush of her adventure. "So?"

"I'll take you back."

She stopped long enough to give him a patently horrified look. "I'm not riding the same horse as you. That's not done here."

He grabbed her elbow and drew her up short. "You are the most maddening person, male or female, I've met in my entire life!" He realized he was shouting and lowered his voice so that she had to strain to hear him. "You just waltzed into a police station, leveled a derringer at Dee Kelly, and now you're worried what people may say if we share a horse?"

"I thought we had already established that where I go I walk. I don't waltz." She smiled.

He stared at her. "You're just so full of yourself, aren't you? I've seen cats lickin' stolen cream off their whiskers that weren't half so pleased with themselves as you."

If anything, her smile became broader. She just couldn't seem to help herself.

Neither could Jarret. His hand snaked from her elbow to the small of her back, and he hauled her flush to his body. Bending his head, his mouth slanted across hers. Hard.

There was only a hint of resistance before Rennie gave herself up to the touch and taste of him. Her arms circled his neck, and she felt herself raised on tiptoe. His mouth moved over hers hungrily, and she reciprocated in kind, oblivious to the small crowd that had surrounded them. She pressed herself against him, her eyes closed, her lips warmly searching. She breathed in his heady male scent, the leather duster, the lingering fragrance of his shaving cream.

The kiss was sweet and tart. The kiss was pure Rennie. Jarret wanted all of her and knew he could have none of her.

Not on Jones Street. Not anywhere.

He set her away from him as the gathered crowd applauded lightly. Rennie took refuge in the absurdity of her situation, brazening it out by making an elaborate curtsy to her admirers. Her composure shattered as she recognized one face among many.

Jarret felt her stiffen beside him. He glared at the gathering, then cut a path through them, Rennie in tow, when they failed to disperse. "What's wrong?" he asked. "There's no color in your face."

What was there to be gained, she wondered, by telling Jarret the truth? She had seen one of Hollis's good friends in the crowd. Not only was James Taddy a friend, but he had served as one of the ushers at St. Gregory's. He had recognized her and he had recognized Jarret, and Hollis would hear of it before she made it uptown.

"Rennie?" Jarret said, prompting her as she drifted away.

She fought for a smile that would ease his mind but could find little humor in what had just happened. "You mean what's wrong besides the fact that I've made a public spectacle of myself?" she asked. "I'd say that about sums it up, Mr. Sullivan. I'm generally not at the center of some public stunt. That's the sort of thing we like to leave to Skye. She excels at it."

"Then, you've done credit to her tradition," Jarret said dryly. He could still taste her on his lips and feel the outline of her body against him. Beside him, she was no longer giving him the slightest encouragement. He raised his hand as a hack turned the corner from Lafayette. The hansom cab stopped, and Rennie climbed aboard, this time eschewing Jarret's help. He looked at her oddly, but she avoided his eyes. Jarret knew then that he had completely overstepped his bounds and overstayed his welcome.

During the hour, he made arrangements to leave New York.

* * *

The station was crowded and noisy. Most of the benches were taken by women with wide skirts and trunks the size of small armoires. Husbands stood directly behind their wives, stoic in the face of boredom, their eyes darting occasionally to an unaccompanied female. Their interest waned in direct proportion to the number of bags, valises, and trunks the porters pushed behind her.

Jarret found it fascinating. He leaned against a pillar, resting on his good shoulder, his lone valise at his feet. His sweat-banded felt hat was out of place among the derbies and bonnets, his leather duster not at all fashionable among the tailored jackets and capes. He smiled ruefully as he considered he would be out of place until he reached Kansas City, perhaps even as far as Denver. Thanks to men like Jay Mac laying rails down wherever there was an open space, train travel simply moved people from one civilized settlement to the next, and the settlements were very nearly all the same.

Jarret suspected there were a lot of people in the station now who would disagree with him, but it didn't change his mind. He was hungry for the sight of the plains and the wild, challenging beauty of the Rockies. He missed dipping his hands in cold mountain streams and slaking his thirst with crystal clear water. He missed drinking coffee as thick as ink, playing cards in a quiet saloon, and laughing at a ribald joke told by a bawdy woman.

He was glad to be going back. More or less. There was at least one thing he would miss about New York.

Caught in his own musings, Jarret didn't understand that the commotion nearing him was *about* him until he was surrounded. He gave a cursory glance to all three men and continued to lean casually against the platform pillar. "Can I help you, gentlemen?" he asked quietly.

James Taddy didn't speak to Jarret, but to his companions. "It's him, all right. Do you recognize him?"

When Taddys friends were slow to answer, Jarret spoke. "It's all right, fellas. I recognize all of you. Miss Dennehy's wedding. The three of you were standing up for Hollis Banks."

"See?" Taddy said. "He admits it. Now ask him about this morning on Jones Street."

Jarret's face didn't register any surprise, but he felt Taddy's words as a blow to his midsection. There was no longer any doubt about what Rennie had seen. One glimpse of Hollis's friend in the crowd reminded her of all she was risking with that kiss. Jarret's glance slid over the trio, assessing the danger.

The one who did the talking was a bully, brawny in a way that suggested he did not have to be a good fighter because most people were intimidated by his size. His blond-haired friend was slight but probably agile, and the darker, dapper companion was heavy-footed. Under normal circumstances Jarret would have been wary of them but not greatly concerned. His bum shoulder changed the circumstances.

Rennie should have told him what she'd seen. At least then he would have been alert to the possibility of trouble. He was staring straight at them, but he knew he'd just been blind-sided by Hollis Banks.

"What can I do for you fellas?" he asked.

James Taddy traded looks with his friends. The slightest nod of his head gave Jarret all the warning he was going to get.

Jarret ducked the first blow that the blond shot in his direction. The blond's fist connected with the pillar, and he howled in pain. Heavy-foot was more fortunate, and Jarret less so. A hammering fist caught Jarret under the jaw and sent him reeling backward. A second blow from Taddy spun him around. Before he could throw a counterpunch the blond danced in and unerringly found Jarret's injured shoulder. The sharp jab made Jarret nauseous with pain. He slumped, trying to protect his shoulder and reach for his gun. The pain arced across his shoulder and back and down his arm. It never reached his wrist. His fingers were numb.

Fear gripped him. He blocked a punch to his face with his left arm, but that made him vulnerable to the blow at his midriff. Taddy's brawn dropped Jarret to his knees. Heavy-foot kicked him squarely on his injured shoulder. This time the pain was so great that Jarret slumped sideways.

As he struggled to remain conscious he was vaguely aware of whistles blowing in the background and people scurrying along the platform. He thought it must be the train coming in and cursed his luck for missing it. His three attackers swam in and out of focus.

"Come on," Taddy said. "That's the cops. There will be hell to pay if our families find out about this."

The blond was bent over Jarret's valise, rifling the contents. "In a minute. Hollis said to get the money if we could." His fingers curled around a piece of paper. He pulled it out and saw he was holding a draft for five hundred dollars. He glanced at the signature. He swore softly. "Look at this! It's the reward money for Mrs. Kelly!"

Impatient, Taddy bent over Jarret and patted down his pockets. He found Jay Mac's personal draft for ten thousand dollars in Jarret's vest. "Here's what Hollis wants," he said. "Let's go. We're attracting too much attention."

The blond straightened, curled the reward check around his finger and deposited it in his pocket. He grinned down at Jarret. "Seems like there should be a reward out on you. You can't go around stealing another man's woman." He plunged the pointed toe of his shoe sharply into Jarret's groin.

When the police arrived Jarret was unconscious and the assailants had fled.

160

Chapter Six

January 1877

Jolene Cartwright rolled lazily out of bed. The plank floor was cold beneath her feet. "Should get a rug," she mumbled to herself, curling her toes. She reached for her stockings lying over the arm of the nearby rocker and padded quickly to the window seat on tiptoe to put them on. She sat down and glanced back at the sprawled figure on the bed. No amount of movement or talking to herself was likely to wake him up. Jarret Sullivan was sleeping off the dregs of a sloppy two-day drunk.

Jolene slipped on one silk black stocking, then the other, smoothing each over the finely curved length of her calf. She secured them with powder blue garters just above her knees, then adjusted the belt of her robe and arranged the collar so that her cleavage was visible. "Not that it matters," she grumbled, darting a look at the bed again. "He's more interested in my bed than my breasts."

"I'm awake, Jolene," Jarret muttered wearily. His head throbbed, and his brief attempt to open his eyes blinded him. He pulled the pillow over his head.

"No kind of awake from what I'm seeing," she said sharply. Jolene leaned toward her dresser and snatched her hairbrush from the top. She rapped it several times against the windowsill just to annoy Jarret before she dragged it through her hair. The harsh snores rising from the bed told her all she needed to know about being ignored. She raised the brush, tempted to throw it, then thought better of it. The covers had slipped over Jarret's thighs, baring his backside.

Jolene took a good, long look at Jarret's taut flanks. "How's a woman supposed to stay mad at a man with bottom cheeks like that?" She began brushing her chestnut hair again, with lazy grace this time, and let her gaze wander away from her bed to the street below her window.

Echo Falls didn't stray much from the pattern of most western towns. Its single wide thoroughfare was named Main Street and every sort of common business was set on either side. There was a barbershop and bathhouse where a miner could get a shave and a soak for two bits. Soap was a penny extra. The mercantile sold a variety of goods from candy and calico to pick shovels and treasure maps. The druggist kept jars of medicines along the rear wall of his store but made most of his money on liniment and hair tonic. Both brands, peculiar to Echo Falls, had more alcohol than a straight shot of whiskey from either Bender's or Bolyard's saloon. That was because Nick Bender and Georgie Bolyard never served any liquor that hadn't been cut with spring water.

Jolene chuckled to herself as Jarret shifted on the bed and groaned softly. From the looks of it, he had been drinking his whiskey with a hair tonic chaser.

She pressed her smooth cheek against the cool windowpane and found she could see almost to the livery at the end of town. There was little activity along the street. Sunday morning in Echo Falls was generally quiet. People who met for services did so in the dining room of Shepard's Boardinghouse, just as they had done every Sunday since lightning struck and burned the church in July. The building fund for a new house of worship was growing slowly. It wasn't that the citizens of Echo Falls didn't care about a new church; it was just that Mrs. Shepard offered the best cinnamon buns after service, and they were in no particular hurry to abandon her dining room. Everyone was remarking that Reverend Johns was putting on a little weight communing as he was with Widow Shepard and her hot cinnamon rolls. As the Reverend had been in to see Jolene and her girls only a few days ago, it was an opinion she shared with the rest of Echo Falls.

Jolene pulled back from the window, twisting her hair in a coil at the back of her head and fastening it with a few pins. Her eyes wandered to the towering peaks that rose north and west of Echo Falls. They were shrouded in thick clouds that meant snow was coming on the back of the wind. The rutted and pockmarked street was already freezing. The sloping roofs and grandiose false fronts of all the stores would be blanketed with snow by dinnertime.

A movement on the sidewalk across the street caught her eye. Jolene's room was on the second floor of Bender's Saloon. There had always been a friendly rivalry between Bender's on the south side of the street and Bolyard's on the north side of Main. Jolene often exchanged a wink and wave with the girls who worked the upstairs rooms of Bolyard's. And why not? With more than a dozen men to every one woman in Echo Falls and the surrounding mining camps, there was plenty of business to go around. That's why Jolene was so surprised that Georgie Bolyard was tossing a woman out of his saloon and onto the street.

Jolene laughed out loud as the woman brushed off the back of her sable redingote, straightened the slant of her fashionable fur-trimmed hat, picked up her matching muff, and marched back into the saloon. Obviously she didn't set any store by Georgie Bolyard's temper.

"Jarret!" Jolene called. "Oh, come here. You've got to see this." As she spoke she saw Georgie's broad face and broader belly pass back and forth in front of the saloon's large window. He was pacing off his territory, looking apoplectic even from Jolene's distant view. "Georgie's lookin' like he's swallowed the fires of hell!"

Jarret groaned, yanked the covers around his waist, and nudged the pillow off his head. He risked opening one eye. It was painful but worth it to see Jolene's silhouette at the window. The blue silk wrapper she was wearing outlined her curves, and her black stockings were like a shadow on the line of her legs. She turned to look at him, and he noticed her eyes were the exact same shade of chestnut as her hair. He tried to recall the events of last night and, failing that, hoped he had at least treated her kindly. Jolene was more than an occasional lover; she was a friend.

"Come back to bed, Jo," he murmured. "Forget about Georgie."

Jolene waved him off. "You're missing it all. Georgie's likely to go off like a Roman candle any minute."

Jarret's right hand squeezed around one corner of the pillow. His grip was tight enough to allow him to heft the pillow in Jolene's direction. She caught it easily, laughing. Jarret looked away, hiding his unreasonable, immediate anger. He hadn't wanted to hurt Jolene when he'd flung the pillow, yet he had pitched it with all his might. The momentum had barely carried it across the room.

"Uh oh," Jolene said, turning her attention to the street again. "Here comes the woman again and . . . there goes her hat. You know, Jarret, I think I'd like a little fur piece like that. It's all the rage back East."

"How would you know?" asked Jarret. He rose slowly, every muscle aching. "You haven't been east of Denver in two years."

"I leaf through Mrs. Dodd's fashion books the same as every other woman in Echo Falls."

"Pardon me. I hadn't realized." His eyes skimmed her attire. "Your wardrobe is usually so . . . umm . . . modest."

The play on words was not lost on Jolene. "Very amusing." She tossed the pillow back at him, but it was wide of the mark. He didn't even attempt to get it. On the sidewalk below, the woman was straightening her hat again. She looked up and down the street as if she expected some assistance, and finding none, she charged right back in the saloon. "She doesn't seem the sort who needs the money," Jolene said. "But then, maybe she's a high-priced whore. No wonder Georgie's throwing her out. He hates payin' his girls more than five dollars for a night's work."

That reminded Jarret. He picked up his jeans and rummaged the pockets of his Levis. He found a ten dollar gold piece. "I must have had a good night at the tables."

"Unless you started with twenty."

He stilled. "Did I?"

"No. You were down your saddle, your horse, and your Remington at one point."

"My God." Jarret shook his head, hardly crediting his stupidity. "What was I? Two? Three sheets to wind?"

Not looking away from the street Jolene held up four fingers.

The way his head felt, Jarret could believe it. He dropped the gold piece on Jolene's nightstand, got rid of the sheet hitched around his waist, and started to dress.

"You know, Jarret, not much happens on a Sunday morning. You're missin' something folks here are going to be talkin' about for the rest of the winter." She chuckled. "By God, Georgie's just tossed her muff into the street. She's not taking the bait. He's going to have to throw her out bodily if he wants to get rid of her." She was thoughtful a moment. "Do you suppose Georgie's got a wife he hasn't told anyone about?"

"That would surely anger the wife we all know he has." Jarret buttoned his shirt and tucked in the tails before he crossed the room to Jolene. The floor was cold beneath his bare feet. "You really should think about getting a rug."

Jolene shot him a sour look.

Jarret sat beside her to put on his socks. When he got them on he finally turned toward the window. The street between the two saloons was vacant. "It's quite the entertainment," he said, tongue in cheek.

"Be quiet and watch."

He was patient for all of two minutes. When no one came or went out of the saloon, Jarret stood. "Do you have any headache powders?" he asked, massaging his temples.

"On my dresser. Behind the perfumes. Do you want me to mix them for you?"

He closed his eyes and rubbed the bridge of his nose. "No, I'll do it. Don't trouble yourself."

"I won't." Jolene smoothed the sleeves of her wrapper. "My word, she doesn't give up," she said admiringly as the street entertainment started again. "Oh, wait, here comes someone from the livery. He must have come to town with her. I don't recognize him either." Jolene watched the woman wave to the man to get his attention. She disappeared into the saloon again.

Jarret poured a teaspoon of headache powder into a tumbler and added water. The mixture fizzed. He put down the spoon and carried his drink back to the window. He saw the man who was hurrying down the planked sidewalk. "That's Duffy Cedar. He's done a fair amount of prospecting in these parts. I've only known him to come to town when he needs supplies. You say he's got a woman with him?"

"More like she's got him with her."

Jarret knocked back his drink. It was like sucking on a lemon. His entire face puckered. "I swear I'm not going to drink again," he said.

"You've said that before."

"I mean that headache powder."

Jolene smiled and caught Jarret's sleeve as he turned away. "So why's Duffy trailin' after a skirt?"

Jarret allowed himself to be held. "Is it a pretty skirt?"

166

"Can't tell beneath all that fur. It sure is expensive, though."

"Then he's probably been hired as a guide. He does that sometimes for city folks lookin' for a mine." He eased himself out of Jolene's light grip. "I'm going downstairs and see if I can't get Nick to open up the kitchen early."

"You'd have more luck getting him to open up the bar." She gave him a cursory glance. "Aren't you going to shave? You look like hell."

"I don't think Nick cares."

Jolene found her brush and tossed it at him. "At least brush your hair."

Grinning, Jarret ran the brush through his tousled hair a few times. "Better?"

"Well, at least you won't scare the other girls."

Jarret set down the brush. "Eggs?" he asked. "Coffee?"

"Chocolate."

"Bacon?"

"A raft of it."

"I'll bring a feast," he promised.

Below stairs, Nick Bender was nowhere to be found. Jarret helped himself in the back kitchen, figuring he had paid Jolene enough to be entitled to a little breakfast. It didn't take him long to scramble eggs and fry the bacon. The aromas of coffee and chocolate mingled in the steamy air. Jarret served up two plates and poured Jolene's hot cocoa. It was when he was holding the pot of coffee that his hand went numb. He managed to jump out of the way as the pot slipped out of his fingers. Coffee splashed on the stove and on the floor. The pot and lid clattered loudly, nearly covering Jarret's angry string of curses.

Shoving aside the plates furiously, he shook out his arm and shoulder, trying to bring back some strength to his hand. Almost immediately the tingling returned, and he could even feel the pulse in his thumb. Ignoring the mess he'd made, Jarret stalked out of the kitchen and went to the bar. He found Nick Bender's cache of good whiskey and opened a bottle.

Jarret had always despised men who looked for solace in drink. His thinking hadn't really changed. Now he simply counted himself as one of those he despised.

Jolene appeared at the top of the stairs. "It's a little early, don't you think?"

Jarret held the bottle neck in his left hand. There was no sense in taking a chance with whiskey. "Leave it, Jolene."

"I thought you were making us breakfast," she said.

"Leave it."

"Don't bother coming back upstairs. My door's locked to you." She pivoted, huffing, and beat a path back to her room.

Jarret watched her go and told himself it didn't matter. He took another long swallow of liquor, relished the burning all the way to the pit of his stomach, then set the bottle hard on the counter. In spite of the jolt of whiskey, or in part because of it, he still couldn't think clearly. Anger was a haze clouding his reason.

He stared at his hand, clenching and unclenching the fingers until he felt no connection to the appendage, until he could look on it as though it didn't belong to him. At precisely that moment he smashed it into the wall.

The sharp edge of anger was blunted by pain. Jarret examined his bruised and bleeding knuckles dispassionately. He put away Nick's whiskey and walked to the window at the front of the saloon. A glance at the sky warned him of the impending snow storm. It wasn't a concern now. He had no plans to leave Echo Falls any time soon. There wasn't a bounty that interested him; there hadn't been for six weeks. That was going to have to change. He didn't have enough money to see him through the winter. According to Jolene he had come close to losing the tools of his trade last night.

His laughter was bitter as his gaze dropped to his right hand. Strike that, he thought. He'd already lost the most important tool of his trade. His saddle, horse, and Remington were superfluous. Small wonder he had anted them up.

On the train ride from New York to Denver he'd consulted doctors in Pittsburgh, Chicago, St. Louis, and Kansas City. Over time drink had lent a certain vagueness to the memory of their pitying faces, even if it had never dulled their words. Not one of them had held out much hope that he would recover full strength in his right hand.

Hollis's friends had been thorough in the damage they'd inflicted. He would never be the bounty hunter he once was; word of his problem had spread. Some day soon a bounty was going to face him down—and still be there after the dust settled. Mountain ranching, with its harsh physical demands, was out of the question now. It hardly mattered that his money had been stolen. He would have only been staking an empty dream.

Revenge had soured Jarret's mind for a while, but it was not a satisfactory solution. Jarret couldn't bear the thought of letting Banks see how successful his thug tactics were. Revenge, by its very nature, meant making yourself vulnerable, letting the other person know how much they had been able to hurt you. Jarret kept a whiskey bottle close by to dull the hurt and accepted bitterness as a constant companion. Most days it gave a flinty edge to his dark blue eyes, but when he thought of Rennie bitterness became his armor.

Of all the dreams he had entertained, none were as hard to dismiss as those of Mary Renee. He depended on whiskey to keep his mind as numb as his arm. Sometimes it even worked.

Jarret thrust both hands into his pockets and rocked gently on the balls of his feet. Across the street the doors of Bolyard's Saloon were flung open. Duffy Cedar was hustled out by Georgie. A moment later he was followed by a feminine fur ball that bore an astonishing resemblance to . . .

Rennie put her hands on her hips and stared down at a cowed Duffy Cedar. "You're not going to let him get away with that, are you?"

Duffy leaned against the outer wall of the tavern and plucked a toothpick from his pocket. His sheepskin collar hid most of his face, but his gap-toothed smile was evident. The toothpick fit neatly in the gap. "You heard him, ma'am. More times than I did, and that's a fact. He don't want you here, and he's not puttin' you up. It don't matter how many spare rooms he has; they're all for workin' gals, and that ain't exactly what you had in mind when you came here."

Rennie glared at her guide. "I thought you said we'd find Jarret Sullivan in Echo Falls. That's why I'm here."

"And Georgie tol' you he ain't seen him in two days. Mos' likely Sullivan's gone trackin' in the hills."

The *hills* to which Duffy Cedar referred were the most daunting fortress of rock that Rennie had ever seen. "Then, we'll follow him there."

"Like hell." He said it pleasantly enough, twirling the toothpick.

Rennie stepped off the sidewalk to pick up her discarded muff. Bits of frozen mud stuck to the fur. She brushed it off and pushed her cold hands into its pocket of warmth. "Listen, Mr. Cedar," she said patiently. "I hired you because I was told if I wanted to find Jarret Sullivan, you were the one who could track him. Well, we've come to Echo Falls, and I refuse to accept it's a dead end. Since Mrs. Shepard's Boardinghouse is full and Mr. Bolyard won't give me a room here, I'll have to try Bender's."

"Ma'am," Duffy said politely, pushing away from the wall. He pulled out the toothpick and spoke slowly, as if to a child. "Bolyard's place is mostly a saloon with a few workin' gals to liven it up. Bender's is mostly for workin' gals who sell a little liquor on the side." Lines at the corners of his eyes deepened as he squinted at Rennie. "You take my meanin', ma'am?"

"Bender's is a brothel."

Duffy choked a little and coughed to cover it. "That'd be my meanin', ma'am."

"I see."

"Nick Bender ain't any more likely than Georgie Bolyard to take you in."

"Well," Rennie said after a short pause. "We'll never know unless I ask."

Duffy started to object, but his focus abruptly shifted from Rennie to a point beyond her shoulder. The doors to Bender's Saloon opened, and a man stepped out onto the sidewalk. Duffy Cedar whistled softly. "I'll be damned. Ma'am, you must've been born under a lucky star."

Following the direction of Duffy's gaze, Rennie turned. Her insides knotted with a mixture of relief and dread. The first part of her search was over. She had found Jarret Sullivan.

He didn't halt his approach until only six inches separated them. "I can't imagine what brings you to Echo Falls," he said tightly. "But there's a storm coming. Make sure you're out of town in front of it." His cold, blue eyes shifted. "You, too, Duffy. You don't want to get holed up here with this bitch."

Rennie stared, open mouthed in Jarret's wake, as he made his way back to Bender's. On the second floor of the saloon a movement in one of the windows caught her eye. She looked up and saw a woman struggling to open it.

Jolene cursed the rattling panes of glass that wouldn't budge. She knew she had the woman's attention now, and she didn't want to lose it. A sudden burst of strength loosened the window. It flew up, letting in a blast of north wind. Jolene poked her head out. "Is there some problem I can help you with, ma'am?" she called.

From just beneath the porch roof of the saloon she heard

Jarret bellow, "Stay out of it, Jolene!" It was enough to harden her conviction that she should be involved. Now that Jolene had had a second look, the woman standing in front of Bolyard's was not entirely unfamiliar to her. She had seen the woman's photograph on two occasions that she could remember: once when Jarret had asked her to find a few loose dollars in the bottom of his valise and once when she had caught him studying it in the middle of the night. He wouldn't tell her who it was or where he got it, but the bleak and bitter cast to his face as he'd put it away made her feel as sorry for the woman as she did for Jarret.

Now she was just damned intrigued.

"Never you mind, Jarret!" She called again to Rennie. "There something I can do?"

Rennie shielded her eyes from the peculiar glare of the gray sky behind the saloon. "Mr. Sullivan says there's a storm approaching," she called back. "There's no rooms to be engaged either at Bolyard's or Shepard's. Might there be something in your establishment?"

It tickled Jolene to hear the whorehouse being referred to as an establishment. She smiled brightly. "I'm sure there's a room to be had here. If not, you can share mine."

Jarret backed up into the street so that he could see Jolene at her window. "This is not funny, Jo. You don't want her staying here."

"This doesn't concern you."

"Like hell it doesn't." He shot Rennie an impatient look over his shoulder. "Nick won't let you stay."

Rennie called to Jolene. "He says someone named Nick won't let me stay."

Jolene dismissed that notion with a wave of her hand. "Let me worry about Nick. Do you have bags? Trunks?"

"A few things at the livery." She turned to Duffy. "You'll get them, won't you, Mr. Cedar?"

He grinned, twirling his toothpick again. "Be happy to, ma'am. Won't take but a few minutes."

"I'll be inside."

Duffy nodded and was off. Rennie began walking toward the saloon. When Jarret blocked her way the first time, she tried to step around him. When he blocked her a second time, she raised her head defiantly. "Let me pass, Mr. Sullivan."

"No."

Her emerald eyes grew stormy. "Do you own this street?"

"No."

"Then, you have no right to block my way."

"You're not staying at Bender's."

"Oh? Do you own the saloon, then?"

"No."

"Then, you have no right to keep me from staying there."

"It's a *brothel,* Rennie."

"I know what it is," she said. The wind stirred her skirts, ruffled the fringe of fur across her forehead, and blew angry color into her cheeks. "If it doesn't keep you from frequenting the place, then it shouldn't bother me. Frankly, I'm bone weary. I've come from Denver across some of the hardest land I've ever seen. I've spent three nights out of doors, sleeping on the lee side of Duffy's dog for warmth. I'm not going anywhere but Bender's Saloon. I can go around you or I can go through you, but trust me, Mr. Sullivan, I *will* go."

From the upper window Jolene applauded. "Well done. Well done."

Jarret was distracted long enough for Rennie to get past him. He reached for her, caught sight of the bruised knuckles on his right hand, and withdrew. How long could he have held her anyway?

It was a relief to Rennie to come out of the cold. She stamped her feet, warming herself, and buried her face in the muff.

"Fix her a drink, Jarret," Jolene called from the top of the steps. "You know where Nick keeps the good stuff. I'll be down in a moment."

173

"Do you want a whiskey?" Jarret asked sullenly.

Rennie lowered the muff. "No, but I'd like a sherry."

He scowled. "I don't expect you could find sherry within eighty miles of here."

She blinked at his tone and said as graciously as she could, "Then, whiskey will be fine." Rennie looked around while Jarret fiddled behind the bar. Except for the decidedly Rubenesque curves of the partially clad woman in the painting above the bar, Bender's was very like Bolyard's as far as Rennie could see. The interior was dimly lighted and starkly functional. The brass footrail along the length of the bar dully reflected the oil lamplight. A half dozen round tables and three times as many chairs took up most of the scarred wooden floor. The open staircase was steep and narrow, and the balcony above stairs offered a view of four rooms and a hallway that led to the others.

Rennie accepted the drink Jarret slid across the bar. "It's very quiet here," she said.

"It's Sunday. Not much point stirrin' on a Sunday morning unless you're going to services."

"Aaah," she said, understanding dawning. "The gathering at Mrs. Shepard's."

Jarret nodded.

Jolene sprinted lightly down the steps. Her bronze brocade gown was an elegant complement to both her hair and eyes. She held out her hand warmly to Rennie and looked at Jarret for the introduction.

"Jolene Cartwright, this is Miss Mary Renee Dennehy." Jarret stopped and addressed Rennie. "Or is it Mrs. Hollis Banks by now?"

It was the sneer in his voice that decided her. Jarret didn't need, or deserve, to know everything. "It's just Rennie," she said to Jolene.

Jolene released Rennie's hand. "It's a pleasure, Rennie. And you call me Jolene. Or Jo. No sense in bein' formal here, not when you'll be spendin' some time with us."

"She's not staying here," Jarret said again.

Neither woman glanced in his direction. Duffy Cedar dragged in Rennie's trunk and dropped her large valise on the floor. "Where you want this?"

Jolene spoke up. "There's a room at the end of the hall that's vacant. Third door on the left. Jarret, why don't you help him?"

Both of Jarret's dark brows rose. "Like hell," he said. Then he walked off toward the kitchen.

Jolene saw Rennie's eyes follow Jarret, and there was no mistaking the despair in the younger woman's expression. She reached out and patted Rennie's hand. "It will be all right," she said gently. She raised her voice to Duffy, who was still standing by the door, shifting his weight impatiently from one foot to the other. "Upstairs with them."

Muttering to himself, Duffy hefted the trunk and grabbed the valise. "Could use a drink myself," he said as he passed the women at the bar.

"It will be waiting for you when you get back," Jolene told him. She went behind the bar and placed a bottle on the table along with a clean shot glass. "We'll leave this for him. Why don't you and I go to the kitchen? Have you had any breakfast?"

As if on cue, Rennie's stomach rumbled.

Jolene laughed. "I suppose that answers my question. C'mon. This way."

Jarret looked up when the women walked into the kitchen. His expression was both sour and forbidding. The evidence of his earlier accident with the coffee was cleared, and a fresh pot was brewing on the stove. "I guess a person can't get any peace around here."

"Ignore him," Jolene told Rennie. "Have a seat and I'll fix breakfast. Eggs and bacon do right by you?"

Rennie sat opposite Jarret. "That would be wonderful."

"That's because you haven't tasted it yet," Jarret said. "She's no Mrs. Cavanaugh."

Jolene saw the remains of Jarret's earlier attempt at breakfast in the sink. "Apparently neither are you," she said, pointing. She put on an apron and busied herself with the preparation. "Who's Mrs. Cavanaugh?"

"Our cook," Rennie said. "She sends her regards, Mr. Sullivan."

"You've come a long way to tell me that," Jarret said. He got up and poured himself a cup of coffee. He sat again without offering any to either Jolene or Rennie. "Dare I hope you'll return my regards immediately?"

"I have no plans to leave Colorado soon," said Rennie.

Jarret stared at his coffee, scowling.

Rennie opened her mouth to speak, but behind Jarret she saw Jolene shaking her head, indicating she should keep her silence. Rennie surprised herself by taking the other woman's advice.

Jolene cracked four eggs in the skillet. The yolks broke in three. "Looks like we're having scrambled," she said, grinning over her shoulder at Rennie. "You still feelin' a chill?"

Self-conscious, Rennie removed her hat, muff, and coat and laid them over an unoccupied chair. She was wearing a dark red woolen gown trimmed with black piping. The cut was severe with long, tight sleeves and a high collar that covered her throat. Except for small jet beads in her ears, she wore no jewelry. Smoothing the taut front of her dress, Rennie went to the stove and poured coffee for herself and Jolene. She was aware of Jarret's eyes following her, boring into her back. Her hands shook.

"Milk's on the back stoop," Jolene said.

Rennie retrieved the stoneware jug and added a little to her coffee. She sat at the table again and sipped her drink. Although Jolene maintained a light stream of one-sided chatter as she worked, the silence between Rennie and Jarret was obvious and strained.

Jolene set a plate in front of Rennie and served her. The scrambled eggs were dry, and the bacon was black at the edges. Rennie didn't blink. "Thank you. You've been so gracious."

Looking at the burned fare, Jarret smirked.

"You're welcome," said Jolene. "You wouldn't get this at Mrs. Shepard's."

"That's a fact," Jarret said dryly.

Ignoring Jarret, Rennie addressed Jolene as she sat beside her with her own plate. "I couldn't get any help from Mrs. Shepard. When I saw the number of people in her dining room, I assumed it was because she had no vacancies. Now I understand that's where the church service was conducted, so perhaps she had room after all."

"I'm certain she did," Jolene said. "But you were traveling alone and—"

"Mr. Cedar was with me."

Jolene smiled gently. "I don't think that would have counted for much in the widow's eyes. She took one look at your fancy clothes and made an assumption about you. That's probably why you were directed to Georgie's."

"She thought I was a—"

"Whore," Jarret interjected.

Rennie was mortified. Not for herself, but for Jolene. Her dark emerald eyes narrowed on Jarret.

"Oh, honey," Jolene said. "Don't take offense on my account. I got Jarret's money on my bedside table, provin' the sort of woman I am." She tilted her head in Jarret's direction and batted her eyes. "And the sort of man he is."

Ruddy color flushed Jarret's lean features. His chair scraped against the floor as he pushed away from the table. He poured himself more coffee and stood by the stove, leaning against a butcher block table.

The revelation that Jarret had shared Jolene's bed made Rennie fight for composure. She was bothered by the fact that she was bothered at all. She hadn't expected that when she'd made her decision to come west. Not that she would have changed her mind, or *could* have changed her mind, but at least her reaction wouldn't have taken her by surprise.

"If Mrs. Shepard wouldn't let me in," Rennie said to Jolene, "why did Georgie throw me out?"

"He knows a lady when he sees one," said Jolene.

Rennie's gaze didn't waver from Jolene. "So do I," she said softly.

Now it was Jolene who flushed scarlet. She bent her head and began to eat.

Jarret leveled his coldly remote blue stare at Rennie. "I think it's about time you tell me why you're here," he said. "I can't imagine with Duffy as a guide that you've lost your way."

"I came to find you," she said calmly.

"And you have. Now why?"

He was the same and somehow not the same, Rennie thought. The sapphire eyes that were so startling were distant now, without any trace of humor. The amused smile was absent as well. The patrician nose, the sun lines etched at the corners of his eyes, and the long, dark lashes were all familiar features of a face that was oddly unfamiliar now. Weight loss showed in the way his shirt lay across his shoulders, in the worn band on his belt that was notched one keeper more tightly, and in the tautness of his skin beneath his day-old beard. He spoke curtly, without the drawl that hinted at some private enjoyment of the moment. She recalled that he had always been capable of sarcasm to make a point, but that no longer seemed to be his intent.

Jarret Sullivan was just plain mean.

Rennie set her fork aside. Her hands folded around her coffee cup. "I had thought you would understand my being here immediately," she said. "Have you heard nothing of what's happened to my father?"

His dark brows pulled together in a faint frown. "News is slow to get to these parts."

"Not that slow," Jolene said, giving Jarret a significant

look. "A person who spends most days starin' at the bottom of a glass doesn't hear too much."

"Shut up, Jo," he said.

Jolene let his order roll down her back. "What's this about your father, Rennie?"

"He's disappeared."

Jarret returned to the table and sat. "What do you mean he's disappeared? How can a man like Jay Mac go anywhere he can't be found."

Jolene whistled softly. "Your father was John MacKenzie Worth?"

Rennie nodded. "You know him?"

"Doesn't everybody?" she asked. "Guess he was about as well known as President Grant."

Jarret jerked his chin in Jolene's direction. "Why are you speaking of him in the past tense?"

"Because he's dead." She glanced at Rennie. "I'm sorry, Rennie, but that's the word in all the papers that come to Echo Falls. *Rocky Mountain News* carried it on the front page. It was quite a story."

"I know," Rennie said. "My sister Michael wrote it."

Jolene's forehead furrowed as she raised her eyebrows. "Now you're makin' no kind of sense."

"You've got that right," Jarret said. "Rennie, what are you talking about? Is Jay Mac dead or isn't he?"

Rennie's eyes lowered. She stared at her hands. Her fingertips were pressing whitely against the cup she held. "It depends on who you ask," she said softly. "Michael believes he's dead. She doesn't want him to be, but she can't convince herself otherwise. Ethan says Jay Mac probably couldn't have survived the wreck. Mary Francis has accepted it. Skye and Maggie, too. Mother's in mourning, but she still doesn't believe it's true. It's for her that I had to come." She paused a beat then admitted, her voice a mere thread of sound, "And for me. We both need to know what happened."

Jarret looked to Jolene for more of the answer. "What did the papers report?"

"Jay Mac Worth was on the train that wrecked near the Iron Ridge Pass a few weeks back."

"Six weeks," Rennie said. "It was six weeks ago. December sixth." She raised her eyes to Jarret. "You didn't know?"

He shook his head. "I never heard anything. Not about the wreck. Certainly not about Jay Mac."

Jolene's chestnut eyes darted between the two of them as she went on. "Sixty people were killed in the wreck, including all the crew except one porter, I think. The train jumped the track at some place called—"

"Juggler's Jump." Rennie and Jarret spoke at the same time.

"I know the place," Jarret said when Rennie gave him a questioning look. "It's a dangerous curve, and there's no place but down from there. I'm sorry, Rennie."

He said it as if he meant it, and he said it as if Jay Mac were certainly dead. Rennie shook her head. "His body's never been found," she said. "Ethan traveled from Denver to direct the search and couldn't find my father's body. Everyone but Jay Mac was accounted for."

"There could be good reason for that," Jolene said quietly. "This country's wild, Rennie, and unpredictable."

"My brother-in-law said the same thing," she said.

Jarret's tone was blunt. He could not spare her pain *and* have her come to her senses. "You should have listened to Ethan. He knows this country. He wasn't—"

"He says you know it better." There was a challenge in Rennie's voice. She had not come so far to be turned away easily. "When I wrote to Ethan and Michael and told them what I intended, Ethan said you were the person I needed to see."

"And now that you're seeing me?"

"I want to hire you, Mr. Sullivan. I want you to take me to Juggler's Jump and help me find my father."

180

Jolene was watching Jarret carefully. He looked as if he was regretting leaving his bottle at the bar. She was not surprised by his reply.

"I'm not for hire," he said tersely.

"But—"

Jarret got up from the table. "Forget it, Miss Dennehy. I'm not interested." He left the kitchen before she could get in another word.

Jolene sighed and looked at Rennie curiously. "Did you really think he would help you?"

Rennie pushed her plate away. "I thought he would take the money. He has before."

"Doesn't look like he wants it this time. Look, honey, he's probably just tryin' to save you the heartache and the money."

"He doesn't care about my heart."

"He doesn't care all that much about money."

Rennie was skeptical. Jarret Sullivan was a bounty hunter. If that didn't entail a serious interest in money, then Rennie couldn't imagine what did. He had accepted ten thousand dollars from Jay Mac to interfere in her life. He wasn't merely interested in money. He was greedy. She assumed her mistake in dealing with him was not naming the amount she was willing to pay. "Where has he gone?" she asked.

Jolene shrugged. "I don't rightly know. Upstairs, maybe. Or back to his cabin. He has a little place on the outskirts of town. Won it in a poker game a few months ago." She shook her head as she read what was on Rennie's mind. "I don't advise going after him now. He's got a sore head for one thing, and he likes his privacy for another. Give him some time to think about your offer."

"I don't have time," Rennie said. "You said yourself that snow's coming this way. All trace of my father's trail could be lost if I don't start out now." Dismissing Jolene's advice, Rennie grabbed her coat and ran after Jarret.

Duffy Cedar was the saloon's sole customer. As soon as

181

he saw Rennie come out of the kitchen, he knew who she was looking for. He lifted his glass of whiskey and pointed toward the street.

Rennie shrugged into her coat on her way out the door. She saw Jarret walking toward the livery and called to him. When he didn't hear her, or pretended not to, Rennie raised her skirts and ran after him. She caught up to him in front of Henderson's Mercantile.

She reached for his arm and brushed his coat sleeve. "Mr. Sullivan, please have the decency to stop while I talk to you."

He did stop. So suddenly, in fact, that Rennie nearly barreled into him. He made no attempt to steady her as she rocked on her feet. "What is it you want?" he asked with icy impatience.

"I've gone out of my way to find you," she said. "The least you could do is hear me out. I'm prepared to offer you fifty percent more to find my father than he offered you to stop my wedding."

"Fifteen thousand dollars?"

"That's right." Had she piqued his interest?

"Go home, Miss Dennehy."

Rennie rocked again on her feet as if hit a second time. He may as well have said "Go to hell." It was delivered with the same venom. "I'm going to Juggler's Jump," she said. "With or without you, I'm going to find what's become of my father."

"Without me." He started to walk away.

"Twenty thousand dollars."

Now he did say it. "Go to hell."

Rennie didn't try to follow him. She waited until he had disappeared into the livery; then she returned to Bender's Saloon. Jolene was waiting for her.

"He didn't change his mind?" asked Jolene.

Rennie shook her head. "You were right about that." She glanced around. "Where's Mr. Cedar?"

"Under the table."

"Too much drink?"

"See for yourself. He's under the table."

Rennie's attention shifted from the seat Duffy had occupied to the area beneath the table. Duffy was flat on his back, eyes closed, the empty bottle of watered-down whiskey beside him. His chest rose abruptly as he snored. "I suppose there will be no help from that quarter," she said, disgusted.

"What do you mean?"

"If Mr. Sullivan won't help me, then I have to find someone who will."

"You're not going to find anyone to set out this afternoon. There's not that many fools in Echo Falls. Maybe not in all of Colorado. Not with the blizzard that's comin' this way."

Rennie took off her coat and folded it over her arm. "What am I supposed to do, then, Jolene?"

She shrugged. "What most any of us do at times like this. Wait."

Waiting was not what Rennie did best, but she didn't share that with Jolene. "Could you show me my room?" she asked.

"Certainly. It's just about time for everyone else to start risin' around here. That's as good a time as any to make yourself scarce."

Rennie's dressing room at home was bigger than the room Jolene showed her. It didn't matter. It had a bed, and that was enough to recommend it. When Jolene left to find Nick Bender and explain about the new boarder, Rennie unpacked a few toiletries from her valise and laid them on top of the pine chest of drawers. Tilting the cracked mirror on top to an angle that served her, Rennie removed the pins from her hair and brushed it out. When tears came to her eyes she pretended it was the hard bristle brush against her scalp that caused them. The corner of her mind that knew better would not reveal itself.

Rennie removed her dress and shoes and lay on the bed. The mattress was soft and sagged in the middle. The down comforter was warm. She turned on her side and stared out the window. Her vision blurred again as the first snowflakes fell. She drifted asleep thinking about someone other than her father for the first time in six weeks.

The snow lasted two days. Rennie had never seen anything like it. With little to do but watch it fall she grew to know its every tumbling whim. It came in waves on the back of the wind, gusting and swirling, obliterating the mountain peaks, the limber pines, and finally Echo Falls itself. A rope was strung from the back of the saloon to the privy so that boarders and patrons wouldn't lose their way during one of nature's calls. Miners carried great clumps of snow on their boots and created a small flurry inside the saloon when they shook themselves off.

Bender's was busy. Miners who couldn't find their way to the adits and shafts had no such difficulty making their way to the saloon. For two days, in accordance with Jolene's wishes, Rennie avoided the noisy activity below stairs. On the morning of her third day in Echo Falls Rennie had had enough. She went downstairs to escape the boredom and instead found the means of escaping Echo Falls. Clarence Vestry and Tom Brighton would not have been given a second glance in New York. But this was Colorado. Rennie did more than give them a second glance. She hired them. By afternoon she and her guides were headed for Juggler's Jump.

"Why didn't you come sooner?" Jarret demanded, slipping on his gun belt. He pulled it tight, strapping the holster to his leg. He tossed Jolene his saddlebag. "Make yourself useful. There's some canned goods in the cupboard over there. You'll find jerky in the larder. I'll pack my clothes and make a bedroll."

Jolene almost threw the saddlebag back at him. She didn't because she cared what happened to Rennie. "You have no right to speak to me that way," she said sharply. She went to the small kitchen area of Jarret's cabin while he climbed to the loft. "I came as fast as I could. It's nearly two miles, you know, and most of it through drifts as deep as my hip."

Jarret snorted at her exaggeration. "If you hadn't let her go you . . ." He left the rest unsaid.

"It's not like I had any say in it. She didn't come to me, did she, and ask for my help the way she did yours? If I had known what she was up to, don't you think I'd have tried to stop her? I warned her no one in Echo Falls was foolish enough to take her out to the Jump in this weather. I didn't think I had to tell her about thieves like Tom and Clarence."

"I hope you're packing my bags," he yelled down, gathering his clothes and blankets.

"I'm workin' as fast as I can. You want flour? Sugar?"

"Everything. There's an extra bag down there somewhere. Pack it. I'm setting out with two horses. I'll take my Zilly and one of Duffy's. He hasn't left town yet, has he?"

"No, but I don't know if he's going to give up one of his horses."

"He won't have any choice." He clambered down the ladder, bedroll and clothes under his arm. He dropped everything on the square kitchen table, then went for his Winchester carbine and ammunition.

"How far do you think they'll take her?" asked Jolene.

It was something Jarret was not going to dwell on. He added cartridges to the bags Jolene was packing, saying nothing.

Jolene shrank from the look on Jarret's face. Tom Brighton and Clarence Vestry weren't ambitious enough to travel far with Rennie as a millstone around their necks. Jarret had to know that. They would rob her at their earliest opportunity. Whatever else they might do had made Jarret's eyes colder than anything Jolene had faced on her way to his cabin.

Chapter Seven

Rennie was tired. The air was so cold it stung her lungs and so thin each breath was an effort. Pride kept her from complaining; fear kept her from dismounting. From time to time Tom and Clarence would glance back at her and exchange a look that was enough to keep Rennie stiff and upright in her saddle. Only a few hours out of Echo Falls, Rennie was willing to admit that she had made a mistake. She hadn't the least idea what to do about it.

Not once during the trek from Denver to Echo Falls had Rennie been frightened for herself in Duffy Cedar's company. On the train and in the wild he had been patient with her, respectful but not obsequious. His eyes had never strayed over her in an insulting manner. Rennie reminded herself that she hadn't chosen Duffy as a guide, Ethan had. He had known something of the man's character and reputation before letting her go off with him. When Ethan and Michael realized they couldn't stop her from making the journey, Ethan had done what he could to make it a safe one.

It was clear to her that Jarret felt no such responsibility. When he turned her down he must have known that wasn't the end of it, yet he hadn't cared enough to make a recommendation. Duffy Cedar, after finding the drinking end of a bottle, was in no condition to accompany her further. It had been up to Rennie to find another escort and protector to Juggler's Jump.

She'd thought she had found two.

Tom Brighton and Clarence Vestry had not been overly eager once they heard her offer. That would have made Rennie wary. They'd pointed out the dangers, much as Duffy and Jarret had, and Ethan before them. They'd refused to travel with her trunks and pack mules and recommended if she was serious about going, then she had to be willing to travel with less gear and fewer comforts. Rennie was willing to do whatever they suggested to gain their services.

Now it was borne home to her that she had misjudged her companions. Jolene would have probably advised her against going, but then Jolene had been privately occupied with a customer when Rennie had sought her advice. Instead of waiting, Rennie had left her a note. It bothered her now. After all Jolene had done, she deserved more than a hastily scrawled thanks and farewell.

The tips of Rennie's fingers were cold even through her fur-lined leather gloves. Her hat tilted toward the front of her head so that a fringe of dark fur bordered her brows. Like her companions she wore a woolen scarf wrapped around her ears, nose, and throat for additional protection against the wind. They wore their guns at their sides. She carried hers in her pocket.

Her thoughts were spinning in so many different directions that she didn't hear Tom call for a halt. It was when she saw him raise his hand that she pulled up on the reins. Rennie lowered her scarf long enough to ask, "Why are we stopping here?"

"I reckon we come far enough for one night."

Rennie frowned. Tom was already dismounting. He was a lean, wiry man with a swaggering spring in his step. Trudging through the snow lessened his bounce, but not much. "I don't understand," she called after him. "We haven't been traveling long. There's still daylight left."

Clarence followed Tom's lead. He led his horse to the shelter of some limber pines and hitched the mare there. Clarence was shorter than Tom, compact and stocky. He moved slowly and stiffly but seemed to accomplish his tasks in the same time as his friend. "Not enough daylight to get to the next sheltered pass," he said. "We know where we are now. This is a good place to stop. In a half hour we could be caught in the open."

Tom removed his pack from his horse. "You can't stay in the saddle all night," he said to Rennie. "We told you it might be better to wait 'til tomorrow, but you insisted on leavin' today."

She *had* insisted. She had also thought they would travel longer before seeking shelter. "You led me to believe we could ride at night," she reminded them.

"Don't recall sayin' that," Tom said. He looked at Clarence. "You?"

"Don't recall it."

Rennie sat on her horse awhile longer, then accepted she had no choice but to dismount. They had already removed their packs and saddles and were rubbing down their horses. Beneath her the cinnamon mare was getting restless.

She felt aching and cold to the marrow of her bones. It was difficult to get her footing in the snow as she headed for the same shelter of trees as her companions. Her boots slipped easily on the crusty path marked by Tom and Clarence. She didn't ask for help with her saddle and supplies, and she wasn't offered any. Duffy had been more solicitous during their travels, assisting her with some of the heavier work. Somewhat to her regret, Tom and Clarence seemed to have believed her when she said she could care for herself. It wasn't the time to tell them differently.

Rennie worked swiftly and with purpose, pleasantly surprised to discover that she was more competent now than she had been when she started her journey. Duffy's patient teaching was serving her in good stead. When she had finished caring for Albion she went in search of kindling while Tom and Clarence cleared an area for the fire and sleeping. She noticed that when she returned the conversation between the two men ended abruptly, as if she had been the topic. Her heart hammered a bit more loudly in her chest. She dropped the kindling and began building the fire. Without being obvious she checked her pocket for the Smith and Wesson revolver. The shape and weight of it was reassuring. Using the gun was the one qualm she didn't have.

Rennie hunkered down before the fire, warming her hands without removing her gloves. Her skirts were draped around her, and she patiently attempted to dry the sodden hem until Tom asked her to make the coffee.

"I've been told mine's bitter," she said, taking the pot and grounds.

Tom grunted. "As long as it's hot."

"Hot I can do." She frowned as her comment initiated another significant glance between the two men.

Clarence took a small skillet from his pack and laid it over the fire. He dropped some bacon fat in, and when it was sizzling he added beans and pork. Each time there was a lull in the wind the aroma hung in the air.

Behind her scarf, Rennie's mouth watered. She got her tin plate and mug and served herself after the men had taken their share. She was a little surprised to see that there was still some left in the pan. Clarence had prepared more than they needed. Duffy had taught her it was better to have too little at any one meal than to waste a mouthful. One never knew what the future held.

Rennie sat on her saddle and ate slowly, enjoying the

warmth of every bite. The coffee was nearly hot enough to burn her mouth but even that felt good. "Will we start again at first light?" she asked them.

Tom nodded. "That'd be best. You know, ma'am, Clarence and I have been wonderin' what brought you to Echo Falls in the first place. If you're so hell bent — pardon the expression — on reaching Juggler's Jump, then you've come a piece out of your way. Duffy Cedar might have been leadin' you on a goose chase."

"No, Mr. Cedar was a good guide." She tried to remember what she had told them. "I only hired him to help me find Jarret Sullivan. Do you know him?"

"Be pretty hard not to," said Clarence. "Echo Falls ain't that big a town."

"But I understand he only recently settled there. Mr. Cedar wasn't at all certain we'd find him."

"Sullivan travels around a lot. I figure you found him and he turned you down."

"That's right."

"Lucky for us, I guess," Tom said. "Can't imagine he'd turn down the money, though. His pockets are mostly empty from what I see."

"Really?" asked Rennie. "I wonder what he did with — " She shrugged. "It isn't important. Jolene says he plays a lot of poker." He probably lost all Jay Mac's money there.

"That's a fact," said Clarence. He sniggered. "Can't hold his cards any better than he can hold his liquor."

Tom gave a bark of laughter. "Can't hold a candle to us, can he, Clarence? Not when he can't hold a gun." Both men laughed heartily behind their scarves.

Rennie looked from one to the other, trying to make out what was so funny to them. What was clear was that neither man had much respect for Jarret Sullivan. That struck Rennie as odd. It was the one thing she thought Jarret commanded on even short acquaintance.

Tom's muffled laughter ended when he caught sight of Rennie's puzzled gaze. "Take no notice of us, ma'am. It's just a joke between friends." He nudged Clarence with his elbow. "I was wonderin' if we could talk about payment."

The hair at the back of Rennie's neck stood up. "I know I made it clear there would only be money if you took me to the Jump. I gave you money for supplies already. The rest you'll have to wait for."

"The thing of it is," said Clarence, "Tom and me aren't what you would call good at waiting. Not when it comes to the kind of money you've offered."

Rennie's hands slipped into her pockets. "You don't really think I have that sort of money on me, do you? I fully intend to write you a draft for the money when we reach our destination. You can cash it at any bank. Northeast Rail will honor it."

"I understand that," Tom said, nodding. "But it don't really change my mind. I figure it's better to have that draft now. Juggler's Jump is a long way off, and anything might happen to you. What if you couldn't write once we got there? Broke your arm or somethin'? Clarence and me would be out a thousand dollars. That tends to make a man a little nervous."

Rennie strove for calm. "I think you'll both understand how writing the draft now might make *me* nervous." Their genial laughter, meant to disarm her, had exactly the opposite effect. "I think I'll turn in," she said. She stood, picked up her saddle and bedroll and moved them away from the fire.

Observing her go, Clarence said, "You'll be cold over there."

"I'll be fine." She laid out an oilcloth to protect her blankets and clothes and placed a thick woolen blanket on top. Using her saddle as a pillow, Rennie lay down and covered herself with two thinner blankets. Duffy had told

192

her to dress and sleep in layers of clothing and to dry anything that got wet. His advice was serving her well again. Even away from the fire, Rennie was not nearly as concerned with frostbite as she was with the possible sting of her two companions.

Clarence and Tom talked lowly for some time before they added wood to the fire and laid out their own blankets. Rennie didn't release the grip on her pocket revolver until she heard the sounds of their sleep. Even then she waited awhile longer before she sat up.

The night was virtually silent. The wind had calmed, and snow absorbed the footfalls of nocturnal animals. An occasional snap of twigs or rustling in the branches overhead was well beyond the limits of the firelight. Rennie moved with caution and quiet.

She was not confident of being able to find her way back to Echo Falls, but she was confident she understood what awaited her if she stayed. Better to take her chances with the elements than to accept the inevitable attack by one or both of her guides.

Rennie stroked Albion, hushing the mare before she threw on the saddle. She had just finished strapping the girth when she realized the animal had grown restless for another reason. Rennie turned around slowly, dropping her hands to her pockets.

Tom stood a few feet away, his gun drawn. The collar of his heavy coat had been turned up, but his scarf was lowered under his chin. When he smiled he showed two sharp incisor teeth that reminded Rennie of fangs. "You desertin' us?" he asked casually.

"I . . . I was cold," she said lamely. "I thought it would be better to move around."

He laughed without humor. "Movin' around's one thing. You look like you was preparin' to go."

"It's close to morning, isn't it?"

"You know damn well it ain't. We got us another eight hours before it's light enough to leave. What you needed to do was move closer to the fire." He glanced toward the light. "Ain't that right, Clarence?"

"That's right. Over here where I can warm her up."

Both of Tom's wiry brows lifted in question as he looked at Rennie. "Well? What do you think of that? Care to take up Clarence's offer?"

"I don't think so," she said with credible calm.

He nodded, apparently thinking over her refusal. "Then, you may want to consider what I got to say. I'd like you to write out that draft for us now. Seems to me—"

"I'm not going to do that."

Tom went on as if she hadn't spoken. "Seems to me that you were about ready to run out without payin' your debt. Clarence? Howse about you gettin' off your rump and seein' if you can't find what we're lookin' for?" He smiled at Rennie. "If he can't do it, I'll have to search you."

Rennie moved away from Albion while Clarence rifled her belongings for the draft. He found a small, black, leather-bound ledger containing a dozen blank checks.

"Whoooeee," he cried out, holding it up for Tom to see. "Struck silver!" He tossed the ledger to Tom and continued to search. Eventually he found Rennie's cache of coin and bills. "Looks like she's got close to three hundred dollars here! Imagine that!"

"Imagine that," Tom repeated softly, putting his gun away. "You find somethin' for her to write with?"

"Pen and ink," Clarence said, chuckling as he held up both. He shook the bottle. "Not frozen either."

"Good," said Tom. "Her blood would have been my second choice."

Rennie blanched.

Tom motioned to Clarence to bring him the pen and

ink. When he had both he carried them and the ledger to Rennie. "You'll be able to see what you're doin' over here. That's two thousand for each of us, ma'am. We're not greedy."

Signing the draft was signing a death sentence. Rennie knew that. When her hands came out of her pockets she was holding the Smith and Wesson. "Step back, Mr. Brighton," she said. "I'm prepared to use this."

"Better do what she says," Clarence told his friend. "Never did trust a lady with a gun, 'specially not one of them fancy little things."

Tom took a respectful step backward and in the same motion threw the ledger at Rennie. She fired, but the shot went wild as the ledger hit her wrist. She understood then she would never get a second chance.

Rennie was tackled from both sides and shoved to the ground. The fire scattered and singed the fur cuff of her coat. She flailed at the men, hitting out with fists and feet. More by accident than design she jammed her knee into Tom's groin. He howled, backed off momentarily, then drove his gloved fist into her belly. Rennie's scream died in her throat as the air was forced out of her lungs.

The night was suddenly alive with sound. Branches overhead dipped and rustled as birds and small animals fled the woman's reedy cries and the men's labored breathing. The horses whinnied and snorted restlessly; a pack of wolves shied away, then grew bolder.

Rennie's scarf was torn away from her face and tossed toward the fire. Flames licked at the fringed ends. Clarence's mouth mashed hers as Tom tore at the fasteners of her redingote. Hands slipped under the fur and kneaded her breasts through the material of her gown. She did not recognize the wounded, whimpering cries as coming from herself. Bile rose in her throat as a tongue protruded between the ridge of her teeth. She bit down and tasted blood, not sensible of its origin until Clarence reared back and slapped her with the powerful flat of his hand. Tears blurred her vision and froze on her cheeks. She heard the collar of her gown give way beneath Tom's frantic fingers. His leather gloves abraded her skin; the cold air stung her bare flesh. Her moan became a keening cry as his mouth closed over her nipple.

Rennie's hands curled like talons, but sheathed in leather they were ineffective. She grabbed a fistful of Tom's hair and yanked. His teeth pinched her flesh until she let go. She sobbed, gasping for air, as hands—she was no longer certain whose—pushed up her skirt and pulled at her drawers.

"Me first," Clarence said, grunting. "I not takin' your leavin's this time." He fumbled with the fly of his trousers, threw off his gloves, and finished the job. "Hold her down. I don't want a knee in *my* privates."

Tom's hands clamped down on Rennie's shoulders as she fought to sit up. Her neck arched. She screamed. Her knees were violently pushed up and apart and kept separated by Clarence's body. Out of the corner of her eye she saw one end of her scarf erupt into flames. Her fingers curled around the smoldering end, and she pitched it at Clarence's face.

He shouted as fire flared across his broad brow. He clawed at the scarf, throwing back his head and gasping for air. His enraged cry echoed in the hills. It was loud enough to make him deaf to the sound that killed him.

Clarence slumped forward across Rennie's body. Tom leaped out of the way, his feet pumping furiously as he fell on his backside and still tried to scramble for cover. Screaming hoarsely, Rennie pushed ineffectively at Clarence's shoulders. Her fingers tore at the burning scarf covering his head, tossing it away before the flames licked at her own face. The press of fear in her chest was enormous. Her breathing was ragged.

She saw Tom draw his gun and fire into the dark pine woods. Something wet and warm trickled between her breasts. Panicked, Rennie heaved at Clarence's body again, this time dislodging it. She sat up and looked down at herself. Her breasts were smeared with his blood. She raised one trembling hand to her chest and tried to wipe it away. Her tormented eyes searched beyond the limits of the light for her savior in the shadows.

Tom slid behind Rennie. He circled her neck with his forearm, compressing her windpipe until she lay limply against him. Using her as a shield, he kept his gun raised, waving it slowly back and forth in anticipation of another shot.

"You want a turn with her?" he called out. "If it's about sharin' the woman, then I don't mind. Hell, I don't care if you want all of her."

Rennie's hands clawed weakly at Tom's forearm. She gagged.

He gave her a little shake, loosening his grip enough to let her breathe. He yelled again to his enemy in the woods. "She has money. More money than you could imagine. You only got to get her to sign these pieces of paper. She'll do it, too. Slide some sweetmeat between her thighs and she'll do whatever you want."

Rennie tried to cover herself. The torn throat of her gown defied her efforts. She crossed her arms in front of her and drew up her knees. She was trembling so hard it was difficult for Tom to keep his gun steady. He pressed hard on her throat again.

"You hear me?" Tom hollered. "You want some of her or some of her money? You want some of both?" It occurred to Tom that his assailant could be circling in the woods behind him. Holding on to Rennie, he began to slowly turn with her, cocking his head toward the pines as he tried to hear a footfall or a hammer click. "Come and get it!" His breath was hard against Rennie's ear. "Tell him," he whispered harshly. "Tell him you want him." He pressed the barrel of his gun in the soft curve under her jaw. "Tell him, damn you!"

"I want you," she rasped.

Tom waved the gun again. "Louder! Tell him louder!"

"I want—"

The flash of light was almost simultaneous to the gun's report. Tom returned the fire, but the bullet in his shoulder threw his aim wide. Pain seared his chest as the force of the bullet drove him backward. Rennie slumped to the ground. Another bullet, this time in Tom's gun arm, forced him to drop his weapon. He sobbed weakly, clutching himself as he tried to move opposite the shots.

Jarret stepped out of the woods and into the circle of light. His hat cast a shadow across his face but did not hide the tensely ticking muscle in his jaw.

Tom recognized him instantly. "You! What do you want?"

"I thought I'd made that obvious," he said quietly.

"There's no bounty on us. Hell, folks around here say you gave it up. They say you can't shoot straight."

Jarret fired off a shot. It drove harmlessly into the fire, scattering sparks and embers. "Sometimes I can't," he said philosophically. He fired again, this time into Tom Brighton's chest. "And sometimes I can." He put his gun away as Tom's body sprawled in the snow. "It's a crap shoot."

Kneeling beside Rennie, he lifted her head and smoothed back a curling strand of auburn-and-copper-streaked hair. Her face was ashen. Her eyes were closed.

"Rennie," he said her name softly. "Rennie, it's me . . . Mr. Sullivan."

She opened her eyes slowly. The lift of her lashes did not lessen the shadows beneath them. With something akin to wonder she said his name. "Jarret."

His smile was faint, his eyes bleak. "Yes," he said. "Jarret." He cupped the side of her face. "Rennie, I want to get you away from here. We can't go all the way back to Echo Falls tonight, but we should move out. Animals will find the bodies . . . do you understand?"

She nodded shortly. "Whatever you say."

He didn't ask her how she was or if she'd been hurt. He kept her busy, forcing her to make small decisions so that she kept her head and kept placing one foot in front of the other. She was compliant at each turn, moving with the mechanical precision of a child's windup toy. He did not press, merely encouraged. In just under fifteen minutes they were moving along the ridge toward Echo Falls.

They rode for almost an hour before Jarret called a halt. It had been necessary to let Rennie ride with him. Now his horse was straining under the double burden and the rough terrain. It didn't make sense to wear out another mount. He dropped to the ground first and steadied Rennie as she slid out of the saddle. She leaned against him, no strength in her own legs. Jarret carried her to a rocky outcropping, shoved aside some snow and set her down. He returned after retrieving blankets to put under and around her, then he set about making camp.

He pitched his small army tent, hammering stakes into the frozen ground, then laid out more oilcloth and blankets inside. When he went to get Rennie, she was gone.

Jarret's heart settled in his feet. He called her name, his voice a mere thread of sound. When there was no answer he called louder.

"I'm here," she said, stepping into the flickering lantern light. Her arms were full of kindling. "You'll want a fire."

"I'll take that," he said, sighing. There was no sense in railing at her for disappearing. She was trying to be helpful. "You go on inside the tent. You can take the lantern

199

with you. I'll be able to see well enough to start the fire."

She hesitated, uncertain. "You'll be here?"

"I'm not going anywhere," he said.

"All right," she said finally. She picked up the lantern and ducked into the tent.

Jarret's fire was built more to keep animals at a distance than it was for warmth. He waited until it was blazing on its own before he tended to the horses. As he worked, his eyes strayed to the tent. Rennie was a silhouette against the canvas.

She had removed her coat and gown and unpinned her hair. The shadow curve of her body was perfectly formed. He could make out the line of her shoulder and arm, the slope of her breasts, and the tapering curve of her waist. He watched her rummage through her valise, her movements nearly frantic until she found what she wanted. She bent forward to the front of the tent, and for a moment her arm was visible as she slipped it through the flap. She scooped a handful of snow and retreated. Then, with washcloth and snow in hand, she began scrubbing herself with rough and furious strokes. Jarret turned away.

By the time Jarret was finished, so was Rennie. He passed her some more of her personal belongings through the flap. While she put on a flannel nightshirt, he set about laying out his bed by the fire.

"Jarret?" she called. There was a hint of anxiousness in her voice.

"Right here," he said.

"What are you doing?"

"Getting ready to go to sleep."

"Out there?"

He stretched out on his blankets and turned to face the fire. "That's my plan."

"Then, I'm coming outside, too."

He bolted upright. "Stay where you are, Rennie. It's too

200

cold out here. You'll be more comfortable in the tent."

She poked her head through the flap. "So would you."

"I'm fine."

She shook her head, retreated, and began gathering her blankets. She stopped when the flaps to the tent opened and Jarret tossed his things inside. "You changed your mind," she said as he hunkered down and filled the opening.

"I wasn't given much choice." He crawled inside as Rennie hastily made room for him. "Are you sure this is what you want?"

She looked away and smoothed the waves in the blankets under her. Her hair fell over her shoulder and curtained the side of her face. "I don't want to be alone," she whispered. "I'm afraid."

Her admission made Jarret's insides clench. Proud, willful Mary Renee Dennehy acknowledging her fear was not something he had ever expected to hear. "All right," he said quietly. "Lie down and I'll tuck you in."

She giggled a little at that. "You sound like Jay Mac." She obligingly stretched out on the blankets.

"I'm not your father, Rennie."

"I know." She fastened the last button of her nightshirt, closing it at the throat while Jarret covered her. "I didn't mean—"

"I know what you meant," he said gruffly. Jarret blew out the lantern and set it outside. He closed and tied the flaps, then rearranged his own bedding. Between them they shared her heavy fur coat and his sheepskin-lined jacket.

They lay facing one another, neither moving, hardly breathing. They could feel each other's stiffness and discomfort, but they didn't know how to alter it. Jarret would have never reached for Rennie without her permission, and Rennie did not know how to ask to be cradled.

201

"How did you find me?" she asked at last.

"Jolene told me you left." His voice was soothing, a husky whisper that eased the tension between them. "I had to come after you."

"I didn't plan it that way," she said. "I never thought you would follow."

"I know."

She shuddered a little and quite naturally moved closer to Jarret. Her knees bumped his. Self-conscious now, she started to scoot away.

"No," he said. "It's all right. You can stay where you are. You're shivering."

Rennie relaxed slowly, warmed as much by his voice as his nearness. Tears dripped slowly from the corners of her eyes. "I act foolishly sometimes." She spoke so softly it was almost as if she had only mouthed the words. "But I'm not a fool, Mr. Sullivan."

Because she couldn't see him, he smiled. "You called me Jarret before," he said. "And I've never thought you were a fool."

She shook her head, not believing him. "It's kind of you to say so."

"I'm not particularly kind, Rennie, you should know that. I'm not saying it to spare your feelings. You *did* act recklessly tonight, but I don't confuse that with you being a fool." And, in part, he blamed himself for not appreciating the depth of desperation that was her motivation. If he had understood that, he could have predicted what she would do next. Her experience with Tom Brighton and Clarence Vestry could have been prevented. "I know now what it means for you to find your father, what you'll risk to make that happen. I should have realized it earlier."

For a moment she was hopeful. "Then, you'll help me?"

"I didn't say that," he told her. He felt, rather than saw, her disappointment. "We'll talk about it later. You should

202

sleep now. Are you warm enough?"

"Mostly."

"In this weather that's not good enough. You can come closer if you want."

"I don't —"

"I won't hurt you, Rennie."

"You didn't have to say that." She hastily swiped at her tears and rubbed the salty traces from her cheeks. "You may be the only man I *can* trust."

He would have liked to ask her about Hollis Banks, but it wasn't the time. She followed her enigmatic statement with turning on her side away from him and fitting the contours of her body warmly to his. She stiffened briefly when his arm curved around her waist, but when he started to remove it, she grasped his wrist and held it there. Her fingers knotted with his. In minutes she was asleep.

It was the sound of an animal in pain that woke Jarret. Outside the tent the horses pawed the ground restlessly. He fumbled for his gun, found it, and waited for the cry to be repeated. He did not have to think about what he would do. A half-crazed animal might not shy away from the fire. It could attack the horses or the tent. The only sure way to end its suffering was to end its life and Jarret was prepared to do that.

Until he realized the animal was human.

Jarret laid his gun aside as Rennie screamed again. The night terrors had shrunk her body into a tight, guarded ball under the blankets. Her knees were drawn close to her chest, protected further by the arms that clasped them. Her head was bent. The entire length of her neck and spine was a rigid curve.

He did not ask for her permission now. He reached for

her, circling with his arms, hauling her against him in an embrace that was more powerful than tender, more securing than security. He held her, rocking, even after his right arm went numb from shoulder to fingertips. The feeling returned intermittently, much as it did for Rennie as she woke and confronted the horror and pain, then retreated into an insular void.

She gasped for air as her body shuddered with great wracking sobs. Tears flooded her eyes and spiked her lashes. Her fingers curled in the material of Jarret's shirt, gripping it as she might a lifeline. She pressed her forehead against his shoulder. Crying came from deep within her, from a broken spirit and wounded soul.

He stroked her hair with fingers that could not always feel it. His chin rested against the crown of her head. He repeated her name, calling her Rennie at first, then Mary Renee as he suspected her family might at such a time. In some manner he reached her. She whimpered, snuffled. He drew a handkerchief out of his pocket and thrust it in her hand. She didn't seem to know what to do with it at first.

"Instead of my shirt," he said lowly.

The words washed over her. It took her a moment to absorb them. She became aware of the way she was huddled against him, curved so tightly to his body that she might well have been part of him. Embarrassed, she began to ease herself away.

"No," he said. "You're fine. Take the handkerchief and wipe your face."

Her fingers unwound stiffly as she released his shirt. Rennie dabbed at her eyes and gently blew her nose.

"Blow," he said. "Like you mean it."

Her eyes filled again. It was his peculiar, rough-edged kindness that undid her. Her unseen smile was trembly as she lifted the handkerchief and blew for all she was worth.

His chest heaved once in a silent chuckle as she started to return it. "No, you keep it." Then, because he was not certain that he liked the fact that she could still make him laugh, he said, "There's still a lot of night in front of us. You may need it again."

The thought that the nightmare might be repeated caused Rennie to tense. "I won't sleep, then."

He wished he had said nothing. "You're not disturbing me," he said when she tried to slip off his lap. "Unless you're not comfortable."

She stayed where she was. "No, I'm fine. I thought you must want to get rid of me."

All the time, he thought, but for reasons that were no longer so clear in his mind. "No, I don't mind holding you."

She nodded, comforted. She reached for her coat and draped it around her shoulders so that they both could share the warmth. "I was dreaming about those men," she said.

"I thought it might be that."

"I wish I had killed them."

He said nothing, stroking her hair from her shoulder to the base of her spine, encouraged by the tension seeping out of her.

"I had a gun."

"I know. A Smith and Wesson pocket revolver. I found it."

"I would have used it."

"I know that, too."

She laid her cheek against his shoulder. Her breath was warm on his neck. "Do you regret killing them?"

"There's never any pleasure in killing," he said. "But them . . . I came close. No, I don't regret it . . . and I'm glad it wasn't you." Jarret shifted his weight and Rennie's. "Let's lie down. You never know, you might sleep." And he had been getting a little stiff—in all the wrong places. He thought he had managed to move her before she felt the swell of his groin.

Even inside a pair a thick woolen socks, Rennie's toes were cold. She rubbed her feet against Jarret's legs as he stretched out beside her. She was too intent on finding a comfortable position for herself to hear his sharp intake of breath.

"Comfortable?" he asked, gritting his teeth as she settled down. He swore; she purred. It wasn't enough that she used his leg like a scratching post, snuggled against him with feline grace, or watched him with emerald cat eyes. She had to purr, too. "Try to get some sleep."

Minutes passed where neither of them closed their eyes or thought about sleeping.

"Rennie? What's wrong? You're wider awake now than you were a while ago."

She was, but she didn't know how he knew that. She'd been careful not to move, to breathe evenly, to lie relaxed beside him. "I can still feel their hands on me," she whispered.

Jarret didn't know what to say. If he could have absorbed her pain, he would have.

"I washed myself. You know, scrubbed. It doesn't matter. I can still feel the pressure of their fingers, their mouths."

"What can I do?"

"Take it away."

He shook his head. "I can't do that, Rennie. I wouldn't know how."

"Then replace it."

"What?" He could barely breathe.

"Replace it," she said. "Put your hands where theirs were, your mouth where they touched me."

"You don't know what you're saying." Or asking, he

206

thought. If he touched her in the way she suggested, it wouldn't end there. "What about Hollis Banks?" he asked.

"Hollis isn't here," she said bluntly. "You are."

"That's selfish, Rennie. Even for you it's selfish."

His observation stung. The truth of it cut deeper. "I can never seem to do the right thing around you," she said.

"Go to sleep," he told her. "Right now that would be the right thing."

The scent of her was like that of a heady wine. It tantalized and promised. The fragrance of musk and lavender lingered, mingled. Her lips were soft, pliant and mobile beneath his mouth, returning his kisses and searching pleasure on her own. He traced the ridge of her teeth with his tongue. Her mouth opened. If there were a taste for yearning and hunger, then he tasted them now.

Her hands cradled his head, holding him to her. Her fingers wound in his hair. She explored with her lips, teeth, and tongue, making forays across his jaw, his cheeks, the cord of his neck. What she felt inside herself now was powerful, a desiring that pushed her beyond the boundaries of reason. Having him consumed her; the consummation was everything.

The force of her own emotion woke her. Rennie gasped, trembling in the wake of her dream. Jarret was asleep beside her. One of his hands lay across her breast, cupping it through the material of her nightshirt. Her flesh felt oddly swollen beneath his palm; the nipple was distended. She drew up her knees slowly, uncomfortable with the vague sense of aching between her thighs and the sudden conscious thought of an emptiness there. There was a peculiar, fading tension in her muscles, a prickling, not unpleasant sensation that she felt skittering just below her skin.

What had just happened to her?

"Jarret?"

He didn't stir. "Hmmm?"

She turned toward him. His thumb grazed her nipple as his hand slid away. An unfamiliar coil of heat radiated sparks from her breast to her womb. Rennie moved closer and raised one leg across his. She pressed her pelvis against his hip. The ache inside her was numbed for a moment. She exhaled softly, her breathing a sigh. Then the need for something more returned with a vengeance until it was almost a physical pain.

Rennie raised her face toward Jarret's, rubbing against him as she moved. Her lips grazed his mouth. Her thigh grazed his sex.

She had Jarret's complete attention now. His eyes opened wide, then closed again, surrendering as her mouth moved over his. His hands cupped either side of her face and stilled her, drawing her back so that she was only touching him with her breath. His voice was husky, whiskey laid over velvet. "Is this what you really want?"

She didn't know what she wanted, but she understood that he did. She was willing to let him teach her. "It must be," she said. "I ache when I'm not touching you.

His resolve collapsed with her softly spoken admission. "Do it, then," he whispered against her mouth. "Touch me."

Jarret found her kiss familiar in an odd sort of way, as if the taste of her was already on the tip of his tongue and he was reacquainting himself with the texture and tang. Her mouth moved over his, nibbling at his lower lip, sweeping her tongue on the sensitive underside of his upper. He tried to catch her lip in his teeth, but she dodged him, spreading hungry, tormenting kisses across his brow and temples.

The blankets tangled between them but they were a minor nuisance compared to his shirt. He laid his hands over Rennie's fingers as she tugged at the buttons. "I'll do it," he said.

Her lips brushed his knuckles as his hands worked. She helped him pull the tails of his shirt free of his jeans. Her palms learned the shape of his chest, the tension of his flesh, and curve of his rib cage. The tips of her nails skimmed his tautly ridged abdomen. His ragged, indrawn breath caught her by surprise. She touched him again, lightly, and felt his hard belly contract under her fingers in anticipation of her touch.

Jarret's hand closed around her wrist, stopping her as her fingers edged just below his jeans. He hauled her upward so that he could have her mouth again. She gave it to him obligingly, engaging his tongue and lips in sweet battle.

Cupping her buttocks in his palms, Jarret pressed the cradle of her thighs against the hard ridge in his jeans. His intimate kiss mimicked the grinding of her hips on his. He turned Rennie so that she was lying mostly under him. His hands pushed her nightshirt higher. He swallowed her gasp as his hands caressed her breasts.

He buried his face in her neck. "Do you want me to stop?" he asked. He felt, rather than heard, her denial. He traced the line of her neck with his tongue and placed a hard, biting kiss in the arched curve of her throat.

His thumbs worried her tautly swelling breasts and pebble-hard nipples. He abandoned them only long enough to slide his palms along her ribs and the tapering curve of her waist. She moved restlessly under him, imprinting his back with the press of her fingertips. Her thighs parted and when his hand dipped lower, past her flaring hips, and his fingers nested in the soft mound between her thighs, he discovered she was warm and wet and ready for him.

And not ready.

Her entire body stiffened at the questing, sexual caress of his hand. He did not move it away, but his fingers no longer moved. "Rennie? I can still stop."

She could hardly hear her own voice. She willed him to understand. "Do you have to touch me there?"

"No, not now," he said, laying his forehead against hers. Their noses bumped. He kissed her with bruising, carnal frankness, and when it was over his hand rested lightly on her hip. "You tell me where," he said. "Tell me where you want to be touched."

For a moment she couldn't say anything. She could only make out the shadowed profile of his face in the darkness. It was both menacing and erotic. She raised one hand and found his cheek, caressed it, her breath catching when he turned his mouth toward the heart of her palm and nipped the fleshy ball of her thumb with his teeth.

"Like that?" he asked, imagining her siren's smile in the darkness.

She took the hand that was on her hip and drew it to her breast. "And here," she said. It was not only his hand she wanted there, but his mouth, and he seemed to know what she could not ask for. His breath was hot on her skin, his mouth hotter. She felt the tug of it, the wet and warm suck as his lips closed over her flesh. It was just not in her breast that she felt it, but deeper, deeper than her thrumming heart, or the fiery run of blood in her veins. Sensation ran under her skin along the length of her nerves and made her feel a hot, aching void between her thighs.

She almost asked him to touch her there again, but he had moved his attentions to her other breast. Her mind and her voice could not give rise to a complete thought. Rennie's fingers tangled in his soft hair. She stroked the back of his neck.

Nothing he did to her was like anything that had been done to her before, yet the caress of his hands on her body was tantalizingly familiar. She remembered the dream that had sent her into his arms—the second one—and she wondered if she were merely dreaming again, wondered if his touch was a continuation of something not of substance, but of wanting.

The edge of his tongue tracing a line from the center of her breasts to her belly was pleasantly rough. His exploration of her navel tickled.

"It does?" he asked when she told him. "Prove it."

He thought his heart might outrace him as she turned the tables, or that he would melt, or simply come out of his skin. He allowed her to lever him onto his back and raise herself over him. She breathed excitement into his chest with her mouth, flicking his flat nipples with the tip of her tongue, raising them as he had raised hers. She slid over him while his fingers sifted through her silky waterfall of dark red hair. Rennie's mouth worked its way down his flat belly and nipped the skin just around his navel.

"That didn't tickle," he said.

She kissed him there. "I must have done something wrong."

Jarret reached under Rennie's shoulders and drew her up so that she lay flush to his body, her head even with his. Her nightshirt slipped over her breasts. His jeans were rough on her naked legs. "Rennie." He said her name quietly, seriously, his voice edged with suppressed passion. "You know what comes next. If you want me to stop, say it now."

"I don't want you to stop."

"I hope you mean it," he whispered against her mouth. He kissed her, turning her on her back. His hand slipped between their bodies. His knuckles brushed her thighs as he unfastened his fly and drew himself out. She raised her knees slightly when he moved between her legs. She quivered beneath him; her breath rasped at the back of her throat. "Wrap your legs around me," he told her. His fingers curved under her buttocks, raising her.

Rennie wanted him. She *did*. But at his entry she tried to get away, bucking, and forced a deeper thrust. Jarret stilled, holding himself steady within her. He felt her close around him as she tried to expel his body. The grip of her velvet walls was an agony of pleasure. He lowered himself over her and rested his weight on his forearms. His mouth nudged hers.

"You should have told me you were a virgin," he said.

"I thought you knew." She could feel her body stretching to accommodate him. "Those men . . . they didn't . . ."

"Sssh," he whispered. Her tentative movement ceased. "I know what happened tonight. I thought in the past nine months that Hollis—" He settled himself more fully against her, driving a little deeper. "That you and Hollis would have . . ."

She moved again, this time to accept him. "No . . . we never . . . I—"

Jarret cut her off, slanting his mouth across hers. His hips rose, fell. He felt the tightening of her legs along his flanks. On the next thrust she rose with him.

The rhythm of their joining threatened to spiral them out of control. Urgency overwhelmed them. Rennie's nails scored Jarret's back. His mouth seared her flesh. Their breathing was harsh, their sentences incomplete and husky. Rennie felt as if she were riding a great wave of tension, extending her entire being for something just beyond her grasp. She was lifted, stretched. Her fingers splayed and her neck arched. She reached outside of herself . . .

It happened without warning. He was with her, guiding their movements, matching the frantic, hungry rhythm of their coupling, and then he was collapsing, not replete in the aftermath of lovemaking, but empty in the aborted attempt as his shoulder, arm, and hand gave way beneath him.

His body lay heavily on hers, not comfortably, but crushingly. In a heartbeat humiliation became blinding anger. Jarret withdrew from her, swearing viciously as he sat up. He pushed aside the blankets impatiently and fumbled with his jeans, buttoning the fly. When he felt Rennie's tentative touch on his shoulder he jerked away.

Dazed, Rennie let her hand fall. "What is it, Jarret? What's happened?" When he didn't answer she asked, "Have I done something?"

"Too damn much," he said tightly. "This was a bad idea from the beginning. I was a fool to think otherwise."

"I don't understand."

He glanced over his shoulder, but he could barely make out her profile. "Look, I'm sorry you weren't pleasured, but it's over. The next time you're feelin' frisky find some other man to ride you. I'm not interested."

She recoiled, stunned.

Her silence unnerved him. He swore again, raw, ugly words this time that did nothing to cleanse his wounded pride. He grabbed a fistful of blankets in his left hand and headed outside toward the fire. "Be ready to leave at first light," he said. He dropped the flap back in place and turned his back on her first jarring sob.

Chapter Eight

Rennie's movements were stiff and slow as she crawled out of the tent. Her bones ached with cold. The sun had risen an hour earlier but gave no indication of warming the day. Its bright light cast a glare across the crusty snow and forced Rennie to raise her hand to shield her eyes.

Jarret was hunkered beside the fire, his back to Rennie. He didn't acknowledge her approach except to point to the dry log at his right where she could sit. When she was down he handed her a tin mug of coffee without once looking in her direction.

Wrapping her gloved hands appreciatively around the hot mug, Rennie raised it to her face. She breathed deeply of the steam and aroma, then sipped it carefully. The heat on her tongue felt good. Her teeth stopped chattering. "When will we be leaving?" she asked. The horses, she saw, were saddled, and with the exception of her belongings and the tent, they were also packed.

Jarret poked at the fire with a stick, stirring the flames a little higher. "Depends," he said laconically. "You want some breakfast?"

She managed to keep the sarcasm out of her voice. Her words made it unnecessary. "In spite of your gracious offer, I think I'll just have the coffee."

For the first time since she joined him, Jarret bothered

to glance in her direction. Instead of staring her down, he simply stared.

The raised collar of her fur coat and the lowered brim of her fashionable little hat couldn't hide the damage that had been done to her. Rennie's skin had no glow and very little color. Tear tracks marred the chalky curve of her cheeks. Her eyelids were swollen, and the tip of her nose was an unnatural shade of pink. There was a purplish bruise and more puffiness along the left side of her face.

Jarret could only imagine what other marks her body bore. He remembered seeing Tom's savage mouth on her breast; then he remembered his own there. His stomach knotted and his teeth clenched. He pitched the cold remains of his coffee on the fire and stood. "I'll knock down the tent," he said. "Be ready to leave when I am."

Tears gathered in her eyes, but she blinked them back. Rennie watched him stride away and begin working with swift, efficient motions. She gingerly touched the side of her face and felt the ache and swelling along her jaw. She didn't clearly remember who dealt her the vicious slap, but she would never forget Jarret's accusatory stare as he looked on it. There was but one interpretation for his cold, angry look that Rennie could find: he blamed her for everything.

She finished her coffee and was waiting beside her mare when Jarret finished with the tent. He gave her a leg up into the saddle. It seemed to Rennie that his touch was especially impersonal, as if he couldn't bear even the most inconsequential contact. She settled herself cautiously against the saddle, more aware than ever of the aching tenderness between her thighs. She felt Jarret's unwavering stare on her again, his disapproval, and she ignored both.

Jarret made certain all the straps on Albion were secure. "What do you have on under there?" he asked.

Rennie blinked. "I beg your pardon?"

He lifted the hem of her coat and her gray, brushed wool dress. "Under here," he said impatiently. "What are you wearing under?"

She flushed scarlet. "I don't think that's any of your concern."

Steadying Albion before the mare bolted away under Rennie's nervous handling, Jarret said, "It is if you can't ride because your bottom's frozen to the saddle. What kind of woman traipses across this country in a dress like you're wearing anyway? Don't you have riding clothes? Or a lady's saddle?" He sighed. "Forget that. You wouldn't get twenty yards in this terrain on one of those."

Mustering what dignity she could, Rennie replied, "I made it this far without your advice, Mr. Sullivan."

His voice was cold. "You made it this far *against* my advice, Miss Dennehy, and before you forget, without my help you'd be dead. Now, what are you wearing under there?"

"Flannel drawers and woolen leggings."

Satisfied, Jarret turned away and mounted. "Stay close," he said. He snapped Zilly's reins and urged her forward.

The ride back to Echo Falls was accomplished with little conversation. Except for a few terse directives on how Rennie should handle her mount, he was silent. Rennie only asked once for a halt so that she could relieve herself. After that Jarret stopped at regular intervals. Rennie assumed it was because he didn't want to hear from her again.

The sky was relentlessly blue. The beauty of it was lost on Rennie. She had a headache from the constant glare of the sun on the snow. When she tried to shield her eyes she slipped in her saddle. When she tried to close them altogether she grew afraid.

Once Jarret slowed Zilly as the path widened and let

Rennie come abreast. Without a word of his intention he took Rennie's hat off her head and replaced it with his. He adjusted the brim low so that it shaded her eyes, then urged Zilly forward again. A moment later Rennie's fashionable fur piece went sailing and skittering down the mountainside. She thought she heard him mutter, "Damndest thing I ever saw," but she wasn't sure.

Sometimes they traveled under a green and white canopy of pines. Snow drifted down as the boughs were gently jostled by their movement below. Looking up, entranced by the balanced beauty of the snow on the greenery, Rennie caught a clump of it right in the face. She sputtered, spitting out snow and a pine needle, and rubbed her face clean. When her vision cleared she saw Jarret had stopped and was looking back at her, not impatiently this time, and not with vicious amusement, but with an odd, almost indulgent expression in his eyes. It vanished the moment Rennie intercepted it. She believed she had mistaken the look.

They reached Echo Falls in the early afternoon. A few heads turned as they rode along Main Street. A merchant sweeping off the sidewalk in front of his store waved to Jarret. Rennie kept her head low and her shoulders hunched. As they approached Bender's Saloon she pulled her horse up.

Jarret halted. "What are you doing?"

"This is where I'm staying."

"No, it isn't." He raised his hand, cutting her off. "No arguments."

She simply didn't have the energy to argue. "All right."

He made a small concession. "I'll tell Jolene where you'll be." He dismounted, tethered Zilly and the packhorse, and disappeared into the saloon. A few minutes later Jolene joined him on the sidewalk.

Jolene's welcoming smile was incongruent with the worried, searching gaze she turned on Rennie. "I'll visit later today," she said, "just to see how you're settlin' in."

Rennie nodded. "I'd like that."

Jolene laid her hand over Jarret's forearm and gave him a gentle squeeze. "I'll see how you're doin', too."

"I'm not one of your charities," he said, stepping off the sidewalk.

Rennie noticed that Jolene was not put out in the least by Jarret's cold shoulder. "That's right," she said. "I'm your friend."

He halted in his tracks, turned, and gave Jolene a light, quick kiss on the cheek. "Don't let me forget that."

"As if I would." She waved to Rennie. "Don't let him bully you, honey."

Rennie nodded, but there was no conviction in it. She lifted her hand in response to Jolene's farewell and nudged Albion forward. She didn't think the sudden unsettled feeling in her middle was due to hunger.

Rennie slowed again as they came upon Mrs. Shepard's boardinghouse.

Jarret turned back and rapped out impatiently, "What is it now?"

"Isn't this where I'm staying?"

"No. Did I say it was?"

"No. I just assumed. But where—"

"My place." Without bothering to see if Rennie was following, he gave Zilly a kick and started again.

Rennie brought her mare abreast of his. "Wouldn't it be better if I stayed with Mrs. Shepard?"

"It'd be a whole lot better," he said. "Except she doesn't have any room. She never does when the snow flies. All the miners who can afford it pack up their tents and head for her place. Besides that, Jolene's expecting you to be with me."

"I don't think I want to stay with you."

He shrugged. "Nothing's keeping you in Echo Falls. You can leave for Denver any time you want. I saw Duffy back at Bender's. Once he's sober, he'll take you back."

"I'm not going to Denver. I'm going to Juggler's Jump."

"Not today, you're not."

Her sigh was an unhappy surrender. She stared straight ahead as the trail began to climb. "I suppose that means I'm staying with you."

"I suppose it does."

They had shared a house before. Rennie had no difficulty seeing how this was going to be different. From the outside the rough log cabin looked no bigger than the parlor room of her own home; from the inside it appeared even smaller. A stone fireplace took up most of the length of one wall. A small table with two chairs—one of them askew on slightly uneven legs—was situated near the hearth. There was a sink and pump, a large iron stove, open shelves with a mismatched assortment of dishes, and a larder mostly filled with canned goods. At the foot of the Boston rocker was a braided rag rug, frayed at the edges and stained with muddy footprints at the center. A storage bench, doubling as a window seat, offered the only other place to sit.

Opposite the fireplace was a narrow, rough-hewn pine ladder which led to the loft. Nearby a curtain partly shielded the wooden bathing tub. And as if she didn't already know, Jarret made a point of mentioning the privy was outside.

"Wood's over there," he said, indicating the canvas sling beside the fireplace. "There's more out back. You better start a fire while I take care of the horses and get the rest of our things. You can do that, can't you?"

She nodded.

219

"Good." He took back his hat, ducking his head as he went outside.

Rennie closed the door after him and leaned against it. "Yes, I can build a fire," she muttered to herself. "But I don't know if I have enough strength to strike a match, let alone lift the wood." She forced herself to push away from the door before she simply melted down its length. Setting one foot in front of the other, her mind devoid of anything but her task, Rennie managed to have a fire blazing in the hearth by the time Jarret returned.

He checked her work, carried in some more wood from the shed, and fired up the stove as well. "Can you get your things up to the loft?"

Her look at the ladder was skeptical, but she was game. "I can do it." She picked up her bedroll and belongings. "Where will you sleep?"

He paused long enough in his unpacking of their foodstuffs to point out the window bench.

Rennie's eyes went from his six-foot-plus frame to the four-foot-maybe seat. "That's ridiculous." She was about to argue, but he silenced her with a single, unamused look. Shaking her head at his unreasonable stance, Rennie went to the ladder. It took her several trips to carry all her things to the loft. She was actually grateful that some of her belongings were still at Bender's Saloon. She couldn't have made another trip up or down the ladder.

"Are you ever going to take off your coat?" asked Jarret as she approached the stove. "I'm not going to attack you, you know."

Stung by his tone, Rennie slowly unfastened her redingote. Until her exertion back and forth to the loft, she had been cold. She didn't tell him that.

Jarret pointed to a row of pegs near the front door where his own coat was hanging. "Over there."

Rennie hung it up. "Can I help you?" she asked. He was

220

making noodles, cutting the dough in even strips and dropping them into boiling water. Pan gravy was simmering on another burner.

"Can you cook?"

"No."

"That's what I thought." He jerked his chin toward the table. "You can set that. Look around, you'll find everything you need."

She would have bit her own tongue rather than ask him to show her where anything was. When she needed something that was beyond her reach she simply dragged a chair over to the shelf, stood on it, and got it down herself. That brought another caustic remark from Jarret.

"Don't be a martyr," he said, watching her push the chair back. "Next time say something."

Rennie finished setting the table, then sat in the rocker, her back to Jarret and her feet on the stone apron of the fireplace. What pins remained anchored in her hair, she finally removed. She combed out her hair with her fingers, letting it fall over her shoulder as she carefully sifted through the knots and tangles.

Jarret banged the table as he set down the kettle of noodles. He saw Rennie jerk. He was sorry for that but glad she stopped her tuneless humming. It was just a little too cozy with her sitting in front of the fire, the polished colors of her hair in full flame while she idly rocked and sang to herself. "You can't carry a tune," he said.

She wasn't at all offended. "I know. Absolutely tone deaf." She stopped rocking. "I'm sorry. It bothered you, didn't it?"

"No," he said shortly. At least not the way she thought it did.

His answer hardly mattered to Rennie. She had already decided she would never do it again. She continued to rock and fiddle with her hair.

221

"Dinner's ready," said Jarret. "It's not much, but it'll hold us until Jolene brings some fresh supplies from town."

Rennie started to coil her hair.

"Leave it," he said. "Your headache will go away faster if you leave it down."

She pocketed her pins and made a loose braid, then joined Jarret at the table. Her mouth watered as he set a heaping portion of the noodles and gravy in front of her. She bowed her head in prayer, and when she looked up she saw Jarret was watching her. Misinterpreting his attention, Rennie touched the swollen left side of her face. "Does it look as bad as it feels?" she asked.

"Worse."

She simply nodded, accepting the fact, and dropped her hand. She picked up her fork and began eating. The thick noodles were tender, and the gravy wasn't bland as she had thought it might be, but richly seasoned with paprika and onion.

Jarret watched her a moment longer. The lines at the corners of his eyes were more deeply etched. His dark brows pulled together in a thoughtful frown. "You're not at all vain, are you?"

Rennie had no idea what he was getting at. Her guard went up. Her eyes were wary, and her laughter hinted at her vulnerability and self-consciousness. "I'd have to have something to be vain about, wouldn't I?" She dropped her gaze and began eating again, hoping it was the end of the subject.

It was, but only because Jarret didn't know how to tell her that her hair was a bewitching combination of colors and textures, radiant even beyond the firelight. Not only didn't he know how to tell her, he wasn't certain he wanted to. As a result they ate their meal in silence.

It was dusk when Jolene arrived. Rennie was sitting at

the window seat, reading one of the yellowed newspapers that had lined a shelf before she confiscated it. She started to get up to help Jolene with the supplies she brought, but Jarret motioned her down again.

"I'll help her," he said. "It won't take all three of us. There's not that much." He shrugged into his coat and stepped outside. A few minutes later Jolene preceded him into the cabin, her arms filled with offerings from Bender's. Jarret stomped, shaking snow off his feet, dropped his own load on the table, and helped Jolene with her cape.

Rennie's eyes widened at the flannel shirt and snug jeans Jolene was wearing.

Seeing Rennie's expression, Jolene looked down at herself and laughed. "Got no drawers but the flimsy kind, and it's no kind of weather for them. I can't abide the wind blowin' up under my skirts and chillin' my—"

"Jolene," Jarret said warningly.

"My bottom," said Jolene, dimpling. "What did you think I was going to say?"

Jarret merely rolled his eyes at her and continued to put things away.

Jolene turned the rocker toward Rennie, sat down, and propped her feet on the edge of the window seat. "The girls are soberin' Duffy up. Should be tomorrow or the day after that he'll be able to take you back to Denver, or at least as far as Stillwater, where you can get the train."

"Ask him if he'll take me to Juggler's Jump."

Jolene hesitated, half expecting Jarret to interrupt. When he didn't she said, "Are you sure that's what you want to do? You had a glimpse yourself how the land lays between here and there. Why not go back to Denver and take the train that goes out that way?"

"The accident destroyed the track at the Jump. Shortly after the search ended, snow drifts prevented crews from

223

reaching and repairing it. Parts of the pass are blocked miles before the Jump. An engine can't get close from either direction. There hasn't been any service on that route for a month."

Jarret rested one hip on the edge of the table and stretched out a leg in front of him. "Are you telling me Northeast Rail doesn't have enough manpower, to say nothing of money, to have those tracks cleared and repaired? And as for a search party, do you really expect me to believe that one word from you can't get a hundred men out there?"

Rennie raised her chin a notch and looked past Jolene's shoulder to Jarret. "Twenty thousand dollars couldn't budge you," she said quietly. "What makes you think I can command a hundred men?"

"Perhaps you don't know the right word," said Jarret. When she merely stared at him blankly he shook his head. "Never mind. What about Banks? Can't he do anything?"

"He insisted on the first search party," she said. "The one Ethan headed. When there was no evidence that Jay Mac had survived he called it off. He refuses to begin another."

"He's in charge of Northeast Rail, then?"

Rennie nodded. "He's in charge."

Jarret's mouth curled to one side derisively. "And he didn't even have to marry you."

Watching Rennie's face pale and the bruise become more livid, Jolene snapped at Jarret. "That's enough. It's not like you don't know how to treat a woman decent." She leaned forward and laid her hand over Rennie's knee. "He's been this way since he came back from New York," she said. "Ever since the—"

"Shut up, Jolene."

Jolene blinked at Jarret's tone. She closed her mouth.

The long and uncomfortable silence was finally broken

by Jarret. Folding his arms across his chest, he spoke tersely to Rennie. "Did you ask Ethan for help?"

"He gave me help. He told me to find you."

"Why didn't he bring you here himself?"

"Besides the fact that his leg's in a splint, you mean?"

Jarret let her know with a single raised eyebrow that he was displeased she had withheld that information. "What happened?"

"He says he slid down half a mountain during the search. Michael says it was more like a hundred feet, but she's not letting him out of her sight."

"Michael is the smarter twin," he told Jolene dryly. Then to Rennie, "Why didn't you say this before?"

"I didn't want you put off by the danger."

It was Jolene who gave a husky bark of laughter. "Honey, danger's just a tease to that man. Leastways it used to be." She looked over her shoulder at Jarret and caught his sour look. She merely smiled sweetly. "Quit your glowerin' and go fetch some more firewood. It's getting cold in here."

Jarret knew better than to believe Jolene was cold. He left her alone with Rennie, hoping she could talk some sense into her.

As soon as he was out of earshot, Jolene's smile vanished. She looked at Rennie, searching her features. "How bad did those bastards hurt you?" she asked with quiet fierceness.

"A few bruises." She touched her jaw. "Here." She touched her breast. "Here." There were the other marks, the ones made by Jarret, but she did not mention the brand of his lips on her neck or at the base of her throat. Jarret had not touched her with savage intent. Only at the end, only then, when he had left her bewildered and hurting, had the outcome savaged her. Something of that pain showed in her dark green eyes. "They didn't rape me," she

225

said. "Jarret stopped them."

"I wish I had been there to stop the whole thing."

"None of it's your fault."

Jolene's smile was weak. "I didn't come here to be comforted by you," she said. "Well, then again, maybe I did. I feel so damn guilty. Jarret, too. He was absolutely wild when I told him you left. Couldn't get out of here fast enough." She studied Rennie's pale face again, her unhappy, heavy-lidded eyes, and folded hands. Jolene recognized Rennie was holding herself together by sheer force of her will. "So what happened after," she asked, "between you and Jarret?"

Rennie's startled, cornered-fawn look gave her away. Still she bluffed. "What do you mean?"

"You're not that good a poker player," Jolene said. "Not with those eyes. Sad to say, but I've got enough experience to read the signs. Did you turn to Jarret for comfort and things get out of hand?"

She hesitated, turning away to stare out the window. The snow reflected the blue-gray colors of twilight. Beyond the clearing of the cabin the barren trees were spindly silhouettes. "Something like that," she said finally. "Whatever happened was my fault. I thought . . . I don't know . . . that it would be healing. Those men . . . Jarret's not like them . . . he didn't touch me like that. In the beginning he made me feel . . ."

"Desired?" Jolene asked gently.

Rennie nodded. Her lower lip trembled and she sucked it in to still it. She smoothed away tears under each eye with the ball of her thumb. "Yes," she said, "desired. And then . . ."

"You weren't ready."

"No, I was. At least I think I was. I know I wanted him." It struck her that she was baring herself to a near perfect stranger, and yet Jolene seemed exactly the right

226

person to tell. "My sister, my mother, they told me what I might expect, how I might feel, and it was like that, only better."

Sweet Jesus, Jolene thought, had she ever been so naive? She couldn't remember. But it felt good to smile at Rennie's sweet, artless disclosure and admit a certain sadness for an innocence lost. "But," she said, prompting, "I hear a 'but.' "

Rennie's eyes dried abruptly and her voice was hollow. "But then it changed. He became so angry. No, not just angry—furious. I don't know what I did. I think he must hate me."

"I don't think I understand," she said. "What caused the change? You were making love and then . . ."

Rennie couldn't answer. She heard the back door handle turn, and a moment later cold air blasted the cabin. She forced a bright smile. "It doesn't matter. It won't happen again. I know that."

Jolene wasn't as convinced. The cabin was small. The loft was smaller. She touched Rennie's hand lightly. "You'll let me know if you need anything, if there's anything I can do?"

Rennie glanced toward the door as Jarret walked in. She nodded quickly at Jolene, eager to end the conversation.

Jolene came out of the rocker and relieved Jarret of some of the firewood. She teased him, practicing spritely conversation while she helped him build the fire. When he started to take off his coat she stopped him. "I have to be leaving. Walk outside with me and give me a leg up."

Rennie watched them from the window, their shadowed figures blurring into one as they walked arm in arm. She couldn't tell if they were talking but suspected that with Jolene it couldn't be otherwise. Rennie wondered about the confidences she had shared. Were they safe? She thought they probably were. At least when Jarret returned to the cabin he didn't confront her with anything she'd told Jolene.

"She brought some newspapers," Jarret said, indicating the small stack on the table. "You don't have to read the shelf liner anymore."

"I didn't mind. It was interesting."

Jarret's expression was patently skeptical. He carried the stack over to the window seat and dropped it beside Rennie. Taking the top paper, he sat in the rocker and began to read. A half hour later when Jarret looked up, Rennie was sleeping. He went to the loft, retrieved a pillow and blanket, and slipped the former under her head and the latter around her shoulders. She didn't stir.

When Rennie woke the cabin was perfectly dark. The fire had gone out, and the sliver of moonlight wasn't nearly enough to light her way. The window seat was uncomfortable, too short and too drafty. She shifted her position several times before giving up and deciding to go to the loft. She made her way across the cabin with sleepy caution, hoping she didn't trip over Jarret, but too weary to care. The ladder creaked under her weight. Halfway up she realized she had neither her pillow nor the blanket. Her unhappy sigh was loud in the still cabin. She went back.

The sloping loft roof left little room for standing movement. Rennie kept her head low, tossed the pillow and blanket down, and sank to her knees on the feather tick. She removed her shoes, then fumbled with the hooks and eyes on her gown, unfastening enough of them so that she could pull it off over her head. Pitching it to one side, Rennie lay back in her chemise and petticoats, covered herself with blankets and a down comforter, and closed her eyes.

That's when she realized she had been ignoring her body's more basic needs.

She felt like crying. She was so spent, so infinitely weary that the walk to the privy had the appeal of a cross country journey. "Damn, damn, damn," she swore softly, sitting up. Throwing off the covers, she scrambled across the tick and down the ladder. It was when her stockinged feet touched the cold floor that she remembered her shoes.

Completely undone, Rennie leaned against the ladder and wept.

She had no clear idea how long she stood there or how quietly or loudly she sobbed; she only knew that it ended when Jarret slipped one arm behind her back and the other under her knees and lifted her.

"The privy?" he asked.

She nodded, realized he couldn't see her, then said smally, "Yes."

He started walking to the back door. "When you return to New York, never wander off Manhattan Island again."

Rennie felt she didn't deserve to take offense. She was totally inadequate in her own eyes as well as his.

Jarret waited outside the privy and carried her back to the cabin when she was through. He followed her up the ladder, took off his boots, and stretched out on the far side of the feather tick. The spot he had vacated when he went to assist Rennie was still warm.

"You were here all along?" she asked, lying down again.

"Hm-mmm. Until you started wailing. The window seat was a stupid idea."

She had *known* that. She punched her pillow and folded it under her head. "What am I going to do about Jay Mac?" she asked forlornly.

His response was as practical as it was unwelcome. "Nothing tonight, Rennie. Go to sleep."

Exhaustion claimed her again. It was Jarret who lay awake for the better part of the next hour, wondering what he was going to do about Mary Renee Dennehy.

The conversation at breakfast could have been about how they tangled in the night and woke in each other's arms. It wasn't. Neither was prepared to discuss it. What they did talk about was mostly inconsequential until Jarret said, "Tell me what's really going on at Northeast Rail."

There was almost an imperceptible tightening of Rennie's fingers around her mug. "I'm not certain what you mean."

His sapphire eyes darkened and did not waver from Rennie's face. "If I'm going to help you, then you have to start telling me the truth—all of it."

Rennie stood. "Would you like some more tea?"

He gave her his mug, watching her carefully as she tried to shake off her agitation. He stretched out his legs under the table. The shift in weight tipped his uneven chair slightly. "What's happened between you and Hollis?" he asked.

She nearly burned her fingers. "Happened? What makes you think something's happened?" She finished pouring her tea and returned to the table. "Hollis and I are still . . . together."

"Really? Is that because he wants it or because you want it?"

"What did you mean about helping me?" she asked. "Is that your intention? Have you changed your mind?"

"You haven't answered my question."

She was silent for a long time, staring at her reflection in her tea. Without looking at Jarret she said, "Hollis is the one who considers us . . . partners. I broke off with him some time ago."

"Before the accident at Juggler's Jump?"

"Yes," she said carefully. "Before that."

"Why does he still think you're interested in him? You told him straight out that you didn't want him, didn't you?"

Rennie nodded, worrying her lower lip for a moment. "I told him." She sipped her tea; then instead of lowering the mug, she stared at Jarret over the rim. "I told him lots of times. I told his parents. I told my parents. I was tempted to pay for a page in the *Chronicle* to announce the end."

"Why didn't you?"

She shrugged. "It would have been a waste of money. Hollis seemed to have convinced himself and most everyone else that I didn't know my own mind, that I was merely attempting to make him more public with his affections. My mother and sisters knew how serious I was, of course, but even Jay Mac had doubts about my convictions."

"Jay Mac never wanted you to marry Hollis."

"No, he didn't. But he didn't know any longer if I knew what I wanted."

"Did you?"

Rennie lowered the mug. She met Jarret's eyes directly and never wavered. "Yes," she said. "I knew."

Jarret believed her. He sat up, leaning forward, and placed his folded arms on the table. "So you don't want anything to do with Hollis Banks, but he's not ready to let you go. What about since Jay Mac's death—"

"Disappearance."

"All right," he said. "Since Jay Mac's disappearance has Hollis shown any sign of changing his mind?"

"None. Working at the office became increasingly uncomfortable, in the end, impossible."

"You quit?"

She shook her head. "No. I couldn't do that. I took

231

things home at first, and then I made the decision to come here."

"To get away from Hollis Banks?"

"To find my father."

Jarret had little doubt that Rennie was holding something back. He let it pass for now. "So Hollis is in charge of Northeast Rail now."

"Yes. He was appointed by the Board of Directors."

"Your family's been taken care of? Your mother? Your sisters?"

"Jay Mac saw to our welfare." Her voice and eyes were bleak. "None of us will want for anything."

Except for John MacKenzie Worth himself, thought Jarret. "And your father's wife?"

Rennie flinched, but said calmly, "Nina's been taken care of. Everyone has a piece of Northeast Rail."

"But Hollis Banks is running it."

"Yes, that's right."

Jarret got up and added some logs to the fire. He poked at the embers, making sure the flames could breathe. "Rennie, you understand that if we go to the Jump, we may not find anything."

She turned around in her chair, and her eyes were hopeful. "Ethan said—"

"Ethan's my friend. If you asked me who's the finest marshal anywhere in this country, I'd say Ethan Stone. But I don't know all the marshals, Rennie, any more than Ethan knows every tracker. He knows I do bounty work to make my way, but he doesn't know that I'm not much interested in it any longer." He set the poker aside and leaned against the stone mantel. "I may not be the best man you could find for this mission of yours. Have you considered that?"

"No," she said, standing. "I never considered it." He started to say something, but Rennie held up her hand.

232

"Wait, let me finish. If I thought there was anyone better, I wouldn't have swallowed my pride and come looking for you. You left New York without a single word to me, no note, no wire, nothing. You kissed me publicly in front of the Jones Street Station, and then I didn't hear from you again. Your bags disappeared from the house, and then you were gone, too. I wasn't expecting a declaration of devotion—nothing like that—but I thought that in spite of everything we had become friendly adversaries. If nothing else, I thought we enjoyed sparring. Then I discovered you didn't think enough of me to say goodbye.

"I put you out of my life that day. Only something of this magnitude could have made me rethink my decision. So, have I considered you may not be the best man for my mission? No. Quite the opposite. You're the man I want."

Jarret's stony gaze widened slightly as she said the last. It was almost as if . . . no, he warned himself, she was only saying she wanted him to find her father, not that she simply wanted him. One of his brows lifted, and he waited to hear the word she had never said easily in his presence.

"Please," she said. "Will you please help me find my father?"

He took his coat off the peg and put it on. "I'll give you my answer in the morning."

"But—"

"Another day one way or the other isn't going to matter, Rennie. That's one reality you're going to have to face. I think you know what the other is." He put on his hat and went out to tend the horses.

Rennie did indeed know what he meant. Getting to Juggler's Jump held no guarantees. Their search might not turn up Jay Mac, but Jay Mac's body. It wasn't the same thing at all.

When Jarret returned his arms were filled with wood. He shouldered his way in the door and managed to hold

233

the load. A few steps from the fireplace his arm gave out, and the pile thudded to the floor. He swore, kicking one of the logs toward the fire. It knocked the burning stack, and sparks jumped wildly.

Rennie put down her paper and left the window seat. She bent at Jarret's feet and began gathering the logs. "Here, let me," she said. "Before you burn the cabin to the ground."

Jarret hauled in his temper and hunkered down beside her. The fingers of his right hand tingled. He was able to use the hand to push a few logs toward the stone apron. He did most of the work with his left. When he was finished he left the cabin again. This time he didn't return until dark.

Rennie heard him stumble a little as he pushed through the door. It was a good bet he had been drinking. She didn't bother looking up from her dinner, finding it easier to pretend she wasn't angry if she wasn't looking at him. Rennie took a bite of venison stew. It had a slightly burned flavor, but that wasn't going to stop her from eating it, or from giving every indication that she was enjoying it.

Jarret served himself a plate but went to the rocker instead of the table. He dropped heavily into the seat, stretching and slouching. He spooned some of the venison and raised it toward his mouth. "I thought you couldn't cook," he said. He tasted it. "You were right."

"Mine's fine."

"Mine's burnt."

"That's because you were gone so long."

He got up and went to the table, but before Rennie could protect her plate, he had scooped some of her stew onto his spoon. He tasted her fare. It was as difficult to swallow as his own. "Liar. You burned the entire pot."

She shrugged.

He nudged a chair away from the table with the toe of his boot and sat. "What's wrong with you?"

"Nothing." She looked at him now. He had a smile on his face that she could only have described as simple. "You've been drinking."

Since it wasn't a question, Jarret saw no reason to respond to it. He tucked into his stew. On subsequent bites the burnt offering wasn't so bad. He was a little regretful he hadn't been present to watch her prepare it. He'd have had another story to swap with Duffy.

Looking around the cabin, Jarret noticed that Rennie had spent the day cleaning. The rug at the foot of the rocker had been scrubbed, the floor swept, the mantel dusted. He realized the chair he was sitting in didn't tilt anymore. She had even leveled off the legs. The top of the stove had been scoured, and the breakfast dishes were put away. "Looks like you kept yourself busy," he said.

There hadn't been much choice. Remaining idle would have taken her wits. There was also the fact that once she started cooking the kitchen area had quickly become unrecognizable. She had strewn flour from larder to stove, trailed sugar along the table top, upended a pot of boiling water, and spilled her blood while cutting the venison. Cleaning had been a necessity.

Jarret reached across the corner of the table and brushed Rennie's hair at her shoulder. She flinched. His fingers stilled but didn't move. "You have some flour in your hair." When he felt her relax he finished brushing it out.

Rennie pulled back the strands when he was done and smoothed them into a loose coil at her nape. Wisps of red and copper strands fringed her forehead. Ignoring Jarret's chuckle, she buttered a warm roll after cutting off the blackened bottom.

"Your face is looking better," he said. When she

235

glanced at him questioningly, he added, "Swelling's down. The color's still not good."

She had seen herself in Jarret's shaving mirror and discovered she was vain enough not to want to see her reflection for several more days. "It's not so bad," she said.

Jarret didn't think it was either, but he was surprised to hear her say so. He finished his meal in silence.

By the time Rennie finished the dishes, Jarret was steadier on his feet. His simple grin had faded, and he had the beginnings of a headache. He considered retiring early, but as he watched Rennie work he knew what he had to do. When she picked up a pile of mending, he gave up his seat at the window and headed for the kitchen pump. "Do you sew any better than you cook?" he asked, watching her try to thread a needle.

"No," she said. "Not a whit better."

He had to smile. She was so matter-of-fact about it. "Better than you sing?"

"Worse."

"Good thing you build bridges, then."

She ducked her head so that he wouldn't see she was fighting back laughter. "It's a very good thing."

Jarret filled a large pot with water and began to heat it. He hooked a kettle of water over the flames in the fireplace and added two smaller pots to the stove. The windows in the cabin soon misted. While the water grew hot Jarret cleaned out the wooden bathing tub. He could feel Rennie's eyes on him, but he couldn't catch her at it. Every time he looked in her direction her lids would have just lowered over her mending.

Jarret carried the pots of hot water in his left hand and filled the tub where it rested behind a yellow cotton curtain. By the time he added a bucket of cold water from the pump, Rennie was on her feet and moving toward the ladder.

"Where do you think you're going?" he asked.

She pointed to the loft. "I'll wait up there while you bathe."

"I didn't drink away all my money at Bender's. I paid two bits for a bath in town. And a penny more for soap." He rubbed his chin. "I had a shave, too. This is for you."

"For me?" Rennie could hardly take it in. "You did this for me?"

Her ingenuous pleasure rubbed Jarret the wrong way. From her attitude one would think he had never shown her any favor. He turned away. "I'll get you some towels," he said gruffly.

His attitude confused Rennie, but she refused to let it overshadow her pleasure. She quickly climbed the ladder to the loft and flung her belongings in every direction searching for bath salts and soap.

"What are you doing?" he called up. "The water's getting cold."

She told him. "They must be with the things I left with Jolene." Rennie squirmed out of her gown, slipped on her nightshift, and clambered back down the ladder. Jarret was gone, and there was more water heating on the stove. Rennie slipped behind the curtain, undressed, and slid eagerly into the water. It was wonderfully warm, lapping her breasts and, when she inched lower, her shoulders. Jarret had laid a towel on the seat of a chair. Rennie picked it up, folded it, and placed it over the back of the tub so that it pillowed her head and neck. She closed her eyes and vowed to stay just where she was until the spring thaw.

The yellow curtain fluttered as the cabin door opened. "I'm here," she called so that he wouldn't invade her privacy.

He did anyway. His hand slipped between the curtain and the wall. In it was the bath salts. When she had relieved him of that he held out the lavender soap. "I brought back your trunk from town. I forgot I left it in the shed with the horses."

She added the salts to her bath. Her skin seemed to absorb the fragrance and soft healing powers of the water. Rennie rubbed a little soap onto a cloth and began to wash with leisurely strokes. Because her eyes were closed again she didn't see Jarret poke his head in long enough to add hot water and make certain he didn't burn her.

"You stay on that side of the curtain," she told him. She looked down at herself after he'd withdrawn and was satisfied he hadn't seen more than her bare shoulders. "If you recall, I offered to go to the loft while you bathed."

"If you recall, I didn't." They were lovely shoulders, he thought.

Rennie was too content to make an issue of it. "I'm going to sleep here tonight," she said.

"You won't be comfortable."

"Nothing will convince me of that now." She raised one leg and began soaping it.

On the other side of the curtain Jarret tortured himself imagining what she was doing. "Do you need any help?"

Rosy color came to her cheeks. Though it felt like her spine was melting, she managed to put some starch into her voice. "Jarret, I've been bathing myself since I was five years old."

"An oversight on my part."

"You're incorrigible."

He deliberately misunderstood. "Encouragable? You're right. One word from you and I—"

"I-N-C-O-R-R—" She stopped. "Oh, never mind. You know perfectly well what I said. And I'm not talking to you anymore. It takes too much energy."

A moment later the curtain was pushed aside. "I could move closer," said Jarret. "You wouldn't have to yell."

238

She tossed her wet washcloth at him. "Make yourself some coffee and drink it black. You need to sober up."

Jarret peeled the washcloth off his face and tossed it back.

Rennie nearly took the bait, coming close to rising above the water line in order to catch the cloth. At the last moment she realized his trick and remained where she was. She wagged a finger at him. "That's quite enough of your foolery."

Unabashed, Jarret retrieved the cloth, dropped it in her hand, and left her alone while he made coffee.

Rennie dropped below the water altogether, soaking her hair. She lathered it up and scrubbed her scalp. It was only when she needed a rinse that she went begging for Jarret's services.

"I'm drinking coffee," he told her.

"Don't be horrid. Just bring me a pot of warm water. It doesn't have to be hot." She added quickly, "Not icy cold either."

"You're very particular."

"Please."

"I like that word." He set down his cup and took a pot of water off the stove. He dipped his fingers in it to make certain it was neither too hot nor too cold. This time upon entering Rennie's oasis, Jarret pushed the curtain entirely aside. She sank lower in the water, her knees drawn toward her chest. Her dark red hair was a soapy crown on her head, the tiny bubbles a row of diamonds. Jarret knelt beside the tub and raised the pot.

She looked at him suspiciously. "That's not cold, is it?"

"It was a temptation," he said, "but, no, it's not cold."

Rennie closed her eyes, screwing her face in anticipation of the waterfall. Instead Jarret let the water trickle over her head. Lather slowly cascaded over her forehead, closed lids, and cheeks. She relaxed as the crown of hair was undone and lifted her face to the gentle splash of the water.

Jarret's touch was light as he smoothed away the damp rivulets of hair that uncurled along her temple and cheek. The backs of his fingers were tender as they brushed the discoloration along her jaw. His thumb was a whisper touch across the spiky edge of her lashes. He sifted through her damp, silky hair as he rinsed it, then laid it over her shoulder. The dark ends of red and chestnut floated on the water and clung to the curve of her breast.

He set the pot aside when the last of the water trickled out. Rennie's face was still raised toward him, close enough now that he could feel her warm breath on his cheek. She hadn't opened her eyes.

"Is that all?" she whispered.

He stared at her. The velvet lashes. The sheen of her skin. The damp mouth. "No," he said huskily. "I don't think it is."

His mouth lowered over hers.

Chapter Nine

The first touch was tentative. The second less so. When Jarret's mouth settled over Rennie's a third time, all hint of hesitation had vanished. His lips captured her sweet response. The kiss deepened.

Ribbons of mist rose from the surface of the water. Rennie raised her hand. Water lapped gently against the side of the tub. She touched her fingertips to the damp curling ends of Jarret's hair at his nape. Water trickled beneath his collar. A droplet traced the length of his spine. It was as if Rennie had touched him there.

He needed her to touch him everywhere.

Jarret cupped the side of her face. His thumb whispered along the arched line of her throat. Beneath it he could feel her pulse, first the steadiness, then the racing. His lips moved to the corner of her mouth and slid lower, along her jaw to her ear. Her breath caught as he teased the lobe with his teeth and the curve with his tongue.

Rennie felt the heat of Jarret's touch against her skin. His thumb seemed to fire her pulse. His fingers trailed slowly down her neck to her shoulder, then passed lightly back and forth across her collarbone. His mouth was at her temple and then the corner of her closed eyes. His hand was beneath the water, sliding along the slope of her breast. Her skin flushed. The rose tip of her nipple hardened. His hand moved between her breasts and held her heartbeat in the heart of his palm.

Hot tears stung the back of Rennie's lids. Her cry was small, panicked. She sat up, pushing Jarret's hand away, and turned her face so that his kiss had no target. Water splashed over the side of the tub as Rennie drew her knees protectively toward her chest. She hunched forward. Rennie didn't have to see Jarret to know that he was withdrawing. She felt it.

Jarret stood. He looked down at her bent head for a long moment, at her hunched shoulders, and at the dark hair swirling on the surface of the water. "It seemed like you were willing," he said lowly.

She nodded, her cheek against her knees. She couldn't look at him, afraid to let him touch her, afraid not to. Her confusion only added to her fears. She tried to speak, tried to tell him what she was thinking, but her mouth was dry. She remembered other hands, less gentle hands, and she remembered how once before Jarret's loving comfort had turned to fury and how the fury had been turned on her. Cruel memories made her shudder.

The folded towel Rennie had used as a neck rest slipped into the water. Jarret reached for it, careful not to touch her. In spite of that he saw her flinch. Angry for reasons he could not clearly define, Jarret pitched the sodden towel. It slapped the floor and sprayed droplets of water on his boots. He found a dry one for her, tossed it on the nearby chair, then slammed out of the cabin.

Rennie did not immediately reach for the towel. She remained in the tub until the water was cold and her skin was colder, until the heat of Jarret's touch seeped out of her. The sensation was only temporary. Picking up the towel, she discovered it was dry, but not fresh. Jarret's scent lingered. The fragrance of his shaving soap remained. She used it, not because there was no other choice, but because she *wanted* him to cover her. Rennie's stomach knotted as she fought another rising wave of panic.

Keeping busy helped her not think about it. She emptied the tub, tossing buckets of water out the back door. She mopped the trail of puddles on the floor, then put away the pots Jarret had used to heat the water. When he still hadn't returned, Rennie straightened things in the cabin that didn't need straightening. She poked at the fire, carried in wood, and trimmed the wicks in all the oil lamps. For a few minutes she stood barefoot on the small front porch in her nightshirt, looking and listening for some sign of Jarret. Snow flurried as wind soughed through the trees, but there was no other movement. Finally she went to bed.

Jarret entered the cabin with infinitely more care than he had left it. He was quiet as he shrugged out of his coat and boots. He padded across the floor and stoked the fire before he climbed the ladder to the loft. Stepping over the mound of blankets that bundled Rennie, Jarret stripped to his drawers, then lay down on the feather tick. He sighed when blankets were pushed in his direction.

"I thought you were sleeping," he said. It was what he had wanted to believe. He drew the blankets around him carelessly.

"You went to Bender's," she said. She despised the fact that her tone was faintly accusing. He had a right to go wherever he wished, whenever he wished. "I'm sorry. I didn't mean it the way it sounded."

"Yes, you did."

"You're right," she said after a moment. "I did."

"What I do is my business."

Still curled fetally, Rennie turned on her side toward him. She could have stretched out her arm and not been able to touch him, but it seemed that more than a physical

243

distance separated them. "Yes, I know that. I was worried."

"About me?" he asked. "Or about yourself?"

Rennie would not let herself be riled. "Both," she said. "But mostly about you."

His voice was sharp. "What did you think I was going to do? Get drunk again?"

She nodded, realized he couldn't see that, and said, "Yes, I thought you might get drunk."

"I didn't."

"No," she said. There was a hard, aching lump in her throat. It was difficult to speak. "No, you didn't. You were with Jolene."

Jarret didn't answer immediately. He stared straight ahead in the darkness and wondered what he should say. He knew what she thought, and he knew the truth. The two were not the same thing. "How did you know?" he asked finally.

Rennie closed her eyes briefly. "I can smell her on you."

"I see."

"She favors rose-scented soap."

"That's true."

Rennie's hand curled around one corner of her pillow. Her fist clenched as did everything else inside her. "You're not denying it, then."

"No," he said quietly, tiredly. "I'm not denying it."

It shouldn't have hurt so much, Rennie thought. She shouldn't have felt betrayed. Telling herself that changed nothing. The feeling remained. "Are you taking me to the Jump tomorrow?"

"I haven't decided."

Rennie wondered if that was really the truth or if he simply didn't want to go another round about it. "When will you know?" she asked.

"When I know."

It wasn't a satisfactory answer. Rennie folded her pillow under her head and blinked back burning tears that seemed to well up from nowhere. She spoke haltingly. "When you kissed me before . . . I wanted you to—I . . . I liked it when you kissed me."

"I don't want to talk about it. Go to sleep."

"No, not yet. You've been gone, with someone. I've been alone here with only my thoughts. I tried to keep busy, tried not to think, but then I came up here and it was either sleep or think. I couldn't sleep and I couldn't *not* think."

Jarret said impatiently, "What is it you want to tell me?"

His tone stung her, but Rennie went on in a voice that was barely audible. "I wish I had let you do more to me."

"Shut up, Rennie."

"I wish I hadn't stopped you."

Jarret's arm snaked out in the darkness and unerringly found her wrist. He yanked her hard across the space that had separated them and trapped her other hand. He held them firmly on either side of her face.

It happened so quickly that her surprise was after the fact. She stared up at him, searching his shadowed profile. She felt his angry tension in the tightness of his grip and in the hard leg that lay diagonally across both of hers. His taut and raspy voice was merely an extension of that same tension. She flinched at the harshness of it.

"What the hell do you want from me, Rennie?" he demanded. "Are you naive or spiteful? Or can't you make up your mind?" He pressed his groin against her hip and let her feel the hardness of him that was all angry desire and tense need. "Don't talk to me about what you wished happened unless you wish it now. Do you, Rennie? Is that what you want?"

"I don't," she said at first. Then, "I don't know."

He swore softly and gave her wrists a little shake. "Why did you start this? I came back here tonight perfectly willing to pretend you were sleeping. Why the hell didn't you give me the chance?"

"I only meant to—"

Jarret let her go and sat up. He closed his eyes and rubbed them with his thumb and forefinger. "What you meant," he said caustically, "was to influence me to take you to the Jump."

Now Rennie sat up. "Take it back," she said quietly.

"Take what back?"

"I'm not a whore," she said. "Take it back."

He shook his head. "I've been with practiced whores who were less skillful than you."

The cruelty of his remark simply took Rennie's breath away. Her chest hurt and her throat seemed to close. She held herself stiffly, as far away from him as she was able. When she could finally speak her voice was brittle. "You've changed," she said without inflection. It was not an accusation, merely a statement of fact. "It doesn't take whiskey to ruin your vision. You're so full of hate and anger and sheer cussed meanness that you can't see straight even when you're sober. If I can't get you to take me to the Jump for the right reasons, then I don't want your help for the wrong ones."

A long silence followed her words. Jarret lay back on the tick and turned toward the wall. "I don't always know about right and wrong around you." It was all the admission he was prepared to make. "Go to sleep, Rennie."

It wasn't a long sleep. Jarret woke her at dawn. He was already shaved and dressed. A bedroll lay at his feet, and elsewhere in the loft their packed bags were stacked. His arms were braced on the beams on either side of the sloping ceiling. He stared down at her while she stretched sleepily and pushed wayward strands of hair from her face. She smiled up at him.

The rare and beautiful smile, the unguarded pleasure in her face, nearly rocked Jarret back on his heels. He realized it meant nothing, that she was hardly awake, but he could not let her see the same vulnerability in him. He stared back stonily. "If you want to go to the Jump, be ready in thirty minutes."

Rennie watched him turn and take the ladder. She had no awareness of her fading smile, just as she had no awareness that it had been radiant and welcoming a moment before. She stared at the point where Jarret had disappeared over the edge of the loft and tried to imagine the hard journey ahead with a man who hated her above everything else.

Jarret had their mares saddled and the third horse strapped with their supplies by the time Rennie joined him. Beneath her redingote she was wearing the clothes he had set out for her. She felt his eyes run up and down her swiftly, making his own assessment.

"Everything fits?" he asked. "The trousers? The shirt?"

She nodded. "These clothes belong to Jolene."

"Belonged," he said, emphasizing the past tense.

"She gave them to you?"

"She sold them to me." There was no rancor in his voice.

"They're comfortable."

He handed her Albion's reins and held her gaze for a moment. "But you're not comfortable."

Her eyes darted away. She mounted without assistance. "Not entirely," she said. "I'm not used to—"

"Wearing a whore's clothes?"

Rennie understood then that Jarret, for whatever reasons, was spoiling for a fight. She refused to be provoked.

247

If he wanted to back out from his agreement to take her to the Jump, then he would have to do it on his own. She wasn't giving him cause.

When he was ready to go Rennie chose to follow rather than ride abreast. Jarret never indicated he wanted it otherwise.

Rennie discovered early on that Jarret was not going to make any allowances for her inexperience or her gender. He altered the pace and chose breaks based on the needs of the horses. He expected Rennie to be able to ride long hours and then be useful when it was time to make camp. On the trail she was given the same attention and deference that Jarret gave to the packhorse's supplies. He couldn't have demonstrated any clearer that she was just so much baggage. At the camp he tersely ordered her around. There she was another pair of arms and legs to fetch and carry.

He didn't make her cook.

At night they shared the tent but not the blankets. They never woke in a tangle or traded a glance. They rarely spoke. Rennie realized that after three days on the trail Jarret and she had exchanged only a few dozen words. She no longer recognized her own voice, but she was getting used to the raspy, staccato orders that Jarret delivered.

The terrain was uneven. Flat stretches opened up to steep descents or sharp ascents. It seemed to Rennie that she was always leaning forward or backward in her saddle. Sprawling juniper shrubs kept the ground from being relentlessly white and rocky, and all around were great forests of ponderosa, lodgepole, and limber pines. Snow defined the slender skeleton branches of the aspens. Mountain streams rushed cold and fast, sometimes beneath a thin layer of ice so that the water looked as if it were under glass. Rainbow colors were captured in the melting tips of icicles. The air was crisp, the snow glazed and crunchy.

For the most part wildlife kept its distance. Rabbits scattered, birds soared, and deer stilled in the presence of the travelers. Rennie sensed more activity at night. Beyond the crackle of the fire and Jarret's soft breathing, it seemed she could hear all of nature's sounds. Pine cones thudded to the ground as predators and prey engaged in a life and death dance. Rocky inclines shifted when animals sought safety in higher ground. The rush of icy water changed its cadence when the chase cut its path.

Rennie found it surprisingly easy to sleep.

It was dawn on the fourth day of travel before Rennie was the first one to wake. She eased out from under the blankets and escaped the tent without rousing Jarret. The sky was gray, and the encampment was shrouded in a cloud. The sun was a blur of light rather than a beacon. It hardly seemed powerful enough to burn off the mountain mist. Rennie knew they would have to travel anyway.

After washing at the stream and seeing to her own needs, she took care of the horses. She had just finished making a better fire when Jarret crawled out of the tent. He took one look at the sky, another at her, then scowled at nature in general. Rennie supposed the scowl was a greeting. When he turned his back and headed for the stream she merely shook her head in unhappy acceptance.

The brisk bathing and shave did nothing to alter Jarret's disposition, but he looked a shade less menacing. He began preparing breakfast while Rennie pulled up stakes on the tent. Out of the corner of his eye he watched her work. Her movements were clean and efficient, and she went at her task with more energy than she had shown on any previous morning. It seemed to Jarret that not only had Rennie survived the demands of the journey, she had adjusted to them.

"Coffee's ready," he said.

Rennie dropped the hammer and stakes on the flattened tent canvas and went for her coffee before it got cold. She sat on a log on the opposite side of the fire from Jarret and held the tin mug in both her gloved hands. The rising steam warmed the tip of nose as she raised it to her face.

Breakfast was stew left over from the night before. When it was ready, Jarret let Rennie dish out what she wanted, then ate the remainder straight from the pot.

"By midmorning we should reach the rails," he said.

As much in reaction to the sound of his voice as to the content of his statement, Rennie's head jerked up. "We're that close?"

He nodded curtly. "We'll follow the tracks to Juggler's Jump. You'll find the traveling easier."

She couldn't seem to help herself from pointing out, "I haven't complained."

"It wasn't an accusation," he said. "I'll find the traveling easier, too."

Rennie ducked her head and continued eating, angry with herself for having taken his comment so personally.

"We should reach the Jump by early afternoon."

She nodded, her mouth flattened in a grim line.

"We'll be approaching it from above. I'm not certain how we'll get down to the wreck. That could take most of the day."

"So long?" Anxiety clouded the emerald eyes she lifted in his direction.

"We'll see," he said tersely.

The subject was closed. Rennie finished her meal in silence. When she was done she took their utensils to the stream, washed them, then completed packing the tent. Jarret put out the fire and saddled their horses. They worked separately but together, skirting each other by design more than chance, as if their motions were choreographed by an unseen hand.

They reached the tracks laid by Northeast Rail sooner than Jarret had expected. Riding single file along the tracks, they hugged the mountain side of the curve during the slow, gradual descent. Occasionally Jarret looked over his shoulder at Rennie, just to reassure himself of her presence. She had not recovered her color since he'd told her they would reach the Jump today. The full impact of her decision to search for her father was confronting Rennie squarely. Jarret wondered if she would be bent or broken by the pressure.

He held up one hand, indicating a halt, as he drew up on Zilly's reins with the other. Ahead of him the tracks disappeared beneath a wall of rock, snow, and ice. Swearing softly, he dismounted and walked ahead to investigate the obstacle. Above him and to his right a wide path had been cut through the trees and shrubs by the force of the avalanche.

Rennie came up behind him and stared forlornly at the blockade that was nearly twice as tall as Jarret at its peak. It was impossible to tell its depth. "What are we going to do?" she asked.

Jarret shook his head. "You said the tracks were blocked in places, but I didn't expect *this.*"

Rennie hadn't either. "Can we get around it?"

"We can," he said, "but it will take us a week to reach the Jump by another route. We'll have to retrace our tracks more than halfway. I don't have enough supplies to do that. I'll have to take time out to hunt for game, and that's going to add to the journey. I had planned to make camp at the site of the wreck and do tracking and hunting then."

"Well, we can't dig through *that,*" she said.

He gave her a sideways glance, his mouth pulled to one

side in derision. "I may not be an engineer," he said, "but I figured that out on my own."

She ignored him. "If we can't get around it, and we can't get through it, then we have to get over it."

"You're not listening. I said we can get around it. It will just take longer."

"Unless you're telling me that going over it is impossible, then going around isn't a choice as far as I'm concerned."

Jarret tipped back the brim of his hat with his forefinger and let his eyes scan the terrain of the blockade. "Truth is, Rennie, I won't know if it's impossible until I've tried it and failed. What I know is that it's dangerous. Are you willing to risk your life? Take a good look over the side of the mountain before you answer that; see where the rest of the rock and snow landed that didn't get stopped on this lip of land."

Rennie didn't look. She knew what was down there, and she knew what was behind her. She was willing to take a chance with what was ahead. "I want to try getting over it, but I won't ask it of you. If you want to turn around, I'll understand and I'll follow."

"So it's up to me."

She nodded.

He turned toward her, and for the first time in four days he touched her, lifting her chin in the cup of his hand. She didn't flinch, but stood there stubbornly, color washing her cheeks as he took the full measure of her resolve. "If you so much as stub your toe getting over this thing, I'll make your life miserable."

She smiled brilliantly, warmly, but Jarret didn't see. He had already turned away, his decision made.

Rennie helped him remove some of the load from the packhorse and distribute the supplies to Albion and Zilly. When that was done they worked together trying to reconstruct the face of the avalanche so that they and the horses would have better footing. They packed the snow where it was loose and moved rock when it was possible. The going was slow. Rocks that seemed to hold at first merely rested on layers of pebbles. When they shifted, sliding like ball bearings, the rocks would shift in turn. Rennie bit her lip every time she heard the sound or felt the earth give beneath her. The alternative was to scream.

When Jarret and Rennie reached the top they saw that the remains of the avalanche stretched nearly fifty yards in front of them. It also sloped gradually toward the tracks again, putting them at the steepest point at the outset. Rennie waited at the summit while Jarret climbed back down to bring the horses. She watched him gentle and calm them when they shied at the start of the ascent. Rennie never doubted he would get them to move; she had witnessed his success with the recalcitrant packhorse often enough to be certain of the outcome. Somewhat to her chagrin she realized he had occasionally used similar techniques with her.

"Must be I've got more horse sense than common sense," she muttered to herself as Jarret crested the ridge.

He glanced at her, and for a moment the old easy smile was back. "Don't flatter yourself," he said dryly.

Rennie knew the air wasn't a single degree warmer than it had been a second ago. It only felt that way. Without another word, and hiding her secret smile, she carefully picked her way across the rock and ice.

It wasn't until they were all safely on the other side that Rennie realized the scope of their accomplishment. Looking back at the barrier they had just defeated, she saw the precarious balance of rock on rock. The snow and ice that had been nature's glue was melting much faster than Rennie had noticed while traveling over it. Without warning an entire section of glistening rock and snow slipped over

253

the mountainside. It thundered at first, then echoed eerily as it came to rest farther down the slope.

Jarret was soothing the horses, but his attention was on Rennie. "Are you going to be sick?" he asked.

She swallowed hard and took an uneasy step back from the edge. She stumbled on a railroad tie behind her and fell on her bottom on the track. "At least I managed not to stub my toe," she said wryly, raising slightly bemused eyes to Jarret.

He transferred the reins to his right hand and reached for Rennie with his left. He pulled her to her feet. They touched along the length of their bodies for the briefest of moments before he released her. They both felt the same frisson of awareness, but only Jarret knew precisely how close he had come to kissing her.

Rennie brushed herself off and adjusted the scarf around her neck. Game again, she took Albion's reins from Jarret's hand and led her mare along the stretch of tracks. Once she was walking it was easier to pretend she wasn't shaking quite as badly as she first thought.

There were no other blockages along the track. Jarret and Rennie reached the curving abutment known as Juggler's Jump at midday, earlier even than Jarret had anticipated. While the tracks followed the curve of the mountain closely and blasting had widened the shelf, the Jump itself reached out beyond the mountain's face.

Rennie and Jarret stood a few steps back from the edge. Four hundred feet below them lay the twisted wreckage of No. 412.

"I make out four cars and a caboose," Jarret said. Snow had long since covered most of the damaged cars, and trees that had been felled in their careening spill off the mountain also blocked the view. "Is that what you understood?"

She nodded. The caboose lay completely on its side, identifiable only because some small patches of red were still visible. Three of the cars were more difficult to distinguish because they were buckled and fused, altered beyond their normal rectangular shape to something that had no well-defined shape at all.

The fourth car was something else again, and it was the one that held Rennie's attention. Even before the wreck it had been different from the others. Jay Mac had insisted that his private car be equipped with both function and comfort in mind. It was only on the outside of the car that he permitted embellishment that served no purpose except to set it apart. The Worth crest appeared on both sides of the car and again on the roof. Jay Mac's private car was the only one in a mostly upright position. Its tilt against a row of sheltering pines meant snow had not clung so tenaciously to its roof. When she looked carefully, Rennie could see the gold leaf coat of arms against the shiny black background.

She pointed it out to Jarret. "That's my father's car," she said. "Ethan told me I'd find it nearly upright. You can tell from here that it's hardly damaged."

Jarret couldn't tell anything of the sort, but he didn't say so. Just because it landed that way didn't mean it hadn't somersaulted in the air on its way down. Neither did it necessarily mean Jay Mac had had a better chance of surviving the crash.

"How do we get down there?" she asked.

"Well, we can do what old Ben Juggler did . . ."

"I'm not jumping."

"Then, we keep on walking. We'll take the tracks to their lowest point, then cut back through the woods. It's not as steep an incline as it seems. Which is why Juggler finally settled on a gun to end it." He grinned. "Jumpin' here didn't do the trick."

She stared after him as he walked away. "You're making that up."

He raised his right hand. "Swear to God."

Rennie couldn't see, but she suspected he was still grinning. She picked up Albion's reins and fell into step behind him.

It was one of those things that shouldn't have happened, an outcome for which neither one was prepared. After giving their horses a rest along the track route, they shifted the supplies back to the packhorse and mounted their own. Neither Albion nor Zilly found the ground they had to cover any more difficult than anything that had come before. Looking up at Juggler's Jump from below, Rennie could see that Jarret was right about the mountain's incline. It only became steep, and virtually impossible to ascend or descend, where it rose vertically to support the tracks.

The terrain they covered now seemed a gentle slope in comparison to the view from above. She thought later that it may have been the ease with which they were moving, or a touch of unwarranted confidence that they had finally reached a milepost on their journey, that made them careless.

Rennie didn't see the rabbit that charged under Albion's hooves until her horse reared. She managed to hold her seat, but Albion faltered on the landing and nearly went down. His attention caught by what was happening over his shoulder, Jarret wasn't prepared for Zilly's misstep. He tried to right himself in the saddle, grabbing the pommel, but the tingling in his hand prevented him from having a good touch. His panic was only momentary, yet Zilly felt it. She stomped restlessly, dislodged some rock, and began sliding.

Jarret regained some control by leaning forward in the saddle and letting Zilly do what she did best. The mare's legs scrambled for purchase, then charged ahead. It was a wild ride to the bottom, and Jarret thought for a moment he and Zilly were both going to make it safely. That was until he saw the fallen ponderosa. It lay on a slant, the bough end caught in the crux of another tree, barring his route like a gate four feet off the ground. He tried to use his knees and legs to redirect the mare's path, but she was too frantic to feel his movements and understand them. Jarret was helpless to stop Zilly from making the jump, and with no strength now in his right arm he couldn't hold on. He lost his seat going up, and unlike Zilly, never cleared the gate.

Rennie was more than halfway to reaching Jarret when she saw him tumble. She saw the fallen pine, realized Zilly was going to make the leap, but never thought it would be the thing to unseat Jarret. He came away from his mount as if the saddle and reins had suddenly been greased.

By the time she reached him Zilly had calmed and wandered back to where Jarret lay. The mare leaned her head over the tree and tried to nudge Jarret awake. Rennie knelt at Jarret's side and pushed Zilly's nose forcefully out of the way. The mare took the direction and meandered away.

His breathing was shallow but even, and Rennie found his pulse easily. She shook him gently several times, saying his name. When he didn't respond she took off her gloves and removed his hat. Her fingers delved into his hair as she carefully felt for bumps or breaks in his skin. She found a large goose egg just behind his right ear. The little bit of blood didn't worry her; the size of the swelling did. At that moment she would have given everything she owned for a bit of her sister Maggie's healing knowledge. It seemed to Rennie that being an engineer made her a fish out of water everywhere but in the Worth building—and lately even there.

The wreckage they were trying to reach was still a good distance from where they were, though now the way was mostly flat. Rennie knew she couldn't lift Jarret, and neither could she leave him where he lay. She considered making camp right there, but Jay Mac's private car kept coming to her as a better alternative.

After assuring herself that Jarret had no other obvious injuries, Rennie rolled him carefully onto a blanket and covered him with others. Working swiftly, she built a small fire that would keep some of the chill at bay. She tethered Zilly and the packhorse and mounted Albion. The mare covered the ground quickly to the site of the wreckage.

Rennie knew she was not going to find her father inside his private car, so she did not steel herself before entering. She wasn't prepared for the rush of emotion any more than she was ready for an environment gone slightly awry. Both of them made her gasp.

Rennie held on to the door to maintain her balance. The car was more than a few degrees off level, held from tipping over by the row of sturdy ponderosas. Everything in the car that wasn't secured had fallen to one side. The things that were secured, like the bed and dining table, were just enough at an angle to be disorienting. Rennie found herself tilting her head in an effort to diminish the dizzying sensation.

There was nothing so simple she could do about the rush of emotion. This was her father's place, and she had never been in it save in his presence. It didn't seem it should *exist* outside his presence. Had the car been perfectly level, she would have still felt the nauseating disorientation.

Tears blinded her briefly, and when she lifted one hand

to brush them away she slid a little on the uneven floor. She kept herself upright by holding on to the door and bracing her other hand against a secured end table. Making her way across the length of the car was like walking on a ship permanently listing from the windward side.

The Franklin-style heating stove was the purpose of her trip. It was cast at the same odd angle as everything else, but when she checked its hinges and seams everything seemed to be in order. The vent pipe was intact, and Rennie could see no reason for not using it. It would provide Jarret with the warmest night he'd had since leaving Echo Falls.

Now she only had to get him to it.

The caboose had the things she needed. Because it was on its side she had to go through a broken side window and drop in. She brushed snow off the storage chest and found an ax, hammer, nails, and rope. They were the tools she needed immediately. She also removed a crowbar and four wrenches with varying handle lengths and different size box ends. Her efforts at pushing open either end door from the inside proved useless. Snow blocked both exits, and the hinges were on the outside. After tossing all the tools she needed through the window, Rennie dragged the storage bench under it, stood on it, and hauled herself through the opening.

Once on the outside she set about clearing one of the doors of snow and ice. Rennie used the hammer to tap out the hinge pins and remove it altogether, then she took off the door handle. She drove nails into the door's top rail so that half their length was exposed and attached the rope ends securely. She pulled on the rope handle, and with a little effort the door glided across the snow.

"Not bad for a sled and stretcher," she said to herself. Rennie slung the rope around the pommel of her saddle, making certain there was enough length to keep the door

259

from chipping at Albion's fetlocks. She mounted and urged the mare forward, using her legs to guide the horse while her hands controlled the slack on the sled. After a little trial and error, Rennie was able to keep the door from slipping too much to either side.

By her own estimation she hadn't been gone much above thirty minutes. Jarret was still unconscious. Rennie touched his forehead with the back of her hand, and then his chest. He had lost only a little body heat, and she grew more confident that her worst fears would not come to pass.

Rennie used the blankets like a ramp to roll Jarret onto the sled. She secured him with ropes from their own supplies. Surveying her handiwork she was struck by the fact he was trussed up like Gulliver. "Wait until you wake up in the private car," she told him. "You'll think you've arrived in some fiendish version of Lilliput."

She sighed when he didn't answer her. "All right, Zilly," she said, untethering the mare. "It's your turn to pull." Grabbing the mare's cheek strap, she held Zilly's head steady and gave her a stern look. Zilly didn't move. It wasn't the technique Jarret used to calm the skittish mare, but it worked for Rennie. "As long as we understand each other," she said.

Getting Jarret back to the car was not the hardest part of the task that Rennie faced. She had to get him inside. Rennie judged the hours of daylight left and decided that she could not take the time to build another fire. She made certain Jarret was bundled and sheltered from the wind, then gathered her tools and went back to the caboose.

After examining the exposed wheels on the caboose, she chose to remove the one least damaged by the crash. The groove that had held the track was still smoothly curved, not flattened as it might have been. If the brakeman had

had any warning of what was going to happen, there would have been an effort to apply the handbrakes. A heavy hand would have resulted in flattened wheels, but probably not altered the fate of the passengers. Now the smooth wheel groove would help save Jarret's life.

It took more in the way of brute strength than cleverness to accomplish the task. What Rennie wasn't able to achieve with the long-handled iron wrenches, she was finally able to do with the crowbar. When the wheel was off she rolled it over to the private car.

It was too difficult to work in her heavy coat, and her efforts had already overheated her. Rennie took it off and laid it over Jarret. Standing on the slanted balcony at one end of the car, Rennie reached as high as she was able and drove a spike halfway into the wall just above the door. The wheel was heavy, but not as awkward to lift as Jarret would have been. Still, Rennie knew she had one, possibly two, chances to thread its center hole with the spike. She probably wouldn't have the strength to lift it after that. It didn't help her confidence when she considered how much trouble she had threading a needle.

She hoisted the metal wheel in her gloved hands, braced it on the balcony railing for a moment, then raised it over her head. She felt the spike catch the hole, then felt the wheel slip. It flashed through her mind that she was not very good at hanging pictures either. The wire never seemed to catch the nail. Swearing sometimes helped.

Rennie heaved again, turning the air blue with her colorfully vulgar and descriptive language. This time the spike held the wheel. It was left to her to find a nut that would keep the wheel from spinning off the spike as it turned. There was nothing that fit exactly right, but Rennie improvised by using a nut that was slightly larger than the spike and making it tight with small wedged-shaped pieces of wood that acted as shims. Tentatively she spun the wheel. It stayed firmly in place.

A double pulley system would have been better, she thought, but her single one would have to do.

Rennie arranged Jarret in a sling of blankets and rope; then she ran the length of rope over the groove in the wheel and fastened the end to Zilly's saddle. She opened the door to the car so that it would be easy to swing Jarret inside once Zilly started to walk forward. The problem was getting Zilly to move while Rennie guided Jarret's sling.

Rennie solved it by tossing a few stones at Zilly's hindquarters. Jarret was dragged toward the car the moment the mare lurched forward. Rennie steadied the sling and encouraged Zilly to keep moving. Jarret bumped against the balcony's iron steps. Rennie protected his head. The wheel above her groaned as Jarret was lifted off the ground. Zilly moved ahead. Jarret was jerked higher, and this time Rennie was able to get her arms under him, cradling his unconscious form. She called to the mare again, and now Jarret was lifted as high as her waist. Rennie eased him toward the open door and jerked on the taut rope, bringing Zilly back.

It took a few more minutes of alternately pleading with the horse and cursing her for Rennie to get Jarret lowered to the floor of the car. When he was down she cut the sling free.

Rennie now had him inside, but she didn't have him warm. As soon as she tethered Zilly she cut wood for the stove and built a fire. Once she boarded two shattered windows with strips of wood from the caboose, the car began to heat. Rennie was of no mind to bring Jarret to the bed. She brought the bed to him, laying out the mattress in the same direction as the slope in the floor so that he couldn't roll and hurt himself. After untying the knots that secured him, Rennie rolled Jarret carefully onto the mattress.

It took all her emotional strength not to simply collapse beside him.

Making him as comfortable as she could, Rennie then took care of the horses, giving special attention to Zilly, who was lathered from the labor. Rennie carried in their supplies, stacking them against one wall. She was just finishing with the last of them when the sun went down. Twilight didn't last long. Rennie found two oil lamps minus their glass globes. They required a level place to rest, so she remounted a shelf on the wall. The effect was quite peculiar. The shelf was parallel to the ground beneath the car, but askew of everything else in the room.

Rennie laid the hammer aside and lighted the lamps. She worked for another two hours, clearing broken glass and damaged, unusable items. She became adept at walking the length and breadth of the car without faltering, though she imagined she looked rather less attractive than a mountain goat. Finally, because she was too tired to walk to the nearby stream, she melted snow for drinking water and lay down beside Jarret when she had her fill.

She bathed his face with the remainder, then let the pot slide away. Covering herself with the blankets, Rennie curled closer to Jarret than she had on any previous night since beginning the journey. Laying one arm across his waist, she rested her head against his shoulder.

When she fell asleep, exhausted almost beyond bearing, it would have been difficult for an observer to tell who was the more unconscious.

Jarret woke in the middle of the night. He had no clear idea where he was. He remembered the last moments of the wild ride on Zilly's back and nothing after she jumped the fallen pine. He wondered why he was sleeping on a slant, why his entire body felt bruised, and why Rennie was close enough for him to feel her heartbeat. Her heartbeat was a soothing thing. He had no trouble falling asleep again.

Rennie felt a chill prickle her skin. It was surprising because she realized she was under a mound of blankets. Even the air was warm. It didn't seem to matter. The cold started bone deep and rose only as far as the surface of her skin. It never seeped out of her completely. In moments she was shaking uncontrollably.

Jarret laid his palm against her face. Her jaw was clenched, yet somehow Rennie's teeth still chattered. Under the roughened pads of his fingers he could feel the muscle ticking in her jaw. It went on for several minutes before she fell into a restless, shallow sleep. The damp cloth he held in his hand was useless against her chill.

Standing, Jarret dropped the cloth back in the pot of water he had placed on the car's only level shelf. He knew how it had come to be that way. Rennie's cleverness made him smile.

In the past twenty-four hours he had seen a lot of Rennie's handiwork: the boarded windows, the stacked supplies, the door that had doubled as a sled, the tended horses, and oddest of all, the caboose wheel above the door. It took him a while to figure that one out, probably longer, he thought, than it had taken Rennie to conceive and construct it.

Looking down at her pale face, Jarret's smile turned grim. All of Rennie's efforts on his behalf had resulted in her own illness. The irony would not be lost on her. It was merely one more of her best intentions gone awry. He sighed. "You, sweet lady, might have been born with a silver spoon in your mouth, but it's a sure bet it was tarnished."

He left the car and tended to the meal he was preparing outside. The stove was good for heating, but it didn't work for cooking. When Rennie was better he looked forward to asking her why she hadn't corrected that small problem. She certainly had set about fixing everything else.

Jarret ate his beans and bread sitting in a chair propped against the canted wall. When he was done he spooned warm tea past Rennie's bluish-tinged lips. Afterward, because he thought he could tend to her better, Jarret moved Rennie and mattress back to the built-in bed frame. When he tried to put the covers back on she kicked them off. She was no longer shaking; her skin was on fire.

Retrieving the wet cloth, Jarret wiped damp tendrils of hair from her forehead. He smoothed it over the unnatural glow of her face. The sheen of clammy perspiration touched her upper lip. He wiped it away also.

Her nightshift became damp, and he exchanged it for one of his shirts. Aware of his attentions, Rennie pushed weakly at his hands as they fastened the buttons. "Don't touch me," she said.

"I won't." Jarret watched Rennie's hands slip to her side. Her agitation disappeared. She seemed satisfied with his promise even though he was still closing the shirt. He stayed with her until she slept again.

Rennie woke slowly. Her lashes lifted, fluttered, and closed again. She stretched tentatively, groaning with the effort of her movements and the deeply felt aches. Turning on her side, she slipped one arm under her head and opened her eyes. A small wave of nausea accompanied her disorientation.

The private car no longer listed to one side; only the shelf had been left hanging on the wall at an angle. The oil lamps had been placed on the perfectly level dining table and most of the room's contents returned to the positions they were meant to have. That Jarret had left the shelf canted proved he still had a sense of humor, even if it was at her expense.

It was a small movement at the end of the bed that gave his presence away. Rennie's attention shifted. Her disorientation returned, more profound this time, and for reasons that had nothing to do with the tilt of the shelf or the lack of it in the bed. She said the first thing that came to her mind: "You're smiling."

Jarret realized that he was. His grin deepened at her observation. He leaned forward and touched the back of his hand to her forehead. Her skin was dry, her temperature no different from his own. "You'd think I'd never done it before," he said.

"You haven't." Her voice was soft and raspy from lack of use, hardly recognizable as her own. "At least not in recent memory."

The tips of his fingers trailed along her cheek. "That so?"

She nodded. She felt his fingers drop away from her face, touch her shoulder briefly, then leave her altogether. She experienced an odd sense of loss. Aware she was staring at his hand, Rennie deliberately shifted her attention to other parts of the room. "You've been very busy," she said. "You righted the car."

"Noticed that, did you?"

His gentle teasing raised her own smile. "How did you do it?"

"You'd be amazed at what three horses and a jackass pulling in the same direction can accomplish."

"A jackass?"

"Me."

She studied his face. His grin had disappeared. The set

of his mouth was solemn, the deep blue eyes unwavering. "Are you apologizing for something?" she asked.

He shook his head. "I'm apologizing for *everything.*"

Two faint lines appeared between Rennie's brows as she frowned. "I don't think I understand," she said.

"Self-pity's a cancer on the soul," Jarret said. "I nearly lost mine." He smoothed the twin lines between her eyes with his thumb. His smile returned. "Do I have to list all my transgressions before you'll accept an apology?"

"No," she said. An abrupt yawn dislodged his hand, and she was sorry for that. "You just have to tell me if I'm dead or dreaming." His laughter was so unexpected and so unfamiliar to her that Rennie's eyes widened a little before they closed completely. "I'm dreaming I'm dead," she murmured. "That must be what's happened."

Jarret had planned to tell her differently, but he saved his breath. She fell asleep as suddenly as she had wakened.

Chapter Ten

It was dusk when Rennie woke again. This time the car was empty. She sat up, pulling the heaviest blanket around her shoulders. The floor of the car was cold on her bare feet, but the air was warm. She padded over to the stove, threw in some wood, then warmed her hands in front of the fire before shutting the grate. Straightening, she caught a movement out of the corner of her eye.

The unbroken windows of the private car were frosted, so the image outside was a blur. Rennie placed the flat of her hand against the frozen pane and melted the ice. She stared through the clear, dewy outline of her palm print.

Jarret's fingers were stiff with cold. He twisted Rennie's wet nightshift, wringing out the water, then laid it over a rock. He bent beside the swiftly rushing stream again, catching one of his own shirts before it was swept away. He washed it quickly, wrung it out, then gathered up the pile of iced laundry and started back to the car.

Over the top of his armload of clothes he saw Rennie standing on the balcony of the railcar, shaking her head in disbelief. "Get back inside," he told her.

She did, but only so that she could hold the door open for him. He entered the car, stomped snow off his boots, and dropped his load of wash on the table. Rennie closed the door and began hanging things on the rope she had strung across the width of the car.

"You should be in bed," he said. He looked down at her bare feet. "Put some socks on."

Rennie stopped long enough in her work to salute him smartly.

"Very amusing," he said dryly, but he didn't mind her cheeky grin in the least. It had been a long time between smiles. He counted himself fortunate to have raised one so quickly, even if it was sassy.

Rennie rummaged through the drawers built in beneath the bed while Jarret rubbed his hands by the stove. She put on a pair of socks and started working again. Water droplets rapped a pleasant tattoo on the floor as the laundry melted.

"How are you feeling?" Jarret asked.

"A little stiff," she said. "A little tired. But nothing more than that. My constitution's strong. I recover quickly."

The hint of a smile touched his mouth. "Define quickly," he said, turning away from the stove.

Rennie propped up the sagging clothes line with the high back rails of one of the dining chairs. "As quickly as you," she said, snapping out her crisp nightshirt.

"Rennie," he said gently. "I was out for less than twenty-four hours."

She nodded, laying her shirt over the line. "I know."

Jarret caught her gaze, held it. "That was nearly a week ago."

Rennie's hands stilled in the process of smoothing out her shirt. "You don't mean that." But she could see that he did. "A week," she repeated dumbly. "How can that be?"

"Six and a half days," he said. He took a step toward

her. "Are you all right? You're not going to faint, are you?"

"I don't faint." She saw him trying to tamp down a smile. "Well, I never did until I met you. And if you recall, on both those occasions you were fairly squeezing the life out of me." In spite of her words about her fitness, Rennie slipped through the curtain of laundry and sat on the edge of the bed. Her heels hooked on the bed frame, and she modestly pulled the hem of Jarret's shirt over her knees. "I had no idea it had been so long." She glanced at him. "I'm sorry. I didn't intend to be so much trouble."

Both his brows came up. He ran his hand through a tuft of dark blond hair at his temple. "Trouble? I didn't have to make a winch to lift you inside the car or tear off the caboose door to improvise a sled. You had most everything cleared and cleaned by the time I came around." He sat beside her. "Of course, you did leave it to me to level out the car. I had to use brute force."

"Not an elegant solution, but an effective one. I was thinking along the lines of levers and fulcrums." She gave him a sideways look and a wry smile. "Elegant, but probably impractical."

"Probably." He would have liked to have seen her try. When she dealt with creative practicalities, no one could hold a candle to her. It was only when she crossed his path that she couldn't seem to find her way.

Rennie's shoulders sagged as she considered how much more time had been lost. "It snowed again, didn't it?"

"Only this morning. For most of the week it's been warm. I did some hunting, tracking. Poked around a little on the mountain slope." He reached into the pocket of his shirt. His fist closed around the object he pulled out. "Rennie, I don't want you to get your hopes up—I don't even know if it means anything—but I found these about halfway up the mountain. Sun on them caught my eye."

270

Rennie's gaze dropped to Jarret's closed fist as he turned it over in front of her. The fingers unfolded slowly. "What is —" But she stopped because she saw what it was. In the heart of Jarret's palm he held the twisted wire frames and chipped lenses of her father's spectacles. Hardly breathing, more than a little afraid she was imagining their existence, Rennie carefully lifted them. Her fingers trembled as she traced the bent and fragile stems and the curve of the lenses.

"They could be anyone's," Jarret said, watching her closely. Curling strands of hair fell over her shoulder as she bent her head and studied the glasses. Her skin was pale, and the bones of her wrists seemed impossibly fragile. "For all I know, they could have been Ben Juggler's."

Rennie shook her head. "*I* know," she said firmly. "They belong to Jay Mac." She unfolded the stems and raised the spectacles so that Jarret could see. "I have a pair nearly like them. So does Michael. They all have this small diamond-shaped etching on the stem. That's the jeweler's mark. How many people on the train do you suppose bought their spectacle frames from a New York jeweler? Or would have lost them over this particular mountainside?"

It was the sort of confirmation he had hoped for but never thought he'd get. Yet it wasn't enough. "Where did your father keep his spectacles when he wasn't wearing them?"

"In his vest pocket. He had to. He lost them otherwise."

"What about at night?"

"At his bedside, I suppose. Jay Mac really can't see very well without them."

"Did these cars jump the track in the day or at night?"

"It was early evening, at dinner. That's why more people weren't killed. There were a lot of passengers in the dining cars forward of the ones that left the track."

"So your father would have been wearing them or carrying them?"

"That's right."

It was enough for Jarret to make his decision. Jay Mac *and* his spectacles had been thrown from the tumbling private car. Perhaps he had been standing on the balcony, enjoying the view when disaster struck; perhaps he had crashed through a window. However it had happened, it seemed likely that Jay Mac could not have been easily separated from his spectacles during the accident. That could only mean they were separated later. Other than the spectacles there had been no evidence of Jay Mac on the mountainside: no blood, no bone. It was almost as if he had walked away from the tragedy.

The tantalizing possibility existed that John MacKenzie Worth was still alive.

Jarret took back the spectacles, wrapped them carefully in a handkerchief, and laid them aside. "Rennie?" She was so still, so pale. "Rennie, why don't you lie down?"

"No," she said, touching her fingertips to her temple. She massaged it gently, thinking. "No, I should be helping you."

"Helping me do what? There's nothing to be done."

She pointed to the damp clothes still on the table. "The laundry. Our dinner. Something. I should be doing *something*." Rennie started to rise, but Jarret placed his hands on either side of her waist and drew her back to the bed. She didn't protest, letting him tuck the blankets around her and plump a pillow under her head.

"The runt of the litter has more strength than you," he said, looking down at her. "Right now you should be taking advantage of the fact that I'm treating you like a princess." He started hanging up clothes. "You have exactly two days to enjoy it. By then I figure you'll be ready to travel and I won't make any allowances. You know that."

272

She nodded slowly, hardly believing her own ears. "We're going to look for Jay Mac?"

"We're going to look," he answered. Then he felt the full force of her beautiful smile.

"I doubt princesses anywhere in the world are treated half so well," Rennie said. She was kneeling over the edge of Jay Mac's copper hip bath. The tub was tarnished and battered, but the seams had held. Just now it was filled with a little hot water and a lot of Jarret Sullivan. He leaned forward while Rennie scrubbed his back.

"I didn't make you haul the water," he said. He closed his eyes as she moved the cloth in a circular motion up and down his back. Every stiff, corded muscle seemed to melt under her gentle manipulation. "In fact, if you recall, I offered to take *my* bath in the stream."

It had been a ridiculous suggestion. "It made as much sense as you offering to sleep on the window bench in your cabin," she said. Rennie stopped scrubbing long enough to adjust the towel that was wrapped around her wet hair. She tucked in the ends, securing them, then pushed at a tendril of hair across her forehead. "What time will we leave in the morning?" she asked, running the washcloth along his shoulders.

"Trains run on a schedule, Rennie."

"So do people."

"In New York, maybe. Not here. We'll leave when I wake up."

"It's a good thing you're not running a railroad."

He took the cloth from her as she began to wash over his scarred shoulder. He did it casually so that she wouldn't question his intent. There was no physical pain in her touching him there; the pain was of a different nature, one he had no desire to share.

273

"It's a good thing you're not a handmaiden. You're too easily distracted." And too distracting. He had purposely found things to do outside the car while Rennie was bathing. He had suggested washing in the stream for reasons that had little to do with modesty or privacy. Standing would have cleared that up for Rennie right away. "Why don't you jump back in bed?" he said, glancing at her bare feet. "And put on a pair of socks. I'm not letting you get near me with those ice toes of yours."

Rennie sighed, turning her back as she crawled into the bed. She towel dried her hair and combed it out. By the time she was situated comfortably under the blankets and facing him again, he was wearing a pair of drawers and hunkered in front of the stove adding wood. The light from the fire gave a bronze cast to his hard, lithe profile. Droplets of water on his shoulders and chest captured the glow. The smooth and sleek slant of his spine drew her eye, and she watched the play of muscle and taut flesh as he lifted more wood.

Jarret closed the grate and took a few more minutes to empty the hip bath before slipping into bed. "Move over."

"I'm already against the wall."

"There's more room in my tent," he grumbled.

"It's warmer here." She bumped him with her icy feet as she stretched.

"So you say." He turned on his side toward her and drew up his knees slightly. They jostled hers. "At least you wore socks in the tent."

Rennie was quiet long enough that Jarret suspected she was on her way to sleeping. He closed his own eyes. Morning couldn't come soon enough as far as he was concerned.

"Jarret?"

He opened one eye. "Hmmm?"

"Tell me what happened to your shoulder."

Both eyes were open now. She had struck so swiftly, so cleanly, that it took him a few moments to feel the pain that accompanied her question. "You know what happened," he said. "Dee Kelly, remember? The scissors?"

"I remember," she said softly. "But after the doctor saw it you said it was all right. I knew you were in pain, but I never thought it was something that wouldn't heal itself. What did Dr. Turner really say to you?"

"He said I should treat it kindly, favor it for a while."

"But you didn't. Is that what happened?"

"More or less." He slipped one arm under his pillow, propping his head up a notch. "Why are you asking about it now?"

"I've only begun to understand it."

That surprised him. He answered carefully. "Is that so?"

"Until tonight I hadn't thought about it." She pulled back her damp hair and edged fractionally closer. "I don't mean that I'd forgotten what happened to you, only that I hadn't realized there might be some permanent injury. Have you seen a doctor since you left New York?"

"Rennie," he said, affecting an air of tiredness, "I've seen half a dozen doctors. There's nothing that can be done."

Beneath the blanket her hand unerringly found his scarred shoulder. She felt him flinch, but she didn't remove her hand. His skin was warm, her touch light. "It's so small," she said quietly. "It looks like a tiny starburst."

Jarret turned and lay on his back. He dislodged her hand, but only for a moment. Rennie's index finger traced the thin, puckered rays of the scar. "Is it really so fascinating?" he asked.

Her finger stilled. "I'm sorry," she said. "I've made you uncomfortable."

"You don't have to be touching me to do that." He

hadn't meant to be so honest. The words seemed to come out of him separate of his intention.

"Then, it doesn't matter." Her fingertip passed back and forth across the scar. "It hardly seems possible something so small could have made you so mean. I should have carried a loaded gun into the Jones Street Station. It would have served Detra right if I'd shot her."

Her fierce solution brought a grim smile. "Dee had already stabbed me," he reminded her. "But your desire for revenge is duly noted."

"You're making fun of me."

"A little." Now Jarret removed her hand and deliberately put it away from him. If she touched him again, he thought he would come out of his skin. He was rock hard. "It's over, Rennie. I told you there's nothing anyone can do."

In spite of his gritty tone, she persisted. "What is it exactly that's the problem?"

Turning his head toward her, Jarret sighed. The lines of her face were drawn in concern. She returned his regard steadily. Jarret realized that he would never wear her down, that it wasn't her way to be beaten. "You're tenacious," he said. "Do you know that?"

She nodded. "That's what everyone says. Jay Mac says Michael is determined, but I'm tenacious. She knows when to let a thing go and take the route around, but I have a tendency to bite down and hang on."

She certainly did, he thought wryly. He would have sworn he had the teeth marks to prove it. "What is it you want to know?" he asked.

"Does your shoulder hurt?"

"No."

"But sometimes you can't hold things," she said. "Like Zilly's reins. That's why you fell, isn't it?"

Jarret winced a little at the memory. There was no pleasure in recalling his clumsy attempts to regain his balance. He made an effort not to snap at her. "That's why I fell, but it wasn't because my shoulder hurt. Sometimes I have only a little feeling in my arm and hand. My fingers tingle; then they go numb. I can't always get a good grip."

Rennie found his hand under the covers. He resisted at first, then allowed her to close over his fist with both her hands. Her fingers stroked his. She drew her knees higher and raised his hand nearer her breast. Hardly aware of what she was doing, Rennie explored the ridges of his knuckles with an airy, delicate touch. "Those men I hired as guides," she said, "they made some comment about that, but I didn't understand then . . . something about you not being able to hold a gun."

"Most folks around here know something's wrong with my gun hand. In the case of Tom and Clarence, a little knowledge made them stupid."

She nodded. His hand relaxed under her touch and uncurled a fraction. "You gave up bounty hunting because of it."

"Why do you say that?"

"Jolene told me you haven't done any tracking for months."

Jarret had some choice words for Jolene, none of which he shared with Rennie. "Well, she's wrong about me giving it up. I don't go out as often as I used to is all. I'm tracking for you now, aren't I?"

Rennie recognized the truth in his words and the lie they covered. She had no interest in beating down his pride. The nature of his reluctance to bring her to the Jump was clearer now. "Yes, you are," she said. She waited a moment before pressing ahead. "When we were still at the cabin you dropped a load of wood you were carrying. Was that because your arm went numb?" She remembered clearly how angry he had been, how he had kicked the logs and stormed out of the cabin. He had gone to Bender's to drink on that occasion. "Is that why you were so angry?"

Jarret's fist closed tightly, and he almost wrested it from Rennie's hands. "Are you going to bring up every occasion where I've made a fool of myself in front of you?" he demanded.

"No," she said quickly, imploringly. "Please, Jarret, that's not—"

He barely heard her and paid no attention at all. "You've already mentioned my ignominious fall from Zilly and dropping the wood. You were lucky I didn't miss my aim at your attackers. Like I told Tom, it's a crap shoot." He went on, his voice bitter. "Then there was the time we were making love, but I understand your unwillingness to mention that. I'm sure the memories aren't any more pleasant for you than for me. You shouldn't have had your first time spoiled with a man who nearly crushed you in the frenzy."

This time when Jarret started to pull away from her Rennie held on for dear life, dragging his hand to her breast and pressing it against her skin. He could have freed himself—they both knew it—but she wasn't going to let him go without a struggle, and they both knew that as well.

"Rennie," he said, invoking her name with strained patience. He turned toward her. He could feel her heart racing beneath his captured hand. "What is it you want?"

"I want to know what you meant." She pressed her hands over his and went on earnestly. "I don't know what you're talking about . . . about you crushing me when we were . . . when we were . . ."

He used a vulgar expression. "Is that the word you're stumbling over?"

"No. You know it's not. You know it wasn't like that." Her voice rose a fraction. "We *were* making love," she

278

said. "Then, when it was over, you left so furiously. You've never told me what I did wrong. Is it any wonder that I was afraid to let you touch me again? Can you blame me for not wanting to bear that sort of humiliation a second time?"

Jarret's eyes narrowed. He stared hard at Rennie, suspicious. "Why were you humiliated?" he asked.

Rennie closed her eyes briefly, ducking his gaze. "Jarret, please . . ."

"No," he said. "You can't ignore me now, not when you've probed and pushed to just this end. Tell me why you felt humiliated."

She stared down at the hand she held. "You couldn't get away from me fast enough," she said. "You never wanted to touch me in the first place. I was the one who wouldn't let it go. Tenacious, remember?" Her low, nervous laughter was without humor. "I kept after you, and you finally gave in. It even seemed for a while that everything was as it should be. But I know I didn't pleasure you. I'm not so naive that I didn't know there was no satisfaction in it for you. How did you think that would make me feel?"

Jarret shook his head now. "Oh, Rennie," he said sadly. His fist opened up. His fingers threaded through hers. He gave her hands a little shake, willing her to listen to him. "It wasn't you. If you don't believe anything else I've ever told you, believe that. *I* was the one who withdrew, the one who decided there would be no satisfaction in it for either of us. My arm gave way, and I couldn't support myself any longer. When I fell on you . . ."

"You didn't hurt me."

"That's small comfort."

"I didn't even know there was anything wrong."

"That's because you *are* naive," he said. Her fingers were stroking his hand again. Her touch was like a warm breeze over his skin. "It isn't supposed to be like that. I

279

just went a little crazy then. I already knew I couldn't depend on my hand to draw a gun or support my aim. Some mornings I could barely carry a coffeepot let alone an armload of wood. I concentrated on two things: lifting a bottle and bedding whor—women. My experience with you shortened my list of pleasures considerably." His attempt at humor fell short. The comment was too pathetically close to the mark.

Rennie inched closer. "So at the cabin," she said softly, "when you kissed me, it was because you needed to prove something to yourself."

"No," he said. "It wasn't like that. I kissed you because your mouth was damp, your eyes were closed, and your skin was glowing. If I'd wanted to prove something to myself, I could have paid for the privilege at Bender's."

"You did," she said. The memory still had the bitter taste of betrayal. "Remember? You were with Jolene that night."

He hesitated. Finally he said, "I was with Jolene, yes, but not in the way you're thinking. We played cards. Talked. Drank a little. She's a good companion and better friend. I've been with Jolene before in exactly the way you're thinking, but not since you came to Echo Falls."

He offered the admission as if it had been torn from him. Rennie bent her head and kissed Jarret's knuckles. She leaned across the small space that separated them and kissed his naked shoulder.

Jarret's breath caught at the back of his throat. He closed his eyes. "Rennie, don't—"

"Let me," she whispered. "Please, let me."

Her breath was like another kiss on his flesh. Still, he said, "I don't need your pity."

Her lips touched the white starburst scar. "Of course you don't. It's not what I'm offering."

Her mouth was at the curve of his neck. When she moved he could feel the heat in her through her cotton nightshift. The fullness of her breasts touched his chest. He lifted his hand and threaded his fingers through her hair. Her lips sipped on his skin, tasting him in a way that sent a fireball of heat down his spine. "What is it you're offering?" he asked huskily.

"Me," she said. She raised her head and kissed the corner of his mouth. "I'm offering me."

He turned without warning, capturing her splendid mouth with his. His hand held her head immobile. The kiss simply went on. And on. When the pressure of his hand eased, Rennie lifted her mouth a fraction and drew a shaky breath. Her heart was hammering in her chest. She stared at him, at the dark, liquid centers of his eyes, at the sliver of sapphire ringing them. She was drawn into his desiring.

Rennie explored the planes and angles of his face with her mouth and fingertips. Her mouth traced his jaw, his chin. She nudged his nose with hers, teasing, then kissed him full on the mouth with almost savage passion. At her back she felt Jarret's hands slide up and down her spine, drawing her nightshirt higher by slow degrees. With characteristic impulsiveness she sat up suddenly, straddled him, and in a sweeping motion pulled the gown over her head. Jarret watched it sail over the side of the bed, and when he looked back at her he was smiling.

At first it was light and shadow that cupped the upper and lower curves of her heavy breasts. Later it was Jarret. His smile faded. His fingers were a whisper across her skin. Her breasts swelled in reaction; the sensitive rose-colored nipples hardened.

"You're lovely," he said.

She shook her head. Her dark hair fell forward over her shoulders and lay against the back of his hands. "Don't say that," she said quietly, laying a finger across his lips. "Don't ruin it."

Jarret held her wrists and drew her down to him. Gently he rolled her on her back. Her thighs cradled his arousal. "I won't say it if you don't want me to, but that doesn't mean it isn't true." Her tentative smile only confirmed his point. His kiss was tender. It touched a chord in Rennie, and she opened her heart.

Jarret's mouth left hers and trailed down the sensitive line of her neck, nibbling, teasing. The tip of his tongue swept the hollow of her throat. She arched her neck. His smile pressed against her skin, then faded as his mouth slid along her collarbone. He shifted lower. His mouth closed over her breast, and his tongue laved her nipple.

Rennie's fingers curled in his hair. She stroked him with her fingertips. The rhythm was the same as the flicking of his tongue. She pressed harder when he traded teasing for the hot suck of his mouth. It seemed he drew fire right from the surface of her skin. His palm slid over her from rib cage to hip, touching the lower swell of her breast, then the long, gentle curve of her thigh. His lips touched the damp skin just above her heartbeat, then trailed slowly to her other breast. He heard the little catch in her breath as his mouth closed over the nipple and his fingers moved between her thighs.

Rennie's legs parted slightly, urged by the insistent, intimate caress of Jarret's hand. She was not so startled by his touch there, but the sensation of it had the power to make her reel. Her fingers pressed hard into his shoulders as his exploration drew her skin taut. Tension arched her back, raising her to his touch. His mouth left her breast, alighted damply on her midriff, at her navel, then took the place of his fingers as his hands cupped her buttocks.

She said his name, but it had no force behind it, no demand that he stop. Urgency was in her breathlessness, and it drove him on as it was meant to. Rennie's heels pressed into the bedding, and her fingers curled in the sheets. She closed her eyes, and the sparks of light behind her lids gave color to the heat that licked her skin. Jarret's caress made her reach for something outside herself, a pleasure that remained maddeningly elusive even while it shimmered just in front of her. When it seemed she would never grasp it, he gave it to her.

Jarret felt her shudder, felt the tension spin out of her and into him. He drew himself up beside her, rolled on his back, and brought her on top. She lay flush against him, breathing shallowly, her head resting in the curve of his shoulder. His hard groin pressed against her belly. He stroked her hair. "Rennie?" he said huskily.

"Hmmm?"

"You can return the favor."

She tilted her head slightly and kissed the underside of his jaw. "Tell me what you want," she whispered. Her hands moved along the sides of his rib cage. She pushed herself lower, pressing kisses down the center of his chest. Her teeth pulled on the drawstring of his drawers.

It was too agonizingly slow for Jarret. He pushed at his drawers, sent them flying with the same abandon that Rennie had shown, then positioned her astride him.

She looked down at him, puzzled. Her hair spilled over her shoulders in a splendid fall of curls. Her beating heart seemed louder than her voice. "I thought you wanted my mouth," she said.

Jarret pushed aside her curtain of dark hair and cupped the creamy swell of her breasts. "I do," he said, "but here." He pointed to his mouth. When she leaned forward to kiss him Jarret's hands slid around her back and palmed her hips. She lifted at his urging and let him guide himself into her. Her kiss was hard and hungry as her hips moved, taking him in. Her mouth slipped away from his

283

as she straightened. She drew his hands to her breasts again and arched her back, moving sinuously over him as she rocked.

His thumbs passed across her nipples, and the ache there cut the razor-sharp edge between pleasure and pain. Rennie stroked his thighs, the tight flat of his belly, and the taut length of his arms. She watched his face. The firelight cast his features in bronze. The lines at the corners of his eyes deepened as his expression strained with tension. Desire had made the planes of his face tight, the substance of his stare as hard and hungry as the rest of him. She lowered herself over him, pressing her swollen breasts to his chest and the swollen outline of her lips to his mouth. She kissed him long and deeply, moving over him with sensual, feline grace that was the measure-for-measure match of her kiss. While the rise and fall of her hips stroked his arousal, it was her kiss that sent him over the edge.

Turning Rennie suddenly, Jarret drove into her hard. Her gasp excited him; the tiny catch in her breath as she sipped the air made him thrust more deeply. Her arms stretched above her, reaching for purchase at the corner of the mattress. The blankets slipped. Rennie arched. The muscles in Jarret's back bunched. She cried out. He cut it off with his mouth. A pinwheel of fire burst in her belly, then his, and Jarret spilled his seed into her.

It was the tiny, teasing kisses being pressed against her cheek and at the corner of her mouth that woke Rennie. She was wrapped in Jarret's arms, and except where she was covered by him, she was naked. So was he. They lay diagonally across the bed in the abandoned position of their lovemaking. All in all it was a satisfactory arrangement.

She smiled at him, turning so that his kiss took her mouth. It was long and leisurely, desiring but not urgent. "I fell asleep," she said.

"So did I." His hand lay just below her breast. He stroked the underside with his thumb.

"What woke you?"

"You."

"Me?"

He nodded. He raised his hand and brushed the side of her face with his fingertips. "You. I woke up wanting you again."

She reached between their bodies. Her fingers folded around him intimately, but her caress was shy, not bold. "You *do* want me," Rennie whispered. "And I want you." Her shyness vanished, replaced by a siren's smile and eager exploration. She moved lower and took him with her mouth. Jarret sucked in his breath. The deft manipulation of her lips and tongue drew out his selfish passion, doing for him what he had done for her, carrying him to the edge of the precipice more than once while the rush of pleasure lay just beyond his fingertips.

His abdomen contracted as he gave himself up to Rennie's desiring; the line of his jaw tensed. His breathing was harsh and uneven, and when Rennie kissed him on the mouth it was as if he had to draw on her for air. "My God," was what he said when she curled against him as replete as he.

"I know," she said. There was a hint of forlornness in her voice. "More skilled than a practiced whore."

Jarret's words came back to haunt him. He closed his eyes, feeling her pain as his own. "I should have never said that." His fingers sifted through her hair. "Forgive me."

Rennie sat up, pulling the sheet at her feet high enough to cover her breasts. "There's nothing to forgive," she said. *Not when you know the extent of my sins.* She searched his face. "You know you're the only man I've been with, don't you? Even when I . . ." She blushed and looked away for a moment. "I've never done that with anyone."

"I know that," he said gently.

"Do you? Then, you believe me?"

"Why is it so important?" he asked. He reached over the side of the bed and rooted around for a blanket. He found one and hitched it around his hips as he sat up. "You know I can't make the same claim."

Rennie sat up on her knees as Jarret climbed out of bed. She touched his elbow, and her eyes implored. "It just is," she said. "You can't know . . ."

Frowning now, Jarret took her hands. "What's this about, Rennie? Are you embarrassed about what you did? Pleasuring me that way?"

She shook her head. "No," she said quickly. "No, but I don't want you to think that—"

He gave her hands a little shake. "What I think is that you're the most *alive* woman I've ever known. You have nothing to apologize for. Nothing. You try so hard to be reticent and respectful and humorless, but when that surface is scratched, all hell breaks loose." He grinned at her and raised her rare smile. "Frankly, Rennie, I wouldn't have it any other way. I like what happens when you scratch back."

She threw herself into his arms, almost knocking him off his feet. "I suppose you know I love you."

Jarret's embrace tightened. His cheek rested against her curling hair. "There were hints," he said.

Rennie told herself not to expect an echoed declaration, reminded herself that she didn't deserve one. She, more than he, had done things that would forever affect their happiness. These were stolen moments. Still, when the words were whispered against her hair, close to her ear, when they drifted warmly to her consciousness and touched her soul, she felt her heart swell, her throat close, and tears gather at the corners of her eyes. He seemed to know she couldn't speak, that her composure was held together by a slender silk thread, that emotion made her tremble, and that the best thing he could do was hold her in the loving circle of his arms.

It was everything she wanted in that moment.

Rennie was stretched out along the length of Jarret's body. Her head rested in the crook of his shoulder. The flat of her hand lay against his heart. Her nightshift was bunched around her thighs, and her feet were buried comfortably under his calf. Layers of blankets sheltered them from the cold. The fire in the stove blazed warmly, and light filtered through the iron grate. Ribbons of orange light crossed their cocoon of blankets.

She was regretting telling Jarret she loved him. That hadn't been fair. She had wanted him to know more than anything, but she hadn't been fair. Rennie stared blankly at the far wall.

"What are you thinking?" he asked.

She couldn't tell him the truth. She lightly massaged his chest in a circular motion. "How did you become a bounty hunter?"

"That's what you've been thinking?"

Rennie turned her head enough to touch his musky-scented skin with her mouth. "It's what I want to know," she said.

Jarret breathed in the sweet fragrance of her hair and said quietly, "It was more by accident than design. When my parents were murdered I went after their killers."

"You were just a boy then."

"Hardly. I was twenty-two. A man's age by anyone's ruler."

"Did you find the men?"

He nodded. "It took six months, but I found them. I brought one in alive, the other dead. Daniel Border was the first man I killed. I was sick for three days."

"But you didn't give it up."

"I never got used to it either. I bring most of my men in alive."

"And the women?"

"Dee Kelly was the first woman I ever had to track. Next time I'll be smarter. Women don't fight fair."

Rennie rubbed one foot against his calf. Her fingers walked across his abdomen and fiddled with the drawstring of his drawers. "I thought you liked it that way."

"Sometimes," he said, stilling her busy hand. "Sometimes not."

"Have you ever wanted to do anything else?" she asked.

He shrugged. "I was going to save some money . . . try my hand at ranching. I thought about breeding horses, cattle." Jarret stroked her fingers. "What about you? Have you always wanted to run a railroad?"

Had she? she wondered. "I've always thought so."

"Only . . ."

She shifted, settling more comfortably against him. Her knee rested on his thigh. "Only lately I've been thinking I just wanted to be close to my father."

It was quite an admission, Jarret thought, and he understood that Rennie was only thinking aloud, testing the words and motives, searching for reasons of her life's devotion to a railroad. He remained silent, waiting.

"He was always around," she said after a moment. "He never forgot a birthday or a holiday. He was attentive and loving, and none of us have ever doubted how he adored our mother. But it seems to me that Jay Mac was a *force* in our lives, rather than a presence. He rarely asked anything of us; Jay Mac had a tendency to issue directives."

288

Rennie smiled now at the memory. "Mary Francis always accepted them to his face, then did exactly as she pleased. She was so serene in her opposition that Jay Mac barely noticed her defiance until it was a done thing. He was apoplectic when she announced she was joining the convent."

Jarret guessed. "Moira brought him around."

"That's right." She glanced up at him briefly, pleased that he understood. "People often think Mama is completely influenced by Jay Mac, but nothing could be farther from the truth. She's fierce about her convictions, and though she's stayed with Jay Mac all these years, knowing that marriage wasn't possible, I don't think Mama's ever deferred to him on any other issue."

"She's the diplomat."

Rennie nodded. "Always. Skye's been arguing about going to college this past year. She wants to travel first. I doubt Papa would be so adamantly opposed if Skye wanted to travel somewhere he considered reasonable. He'd probably permit a tour of Europe; but Skye's got it in her head she wants to see Africa, and Jay Mac says absolutely not. Of course, Skye's been just as inflexible about her wishes."

Jarret chuckled, imagining Moira in the middle between intractable Jay Mac and fiery Skye. "So your mother's negotiating with both of them."

"Exactly. It's the sort of thing that happens all the time. Maggie mostly goes her own way. She's quieter than the rest of us, almost always an observer in any fray. She talks about being a doctor, but Jay Mac hasn't been very supportive. He's always wanted us to be independent, but when we are he's a little uncomfortable with our decisions."

"He couldn't have been pleased with Michael's position at the *Chronicle*."

"God, no," Rennie said vehemently. "Michael and Papa have always been at loggerheads. She resents him almost as much as she loves him. It's the very rare occasion that she asks him for anything. It wasn't until she met Ethan that she began to have some appreciation for how Mama feels about Jay Mac. Before that Michael was quick to judge them both." Rennie's faint smile was poignant. "You saw them at Michael's wedding. It's plain to anyone with eyes in their head how much they love each other."

Jarret agreed. If Jay Mac hadn't been married when Moira came to work in his home, if she had been Protestant or he had been Catholic, if they had cared a little less about certain conventions and a little more about others, perhaps they would have had a last name in common and five daughters who did not have to struggle with the brand of illegitimacy. He remembered what his own parents had shared, and he felt something inside him stir, a certain longing for permanency and commitment drift through the edges of his thoughts. "What about you and Jay Mac?" he asked quietly.

"I'm not like the others," she said. There was regret in her voice. "I can't listen quietly, then do as I wish like Mary Francis. I don't know how to withdraw like Maggie. I can't wear him down like Skye, and I care too much about pleasing him to charge ahead like Michael."

"I've seen you stand up to him, Rennie," said Jarret. The back of his finger trailed across her cheek and along her jaw. "You challenge him in ways different from your sisters, but you do it."

"Shaking in my shoes."

Jarret laughed. "I bet Jay Mac doesn't know that." He gave a tendril of hair at her temple a slight tug as he wound it around his finger. "What is it that you want from him?"

"I want him to approve of me, of my choices. I want

him to respect my work and acknowledge my skill."

He paused in playing with her hair, thoughtful, his brows drawn together. "Rennie, did you tell your father the problems with putting down rails at Queen's Point?"

Rennie was caught off guard. "I wasn't talking about that."

"Weren't you?" he asked. "What did he say when you showed him your work and your conclusions?"

Behind her lids Rennie's eyes ached with unshed tears. Her voice was barely audible. "He said I should put my own house in order before I tell him how to run his."

Jarret's arm slipped around her shoulder. "I see," he said lowly. He remembered quite clearly listening to Rennie explain her work on the Queen's Point rails, her judgment that the surveyors had been wrong. He also recalled that she was not quite as confident in her abilities as he would have thought, that she was not prepared to argue convincingly in support of her own conclusions. "He's decided to trust Hollis and the surveyors, is that it? The tracks will be laid along the wrong route."

"It's already begun. The work started months ago." She sensed Jarret was going to argue with her and went on. "He's seen me make a mess of too many things to trust my assessment."

"But surely those were personal, not professional." Jarret couldn't imagine that Jay Mac had made a success of every business venture he touched by confusing the two.

"I'm his daughter," Rennie said. "There are different rules. It's what we all fight. I just do it more clumsily than the others." Her low laughter was humorless. "The irony, of course, is that I'm the one who tried to join the battle on his side. Mary Francis chose the convent; Michael, the *Chronicle*. Maggie *will* be a doctor someday, and Skye will go to the moon if she has a mind to. I thought Northeast

291

Rail would bind Jay Mac and me. Instead we spar all the time."

"Your sisters are all doing what they want to do," Jarret said. "Can you say the same?"

Rennie did not answer immediately. She knew what Jarret was asking, and she wasn't prepared to respond in that same vein. Instead she raised herself up, folding her arms on Jarret's chest, and met his gaze squarely. "Right now," she said, "I'm doing *exactly* what I want to do."

When she leaned forward and kissed him full on the mouth, Jarret was glad she was.

"You're awake," she said. She whispered because she wanted to keep dawn at bay. "Does this mean we're leaving soon?"

"It means I'm thinking about it."

Rennie stretched lazily, then curled like a contented cat. She fit her bottom snugly against Jarret's groin. "Think about it all you like. I want to sleep."

"You'll understand if I don't really believe you." He lifted the hair at the back of her neck and nuzzled. She murmured her contentment. The sound of it vibrated against his lips. He smiled, breathing in her fragrance, and kissed her softly.

"Hmmm."

"Like that, do you?"

"Hmmm-mmm."

Jarret's hands slipped around her and cupped her breasts through her nightgown. His thumbs massaged her nipples, provoking them to hardness. She shifted, rubbing her backside against him. "Like that, do you?"

He playfully nipped her neck in response. "There are some things I can't hide from you."

Rennie turned in his arms. "You're not going to let me

sleep, are you?" Even as she spoke Jarret was raising her shift above her thighs.

"That's what I said a few hours ago," he reminded her. "And you didn't listen then."

"That's because you're a very lucky man."

"Thank God." He kissed her mouth with breathtaking thoroughness. Rennie pushed at his drawers and took him into her hands. It took some adjustments, some laughter, but then she was guiding him into her, taking all of him, accommodating the fullness and the heat, and matching his rhythm.

Urgency swept them. Her mouth slanted across his; her tongue ran along the ridged line of his teeth, pressing entry in the way he had pressed his. His lips moved over hers, and he tasted her need as if it were a tangible thing, like succulent oranges or sweet, ripe cherries. The flavor of her kiss was like the fragrance of her hair, capable of reaching him, arousing him just below the level of his consciousness on some deeply felt primal plane.

He was a pressure inside her and a presence all around her. She felt his arms across her back, his legs flush to hers. His mouth touched her throat, her shoulders, her breasts. His skin was warm. Tension arced between them, and the air was dry and crackling. She thought they might spin wildly out of control like Roman candles.

Then they did.

Rennie listened to their breathing slow in unison. She touched her thudding heart as though she could calm it from outside her chest. She glanced at Jarret. He was watching her, the black centers of his eyes slowly receding in the aftermath of their loving. Her shadowed smile appeared slowly. "That was quite something," she said softly, a little dazed.

He nodded, more than a little dazed himself. He had never experienced anything like he had just shared with

293

Rennie. The intensity of the pleasure had driven him hard against her and into her. "I didn't hurt you, did I?"

She shook her head. "No . . . not at all." She touched his shoulder just above the starburst scar. "I think I bit you," she said, equally surprised and embarrassed.

Jarret's brows rose, and he tilted his head to get a look at his shoulder. The faint indentations of her teeth were visible. "I'll be damned," he said. He turned, and his slow grin transformed his face. "You *are* tenacious."

Chapter Eleven

Traveling together was a different experience for them now. Jarret, although he held to his promise of not making allowances for Rennie, was more inclined to ask rather than order. Rennie rode abreast of him often, no longer wary of interjecting the occasional question. The journey had become something to be shared and would never be remembered from the framework of a single person's recollection or viewpoint.

They rode on opposite sides of a narrow, rushing stream with the packhorse following Jarret. The run of icy water was a steady and pleasant whisper in their ears, interrupted only by the crunch of snow beneath the horses' hooves. There was almost no wind. The air was dry and bitterly cold, and the sun offered light, but little in the way of warmth. By the time Jarret decided to stop for the afternoon meal, Rennie felt as if she'd been riding for days.

They sought shelter in the shadowed adit of an abandoned mine. Icicles hung like a fringe of crystal beads from the entrance beam. Rennie ducked beneath them to enter; Jarret broke them off.

"But they were so pretty," she said.

Jarret looked at her as if she'd lost her mind. "You might feel differently with one of them sticking in your back."

Wincing at the image that presented, Rennie said, "I'll remember that." She glanced around, stamping her feet in place to keep warm. Her arms were crossed in front of her, and her gloved hands were buried in the crooks of her armpits. "There aren't any bears in here, are there?"

Jarret unwrapped the long, woolen scarf around his neck and used it to lasso Rennie. He tugged on both ends and pulled her closer. "How would I know? I haven't seen any more of this place than you."

Her eyes widened. "Shouldn't you . . . you know . . . look around a little bit?"

He settled a leisurely kiss on her mouth, raised his head, bussed her on the tip of her reddened nose, and rested his forehead against hers. "You look around for those bears. I'll get wood for a fire." He left his scarf lying around her shoulders and disappeared out the entrance.

Rennie stared after him. The heat of his kiss lingered. She touched her mouth, felt the shape, and realized she was smiling. "I'll stay just where I am, thank you very much."

Their lunch was rabbit stew and pots of hot coffee. Rennie took Jarret's advice and savored the last of their carrots and potatoes. Dinner would be beans and jerky.

Rennie scraped her plate clean. "Maybe we'll have bear meat tonight," she said. "That would flavor those old beans."

Above his steaming mug of coffee Jarret's eyes were amused. "You planning on killing yourself a bear?"

"I thought you might."

"You know where one is?"

She pointed to the dark recesses of the adit where the mine tunnel took a turn. "Hibernating."

"Then, it's hardly fair to wake him," Jarret said, playing along. "We'll let sleeping bears lie."

Rennie wrinkled her nose at him and gathered their plates and utensils. She wiped them clean with snow and a rag, then packed them away. Returning to the fallen timber beam that was her seat, Rennie poured herself the last of the coffee. It was slightly bitter but wonderfully hot.

"We're traveling fairly quickly," she said carefully, swallowing her own anxiety. "I don't recall you pausing but once or twice to look for anything. Are we going someplace in particular or haven't you found what you'd hoped?"

Jarret's forearms rested against his knees, and he held his mug in both hands. "Snows have come and gone a dozen times since the accident," he told her. "The first rescue party to reach the wreck trampled most everything in sight, and Ethan's men scoured wider ground when they searched. There's nothing that I'm likely to find now."

"But you found Jay Mac's spectacles."

"That was dumb luck, Rennie. I doubt lightning's going to strike twice."

She nodded. "Then, you have somewhere in particular we're headed, is that it?"

"That's it." He sipped his coffee. "If Jay Mac was lying near where I found his spectacles when the first rescue efforts were made, it's understandable that he was missed. It would have been dark by the time the surviving passengers and crew on No. 412 could have reached the wreckage. They probably took a route similar to the one we did, bypassing Jay Mac altogether. When Ethan and his search party came to the site days later, Jay Mac had already wandered away . . . or perhaps he was taken

297

away . . . I don't know." He finished off his coffee. His sapphire eyes narrowed slightly as he studied Rennie's pale features and gauged her weariness.

"There's an old prospector in these parts named Dancer Tubbs," he said. "He's not like Duffy Cedar, so don't make the comparison in your own mind. Dancer's been on his own for too many years, more hermit than human. He doesn't have much time for other folks, and he makes a point of avoiding them. The last time I saw Dancer he held me off his claim with a shotgun." Jarret's grin was self-mocking as he gave her a knowing look. "I can tell you, Rennie, I remember more about that shotgun than I do about Dancer."

"But that's where we're going?" she asked.

He nodded. "Dancer moves around in these mountains like a shadow. He knows what happens here, who comes and goes."

"Why didn't Ethan seek him out?"

"I doubt if Ethan knows about him. I told you, the man keeps to himself. I first met him six years ago when I was tracking Brownwood Riley. I had a sense I was being followed — for a time I thought it was Riley himself, circling back on me. I guess it unnerved me. I got a little skittish and so did my horse. I took a spill with him on some rocks. I don't know how long I was out, but when I came around Dancer was there. He shot my bay and reset my dislocated shoulder. Hardly said a word to me. I wouldn't have been surprised if he'd shot me and set my horse's leg.

"He's a hard man, Rennie, and harder to look on. I want you to know that at the outset. He's missing most of his left ear, and the same side of his face is just a scar. As soon as I was healed he sent me out on my own. I didn't have a horse and only a few supplies, but the alternative was a bullet. He won't want you staring at him—he may not even let us get close—but if Jay Mac is alive and somewhere in these mountains, Dancer knows about it."

Rennie swallowed the last mouthful of coffee. "How far are we from his claim?" she asked.

"Last I knew he built himself a little cabin. We'll reach it tomorrow morning."

She set down her cup. Rennie's gaze was level, her mouth set in a flat, serious line. "Then, we should have a plan."

Jarret wasn't listening to her. His eyes were locked on the ominous, amorphous shadow behind Rennie. He raised his hand slowly toward her. His voice was taut and quiet. "Take my hand, Rennie."

She never understood what made her obey without question. Her fingers slipped through his. In the next second she was being dragged full tilt out of the mine, then propelled to one side by Jarret's rough and urgent push. She fell face first in the snow, rolled, and came up on her hands and knees. Spitting out a mouthful of snow, Rennie's head swiveled around, and her eyes darted anxiously. She saw Jarret grab his carbine from the leather sheath secured to Zilly's saddle. He slapped the mare hard on her flank. She scrambled out of the way as Jarret pivoted toward the adit and took aim.

Rennie followed the swing of the carbine. Her eyes flashed on the maple stock, the hammer, the silver-plated lever and trigger guard. In a single panicked glance she took in the unwavering length of the barrel as Jarret steadied his sights. She saw the bear in the same moment he did.

The brown bear cub shook his head sluggishly, raising one paw as if to wipe the sleep from his eyes. He looked around, batted one of the dripping icicles that Jarret had missed, then shied away from the clatter it made when it shattered against rock.

"It's just a baby," Rennie whispered, entranced by the bear's antics and relieved by its size.

If Jarret could have rolled his eyes *and* kept his sights, he would have done so. "It's Mama I'm worried about," he said. The cub poked his head out again and, after a cautious look at both Rennie's and Jarret's still figures, lumbered lethargically out of the mine.

Laggard, Rennie thought. Out of the corner of her eye she saw Jarret lower his gun slowly and scoop up a handful of snow. Guessing his intent, she did the same, packing her snowball so that it neatly fit the palm of her hand. Without a word passing between them they simultaneously fired their missiles.

The cub took one shot on the nose and another on his flank and beat a hasty retreat for the sanctuary of the mine shaft.

Jarret helped Rennie to her feet. "Let's go before Mama decides she wants to play." He gave her a leg up on Albion, sheathed the carbine, and mounted Zilly. Their own departure was no less hasty than the bear cub's.

Rennie rode abreast of Jarret. She glanced over her shoulder at the mine entrance. "You know we left our mugs back there," she told him.

Jarret pulled up on Zilly's reins. "I'll wait here," he said. "You go on back and get them."

Rennie pulled down the scarf that covered the lower half of her face. She poked her tongue out at him.

"Don't get sassy in this weather. You're likely to freeze that way." He gave Zilly a light kick and started off again.

Rennie thought there might be some merit to his warning. She raised the scarf and followed. It was enough that he knew she was laughing.

They made camp that evening in the natural shelter of some rocks. The tent was secured to the scrub pines, and they built a fire big enough to feel the heat inside.

"You're going to have to stop laughing sometime," he said. They were sitting up inside the tent, her body tucked between his raised legs, her back leaning against his chest. Jarret gave Rennie half his jerky. "Here, eat this."

Rennie gnawed on the dried meat. It wasn't any easier to swallow the food than it was to swallow her laughter. "It's just we were both so ready for some terrifying beast and then . . ." She hiccupped. "Excuse me." She caught her breath and went on, "And out came . . . out came this roly-poly sluggard baby bear. The poor thing was more afraid of our snowballs than your carbine."

"I thought you weren't the Dennehy with a sense of humor," he said dryly.

"I'm not."

He made a disbelieving sound at the back of his throat. "You didn't really know that bear was there the whole time, did you?"

Rennie's dark, feathery brows lifted. She nudged him with her elbow. "I'm not completely daft."

"I know." He kissed the crown of her head. "Tell me about that plan of yours, the one our menacing bear cub interrupted."

Rennie explained her idea, pleased that Jarret listened without interruption. When he heard the whole of it, he wasn't immediately criticizing, but thoughtful.

301

"That could work," he said finally. "You know, Rennie, there are no guarantees. Jay Mac may not be alive. Dancer Tubbs may only be able to lead us to a grave or he may not know anything at all. Are you prepared for that?"

Rennie was silent a long time before she answered. She thought about her journey west, the angry battle with Hollis over her right to leave, the teary and troubled face of her mother as she said goodbye. Mary Francis had said a prayer for her. Skye and Maggie had accompanied her to the train station, their faces pale and tense, supportive but uncertain she was making the right decision. In Denver Michael and Ethan had tried to dissuade her from going any farther. She had heard their arguments but couldn't find the logic in them. She had it between her teeth, this sense that Jay Mac was still alive, and she would not, *could* not, let it go.

"How can I be?" she asked with painful honesty. "I've come all this way because I've hoped for a different ending." His hands were folded against her middle, and Rennie laid hers over them. She turned her head and rubbed her cheek against his shoulder. "But I'm glad you're with me," she whispered. "I'll try not to make you sorry you brought me."

Jarret rocked her gently, and when she was asleep he laid her down and tucked the blankets around her, then himself against her. "You couldn't make me sorry," he said, smoothing the back of her silky hair. "Not about this."

Dancer Tubbs tracked the riders for two miles. The man was familiar; his companion was not. He scratched the whiskerless, scarred side of his face, searching for a

name to put to the man. He had a vague memory of
setting a shoulder years ago and a more recent recollection of going toe to toe, barrel to barrel, with his shotgun and the bounty hunter's carbine. "Sullivan," he
muttered to himself. "Damn Irish just walk on any
man's land."

Dancer's eyes shifted to the second rider. Even from
his position in the rocks above them, Dancer could see
it was a woman. A deep crease formed between his
brows as he frowned. She was swaying more in her saddle, leaning weakly forward as though she couldn't keep
her balance. Occasionally Sullivan would reach over and
steady her, but she always sagged limply when he removed his arm.

Dancer lowered his gun but kept track of their
progress. They were headed right for his cabin. "Tres-
passers," he mumbled. His damaged vocal chords gave
his voice a guttural, raspy quality. "Damn Irish squat-
ters." He looked back at his iron gray gelding. "They
think I'm running a boardin'house?" he asked. The gelding pawed the ground nervously, not used to Dancer's
rough voice.

The prospector looked back at the travelers. He
watched Sullivan finally give up trying to steady his
companion and simply pull her onto his own saddle.
She went without protest, for all purposes too weak to
mind the discomfort of riding double. Dancer swore
softly and spit. He put his weapon away and mounted.
It wouldn't hurt to get a little closer and take another
look.

"Do you think he's seen us?" Rennie whispered against
Jarret's coat.

303

"There's no knowing for sure," he said. "He's around here somewhere, though. The hair's standing up on the back of my neck."

"Are you afraid?" she asked.

"I'd be a damn fool if I weren't. A good sense of fear keeps you cautious. The trick is not to let it overwhelm you."

It was too late for Rennie to learn that lesson. Her heart was slamming against her breast, and the chill she felt in her bones had little to do with the cold. Her stomach roiled and she moaned softly. "I think I'm going to be sick."

"Good," he said practically. "It fits the plan." But he held her more securely just the same.

Dancer Tubbs used his gelding to block the narrow trail a mile before his cabin. When Rennie and Jarret rounded the curve they were met squarely by the muzzle of Dancer's Winchester.

Rennie had steeled herself to face the man but never quite believed the reality could be worse than her imaginings. It was. The scars on Dancer's face were set in white relief against his skin, like a hundred twisted webs stacked thinly on one another. His half ear was curled and flattened against his head. The left side of his mouth was pulled taut in a perpetually savage grin. His beard grew down from the right but only covered three quarters of his face. It was thick and ill-kempt, as black as boot polish and long enough to reach the second button of his woolen blue-gray overcoat. A gold braid epaulet dangled from his right shoulder. A saber dangled at his waist.

Rennie tried not to show her alarm, or worse, her

pity. Fear simply knotted up inside her, making it impossible to breathe, and she felt a familiar tide of shadows lapping at the edges of her consciousness. Jarret was holding her too tightly. She tried to tell him. When he realized what was happening it was too late. Rennie slumped forward in a faint.

Dancer's laughter was a high-pitched cackle that sounded as if it were breaking in the back of his throat. He made a stabbing motion with his rifle in Jarret's direction. "You shoulda told her about me, Sullivan. This ol' face of mine sets 'em swoonin'."

Jarret felt a moment's relief that Dancer Tubbs remembered him. He needed every second for negotiations, not introductions. "She's not the kind of woman that's put off by a pretty face, Dancer. She's sickening for something."

"That so?" he asked suspiciously.

"See for yourself." Jarret raised Rennie's chin, lifting her face for Dancer's inspection. He noticed it was obligingly pale.

"What's wrong with her?"

"I don't know. She started complaining last night. I thought it was a ruse, but it appears I was wrong."

One of Dancer's eyebrows arched. He pointed with the rifle again. "Eh? What's this about a ruse? What do you mean? Is she runnin' from you?"

Jarret felt Rennie stir in his arms. He didn't let his relief show. "There's a bounty on her. Three hundred dollars."

"How's that? What'd she do?" He cackled again. "Robbery or murder?"

"Murder. Took leave of her senses one evening and stabbed her husband to death."

Dancer considered that. "He probably deserved it.

305

Don't know many men who don't. Where you takin' her?"

"Denver. That's where I'll get the reward."

The prospector's teeth were bared in a parody of a thoughtful smile. "Maybe I'll kill you and take the bounty myself."

Jarret shook his head. He felt Rennie tense, and a warning squeeze of his fingers was enough to keep her still and silent. "You wouldn't do that, Dancer."

"How's that again?" he asked, his face reddening everywhere but in the web of scars. "And what's to stop me?"

"You're a healer," Jarret called back, inching his horse ahead. "That's why I brought her to you, because you can help her."

"So you can take her back and let her swing from a rope? Seems like a waste of my time."

Jarret was silent, not wanting to overstate his case. He let Dancer think about it.

The prospector fixed his stare on Rennie. He lowered his Winchester by slow degrees. "All right," he said reluctantly, "but you can't stay a minute past her being well."

Jarret nodded. "Agreed. We'll stay only until she can travel again."

Dancer put the weapon away, gave Jarret a brief nod binding the agreement, then swung his horse around.

Urging Zilly forward, Jarret caught up to Dancer. They rode single file until the path widened. A corridor of pines sheltered them. "Have you seen that train wreck by the Jump?" asked Jarret.

"Could be." He glanced sideways at Jarret. "You travel up this way from there? Seems like you been goin' a mite out of your way to get to Denver."

"Don't I know it." Jarret propped Rennie up. Her head flopped forward like a rag doll's. "She's led me a merry chase."

"Don't seem like she'd be able to survive long in these mountains on her own."

"You're seein' the truth of that right now. She would have died of exposure if I hadn't finally caught up to her."

Dancer's mouth puckered whitely as he pursed his lips in thought. His clear, frost blue eyes would have been uncommon in any face, but in one so disfigured they were especially remarkable. Like twin points of searing light, they burned Jarret with their heat. "You got a mighty poor way of makin' a livin', bounty hunter, trackin' folks down only so's they die in civilized country." He gave a short bark of laughter and shook his head slowly. "Thank God I been saved from civilization."

There wasn't anything Jarret wanted to say to that. He stayed abreast of Dancer Tubbs in silence.

The prospector's cabin was built with the timber that had been cleared to make room for it. It was situated on a small knoll, protected by towering pines and aspens on three sides and a wide, shallow stream on the fourth. They splashed through the stream and rode up to the lean-to, where Dancer hitched the horses. Jarret pretended to steady Rennie while he dismounted then helped her slide down into his arms.

"You go on," Dancer said. "Take her inside. I'll see to the horses and your supplies."

Jarret hefted Rennie and carried her to the door. He pushed it open with his good shoulder, and when he stepped inside he let her drop.

"Well, thank you very much," she whispered, stumbling on her feet.

Shaking out his arm, Jarret said, "You're lucky I didn't pitch you in the snow."

"Your arm?"

"Hmm-mm." He didn't give it another thought. He worked his fingers, folding and unfolding them as he looked around the cabin. There was a stone hearth that Dancer used for heat and cooking. The prospector couldn't have been bothered with amenities like a stove. There was also no pump, which meant water was hauled from the stream. The furniture was pine and had been crafted with considerable care. The table surface was smooth and cornered cleanly with hard right angles. Two high-backed ladder chairs had been sanded in a way that brought out the wood grain. Pots and kettles hung on the wall near the fireplace, and a colorful rag quilt covered the bed. Jarret's eyes swung from the bed to the ladder which led to the loft. He was going to investigate what use Dancer had for the loft when he heard the prospector's approach. He gave Rennie a push in the direction of the bed.

Rennie lay on her side on top of the quilt, her knees raised slightly toward her chest and her arms folded across her middle. It was not so difficult to pretend she was sick when disappointment and defeat gnawed at her insides with the power of a living thing.

She had not fully realized her own expectations until she stood on the threshold of Dancer's cabin and saw nothing of her father. She had warned Jarret she wasn't prepared for that eventuality, and she wasn't. No matter how unreasonable the prospect, Rennie had always held a different vision in her mind's eye, one that had her stepping into her father's outstretched arms and being congratulated for her persistence and single-minded determination.

Rennie's soft moan gave sound to the ache in her heart. It was quite real.

Dancer glanced from Rennie to Jarret. "I left your supplies in the lean-to. You go get what you need." He took off his gloves and dropped them on the table. "I'll see about brewing something for her. I got a few herbs that might turn the trick."

Jarret did not want to leave Rennie alone, but he couldn't afford to let his reluctance show. He stepped outside.

Dancer waited until the door closed before he shrugged out of his coat. "That man don't trust you," he said. "He thinks you're gonna get up and walk away." He looked at Rennie thoughtfully. "Could be he's right."

Rennie's eyes fluttered open. Dancer was stroking the ends of his long, black beard. She made the pain she felt work in her favor, but didn't know if it would be enough. She was no actress and never before had any cause to want to be. "I'd like to walk away," she said raggedly, wetting her dry lips. She winced as though seized by another stomach cramp. "But I can't."

"Could be you're tryin' to fool me," he said, turning away. He rummaged through the open shelves, shuffling jars and bottles and tins until he had what he wanted. By the time he had everything set on the table, Jarret had returned to the cabin. Dancer didn't bother looking up as Jarret swung a chair around and straddled it. "She's still here," he said.

"I see that."

Dancer pinched some herbs and stems from each of the tins and ground them together in a porcelain mortar. He hefted the kettle on the hook in the fireplace and found it was empty. "This needs fillin'," he said, handing it to Jarret. When Jarret was gone Dancer placed the grounds in a tin tea strainer. "You know, ma'am," he said in his raspy, damaged voice, "I could kill him afore he steps inside."

Rennie sucked in her breath in reaction, then tried to cover it by curling in a tighter ball. She was afraid to look at Dancer to gauge the effectiveness of her playacting, so she kept her eyes squeezed shut.

Dancer tapped the tea strainer against the edge of the table, waiting for Jarret's return, and continued to subject Rennie to his intense blue-white stare.

Jarret knocked snow off his boots by kicking the door jamb. He held out the kettle for Dancer. "Do you need more wood?"

"Got plenty," Dancer said, taking the kettle. "Put your coat on that peg over yonder and then take the lady's coat. You might put her under the quilt, get her dry and warm." He hung the kettle on the hook and poked casually at the fire, raising the flames. "I offered to shoot you for her, just so's she could get away. I guess she ain't much interested in that right now. We'll have to see what she thinks about it when she's feelin' better."

Jarret finished helping Rennie under the covers. Out of Dancer's sight he gave her hand a reassuring squeeze. "It will be something to look forward to."

Dancer's breaking laughter filled the tiny cabin with sound.

Straddling the chair again, Jarret laid his forearms along the top rail and rested his chin on the back of his hands. "You know much about that train wreck?" he asked indifferently.

"Could be." Dancer tilted his own chair against the wall while he waited for the water to boil. His feet dangled off the floor, so he hooked his heels on one of the leg supports. "That's the second time you mentioned the wreck. Why you so interested?"

Jarret shrugged. "It's kind of a curiosity, don't you think? Not much happens in these parts. Mountains must have been swarming with people for a while."

"Damn near had a parade goin' through here," Dancer grumbled.

"No one bothered you, did they?"

"Ain't many people know where I am." He gave Jarret a sour look. "Can think of about two others save you that coulda found me on purpose."

"Did you ever go down to the wreck?"

Dancer scratched his beard. "Now, what cause would I have to do that? Got no use for pokin' my nose where it don't belong." He tipped the chair forward, landing lightly on his feet, and used a towel to unhook the kettle. He set the tea strainer in a chipped, thick-lipped mug and poured the hot water. "I heard the crash," he said, setting the kettle aside. Fragrant steam rose from the cup. "Seemed like it echoed for near on five minutes. I took a look-see for myself, but folks from the train were already takin' care of it by the time I got there. No sense in hangin' 'round after that."

He slid the mug across the table to Jarret. "You give it to her. She might not want me touchin' her."

Rennie opened her eyes now and made a weak attempt to sit up. "No," she said, her voice almost as throaty as Dancer's. "I'd rather have it from you."

Dancer's eyes widened. "Whooooee," he said, slapping the table. "She don't trust your no-account self." He picked up the mug and carried it over to the bed. "You have to sit up, ma'am. Can't take this down unless you're sittin' up."

Rennie let Dancer help her. She pushed back hair that had come loose from the ribbon at her nape, then accepted the mug. Raising it gingerly to her lips, she sipped. Simultaneous to the brew burning her tongue, the steaming fragrance cleared her head. Her eyes widened a little at the effect.

Dancer chuckled at her surprise. "Got a kick, don't it? Go on. It's good for you." He waited until she had finished all of it. "Now you just put yourself down again. You mind if I touch your head, ma'am?"

Rennie shook her head. She made certain she looked him squarely in the face, her eyes unafraid and not repulsed. The pads of his fingers were calloused and rough, but his touch was gentle. He turned his hand over and laid his fingers across her forehead.

"You're cool enough," he said. "Don't suppose you'll be needin' more than a day's rest afore he's ready to take you outta here." He straightened and spoke to Jarret. "I got work to do at my claim. Just let her sleep. If I remember rightly, you're a fair to middlin' cook. You might fix dinner as payment."

When he was gone Rennie sat up. She tucked in the tails of her shirt and refastened the ribbon in her hair. "What are we going to do now?" she asked wearily. "We got close enough to talk to him, but Jay Mac isn't here. Why didn't you ask him straight out if he knew anything about my father?"

"Because he doesn't trust us yet. It's his nature to be suspicious. He's not entirely certain you're ill, and he can't figure out if you're pretending so you can get rid of me or if we're both pretending to get near him. If he knows something, he may not tell us, and that's worse than him not knowing anything at all."

Rennie pushed her legs over the side of the bed. Her shoulders were hunched and her head bowed. "I just thought . . ."

The chair scraped against the floor as Jarret moved to sit beside her. He put an arm around her shoulders and let her lean against him. "I know what you thought. Let's play it out a little longer and see what happens." Jarret's eyes strayed to the two chairs at the table and then to the loft. "It's too soon to jump to conclusions one way or the other."

She nodded. Her forehead rubbed against his shoulder. Jarret lifted her face and met her eyes. She watched his glance drop to her mouth and linger there. He bent his head and kissed her with sweet poignancy.

Jarret drew back and studied her face. Her tear-washed emerald eyes glistened; her mouth was invitingly parted. He cupped the side of her face and ran his thumb along her lips. "Trust me, Rennie. I can't make any promises about the outcome, but trust me to be doing what's best."

"I do."

He released her and stood. "Why don't you see what Dancer's got stocked in his larder while I have a look in the loft? Set out what you want me to make for dinner. Make certain you look in his dirt cellar. He's bound to have some vegetables in there. I'll get the meat from the curing shed out back."

Rennie wondered what Jarret expected to find in the loft, so while he went to the curing shed she climbed the ladder herself. There were a few trunks, all of them filled with clothes or blankets and the few odd treasures. A feather tick, much like the one Jarret had in his loft, took up most of the floor space. Unlike the smoothly made bed below, no attempt had been made to straighten the covers here. They were lumped together at the foot of the tick.

Shrugging, Rennie climbed down, and when Jarret

313

came back she was rooting through the dirt cellar, picking out the potatoes and turnips that she wanted for their stew. She handed them up to him, then let him pull her out. She saw him shake out his right arm again, but made no comment. It seemed that since his fall from Zilly, he had been having more trouble with it. "Anything interesting in the loft?" she asked.

"Not a thing," he said with forced nonchalance. He gathered up the vegetables, dropped them on the table, and looked around for a knife. "How about pouring some water from that kettle into one of those pots?"

Rennie did as she was asked, slopping water all the way from the fireplace to the table. She looked at Jarret innocently when he scowled at her mess. "Mrs. Cavanaugh hardly ever lets me help in the kitchen. I suppose I'm clumsy at it."

He leveled her with an arch look. "More likely you're clumsy at it because you don't want to help."

"Could be," she said, imitating Dancer's terse response. Rennie sorted through the prospector's larder and laid out spices and seasonings. "I'd check everything twice before you add it to the stew. I don't know what some of these things are. We could poison ourselves." She held each of the open tins and spice jars under Jarret's nose while he continued to peel and slice the potatoes.

"Smells about right," he said after approving all of them.

Rennie put the lids in place and sat down. "How did his face get that way?"

"Mine explosion. It happened a long time ago. Dancer was among the first group of men out here after placer gold was discovered in fifty-eight. At least that's what I've learned from the few others who remember him. He didn't know much about mining and even less about explosives. There was no dynamite back then, and nitroglycerine was all a serious miner had to use. You probably know how unstable nitro is."

"I've had occasion to use it myself."

Jarret's dark blue eyes narrowed, and his brow creased. He looked hard at Rennie, then at the trail of spilled water, then at Rennie again. "Amazing," he said softly, shaking his head.

"Well, I did."

"Oh, I believe you. It's just amazing, that's all." He pushed the turnips and onions in her direction and gave her the knife. "Slice these and not your fingers. I'll cut the venison."

She wrinkled her nose at him but accepted the task. "So Dancer's stayed to himself all these years since the accident?"

"That's right. He accepts a gift now and again from someone who's been helped by him, but he's rarely ever out among people. You can see there's not much around here that came from town."

"Was he a doctor before he came to find gold?"

"Not likely. What he knows about healing, he either learned on his own or was taught by Indians."

"What about that coat he was wearing? And the scabbard? Did he fight in the war?"

"I don't think so. The explosion injured him before then. He probably picked it off some poor frozen deserter who wandered out this way. It adds a little to that madness he has about him."

It certainly did. Dancer's harsh, almost violent laughter was another aspect of it. His damaged, grating voice that sounded like sand over glass completed the effect. "He was gentle when he touched me," she said softly.

315

"There's that side of him. It's what brought us this far, but don't believe he was just whistling when he said he'd kill me so you could go. I think he might do it."

"Jarret! But you told him I was a murderer. Why would he do that?"

Jarret laid his knife down and held Rennie's eyes for a long time. The set of his features was solemn as he searched her face. "Don't you know what a man would do for your smile?"

Rennie looked away. "Don't say that."

"Why not? It's true."

She shook her head, began slicing an onion, and almost immediately cut her finger. Sad tears, pained tears, onion tears—they all stung her eyes. She fought for a watery smile. "See what you made me do?" she asked shakily.

Jarret had only to say her name and the floodgates opened. He came around the table and drew her to her feet. He wrapped his handkerchief around her finger, holding it in place while he pulled her against him. His shirt absorbed her tears. It was more than a minute before she exhausted herself.

"I'm sorry," she said, sniffling. She swiped at her eyes with her bandaged finger. "I suppose I'm at the end of my tether."

"Since it's stretched from New York City to Juggler's Jump, I suppose that's understandable."

A shadow smile lifted the corners of her mouth. "You know the right thing to say."

"Not always," he said, raising her face. "A moment ago that wasn't the case. Aren't I allowed to think you're beautiful, or am I just not allowed to say so?"

"I'm not used to it," she said, her eyes dropping away

from his. "It feels as if you're having a secret laugh at my expense."

Without even realizing it he gave her a small shake. "Nothing could be farther from the truth."

"It doesn't help me hear better."

"What?" he asked. "What are you talking about?"

"You're shaking me," she explained patiently. "It doesn't help me hear any better."

"Oh, God." He looked down at his hands on her upper arms and let her go altogether. "Rennie, I've never made any secret about finding things you do amusing. You can't carry water five feet without spilling it, but you've handled nitro. You can't carry a tune worth a damn, but you have the most melodious voice. You're smart as a whip when it comes to *things,* yet you make the damndest choices when it comes to your own life. I've never known a woman as unconcerned about her appearance as you, but you couldn't make yourself any more attractive to me than you are right now."

He brushed her cheek with the back of his hand and looped one loose strand of hair around his finger. "It's something inside of you that touches me, Rennie, and it comes out in your eyes, in your skin, and especially your smile. If no other men have ever said that to you, then it's because you intimidated the hell out of them."

Rennie rocked back on her heels and blinked owlishly. "Oh, my."

Jarret tapped her on the nose with his index finger. "Exactly."

She sat down slowly. Jarret skirted the table to his own chair. She picked up the knife and returned to cutting onions. He picked up a cleaver and began chopping venison. For a few minutes it was just the sound of Rennie cutting and Jarret chopping. She giggled first. The

317

sound was contagious. Neither one knew why they were laughing, only that it was healing and bonding and right and necessary.

In the quiet void that followed, Rennie said, "If there ever comes a time when you think I don't love you, don't believe it."

He looked at her oddly. "What does that —" He stopped as Rennie's attention dropped to her hand.

"Oh, damn," she said. "I've nicked myself again."

Jarret wondered why he had the impression she had done it on purpose.

Dancer drew a deep breath as he entered the cabin. The faded blues and grays of twilight framed him in the doorway. He leaned his rifle against the wall and hung up his coat and scabbard. "Stew smells good," he said. "Always a pleasure when someone else does the cookin'." He peeled off his gloves and warmed his hands at the fire. He called to Rennie over his shoulder. "How you feelin', ma'am? You still look a mite peaked."

Rennie was sitting up on the bed, feet tucked to one side and her back against the wall. She touched one hand to her face. "I feel better than I did this morning," she said.

He nodded, pleased. "Good. I'll have another cup of tea for you here in a minute." He glanced at Jarret. "Told you it would do the trick, didn't I?"

"You did. I appreciate it, too."

Dancer straightened and went to the larder. The tins were handy this time, and he had what he wanted quickly. He worked at the table in front of Jarret. "I see she's got her fingers bandaged," he said. "You have some trouble here while I was gone?"

"Nothing I couldn't handle," said Jarret. He pushed

away from the table and removed the stew pot from the hearth, replacing it with the kettle. "She cut herself grabbing for the knife I was using." While Dancer's back was turned Jarret winked at Rennie.

Dancer finished pinching and grinding his herbs and accepted a plate of stew from Jarret. "You can give the lady a little if she wants it. Won't hurt her none to put somethin' good in her."

Rennie had eaten earlier in the event that Dancer might not have been so generous. Her mouth watered anyway when Jarret raised an empty plate to ask her if she wanted some. "Please," she said.

Dancer chuckled. "You musta straightened ner out this afternoon, Sullivan. She tries to kill you then, now she says 'please.'"

"She does what she will to get what she wants." He left the table long enough to give Rennie her stew. His grin was for her alone. "Isn't that right?"

"If you say so," she said sullenly.

Dancer spooned in a large mouthful, then talked around it. "She looks like she was cryin' today," he said. "You make her do that, too?"

"I don't suppose I made her do anything. She was crying because she failed to kill me."

The prospector thought that over. "I could still do the job for her."

"I'm certain she's happy to hear that."

Dancer got the kettle and made Rennie's tea. He gave her the mug. "You give it some thought, ma'am."

Rennie put her plate aside and took the hot tea. She had no idea how to respond to Dancer's offer. "What would you want in return?" she asked.

"Just you stayin' here with me. Six months, maybe a year. What you think about that? You willin' to trade his life for some time with me?"

There was no question that the time would be spent in Dancer's bed. Rennie's skin crawled, and she fought back a wave of horror. "I'd be willing to trade," she said softly. Her small smile was coy; her eyes hinted at hidden pleasures.

Dancer's cackling laugh reverberated in the tiny cabin. He threw back his head and did a little jig, slapping his thigh when he was done. He wiped tears from his eyes as he returned to the table. "You're right about that one," he said to Jarret. "She does what she will to get what she wants."

Rennie peeled herself away from the wall. Dancer's abrupt and mad laughter had raised the hair at the back of her neck. She looked down at the mug she held. It was only three-quarters full—the rest of the tea was staining the front of her shirt in an ever-widening circle. She brushed at herself ineffectually with fingers that still trembled.

"I take it that means I'm safe," Jarret said dryly.

The prospector grinned as well as he was able. "I'm not going to murder you in your sleep."

"That's good to hear."

"But I don't know what you're going to do about her."

It was Rennie who responded. "I can tell you what he'll do. He'll tie me to the foot of the bed. He's done it before."

Jarret just managed to swallow his stew without choking. He saw Dancer's skeptical gaze and nodded, confirming Rennie's statement. "I can't sleep with one eye open," he said. "And neither can you. She'd kill us both."

"Seems that way," said Dancer.

When they finished eating Jarret cleaned the plates and utensils at the stream. He returned to find the furniture had been slightly rearranged. The table had been moved close to the bed, and Rennie was sitting up, shuffling cards from a well-worn deck. Dancer occupied one of the chairs set at a right angle to her.

Rennie looked up at Jarret as he entered, her bewildered gaze for him alone, and said, "He wanted to play."

Jarret couldn't fathom it either, but he didn't want to offend Dancer by not joining. The prospector had already gone to the trouble of boiling more water and making fresh tea. He was sitting at the table expectantly, greedily snatching up the cards that Rennie dealt.

Taking up the vacant chair, Jarret picked up his cards. "What are we playing?"

The game was five card draw, and the ante was nuggets of fool's gold that Dancer had collected from his claim. They only played a half-dozen hands before Rennie began to yawn. She was losing anyway, so she divided the last of her nuggets between Dancer and Jarret and lay back on the bed.

Jarret stopped shuffling and put down the cards. "Let me escort her to the privy now," he told Dancer, "or she'll be wanting to go later."

"Certainly," said Dancer. "I'll make some more tea."

Helping Rennie to her feet, Jarret supported her with his strong arm and led her outside. Once they were out of earshot of the house, he said, "It's the tea, Rennie. That's why you're so tired. Dancer's drugging us."

She yawned hugely, too sleepy to be surprised or worried. "I don't think I can fight it, Jarret."

"You don't have to. I'm not drinking any more. I'll keep you safe."

"I know you will."

Her absolute conviction that he was as good as his word made Jarret want to kiss her right there. He quelled the urge until they were just outside the door of the cabin again. Her lips tasted warmly of the tea. "Wipe that smile off your face," he whispered.

The night was inky. "You can't even see that I'm smiling."

"It doesn't matter. I know what you look like when I kiss you."

She gave him a light tap in the middle of his chest with her fist. "Braggart."

It was Jarret who had to tamp down his smile as they stepped back inside.

After tying Rennie's hands loosely to the bed, Jarret played another six hands with Dancer. The prospector won all his nuggets in the end, and Jarret was able to give the appearance of having lost to a better player. Jarret was also able to surreptitiously dump most of his tea between the cracks in the floor boards. It trickled into the dirt cellar with Dancer being none the wiser. When Jarret tiredly indicated he was ready to stop playing, Dancer obliged by helping him make up his bed on the floor. Once Jarret was settled the prospector turned back the lamps and climbed to the loft.

It seemed forever before Dancer Tubbs climbed down again. Jarret could hear more easily than he could see, and what he heard surprised him. The prospector put on his coat and gloves, took the pot of leftover stew from the hearth, picked up a plate and utensils, and carried it all outside. Jarret waited only long enough to assure himself Dancer was not immediately returning. He untied Rennie, grabbed his gun belt and coat, then stepped outside in time to hear Dancer leaving on horseback.

Jarret followed on foot, certain now that Dancer was going to his claim and fairly confident the mine wasn't far from the cabin. As Jarret's eyes became adjusted to the darkness he was able to quicken his pace. The trail climbed by small increments, but the terrain was smooth. Jarret was able to keep the distance between them from widening, and Dancer led him right to the claim.

Pale yellow lantern light illuminated the mouth of the mine. Jarret stayed back, hidden in the rocks and shadows while Dancer dismounted. There was already a mule tethered to a post near the entrance, and Dancer hitched his horse alongside. As Jarret watched, the prospector unhooked the stew pot, a canteen, and the mess kit and walked into the adit. Jarret waited a minute, then moved silently toward the mine entrance. He paused at the lip, not able to see in without revealing himself, but able to hear the conversation inside.

"Thought you might be gettin' hungry," Dancer was saying. "I brung this for you. Good venison stew."

There was no reply, and Jarret guessed the other person in the adit was already eating.

"Take it easy," Dancer said. "You don't want to make yourself sick on it. There's plenty. I made sure we saved you some. The woman didn't eat much, and I only had a plateful myself."

This time Dancer's companion spoke. Although the voice was muted by a mouthful of food, Jarret had no trouble recognizing it. He stepped into the light and looked directly into the startled emerald eyes of John MacKenzie Worth.

Chapter Twelve

"Who the hell is it?" Jay Mac demanded, squinting at
the entrance. "Dancer? Who's there? Is it one of the
killers?"

For a heart-sickening moment Jarret thought Jay Mac
was blind; then he watched the older man pat down his
vest pocket in a habitual, absent-minded fashion, and understood the problem. He stepped closer.

"Is that what Dancer told you, Jay Mac?" asked Jarret.
"That I was a killer?"

"Weren't no lie," Dancer grumbled. "You *are* a killer."

Jay Mac was sitting on the floor of the adit, his legs
stretched in front of him. His back rested against a splin-
tered timber, and he was holding a tin plate of stew in one
hand at the level of his chest. His silver-threaded vest was
rent in a half dozen places, but both shoulder seams of his
shirt had been carefully mended. His trousers had been
patched at the knee, and everything he wore was covered
with a fine layer of rock dust. On the ground beside him lay
a dirt- and sweat-stained knobby pine cane.

"What the hell's going on?" Jay Mac demanded again.
His eyes narrowed farther, and he studied the intruder
from top to bottom. Recognition came when Jarret hunkered down in front of him and Jay Mac's hard stare set-

tled on the amused and reckless slant of Jarret's mouth. "My God," he said softly, unbelieving of what his eyes finally told him. "It's you."

Dancer took away Jay Mac's plate before it was dropped. "You know him?" he asked.

"I know him. He helped me out once." He reached out to shake Jarret's hand. "Too bad you weren't around to help me out a second time."

Jarret grasped Jay Mac's hand firmly. "Stopping weddings is one thing, I don't think I could have done much about that train wreck."

"I wasn't referring to the train—" He stopped. "Oh, never mind. I'm through interfering anyway."

Jarret snorted, letting Jay Mac know what he thought. "You don't look much worse for your ordeal," he said. "I take it Dancer's been taking good care of you all this time?"

"The best of care."

Dancer shuffled away, uncomfortable with the praise and being even briefly at the center of attention.

Jay Mac picked up the plate again and began to eat. "You don't mind, do you? I haven't had anything since this morning."

"Go right ahead. You've been here all day?"

He nodded. "I've been helping Dancer with his claim since I was well enough to work." He showed Jarret one of his hands. It was calloused, with dirt under the nails and rock dust lying in the furrows of the knuckles. "It's been good to work like this again. I come out in the morning and stay most of the day. Today, because Dancer was worried about you, I didn't return to the cabin."

"He led you to believe I was dangerous?"

"That's right, but he was only trying to protect me. How would he know you weren't dangerous?"

"Because he *knows* me. Isn't that right, Dancer?" Jarret

turned to the prospector only to find he had moved. He spun around, facing the entrance now, and saw Dancer standing on the threshold with his Winchester raised. "Put it down, Dancer. I'm not looking for any trouble."

"Neither am I," the prospector said. "You go on your way, leave me and my friend alone, and we'll all be fine."

Jarret stood slowly, raising his hands, palms up, to the level of his waist. "He's the reason I've come," he said quietly, evenly. He didn't want to spook Dancer. "But I think you realized that, didn't you? There's nothing much that gets past you."

"Nothin' much."

"Do you know who my traveling companion is, then?" he asked.

Dancer's chin jutted forward aggressively. "It's a sure thing she ain't never killed no one," he said, almost daring Jarret to contradict him.

"That's right, she hasn't."

"I thought so. And she weren't really sick neither."

"Not as sick as she appeared to be, no, but she was very ill a short time ago. She's not all that strong yet." He paused to let that sink in, then said, "I think you might have a guess about her identity, Dancer."

"Hhmmph."

Jarret suspected Dancer knew and didn't want to admit it to himself or anyone else. Some sort of bond had been forged between Jay Mac and the old prospector in the months since the train wreck, and Dancer was fighting to keep the only human connection he had made in more than twenty years. "Do you want me to say?" Jarret asked calmly. "You know what it means. She's come a long way to find him."

"I didn't hurt her none."

"I know. But if we don't go back soon, she'll wake up and be frightened that we're gone."

Using the cane for support, Jay Mac struggled up to his knees. He squinted in Dancer's direction. "What's he talking about, Dancer? You told me the woman with him murdered her husband."

"That's what he told me," said Dancer defensively, jerking his rifle at Jarret to emphasize his point.

Jarret realized belatedly that Jay Mac wouldn't know any differently. He probably had first suspected that Jarret's path had crossed his because of a bounty. "But it isn't true," Jarret said. "Tell him, Dancer."

"She got your eyes!" Dancer shouted. His face contorted briefly in anger. The web of scars on the side of his face pulsated as his jaw clenched. He raised the rifle, prepared to shoot, then just as suddenly changed his mind. He spun around on the balls of his feet and charged out of the mine.

Jarret leaned a little weakly against one of the support timbers and waited for his heart to still. He glanced down at his useless right hand as the tingling skittered along his skin from wrist to elbow to shoulder. He swore curtly under his breath.

Jay Mac hauled himself to a stand, leaning heavily on the cane. "You took quite a chance not drawing on him," he said.

"There's not much sense in it when a Winchester's already staring you in the face." To say nothing of the fact that he couldn't have drawn if he'd wanted.

"Still, you took measure of the man's character and realized he wouldn't hurt you. It's not in Dancer to hurt a soul." He looked toward the entrance but couldn't see more than a blur of light and shadow. "Don't worry about him; he'll go off in the hills for a while, then come back when he's ready." He turned to Jarret. "What did he mean about the woman's eyes being mine? Who's come here with you?"

"It's Rennie, sir," Jarret said, finding he had it in him to raise a smile. "She's brought your spectacles."

Jarret guided the mule back to the cabin while Jay Mac rode. It was a sight that Jarret wasn't likely to forget, and he let the railroad tycoon know it. Jay Mac wanted to hear everything about how they had found him, but Jarret wouldn't oblige him. "You need to hear it from your daughter," was all he said, and the subject was closed.

Jay Mac leaned on Jarret to get from the lean-to to the cabin. "My right leg's healed fine," he said, "but I just sprained the left one again the other day. Dancer warned me I was trying to do too much, that I wasn't strong enough, but I—"

Holding up his hand, Jarret cut him off. "You don't have to explain, sir. I know about how deep the stubborn streak goes."

He chuckled appreciatively. At the door he paused, and his quiet tone was solemn. "I've got no complaints about Dancer Tubbs," he said. "He saved my life. Still, I doubt you can ever know how glad I am you're here. I couldn't have made it out of here for weeks yet, perhaps not even then, and probably not on my own. I've known for a while now that Dancer wasn't going to help me leave."

"You've made a friend there. No one who's ever met Dancer thought that could happen."

"I know," he said heavily. "What I don't know is if I've done him any favors. That man's been alone for years, but I think it's been a long time since he had to struggle with loneliness."

In a gesture of understanding, Jarret placed his hand on Jay Mac's forearm. "Let's go inside," he said lowly. "Your daughter's waiting."

* * *

It was the fingers drifting lightly across her brow that woke Rennie. She wrinkled her nose, squeezed her eyes tighter, and smiled sleepily. She batted at the hand. "Go away, Jarret."

Jay Mac's usually impassive face showed a flicker of surprise. "It's not Jarret," he said.

Rennie's eyes opened widely and stared into ones very much like her own. "Papa!" She bolted upright and launched herself into his arms. Rennie pressed kisses all across his broad face. "How? When did you—? Where—?" She looked for Jarret. He was standing by the hearth, watching her. "Did you—?" She searched her father's dear face. His dark sandy hair was longer than she'd ever seen it, curling under his collar. He'd allowed his side whiskers to grow into an unruly beard, and his mustache had lost its elegant shape. "You look—" Tears sparkled in her eyes, and her throat closed. She stared at her father mutely.

Jay Mac held Rennie, rocking her much as he had when she was a child. He patted her head lightly, stroking her hair, and saying just the right things in her ear. "You're a wonder, Mary Renee. A perfect wonder."

It was dawn by the time both sides of the story unfolded. Jay Mac refused to say or hear anything until he had washed and changed clothes. Nothing of Dancer's had ever fit him, but now Jarret offered some clothing—all of it slightly too big—and Jay Mac was outfitted in flannel drawers, jeans, a light blue cotton shirt, and heavy woolen socks. His chipped spectacles rested askew on his face in spite of his efforts to straighten and flatten the ear stems. It was only a minor irritant. John MacKenzie Worth pronounced himself a new man.

While Jay Mac washed, Jarret explained to Rennie what had happened as she slept. It hadn't been entirely surprising to him, he told her, because a hermit with *two* chairs and *two* beds had been early evidence that Dancer had company. The prospector's flight into the rocks was especially distressing to Rennie. She couldn't imagine leaving without seeing him again, thanking him, or saying goodbye.

After Rennie's convoluted tale of her trip west to find him, Jay Mac's account of No. 412's derailment could not have been more simple. He had been standing on the postage-stamp-sized balcony at the rear of his private car—and then he hadn't. He had no memory of anything connected with the actual accident and only a vague recollection of wandering in the trees, along the stream, and up and down rocky inclines until he collapsed. The next thing he knew he was lying on the floor of Dancer's cabin. His legs were immobilized in splints. There was a pillow under his head and a blanket over him. He slipped in and out of consciousness, recalled being spooned soggy chunks of bread soaked in broth, and knew his attempts to communicate were ineffectual. By the time his first unbroken memories began he was resting comfortably on a newly constructed bed, and one of the splints had been removed.

Jay Mac's alliance with Dancer was forged over the length of his slow recovery. He knew that the prospector was disfigured, but the extent of the injuries was never clear to Jay Mac, nor was it important. Likewise, Jay Mac believed Dancer Tubbs didn't care in the least that his guest was one of the hundred richest men in the country.

"Truth is," Jay Mac said, winding down his story, "Dancer's gold mine is a *gold* mine, so I don't suppose that my little fortune impressed him much. It's been a long time since I had to earn a man's respect for what I was and not what I owned."

Rennie heard something wistful on the edge of her father's words. "You sound as if you enjoyed it," she said.

He smiled, rubbing his bearded chin. "Sometimes it's good to earn a person's respect the hard way."

Jarret saw Rennie flush at her father's statement and knew she had taken it personally. He had no idea whether Jay Mac had intended it to be a pointed observation, but he keenly felt Rennie's hurt. "We can't travel today," he said, putting down the fire poker. "Jay Mac, you and I haven't had any sleep, and Rennie's not had much more. It would be better all the way around if we caught a few hours now, and again tonight, and took to the trail tomorrow."

There was immediate agreement. It was the sleeping arrangement that caused some distress. Jay Mac could not climb to the loft, so Rennie gave up the bed for him. When she started to follow Jarret into the loft, however, her father cleared his throat disapprovingly. Rennie paused on the ladder and looked down at her father, mute appeal in her eyes. Jay Mac backed away, but not down. "We'll speak of it later," he said.

Rennie crawled into the loft. Jarret had already collected blankets and was preparing to push them over the edge. "What are you doing?" she asked.

"I'll sleep in front of the fireplace. It will be all right."

"Please, no," she said lowly. "Stay with me."

"Your father—"

"We're *sleeping*, Jarret."

He reached for her then, held her. They stretched out on the feather tick and fell asleep in each other's arms.

Dancer approached the cabin the following morning as they were getting ready to leave. He drew his horse to one side of the path and dismounted. Jay Mac watched him and said to Rennie and Jarret, "Go on, wait for me on the trail up ahead."

Jarret led the way. He leaned over in his saddle as he passed Dancer and held out his hand. "Thank you," he said. "If there's ever—"

Dancer accepted the outstretched hand haltingly, shook it once, and waved Jarret on. "Shoulda fixed that shoulder," he muttered.

Rennie wanted to dismount and put her arms around the surly prospector. Suspecting it would be rebuffed, Rennie leaned over in her saddle as Jarret had done and put out her hand. "You're quite a wonderful man, Dancer. I thought so even before my father said he felt the same way."

Dancer shifted his weight and looked away; then he gave Rennie's horse a slap on the flank and sent her trotting toward Jarret.

They waited where the trail widened on the other side of the stream. A grove of trees gave Jay Mac and Dancer privacy. Rennie came abreast of Jarret and leaned forward, stroking Albion's black mane. "What do you think they're saying to each other?" she asked.

"I don't know," he said. "I know what I say to Ethan when we're not going to see each other for a while. I tell him I'll be there if he needs me. He says the same. And we always have been."

Jay Mac came up the trail a few minutes later, riding the packhorse. "Let's go," he said gruffly.

It was hard to know for sure, but behind Jay Mac's chipped lenses, Rennie thought she saw her father's tears.

They rode for several hours before Rennie realized they weren't retracing the trail back to the wreckage. Jarret explained that they needed to take a different route if they were going to avoid the avalanche. There was also Jay Mac's strength they needed to consider. Rennie accepted his reasoning, but she suspected there was something more. When she pressed, his replies were enigmatic, and finally she let it go, finding Jay Mac's questions about family and Northeast Rail more than kept her busy.

They stopped often during the ride so that Jay Mac could stretch his legs, and Jarret called a halt to everything with a few hours of daylight left so that they could make camp. There was no question of who would share the tent that first night and each subsequent night. Jarret laid out his bedroll near the fire, and Rennie and her father took the tent.

"You've asked me a lot about Mother," she said quietly, staring at the shadows that flickered on the canvas ceiling. "And about my sisters. You haven't asked very much about me."

Jay Mac's head was cradled in his palms. He stared at the same flickering play of light as his daughter, and he answered lowly so that he would not be overheard. "I think you know why that is. What would you have me say in front of him? I don't need my spectacles to see the man's in love with you."

"I love him, too, Jay Mac."

"I know that. But you haven't told him, have you?"

She shook her head. "No . . . I couldn't."

"This isn't the way you were raised, Mary Renee."

Before she thought better of it, she said, "It was *exactly* the way I was raised."

The silence that followed was charged.

Jay Mac spoke only when the first flash of anger had receded. "I've never raised my hand to you, because I never thought it was deserved." He added unhappily, "Until now."

Rennie turned on her side toward him. "I'm sorry, Papa," she whispered. In the darkness her eyes beseeched him. "I'm so sorry."

333

"I know you are. It doesn't change what's been said, though."

"I would take it back."

He sighed. "You can't. Like so many things that have ever been done, it can't be taken back." He found her hand and laid his over it, patting it gently as anger receded. "Maybe it's not a bad thing. Some things shouldn't be erased so quickly; some are worth thinking about. I make no apologies for being with your mother all these years, Rennie. Moira's part of me, and apologizing for loving her would be like being sorry for living. I'll never be sorry for that. I regret things, though. I regret that my wealth and my power can't protect my daughters from being called bastards. I flinch a little every time I realize the strength you've all cultivated is going to be turned first on me. I regret that you've needed it because of me. I regret that I can't protect you and that I can't make you learn from any mistakes but your own."

Jay Mac felt the grip on his hand change as Rennie squeezed his fingers. "I never lied to your mother, Rennie," he said. "She knew from the beginning who I was and what I was. There was no question of marriage being possible between us. We understood that at the outset, long before there was any intimacy."

"Papa," Rennie said, uncomfortable. "You don't have to—"

"I think I do. I want you to know that honesty between your mother and me has always been important. When you think of how you were raised, I hope you'll think of that."

Rennie's knees curled up. She did not let go of her father's hand. "I'll tell him," she said quietly. "Please give me time. Let me do it in my own way when I think it's right."

"I love you, Rennie. I want what's best for you. You're my daughter."

"Mama was someone's daughter, too. He wanted the same for her and she chose you." She heard her father sigh. "I think she made the right choice."

Jay Mac smiled. "Just give me your little finger, Rennie. The one you have me wrapped around."

It was two more days of journeying before Rennie understood where Jarret was leading them. She noticed the lay of the land, the winding floor of the valley, the wide stream that cut a meandering path through its center, the hard hillside terrain on either side of the mountain lake that would have made building trestles and laying railroad ties so difficult. Jarret never said a word to them until he had brought them above the valley so that they could see the expanse of it, the grade of the slopes, the waterfall, and the beauty of the barren trees outlined with snow. Noonday light was reflected off the surface of ice-covered lake, and the cascading falls looked as if they were spilling sunshine.

"The mountain town everyone wants to reach by rail lies on the other side of the lake," Jarret said. He pointed to the cluster of wooden buildings nestled among the distant pines. Higher up the mountainside, trees had been stripped to make openings for the mine tunnels and shafts. "That's Queen's Point."

The splendor of the vista faded for Jay Mac. He frowned. "It can't be," he said.

Jarret wasn't surprised by Jay Mac's reaction. "I assure you it is. Across the lake is, what I suspect, one of the richest silver mines in all of Colorado. The problem is, the miners have to bring the ore out by pack mule, and they can't get heavy equipment in here to run the shafts as deeply as they want or process the ore. Up in Madison the folks don't want the railroad. They figure their ore will last out the century that way, and wealth can trickle in and out. At Queen's Point they're not all that concerned with trickling. A geyser of wealth would suit them fine. That's why they want the Northeast to put down rails. The way I understand it is that yours is the first company to offer them a contract that wouldn't gouge them for using the line."

"That's right," said Jay Mac. He dismounted slowly, favoring his injured leg. Leaning on his cane, he limped to the edge of a steeper part of the slope and surveyed the lake to his left and the valley below. "But this can't be Queen's Point," he repeated. "The work is already supposed to be started down there."

Jarret shared a glance with Rennie, then urged his horse closer to where her father stood. "Rennie said something about that to me," he said casually. "It was the first I'd heard about it. Of course, I hadn't exactly been making a point to be informed. I didn't even know about the derailment until Rennie showed up in Echo Falls. I thought as long as we were close you might want to see things here for yourself."

Stunned, Jay Mac could not keep himself from staring out over the valley. He heard Rennie's approach on foot but did not turn. "I had planned to come out this way to see the progress of the line myself," he said.

"I didn't know that," Rennie said.

Jay Mac shrugged. "I didn't tell you on purpose. I wanted to see the lay of this country firsthand, learn for myself if you were right about the valley flooding."

"I thought you didn't believe me about it."

"I believed *you* believed it." He slipped his arm through hers as she came to stand beside him. "You've never understood how I had to do things back in New York. I had

336

people who've been working for me for years, a score of years in some cases, telling me in no uncertain terms that your conclusions were the wrong ones. I approved the Queen's Point project on their recommendations, Rennie, because that's the way things had to be. They had already proved themselves to me. But you're my daughter, and as much as I trust those men, I love you more. I came here because of you, because I had to prove privately that my daughter's judgments were also sound."

His admission took Rennie's breath away. She closed her eyes briefly, prayerfully. "Thank you for that," she said.

Jarret looked on as father and daughter made their quiet peace. He sidled Zilly closer. "I think you can see the valley's ripe for flooding," he said. "When the winter snows melt only a dam could make a difference. No one's going to put one of those here. The project that Rennie proposed would bring the tracks up from the other side of the mountain. There's more work involved, more expense at the outset, but you can see for yourself it won't be a waste of time or money."

Jay Mac nodded. "There's already been incredible waste of both those resources."

"But the project's not yet started," Rennie said. "You haven't—"

Jarret interrupted. "I think what your father's trying to say, Rennie, is that he's already approved payments for materials that aren't here and wages for men who were never hired. Is that right, Jay Mac?"

"In a nutshell."

"You didn't tell Rennie you were coming here as part of your other business, but did you tell anyone at Northeast?"

Jay Mac shook his head. "No. I didn't want Hollis and the others to think I was checking up on them, or worse, questioning their judgment after approving the project. I knew there wouldn't have been a lot of work done yet, and there'd be no problem routing the rails the way Rennie wanted. At the very worst I only expected to show them they could make mistakes as easily as the next person. They would have had to give more weight to Rennie's ideas in the future. I sure as hell wasn't expecting this."

Neither was Jarret. He was so certain Jay Mac must have spoken to someone about his plans. "So no one knew you meant to come to Queen's Point."

Jay Mac looked over his shoulder at Jarret. "No one at Northeast," he said. "But I mentioned it to my wife."

"Moira wouldn't—" Jarret began.

"My *wife*," Jay Mac said pointedly. "Nina."

Rennie felt all the warmth rush out of her body. Her knees grew weak, and her skin was as white and as cold as the snow around her. She sagged against her father, and when he couldn't support her they both stumbled. Jarret leaped down from his horse and hauled them both up the slope to safer, more even ground.

Jay Mac had his cane to lean on; Rennie leaned on Jarret. "What's wrong?" he asked. "For a moment it looked like you were going to faint."

Rennie pushed a strand of hair away from her cold cheek. She was aware of Jarret's steady regard as well as her father's. "I'm just a little dizzy," she said. "It was nothing. The height, that's all." They both knew her, both loved her, and Rennie wondered if she had convinced either of the lie. She kept her head low so that they couldn't see her face and suspect the depth of despair she felt. Her father had wanted her to tell Jarret the truth. It seemed to Rennie the time was nearly upon her.

Jarret helped Rennie mount Albion when she assured him she was recovered. "If there's no business either of you have in Queen's Point, we'll start back to Echo Falls.

338

Jay Mac can send a telegram to Denver and New York from there."

Jay Mac nodded. "It's about time I let a few other people know I'm alive." The way he said it, almost threateningly, let Jarret and Rennie know he wasn't only speaking of his family.

"Please, Jay Mac," Rennie said imploringly, "don't send any message until we've talked about it. Please. I'm thinking of Mama. We should make certain someone's with her when she hears of it."

Jarret raised the brim of his hat and looked at Rennie consideringly. There was a measure of desperation in her voice that struck him oddly. He caught her eyes, but she turned away immediately, not able to give him a hint about what was troubling her.

The remainder of the journey to Echo Falls passed largely in silence. When there was discussion it never dwelled on the revelations at Queen's Point. Rennie avoided being alone with Jarret and, to an equal degree, avoided being alone with her father. She stayed to herself, following at a distance on the trail, or worked at solitary tasks so that she didn't have to strike up conversation.

They reached Echo Falls at night. By mutual agreement they had chosen to travel after sunset so that they could look forward to some simple creature comforts that evening. Jay Mac was exhausted, his legs like leaden weights. Jarret had to help him dismount in front of Mrs. Shepard's Boardinghouse. The widow was happy to make a room for him, though she was less cordial to Rennie. Jarret's quiet insistence helped.

Rennie stayed with her father until he was comfortably settled before she went to her own room. Jarret was waiting for her there, sitting in the room's lone chair, his feet propped on the edge of the bed. He looked up when she entered.

"I thought you'd be gone," she said, shutting the door gently. "The widow surely thinks you're gone."

"I came in the back way. I thought we needed to talk."

Rennie pulled out the ribbon at her nape and shook out her hair. Leaning against the door, she closed her eyes and massaged her scalp. Her weariness was complete. "Please," she said, "can we talk later? I can't think of anything right now save a hot bath and a full night's sleep in that bed." She pushed away from the door, only to find herself bumping hard into Jarret's chest.

He steadied her and held her startled gaze when she opened her eyes. "All right," he said, "but only because I'm thinking of just about the same thing." He kissed her on the forehead. "I could do with less than a full night's sleep if I was sharing that bed with you."

"Oh, Jarret." She slipped her arms around him and pressed her cheek to his chest. "Promise you won't forget that I love you."

"Rennie?"

"Promise."

He rested his chin in her hair. "I promise." Unable to fathom the bent of her mind, he held her just that way for several long minutes, his fingers sifting through her hair. "You're going to fall asleep standing up." He gently prodded her toward the bed. "I'll mention to the widow that you want a bath."

"She'll be shocked," she said, lying down and shutting her eyes. "You're not supposed to be here."

Jarret kissed her cheek. "If you're not at my cabin before sunup, then I'm coming back here, and to hell with Mrs. Shepard or your father."

"Hmmm."

"I mean it."

She brushed aside the finger that was tapping the end of her nose. "I'll be there. I want to talk, too."

Jarret straightened. "It's not the only thing I have in mind."

Rennie buried her face in the thick feather pillow. "Me either."

He wasn't certain that she'd even remember their conversation, much less oblige him by showing up at his cabin. Still, a few hours past midnight Jarret heard the door being pushed open and the familiar light clicking of Rennie's shoes on the floor boards. The glow from the fire reached him as she added wood and stoked the embers. The ladder rattled against the loft as she began to climb.

Jarret lay back and pretended to sleep.

Taking no particular pains to be quiet, Rennie crouched in the loft and stripped out of everything except her cotton shift. She dove under the covers and snuggled against him. He didn't move. Rennie raised herself on her elbows and leaned over him. She brushed his nose with hers. "I think you're faking," she said softly, her breath warm against his lips. "I know just how to touch you to wake you up."

Jarret kept his eyes closed, though it was harder not to smile. He anticipated her fingers fiddling with the drawstring of his drawers, dipping just below the waist . . . which was why he nearly came out of his skin when Rennie thrust her icy feet under his legs. He captured her wrists, wrestled her onto her back, and nuzzled her neck with noisy, playful kisses.

Their foreplay was laughter, but their joining was intense. She was ready for him and he was in her, driving hard. She gasped at the force of his entry, but when he stilled she was the one who arched, driving into him. It was a battle of wills and greedy pleasures where surrender

341

was a victory. She said his name huskily and bit off the sound of his wild pleasure. When he collapsed against her she welcomed the warm sweat-slick weight of him. He shifted to the side, and now she rolled with him, raising her thigh to trap his legs while stretching her other leg against his.

"Sometimes I think if you don't touch me, I'll die," she whispered, "then you touch me and it feels as if I'll die anyway."

"You know exactly the right things to say." Jarret's fingers trailed lightly on the arm that lay across her chest. "The first time I touched you, you didn't like it at all," he said.

"You dangled me off the floor."

"I swept you off your feet."

"You made me faint."

"I made you swoon."

Rennie punched him softly in the ribs. "You were horribly ill-mannered."

"*You* were trying to slap my best friend."

She laughed, remembering. "You must have thought me mad."

"I thought you were wonderful."

"Really?"

"Well, not just at that moment, but it occurred to me eventually." This time Jarret was able to catch her fist before she landed the jab. Her light laughter washed over him. Jarret let it fade away; then he said seriously, "We should talk, Rennie."

"No," she said. "Not yet. Let's sleep."

He did for a while; but the loft became cold, and when he reached for Rennie she wasn't there. Jarret sat up, fear setting his heart slamming; then he heard her below. He leaned over the edge of the loft and saw her. She was sitting on a blanket in front of the fire, combing out her hair with her fingers, separating the damp strands. He had seen her like this once before, in her own room, her dark red hair spilling over one shoulder, her skin drinking in the colors of the firelight. He had wanted her, and there hadn't been a damn thing he could do about it then. There was now.

Jarret hitched a sheet around his waist and climbed down the ladder. He knelt behind Rennie and pulled her hair back. He let it fall through his fingers slowly. His voice was hushed. "I thought you wanted to sleep."

"I did. I couldn't."

"Neither could I, not without you there." He leaned forward and pushed her shift off one shoulder. His lips touched the naked curve of her neck. "You're beautiful." Her skin grew warmer, but she didn't flinch at his words. Her head tilted to one side as his mouth became more insistent, more seeking.

First it was the heat. His mouth on her throat. His hands on her breasts. Then it was the fire. His fingers trailing down her spine. The damp edge of his tongue on her skin. He dropped her shift to her waist. His palms slid along her shoulders, her arms. Back and forth. Learning the shape of her. She leaned back and was tucked against his body, her hair a silky screen between their skin. His hands slipped around her waist. Then lower. He ran his palms from her hips to her knees. Up and down. Gentle pressure urged her thighs apart. Her neck arched. She lent her throat to his mouth, lent herself to his fingers. Tension pulled her muscles taut, made her press herself intimately against him. He caressed; she responded. She breathed shallowly, air never quite filling her lungs. He explored the flat of her belly, pressing hard against her skin. He cupped her breast. The nipple rose. Hardened. He whispered in her ear, against her skin. His words, his mouth, raised a response. "Yes," she said.

343

Again, "Yes." He stroked her. The heat had a center now, the tension focus. The circle widened. His hand between her legs. His mouth sipped the light reflected on her shoulder. "Oh, God," she said. It was hardly a sound at all. Then, "Jarret." She was shattering, trembling. Her head fell forward. He held her, pushed aside her hair, and kissed the back of her neck. Her body was flushed. It cradled him.

They leaned forward together. Her hips were raised. He came into her from behind. A slow thrust. She held the length and heat of him. She rocked. He made a sound at the back of his throat. It was her name. She moved again. He filled her. She thought she could see their reflection in the flames, their bodies twined, joined. The pressing. The sliding. His hips rolled hard against her bottom. The thrusts deepened; his breathing quickened. "Sweet," he said. Her body tightened around him. He held her still, just held her, feeling the velvet tightness of her. The set of his face was taut, desire held in check. It couldn't last. He wanted it to last; he wanted it to last forever. She pushed against him, and he could not help himself, could not help the quick and shallow thrustings. His throat arched. He closed his eyes. His body contracted as he spilled his seed into her.

They rolled apart. Limp. Replete. A touch just then would have been too much.

Rennie moved enough to straighten her shift. It was exhausting work. Jarret wrapped the sheet around him and felt the same. They couldn't have talked if they wanted to. They didn't want to. They slept.

This time Jarret was awake first. A hint of dawn colored the sky. He sat at the table drinking coffee, waiting for Rennie to wake. She slept on her side, one arm propped under her head, the other folded against her chest. He knew the moment the aroma of the coffee reached her. She made a sleepy little smacking sound with her lips. A few seconds later she wrinkled her nose.

"I'm making oatmeal," he said. "Do you want some?"

Her eyes opened, filled with mock horror.

"Coffee, then."

Rennie sat up slowly. Behind her the fire was pleasantly warm. "Coffee will be fine."

Jarret brought the pot over to the table and poured her a cup.

Rising to her knees, Rennie looked out the window. "It's early yet," she said. "I could have slept longer."

"Not if you want to get back to the boardinghouse unseen," he said, "and not if we're going to finally discuss some things." He gave her a considering look. "We *are* going to discuss some things, aren't we?"

Nodding, Rennie came to her feet. She picked up the blanket and pulled it around her shoulders like a shawl. The coffee was hot. She carried her cup to the window seat and sat down, tucking her bare feet under one corner of the blanket. She thought she was going to have to go first, but it was Jarret who spoke.

"I don't know what you've been thinking these last days since finding your father," he said. "I know that you haven't wanted to be alone with me, especially since Queen's Point."

"I'm sorry," she said. "It was easier to stay away than it was to explain. That's still true."

"But you came here anyway."

"I did," she said a little sadly. She sipped her coffee. "I didn't say that staying away was easy, only that it was easier than explaining."

"I see."

Her small laugh held no joy. "No, you don't. But you

will." She looked away from the window and met Jarret's puzzled eyes. "I don't think the derailment at Juggler's Jump was an accident," she said. "I suspect you think the same."

"I did," he said. "I'm not so certain now. Your father said he hadn't spoken to anyone at Northeast about his scheduled side trip. That didn't make sense to me."

"I know," she said. "But you don't know everything yet."

"Such as?"

"The wheels weren't flat," she told him. When he looked at her blankly she went on patiently. "None of the derailed cars had flattened wheels. I looked at all of them. That means there wasn't any attempt to apply the handbrakes, probably because there wasn't time. You'd have thought the brakemen would have been more alert; after all, No. 412 was on her descent. The brakes have to be applied evenly over the length of the entire train to avoid buckling the link and pin couplings."

"Maybe they weren't applied evenly. Maybe that's why the derailment occurred."

She shook her head. "No. I don't think that's what happened. The couplings between the cars that derailed were damaged, but that's explained by the accident itself. The cars twisted and buckled once they left the track. The first car that derailed, however, had no damage to the link. None at all. It was as if the pin had simply been pulled."

"The pin might have broken."

"If it had been weakened perhaps, but not otherwise, not on the descent."

"You realize what you're saying, don't you?"

She nodded. "Someone was willing to let a lot of people die to see that Jay Mac didn't reach Queen's Point. You were thinking it, too. You knew something was wrong when I told you about the work that was supposed to be going on there."

"I knew something was wrong, yes, but I wasn't thinking about murder. That really only occurred to me when Jay Mac said he had planned to visit the work site. It seemed reasonable to suspect someone might not have wanted him to do that."

"And who did you think that would be?"

"You're not going to like it much, but Hollis Banks was my first choice. He's not only good at blindsiding people, he can get others to do his work and keep his own hands clean."

Rennie frowned. She didn't disagree with Jarret's assessment but was surprised to hear it from him. "What do you mean?" she asked. "Surely you got the better of Hollis on both occasions of your meeting."

Jarret rose from the table and went to the stove. He stirred the oatmeal. It was already clumped and gummy. "You're right," he said. "I only met him twice. The third time he sent his friends." He spooned oatmeal into a wooden bowl and added sugar. "I didn't see any point in telling you this before," he said, returning to the table. "But there's no reason not to now. On my last day in New York, while I was waiting on the platform for my train, Hollis's friends—I recognized them from the wedding—came after me."

"Jarret!" She nearly tipped her coffee into her lap. "Why didn't you—"

He held up his hand, cutting her off. "It was over quickly. I wasn't in any condition to put up much of a struggle. Dee Kelly, remember? One of them—I don't recall who anymore—planted his foot right in my shoulder. Later I got a toe in my groin. The blond did that, I think. I know he took the bank draft Jay Mac wrote me. He also took the reward for bringing in Dee."

Rennie's shoulders sagged a little. "Oh, God," she said, closing her eyes. She put her cup down on the narrow window ledge to keep from spilling it. Her hands trembled. She looked at him. "The blond's name is Richard Dunny. He's an old friend of Hollis's. I suppose Taddy and Warren Beecher were the others. Taddy saw me kissing you at the Jones Street Station. He was in the crowd that gathered. That's why I wanted to get away from you so quickly. Taddy must have run straight to Hollis with the story—that would be just like him—but no one ever breathed a word of it to me."

"I didn't think they had." He paused, studying the drawn, colorless features of her face. "Do you think I blame you for what happened to me, Rennie?"

"No, but it would be easier if you did." All the times she had seen him struggle with his arm, she had blamed Dee Kelly for the injury and Jarret himself for not taking care of it. It wasn't so simple. The real damage had been done by Hollis's friends and, in turn, Hollis. It was easy to feel some of the responsibility herself. If she hadn't kissed him in public, right there on Jones Street, with God and Taddy and a dozen strangers looking on, Jarret Sullivan would still have the full use of his right hand and arm. "You know I thought what money you hadn't lost gambling was spent on liquor and—"

"And women," he said, grinning. "Don't forget women."

"It isn't funny," she snapped. "Damn you! You know it isn't funny."

Jarret sobered. "It also isn't in any part your fault. If you want to know the truth, I *did* blame you for a time. There just wasn't any sense in it, and after a while I came to see it that way. I admit it wasn't to my liking when you showed up in Echo Falls, but there were a lot of other reasons for that. I didn't need you here to recall what

348

Hollis had done. I only had to drop a glass of whiskey or miss the grip on my gun to bring Hollis Banks to mind. I had been trying to live with that since leaving New York. Seeing you again made me realize I hadn't been living at all, perhaps not for a long time, Rennie, longer than even I had suspected. Perhaps not since my parents were murdered."

His chair scraped the floor. He went over to the window seat and sat beside her. "You touched me, Rennie. You threw yourself at everything with such tremendous spirit and will; you set a course for yourself and hung on. I admired that. There was a time I thought you might be turning it on me." His smile was tinged with self-mockery and regret. "Who's to say if I was leaving New York because my job there was finished or if I was running scared?"

If only he had given her some hint. She had waited a long time to hear from him. "But you stayed away. There was never a word from you."

"What was I supposed to offer you? I didn't have any money. I couldn't earn it the way I knew how. I didn't see any hope for the ranch I wanted, and I doubted you would ever leave New York." He leaned back against the windowsill and sighed. "And you were still set on marrying Hollis. You haven't forgotten that, have you?"

"No," she said dully. Her eyes dropped away from his profile. "I haven't forgotten."

Behind him, Jarret could feel the warmth of the sun pressing on the glass. He glanced over his shoulder and saw that daybreak was well upon them. "You're not going to make it back to the boardinghouse without being seen," he said. "You'd better go get dressed. I'll escort you back. There's a lot we need to talk to your father about."

"Jarret, I—"

"Go on." When she hesitated again, he said, "Are you worried what Jay Mac will say about you being with me?" He leaned over and kissed her lightly on the cheek. Her skin was cold. He drew back slowly, searching her face. Her emerald eyes were clearly pained, her lower lip swollen where she had been worrying it. "Rennie, you realize, don't you, that I plan to ask Jay Mac for your hand today?"

Her eyes widened. The blanket around her shoulders dropped as she reached for him. "No, you can't do that!"

"What do you mean? I thought it was understood."

"No!" She stood up. "It's not understood at all."

Jarret came to his feet as well. "I'm sorry," he said. "I've never done this before. I should have asked you first."

Her heart was breaking. It was there in the eyes she turned on him. "No," she said softly. "Don't do it. Don't ask."

Jarret was certain he hadn't moved. It was the earth that had shifted under him. He heard her words, but he couldn't make sense of their meaning. "You're not going to marry me?"

"I can't."

"You *can't?*" he asked. The shield that came over his face hardened his features. His deep blue eyes cooled and his jaw tightened. "Or you won't?"

"I can't," she said again. She wanted to look anywhere but at him. She didn't because she owed Jarret a straightforward response. "I'm already married. I married Hollis Banks a month before Jay Mac's accident."

"Rennie." When she hesitated again, he said, "Are you worried what Jay Mac will say about you being with me?"

He leaned

the

her

dryly,

harsh

Chapter Thirteen

He looked as if he were going to be sick. His features were suddenly drawn and gray. In a heartbeat of time his sapphire eyes had become remote. Rennie reached out to him.

Jarret flinched from her outstretched hand and took a step backward. "It's not a good idea to touch me right now, Rennie."

Her arm dropped to her side. He was already turning away from her. "Please," she said, "please, listen to me."

He picked up his mug and filled it at the stove. With the part of his mind that could think rationally he marveled at his ability to do so without spilling a drop. That he could place one foot in front of the other also impressed him. It only proved that the piece she had cut out of him wasn't necessary for the daily business of living. He sat at the table. His knuckles were white on the mug; the set of his shoulders was rigid. "I'm listening," he said with credible politeness. "Though I can't imagine what you have to say that's worth hearing."

The chill between them had become a tangible thing. Rennie kept her distance and implored him with her eyes and her voice. "I know I should have told you," she said.

"Then, we agree on that."

"I didn't think you'd take me to find my father if you knew," she said.

His voice finally revealed the powerful edge of his anger. "I sure as hell wouldn't have touched you!"

"Don't you think I knew that, too?" she asked quietly. "That's as honest as I can get, Jarret. When I first decided to come to Colorado I didn't know I was going to see you again."

He snorted derisively.

"It's *true*," she said. "I thought Ethan would be taking me to Juggler's Jump."

"Your sister's not stupid enough to let you loose with her husband," Jarret said bitterly.

Rennie rocked back on her feet as if pushed. At her sides her hands clenched. She closed her eyes long enough to steady herself, and then she went on. "There's no need to say things like that. Do you think I'm not hurting already?"

"You know, Rennie," he said evenly, "right now I don't give a good damn." He smiled without humor. "That's as honest as I can get."

The words were hurled back at her. Rennie sat on the edge of the window seat, her hands folded on her lap. She pressed on. "I didn't come with Ethan because of his broken leg. He directed me to you. I wasn't certain Duffy Cedar and I would ever find you, and I wasn't certain I wanted to . . . until I saw you again. You made it very clear you didn't want to see me, though. When you finally introduced me to Jolene you made a snide remark, asking if I were Mrs. Banks now. I decided right then I wasn't going to tell you and have you respect me any less than you already did. I cared too much about finding Jay Mac to let that get in the way, and I had no desire to explain my reasons for marrying Hollis. I certainly didn't feel then that I owed you an explanation. I still don't."

Jarret's brows raised a fraction, and he gave her a contemptuous look. "You'll understand if I disagree."

"No," she said. "No, I won't. What I owe is an explanation for why I didn't tell you about the marriage, not why I married in the first place. You were no part of my life then, Jarret. You had been long gone from New York, and if you're being really honest, you know you had no intention of ever seeing me again. Are you suggesting I was supposed to wait for you? Wait for someone who was never coming? We didn't part on those kind of terms. You were so careful never to state anything of what you felt, so careful never to promise, and I admit I wasn't any more forthcoming than you."

Rennie scooted back onto the seat and drew her knees up to her chest. Her bare feet were visible beneath the lace-edged hem of her shift. "Still," she said softly, "I found myself wishing things had been different. For a while I allowed myself to hope that you'd write or simply show up one day. When Michael and Ethan moved back to Denver I thought I'd learn something about you then." She stared straight ahead, shaking her head sadly. "It never happened. It was as if you had disappeared."

Rennie smoothed her shift over her knees and hugged herself more tightly. "So no," she said, "I don't think I have to explain why I married Hollis Banks."

Jarret set his mug on the table and pushed it aside. "I'm not trying to fool myself that it had something to do with me not being around," he said. "It wasn't any secret that you wanted Hollis so you could have more influence at Northeast. I don't know why you thought you had to marry him."

Rennie shot to her feet. "Bastard!" She ran to the ladder and started to climb, intent on getting her clothes and leaving. Jarret caught her by the waist and stopped her. "Let me go!" she said through clenched teeth. She struggled, hanging on to the ladder while he tried to pull her away. "You don't know anything about it!"

"Then tell me!"

She kept her lips closed in a mutinous line and kicked back at him. "Go to hell!"

Jarret got his left arm completely around her waist and yanked. She had to let go of the ladder or let it fall on top of her. She let it go. He turned her around, pressing her back against the slats and blocking her escape with his body. "Now tell me why you were so eager to marry Hollis Banks if it wasn't because of Northeast," he said, his words clipped.

She pushed at his chest. He didn't move. "I wasn't eager."

"Then why, dammit!"

She shouted at him. "Because I was *lonely!*"

Stunned, Jarret let himself be pushed aside as Rennie put some distance between them.

Trembling with the strength of her pain, she escaped as far as the fireplace and picked up the poker.

"Are you going to hit me with that?" he asked, turning toward her.

Her eyes dropped to the poker. Its end was tapping against the floor, an extension of her shaking hand. "I want to," she said, looking back at him. She let it drop. Tears hovered on the rim of her eyes. "You don't know anything about my life in New York. I was never part of the social circles that gave fabulous balls and afternoon teas or drove carriages through Central Park for show. I didn't have friends who invited me to be part of their skating party in the winter or asked me to tour a museum with them in the spring. My *sisters* were my friends."

Rennie swiped at a tear that dripped over her cheek. She took a shallow breath and let it out slowly, fighting for composure. "As for men . . . there were none. Did you think they lined up on Broadway and 50th to call on the bastard Dennehy sisters?" She laughed scornfully. "Jay Mac sent us all to boarding school so we could be insulated from the jibes of the outside world, though I can tell you that no one's crueler than a schoolgirl who thinks your place is beneath her dainty feet. Michael and I were fortunate. We had each other for friendship. When it was time to leave there was no coming out party for us. We weren't part of any debutante balls. We quietly slipped into college and fought every prejudice that was in place to defeat us.

"Michael went to a woman's college, but I took a different course. To study engineering I needed to study with men. To learn the science I had to compete as an equal. My classes were filled with colleagues who resented me at every turn."

Jarret made no attempt to approach her. Almost against his will he said her name softly, feeling her pain.

"No," she said, swiping at her eyes again. "You wanted to hear this." She swallowed the pressure that was building at the back of her throat and gave Jarret her frankest stare. "Men who showed me any attention generally fell into very specific categories. There were those few who simply wanted to pick my brain and score their success on my hard work. There were those who came from families with good social connections, who didn't realize at first that I was one of Jay Mac's bastards. As soon as they found out, they either disappeared — which was much more honorable — or they stepped up the pursuit in order to get me into their bed. After all, what prospects did I really have? Their attitude was that I should have been *grateful* for their attention.

"Other men, whose prospects were perhaps more than my own but with pockets to let, came courting my money. Jay Mac's wealth has always made the issue of my illegitimacy very complicated for New York's middle crust. They want entry into the exclusive homes but lack the finances, but getting the finances means taking me."

She smiled now without rancor. "Do you see, Jarret? They can't decide if I'm a stepping stone to a finer life or a millstone around their neck."

Jarret leaned one hip on the edge of the table, stretching

out a leg in front of him. He returned her level stare, his eyes implacable.

"Michael and I kept going our own way after college. She wouldn't allow Jay Mac to buy her a position at the *Herald,* and she took the job at the *Chronicle.* She had a hard time of it before she was finally accepted, and she was very fortunate to work for someone like Logan Marshall. I didn't have the same harassment at Northeast. No one would have *dared.* All the same, I was never taken very seriously by my colleagues, and mostly I was just plain ignored."

"Except for Hollis," said Jarret.

"No, not really. He was just a little more careful about how he did it. He placated me on the one hand and then did as he damn well pleased on the other." Her angry emerald eyes narrowed. "Don't look at me that way. I didn't always know that about him. Certainly I realized that he was interested in my money and in furthering his connection with my father and his authority at Northeast. I had no illusions about being loved by him, but I thought he genuinely cared about me. In my mind at least, I believed we would work comfortably together."

Rennie leaned against the warm, smooth stones of the hearth. She pushed back the dark red fall of hair that had spilled over one shoulder and crossed her arms under her breasts. "Still, I didn't know if I wanted to marry him. Then Michael returned to New York. She was pregnant. She was miserable. God knows, I wasn't sympathetic. I was horrible to her at first. I didn't understand how she could have allowed herself to become pregnant." Rennie blinked hard, reining in the tears. "Just what the world needed, I thought. Another Dennehy bastard."

Looking not at Jarret now, but at a point beyond his shoulder, Rennie said, "I decided to marry Hollis for a lot of reasons, but the foremost among them that first time was my promise that I would *never* end up like my mother and my sister." Her smile rose faintly now, full of brittle self-mockery. She said, "The second time I planned a wedding with Hollis it was because I had given up hope that I would *ever* end up like my mother or my sister."

When Jarret looked as if he might approach her, Rennie shrank against the stones and kept him back. "You see, I had finally realized what they had, and I was willing to settle for even a pale imitation of it. So I married Hollis. It was a small wedding this time. We did it in St. Gregory's in front of a few witnesses. Jay Mac wasn't there. Neither was Michael or Ethan. Mama cried through the whole service. Mary Francis fiddled with her rosary. Maggie and Skye were wretched. They all knew that what I was doing had much less to do with Northeast than it did with just not being alone anymore." Tears spilled over her cheeks, and now she made no attempt to wipe them away. She pressed her lips together, stuffing back a sob. "It wasn't that I married Hollis for all the wrong reasons, but that I married him for none of the right ones."

She raised the hem of her shift to dry her eyes. When her vision cleared Jarret was standing in front of her with a handkerchief in his hand. "Here," he said. "You never seem to have one of these."

She nodded, hiccuping. "I know. Hollis hates it."

Jarret's mouth flattened. "What else does Hollis hate?"

Startled, Rennie raised her tear-stained face. "What do you mean?"

"I mean what happened between you and Hollis after the wedding? You were a *virgin,* Rennie, when you came to me. Does Hollis hate all women, or is it you in particular?"

"Oh, I see," she said after a moment. She took a shaky breath, composing herself. "You think he's one of those men who like other men."

"Well?"

She shook her head. "No, it's nothing like that. Hollis has someone. A woman. He's had her for a long time, long before the first time I planned to marry. He told me about her on our wedding night as he was getting ready to join me in bed. He said he wanted me to know that I shouldn't expect him to be faithful, not when I had already . . ."

"What? What did he say?"

Rennie sighed, looking away. "Not when I had already whored for you."

Jarret swore softly.

"It's no good being outraged," she said, her eyes accusing. "It's less than what you've said to me yourself."

It was Jarret who had the grace to look away now. "You're right." He crossed to the window and stood staring. The vision that filled his mind wasn't the one in front of him. He didn't see the eddies of powdered snow swirling on top of the crust. He didn't see the pine boughs trembling in the wake of some playful squirrels. What he saw was Hollis Banks standing over his bride and informing her he had a mistress . . . and demanding his own rights in the next breath. He was so certain that Hollis had acted in just that way that his words came out as a statement, not a question. "He tried to press you for his marital rights then."

"Yes."

Jarret turned back to Rennie. She was holding the handkerchief balled in one hand. Her arms were still crossed protectively in front of her. "You refused him. What happened?"

"He beat me."

She said it so matter-of-factly that it took a moment for the words to register. When they did Jarret recoiled as if struck himself. He picked up the mug Rennie had left on the windowsill and pitched it at the fireplace. The pottery shattered, flames hissed as coffee splashed over them, and Rennie flinched, then froze against the stones, afraid of the searing, angry heat in Jarret's eyes. When he took a step toward her she couldn't move.

He saw the still caution in her face, knew that he had put

it there with his unthinking, violent act. "Oh, God, Rennie," he said, stopping in his tracks. "I'm sorry. I just . . ." His hands fell helplessly to his sides. "I think I want to kill him." The admission caught him off guard. He had never once considered revenge on Hollis for the incident at the train station, but the thought that he had hurt Rennie made it difficult for him to breathe let alone think. "No," he said, shaking his head, "that's wrong. I *know* I want to kill him."

Rennie came away from the wall. She raised one hand as if she could deflect his horrible anger and simultaneously prevent him from carrying out his threat. "Don't make me sorry I told you," she said quietly. "I healed. He never had the opportunity to do it again."

Jarret thrust his hands into his back pockets. He let out a breath slowly, searching her face. "I don't know what to say, Rennie."

"It's all right," she said, becoming the comforter. "You don't have to say or do anything. Just hear me out, Jarret. It's the hardest thing I've ever asked of you, and it's the only thing I want."

He nodded. "Go on."

"I didn't just let him beat me," she said. "I gave it back as well as I could. We were spending our first night together at one of the suites at the St. Mark, and I think he was afraid someone might hear me screaming. When he couldn't knock me unconscious he stormed out of the suite." Rennie's short laughter was rife with disbelief. "The most amazing thing was that he really expected me to allow him back in the suite the next morning. He stood on the other side of the door, begging, swearing that he would never touch me again, even promising to give up his mistress.

"He had to leave eventually or risk bringing on the curious. I don't know where he stayed those weeks while we were supposed to be away. I stayed right where I was, letting the bruises heal. He came to me at least once every day, making the same promises, and every day I denied him entry. When the last bruise had faded I opened the door to him because I was ready to leave. I told him there would be no word of what had passed between us to my family, but that I would be seeking an annulment.

"I went home to my family then, and they took me back without asking for a single explanation. I stopped going to work at the Worth Building, and messengers brought my assignments to the house. I have no idea what Hollis told anyone else, or even if anyone else had dared to ask him about me. I know that until word came to me about the accident at Juggler's Jump, it wasn't necessary for me to see him."

Jarret recalled some things Rennie had said to him weeks ago. "Hollis took over the company then."

She nodded. "Almost immediately there were problems — at least to my way of thinking — but Hollis had the confidence of the board just as he had had my father's confidence. Projects that had been on hold prior to the accident were suddenly approved. Hollis would not allow me access to certain information any longer, and he stopped allowing me to work out of my home. He wanted me back at the office, and he wanted me to stop pursuing the annulment." Rennie shook her head, still disbelieving that Hollis had thought she would comply.

"I was inclined to do neither of these things," she said dryly. "Instead I told him I intended to find Jay Mac." She laughed, remembering Hollis's outrage. "I truly think Hollis would have had me committed if he could have avoided the scandal. That was at first. Later I believe he thought it was better to have me out of the way for a while, that if I kept myself busy on a wild goose chase I couldn't interfere in the running of Northeast."

Jarret pulled out a chair and straddled it. "But you said Hollis had the confidence of the board. How were you able to interfere at all?"

"In his will Jay Mac let it be known who he wanted to

manage Northeast, but he divided his interests in the company among his heirs. His wife received fifty percent. Twenty-five percent went to my mother, and the remaining twenty-five was divided equally among me and my sisters."

Jarret whistled softly as he realized the impact of Jay Mac's decision. "Then, the interests were split evenly."

"That's right. Hollis knew my mother and sisters would follow my advice and that it would not always be the same as his. Nina Worth, like the board, was prepared to follow his lead. The potential existed to stop all the activities at Northeast. Hollis wanted my five percent interest to prevent that. As my husband he had the opportunity to get it."

Jarret's brows came together. "Another reason for him to object to the annulment."

Staring out the window, she nodded. "That five percent interest in Northeast was the reason he wanted to marry me in the first place," she said. "It gave him control. Jay Mac's accident gave him opportunity, but our marriage put control in his hands. He had been planning it for a long time."

"The marriage or the accident?"

Rennie turned to Jarret. Her eyes were unwavering, her expression frank. "Both," she said. "Hollis planned both."

Jarret was silent for a moment. He could see that she believed what she was saying. "That's a powerful accusation, Rennie."

"You were thinking it yourself."

"I told you already, that was before Jay Mac said he hadn't informed Hollis about inspecting the work at Queen's Point."

"You're missing the point," she said, puzzled that he did not understand. "Jay Mac did tell someone, and *she* told Hollis."

"Why would—"

"Didn't I say?" asked Rennie. "No, I suppose I didn't. It's what I've been trying to say all along, though. Nina is Hollis's mistress. Nina Worth . . . my father's wife."

Jarret's eyes flickered with surprise. For the space of a minute it was his only reaction. "My God," he said finally. "Hollis told you that?"

"He *relished* telling me that." She did not have to close her eyes to recall how Hollis had gloated, how he had derived so much pleasure from her own stunned reaction. She remembered it more vividly than the beating that followed.

"Does Jay Mac know?"

She shook her head. "I've never said a word to him. If he knows Nina has a lover, then I'm certain he doesn't realize it's Hollis." Rennie scooped up a blanket and returned to the window seat. "It's Nina's ultimate revenge on Jay Mac and the Dennehys. I can't even find it in myself to blame her. She's been married more than twenty-five years to a man who doesn't love her, who has never made any secret of his devotion to his bastard family. I've never even formally met Nina, and I've only seen her a few times; but she's always been a presence in my life. She's quite beautiful, very delicate and reserved. Some might say cold. Jay Mac would.

"Perhaps she and Hollis are merely using each other, or perhaps they're really in love. I don't know the truth, and I don't know if motive matters. What I do know is that the accident at Juggler's Jump wasn't an accident. It was a deliberate attempt on Jay Mac's life and an opportunity for Hollis to seize complete control of Northeast. My husband is responsible for the deaths of more than sixty people, and it was done to cover the fraud of the Queen's Point project."

Jarret said nothing as he took it all in. He felt Rennie's eyes on him, waiting for him to challenge her assertions. He didn't. More to the point, he couldn't. He believed her. "When I showed you Queen's Point it all came together, didn't it?"

She nodded. "At the moment Jay Mac said he'd spoken to Nina, I knew what happened."

"There's no proof."

"I know that, too."

"What are you going to do?"

Rennie stared at the far wall, her shoulders hunched. "I haven't thought that far," she said quietly. "I've only been able to think about the consequences of telling you."

Jarret's fingers pressed against the top rail of the chair. He managed to keep his voice even, his frustration in check. "You married him, Rennie, and you lied to me about it. What is it you want from me? Absolution? Forgiveness?"

She couldn't speak. She stared at him helplessly.

He slammed the heel of his hand against the top rail. "Dammit, Rennie! You didn't give me a choice! Do you expect me to thank you for that?"

Her voice was choked, barely audible. "No. I was wrong. I told you that." She stood, drawing the blanket more tightly about her shoulders. "I was wrong about a lot of things. I don't want anything from you, Jarret. It was a mistake . . . all of it."

Rennie crossed the floor to the ladder, and this time Jarret let her go.

Jay Mac was eating breakfast in Mrs. Shepard's dining room when Rennie entered the boardinghouse. He caught her attention as she paused in the hallway, removing her coat.

Rennie accepted the chair her father held out for her and unfolded the napkin on her lap. "I was with Jarret," she said without inflection.

Jay Mac's green eyes searched his daughter's pale and stoic features. "When you weren't in your room this morning I suspected as much." He poured her a cup of tea and pushed the saucer toward her. "You told him."

Nodding, she raised her cup. She could feel the scalding

heat of the tea before it touched her lips. She drank anyway. Out of the corner of her eye she saw her father wince at her self-inflicted pain. "He was angry."

"You didn't expect otherwise, did you?"

Rennie shrugged. "It doesn't matter what I expected," she said. "It's over now. It was a mistake. I told him that."

"I see."

"Do you?" Her laughter was brief and humorless. "I'm not certain I do. I thought he loved me."

"Did he say he didn't?"

"He didn't have to. It was there in his face, in the way he looked at me."

Jay Mac's voice was gentle. "You haven't given him any time."

Rennie returned her father's gaze unflinchingly. "I committed adultery, Papa. I made him an accomplice. He never said it in so many words, but it was what he was thinking." Rennie set her cup down. "He asked me to marry him. He was going to come here with me today and ask you for my hand." A faint smile crossed her face as she thought about Jarret's desire to honor convention. Only her eyes were regretful. "I had to tell him then. It was painful."

"For both of you."

Rennie's eyes glistened. Her mouth pressed in a flat line. She waited until she gathered her composure. "I don't think I care for any breakfast," she said carefully. "If you don't mind, I'd like to go to my room."

"Of course." He stood and kissed Rennie's pale cheek. He watched her go, a heavy ache in his own heart.

Jarret opened the door to his cabin at the second thunderous knock. He stared at his visitor for several long moments before stepping aside. "I thought you might come. I didn't know if you'd find me or not."

Jay Mac removed his hat and coat and hung them up. He

stomped snow off his shoes while his eyes darted around the cabin. Leaning on his cane, he took a seat at the table. "I asked around. A Miss Jolene Cartwright was happy to give me directions."

One side of Jarret's mouth lifted in disgust. "She would." He leaned against the door, his arms folded in front of him. "You've spoken to Rennie?"

"Yes."

"Then, you know everything."

"I know enough."

"What are you going to do?"

Jay Mac carefully balanced his cane against one of the table legs. His chipped and twisted spectacles rested far down the bridge of his nose. At his temples and at his side whiskers the threads of gray were more pronounced. The lines at the corners of his green eyes were deeply engraved. "Odd," he said, studying Jarret carefully. "I came here to ask that of you."

"I'm not sure what you mean," said Jarret. "You're leaving soon, aren't you?"

"*I* am, yes. I don't know what Rennie will do. I'm going to offer her the opportunity to take over the Queen's Point project. I'd like you to be her foreman. She'll need someone to help her handle the men, at least until she wins them over."

"Under the circumstances I don't think she'll jump at the chance."

"Because you'll be there?"

Jarret shook his head. "Because you'll be *there*. In New York. She's not going to let you go back alone. She's probably not going to let you out of her sight once you're there. She didn't come all this way to find you only to let you risk your life a second time."

Jay Mac pushed his spectacles up his nose. His sandy brows came together, deepening the vertical crease in his forehead. "What the hell are you talking about?"

Jarret pushed away from the door. "The train wreck," he said. "Your wife and Hollis. What the hell are you talking about?"

"You and my daughter coming to your senses."

Both men were quiet. They stared at one another recounting the conversation in their minds. Jarret said, "I thought you talked to Rennie."

"I did."

"Not about the accident at Juggler's Jump."

"No," Jay Mac said. "Was I supposed to?"

Jarret ran his fingers through his hair, sighing. "I thought she would bring it up. Have you sent a telegram east?"

"Not yet. What's this about Hollis and Nina?"

Jarret didn't answer directly. He went to the pantry and found a quarter-full bottle of whiskey. He set out two glasses and poured the drinks.

"It's not even noon," Jay Mac said.

Jarret's smile was grim. "It's that kind of news."

Hollis's smile was grim. "It's that kind of news," he said, pushing a tumbler of Scotch toward Nina. He added another splash to his own glass before replacing the decanter on the sideboard. He raised his glass to Nina in a mocking toast.

Nina was hesitant. Her slender fingers curved around the tumbler, and the weight of it looked too heavy for her delicate wrists. The crown of her pale yellow hair barely reached Hollis's shoulder. She raised her face to him, her milky skin seamless across the fine-boned features of her face. Her eyes were widely spaced with enormous pupils that crowded out most of the cinnamon color ringing them. She was nearing fifty but even under the most unforgiving light looked a dozen years less.

Hollis loved the daintiness of her, the exquisite fragility of her lines, the grace of her movements. He loved lifting

366

her against him, raising her silk skirts and plunging into her. She let him do whatever he wanted, never denied him any privilege with her body, but she never initiated their lovemaking, rarely spoke during it, and never commented afterward. Her cool reserve was never breached. It maddened him, intrigued him. He felt protective when he was near her, powerful when he was in her.

It was hard for him to remember who had first approached whom. He had thought for a long time that the overture was his. Now he wasn't so certain. It seemed to him that she was capable of letting him believe he had come to her because it suited her purpose. There were times he felt in complete control of their association and times when he knew without question that he was being manipulated. There were also times when the lines between the two were blurred, when she gained control by letting him think it was his.

If Nina Worth had been a cat, she could only have been Siamese.

Hollis's broad shoulders lifted as he touched the rim of his glass to Nina's. Gaslight was reflected in the highly polished wainscoting of the study and refracted in the cut glass facets of the tumblers. He sipped his drink, then offered his arm to Nina and escorted her to the loveseat. They sat in unison, turned slightly toward one another. Her nearly black eyes never left his face. Her small bow mouth was damp with Scotch.

"He's alive, isn't he?" she asked. Her voice was coldly elegant, like chilled crystal. There was no resonance to her speech, little nuance of passion or conviction. "That's what you want to tell me."

That she had guessed astonished him. He nodded. "How did you know?"

She shrugged. The narrow black and fitted lines of her mourning gown further emphasized the sleek, graceful line of Nina's figure. "How long have you known?"

367

"Less than an hour. I came as soon as I heard. He's returning to New York." Hollis examined his pocket watch. "In fact, he'll be here in just under thirty-six hours. No. 448 is scheduled to arrive in the middle of the night."

Nina gave no evidence of surprise. "So soon," she said calmly.

He nodded. "I believe it was meant to be a secret. He's been traveling for days it seems. He was recognized by a dispatcher in Pittsburgh who sent the information on to me. I imagine he thought I would want to make a celebration of it."

"Your wife's with him?"

"Yes."

"You should have killed her." She offered the rebuke with the same tone one would offer a practical suggestion. There was no hint of malice. "Her shares would have been yours then, and she wouldn't have gone looking for John."

It amused Hollis that Nina never called her husband Jay Mac. She was of the opinion that it was a vulgar name. Hollis finished his drink. His dark brown eyes studied the cool, poised features of his lover's face. "I don't think it could have been done without bringing suspicion to me. Anyway, we both thought her trip to Juggler's Jump would be fruitless. He should have died in the wreckage. Others did."

"Perhaps there is a mistake."

"There's no mistake."

"Do you think he saw Queen's Point?"

"I don't know. Even if he did there are ways to explain it. It would have been better if he had died, but I'm not completely vulnerable there."

"Do you think he knows about us?"

"Rennie wouldn't tell him. She didn't before he left. I doubt she would later."

"She's very protective of him, isn't she?" asked Nina.

"Very protective."

"It will be difficult to kill him."

"Nina. I told you before. It isn't absolutely necessary."

She did something she had never done before. She picked up his large hand and laid it over her breast. "I think it is."

She let him take her on the floor of the study.

Thirty minutes later she was saying goodbye to him. He's so easy, she thought, watching him walk through the gate. He glanced once over his shoulder, grinned. She didn't miss a beat, raising her hand as she raised a perfect smile. She waved. Nina didn't step back from the threshold until he was out of sight.

After shutting the door, Nina returned to the study. She poured herself a drink and sat down, staring at the floor where she had seduced Hollis Banks. How surprised John would have been, she thought, if he had come upon them, even more surprised to discover she had initiated the encounter. She had never done that with her husband. It would have made him suspicious. He would have wondered what she wanted. Hollis didn't even ask.

Nina sipped her drink. Her hands were steady, her features placid; but a fire burned at the center of her belly, and alcohol fanned the flames.

It was difficult to accept that John was alive. She had planned for so long, accounted for every possibility — except that he would live. The plan had blossomed when she met Hollis Banks, but the seeds had been sown when the whore Moira Dennehy had become her husband's mistress.

It was a succession of insults that helped the plan take root. Moira was an Irish Catholic servant, so far beneath Nina's notice that it still took her breath away to realize she had been usurped by a peasant. John then made his mistress mother to five daughters while Nina had never conceived even once. From the first he had made no attempt to be secretive about his affair. And still, Nina thought, she could have forgiven him all that, could have quelled the rage that roiled her stomach now and ate at her insides like a cancer, if it hadn't been for the final insult.

What she could not forgive, would never forget, was that while he had given her a name, unlimited wealth, and a social position that was enviable even among the city's elite, John MacKenzie Worth had given Moira Dennehy his heart.

Nina finished her drink and set the glass aside. She waited until the liquor settled and the burning sensation in the pit of her stomach passed. The rage that was like a living thing inside her never flickered in her eyes.

She rang for a maid to draw her a bath. She needed to wash Hollis's scent off her skin. Her husband wouldn't have been surprised by that. She had always suffered his touch, much the way she suffered Hollis's. John had seen through her almost immediately and stopped coming to her bed after only a month of marriage. Hollis Banks, her lover of several years, still didn't know what hit him.

Nina rose slowly from the sofa. There was no question of stopping now as Hollis proposed. There was only the question of how to go on.

Rennie sat beside Jarret on the narrow bench seat of the railway car. Across the aisle from them was Jay Mac. He was leaning against the side of the car, his cheek pressed flat to the window and his arms folded in front of him. His spectacles had slipped almost to the end of his nose. His eyes were closed. He had been sleeping for the better part of thirty minutes, oblivious to the rough jostling of the moving car.

Rennie envied her father's ability to sleep. She felt as if she were a single exposed nerve and had felt that way for the length of the journey. Jarret's presence didn't help. Against her wishes Jay Mac had offered Jarret a position as a bodyguard, and again against her wishes, Jarret had accepted. Jay Mac may have felt protected in Jarret's company, but Rennie felt vulnerable.

Her head lolled to one side as her eyes fluttered closed. When her cheek brushed Jarret's shoulder Rennie sat up abruptly. "I'm sorry," she said stiffly.

"You can lean against me, Rennie." He spoke lowly so that his voice wouldn't carry in the crowded passenger car. "I won't think less of you for needing a little sleep. You've hardly closed your eyes since Denver."

She leaned away from Jarret. Her head wobbled against the window. Outside it was dark. The countryside was cloaked in the opaque shadows of night, ink blue and black colored the sky and silhouetted the Pennsylvania hillsides. Occasionally pale rectangles of light would illuminate the windows of distant farmhouses.

"You're a stubborn woman," Jarret said. He turned slightly toward her and placed one arm along the back of the bench seat behind her shoulders. "What are you proving by forcing yourself to stay awake?"

"I'm not trying to prove anything. I can't sleep." She could feel the heat of his arm behind her. The simple gesture of support was too much and not enough. "We're slipping into New York like criminals ourselves. Aren't you the least concerned about what's going to happen?"

"Your father's paying me to worry, Rennie. Not you. We've done what we can to keep your father's arrival a secret. There's certainly not going to be a welcoming party of family at the platform to greet him."

"I wish Mama knew he was coming home," she said wistfully. She pointed to Jay Mac. "He looks older, don't you think? These last days have been hard on him."

Jarret's eyes slipped from Rennie's careworn profile to her father's. There were shadows beneath Jay Mac's closed eyes, and the broad arc of his cheekbones was more pronounced. The side whiskers were more gray than ash, and even in sleep there were tiny white lines of strain at the corners of his mouth. Jarret turned back to Rennie. "They've been hard on you, too," he said.

"If they have been, then you know the reason," she said. "I didn't want you to accept my father's offer."

Jarret was not entirely successful at keeping the bitterness out of his tone. "You would rather have had Ethan accompany you and Jay Mac from Denver."

"That's what I said then and what I still wish had happened."

"Because you think I can't protect you."

Rennie's eyes dropped to where Jarret was flexing the fingers of his right hand. "I never said that," she said softly.

Jarret removed the arm that was cradling her shoulders and faced forward. He propped his long legs on the bench across from him. "You didn't have to, Rennie. There are some things you don't have to say at all."

She wanted to tell him he was wrong, but her own pride kept her silent. Let him think he was the cripple instead of her. He didn't have to know how the arm at her back had tortured her, how his presence was a constant, painful reminder of what they had shared and what he no longer wanted from her. She had been rejected, not the other way around, and Jay Mac's offer to Jarret and Jarret's acceptance had been further proof that her feelings were of little importance. To Rennie's way of thinking, she had been betrayed by both the men she loved.

Perhaps if they had had the opportunity to speak of Jay Mac's offer privately, Rennie thought, she may have been able to convince Jarret to stay behind. She may have risked telling him that it would simply hurt too much to have him as a companion and not a lover. Instead, when Jay Mac and Jarret returned to Mrs. Shepard's boardinghouse, Rennie was presented with a *fait accompli*. There was nothing she could say to change the mind of either man.

When they reached Denver she had tried again. Ethan

had been willing to travel east with them, Michael had been willing to let him go, but Jay Mac had thwarted her, pointing out Ethan's responsibilities to his wife and daughter. Did Rennie want it on her conscience, he asked, if anything happened to Ethan?

How was she supposed to have answered that? she wondered. That she would have preferred Ethan to be hurt rather than Jarret? That she would have preferred her own father's life to be at risk rather than Jarret's? Solomon hadn't been called on to make those judgments, and Rennie didn't try to. She didn't want anything to happen to anyone. She wanted it to be over.

Jay Mac, though, wanted Jarret Sullivan, and as usual, he got what he wanted. It was left to Rennie to stoically endure the pain of her strained partnership with Jarret.

Looking through the sweep of his lowered lashes, Jay Mac studied first the grieving eyes of his daughter, then the impassive features of the man at her side. Love had made them so very foolish, he thought. He wished he was with Moira now. She would know what to do.

Northeast Rail's No. 448 arrived at the New York station minutes ahead of schedule. The platform was a hub of activity even at four in the morning. Well-wishers had come to see off friends and family; others had arrived to greet the incoming hoard. Porters were busy collecting and distributing baggage, and there were lines at both the ticket and telegraph windows. Station officers patrolled the platform, greeting passengers with a jaunty salute and swinging their nightsticks to match the rhythm of their stride.

Rennie, Jarret, and Jay Mac waited on the platform for their bags and trunks. Rennie spoke quietly to her father while Jarret stood off to one side, his eyes scanning the length and breadth of the station. He was not looking for anything in particular, merely looking. It was force of habit more than expectation that kept him studying the scene, but it was experience more than luck that kept his gaze returning to one man.

He was slightly built. His clothes were expensive but ill-fitting. The seams of his stylish jacket drooped over the set of his shoulders, and his trousers were cuffed in opposition to the current fashion, as if they'd been too long. Borrowed? Jarret wondered. Stolen?

A narrow face had been compensated for by large side whiskers and a full black beard. A mustache dropped over the man's upper lip. A bowler was tipped forward, cutting across the man's brow.

He sat alone, moving once when he was joined on the bench by a fellow traveler and carrying his carefully folded newspaper with him. He obviously relished his isolation—which made Jarret wonder why he was spending his time in the train station. He appeared uninterested in the comings and goings of the passengers, so it was unlikely that he was waiting for someone. He showed no interest in the departure board which posted delays at regular intervals. It was doubtful the man himself was going anywhere. He made no attempt to read the bulky newspaper he kept folded on his lap. Occasionally he took an interest in his polished shoes, brushing the toe free of an imagined bit of dust or soot, but mostly he stared straight ahead, his head tilted to one side, the perfect picture of a solitary man lost in solitary thought.

And Jarret knew there was something wrong.

"Let's go," he said, stepping closer to Rennie and Jay Mac.

Rennie protested. "Our bags . . . my trunks."

Jarret placed his hand at the small of Rennie's back. "Now," he said tightly. "We'll get the baggage later. Jay Mac, you stay between me and the train."

Acknowledging there was some urgency, Rennie did not voice another protest. She kept pace with the long-legged strides of her father and Jarret as they headed for the exit.

Jarret glanced behind him. The man on the bench was still there. He was unfolding his newspaper. "Keep walking," Jarret said quietly. "Don't look back." He gave father and daughter a small push forward before he stopped himself and spun on his toes, drawing his gun in the same motion.

Jarret's quarry was no longer on the bench, but standing behind it. The newspaper lay on the floor. The stranger held a gun in both hands. They fired simultaneously. Jarret's shot went a fraction of an inch wide of the mark, catching the assailant in the drooping jacket sleeve instead of the arm. The other bullet also went wide, this time by more than twelve inches. Instead of striking Jay Mac it felled Rennie.

Above the screams of the passengers, above the melee of scrambling travelers, Jarret heard her cry, heard Jay Mac's anguished shout. He stopped his pursuit of the fleeing gunman and ran back to Rennie and her father. Jay Mac was on his knees beside Rennie, gently turning her over. Jarret helped him open her coat. There was a blossom of blood on her left shoulder. Behind them a crowd began to gather.

Jarret raised Rennie's head on his lap and pressed a handkerchief to her wound. His eyes darted through the faces in the crowd. "Did anyone chase the gunman?" he demanded.

"One of the station guards went running in the other direction," someone said. "Maybe he went after him."

Jarret had to be satisfied with that. Rennie stirred against him. He touched the back of his hand to her head as a measure of color returned to her face. "Rennie?"

She opened her eyes and saw the drawn and ashen faces of the two men immediately above her. Beyond them a sea of unfamiliar faces crowded her vision. For a moment it was difficult to catch her breath. She winced at the pressure Jarret was applying to her shoulder. "I think I had the wind knocked out of me," she whispered. "Jay Mac pushed me too hard. I fell."

Jarret looked at Rennie's father. Jay Mac shook his head. "I didn't touch her," he said.

"You're hurting me, Jarret," she said. "Your hand's hurting me."

Jarret knew the pressure of his hand was firm but not enough to give her pain. What she felt, the only thing she felt, was from the gunshot wound. "It will have to hurt a little while," he told her. "We'll get Dr. Turner to look at it, though, as soon as we get you home." To Jay Mac he added, "It's not a mortal wound. She's going to be fine."

"Of course I'm going to be fine," Rennie said with some asperity. "Tenacious, remember?" She tried to sit up and promptly collapsed.

Jarret leaned over her and touched his lips to her forehead. "God, but I love you."

There were tears in Jay Mac's eyes as he helped Jarret lift his daughter. He acted quickly, getting assistance, then dispersing stragglers in the crowd. His natural authority commanded attention and obedience, and in short order he had their luggage collected and a hansom cab waiting for them in the street. Jarret gave a short, impatient statement to the station police and management before he climbed into the cab. The sudden return of John MacKenzie Worth created a stir that nearly overshadowed the shooting. Onlookers gathered again as word spread of the identities of the travelers. Disgusted with the press of the curious, Jarret slammed the door of the cab.

"It will be in the morning papers," Jarret said to Jay Mac. "All of it. The shooting, your return. There's no possibility of keeping it a secret now."

Jay Mac cradled Rennie's head in his lap. He stroked her hair, keeping her steady as the cab rolled forward. "Apparently it never was a secret. What happened back there? Who shot my daughter?"

"I don't know." Gaslight from the street filtered into the cab. Jarret stared at Rennie's pale face. It was difficult for him to think of anything save the fact that he hadn't been able to protect her. "Someone sitting on one of the benches caught my eye. I wasn't certain we were meant any harm at all. I thought he was a pickpocket or a thief making plans for a robbery. It only made sense to leave before he saw us as easy targets." Jarret leaned forward and touched Rennie's cheek with the back of his index finger. "When I looked back he was unfolding the paper in his lap. I saw the gun. I couldn't get you out of there fast enough."

"You probably saved our lives."

Jay Mac's words meant little to Jarret, not when he knew he should have been able to do more. "I pulled my shot at the last moment," he said quietly. "I shouldn't have done that. The assailant got away because I couldn't make myself go for the heart."

Jay Mac frowned. "What do mean? You could have killed the gunman and you chose not to?"

"Something like that," Jarret said. His smile was rife with self-mockery. "I told myself that after Dee Kelly I would remember that women can be as treacherous as any man. In the blink of an eye I forgot that tonight."

Jay Mac's frown merely deepened. "Are you talking about Rennie?"

Jarret shook his head. He leaned back in his seat. "No, sir. I'm talking about the shooter. It wasn't a man who fired that gun. It was a woman."

Chapter Fourteen

Everyone agreed Rennie was a horrible patient. Of the family, Maggie could tolerate her the longest, Mary Francis the least. No one, not even Dr. Turner, quite understood how Jarret could spend so much time in her miserable company. In the week since the shooting she had snapped at everyone a half-dozen times.

Jarret sat in a large, comfortable armchair near the bed. A small table separated him from Rennie. A marble chessboard with ivory pieces was the focus of their attention. Most of the captured men lay on Rennie's side of the board. She was gloating as Jarret's fingers hesitated on his remaining bishop.

He looked up at her, saw her triumphant face, and reconsidered his move. "Your family thinks I'm a saint for putting up with you," he said.

"Don't let Mary Francis hear you talk like that. It's practically blasphemous."

Jarret smirked. "That's how much you know. She's the one who's suggesting I be canonized." He let go of his bishop, watched her swoop down on it with her rook, and sighed. "I'm not nearly equal to your skill," he said. "You should get Jay Mac in here."

"He's only a little better than Mary Francis when it comes to tolerating my company," she said resignedly. "I haven't been very pleasant to anyone." She didn't expect Jarret to deny it, and he didn't. Sighing, Rennie adjusted her position on the bed, plumping the pillows behind her. She winced as her shoulder bumped the headboard.

"Are you all right?" he asked. "Here, let me do that." Jarret fixed the pillows, one at the small of her back, the other at her shoulders. He smoothed the blankets over her lap and moved the table so that she could reach it without straining.

"Thank you." She couldn't quite meet his eyes. "That's better."

"That hardly hurt at all."

"My shoulder's getting better."

Jarret shook his head. He captured her chin and raised it so that she was forced to look at him. "No," he said, "I meant saying thank you." He let his hand fall away as Rennie pulled back, all prickly and defensive now. He cut off the tirade she was preparing by simply laughing at her. A moment later she gave in and joined him.

Jay Mac nudged open the door to Rennie's bedroom with the toe of his shoe. "That sweet laughter is music to *my* ears," he said, elbowing the door closed. He was carrying a dinner tray ladened with slices of ham, parsley potatoes, corn and lima beans. Steam from the dishes had misted his new spectacles. He set the tray across Rennie's lap and wiped off his lenses with a handkerchief. "Why is it no one else can make her laugh like that?" he asked Jarret.

"Perhaps because no one else plays the fool so well," said Jarret.

"Somehow I doubt that's the case," Jay Mac said.

Rennie retied the ribbon that gathered her thick hair at her nape. "You heard it from him," she said, unfolding her napkin. She pointed to the chessboard. "Perhaps you could help him out of his predicament, Jay Mac. This game won't last three more moves if you don't."

Jay Mac sat on the edge of Rennie's bed, careful not to

379

jostle her tray. He studied the board for a moment. "It won't last three more moves if I do. He's coming at you from all sides. Go on, Jarret. You can have in her check."

Startled, Rennie reexamined the board, then Jarret's smug smile. She sniffed delicately, flattening her mouth primly, and went back to cutting her meat. "I think you moved something while I wasn't looking," she said testily. "I refuse to believe I've lost fairly."

Now Jay Mac laughed. He gave Jarret a pat on the back, reminding him dinner would be within the half-hour, and that their appointment was at eight. He kissed Rennie on the cheek, patted her uninjured shoulder, and left.

The door had barely closed when Rennie turned on Jarret. "What appointment? What are you and my father doing?"

Jarret moved his black knight. "Check."

Rennie wagged her fork at him, refusing to even glance at the game board. "I'm not a train. I can't be so easily sidetracked."

"It has nothing to do with you," Jarret said.

"I didn't think that it did. It was a simple enough question."

He gave her an arch look. "Nothing is ever simple with you, Rennie."

"You're doing it again," she said. "I won't be dismissed like that, Jarret. My mother and sisters have been doing it all week. Even Jay Mac won't give me straight answers. Then they have the gall to wonder why I'm so miserable being cooped up in this room. You've been the only one to talk about what happened, what *really* happened."

"I think the others didn't want to distress you."

"Well, I *am* distressed. And I have been since I woke up in this bed with Dr. Turner leaning over me. I'm not used to being shot."

Jarret managed to choke back his laughter. "It's not the sort of thing one gets used to," he said dryly.

"You know what I mean. I think I have a right to know more than anyone, including you, has thought fit to tell me. It isn't fair, Jarret."

Pushing aside the table and chessboard, Jarret stretched his legs in front of him. He recognized Rennie's stubbornness. It was in the shape of her seriously set mouth, in the tension around her emerald eyes. Her feathery brows were drawn fractionally together. The curling strand of dark red hair that lay across her left cheek fluttered slightly as she worked a muscle in her jaw.

Her skin was flushed, not the unnatural, fevered flush that had waxed and waned for the better part of the week, but the flush of frustration and impatience. Two buttons at the neck of her nightshirt had been unfastened, exposing the hollow of her throat and part of her collarbone. She should have looked fragile. With her chin jutting at that defiant angle, with the pulse beating hard in the side of her neck, with the tense rise and fall of her breath, Rennie looked unbreakable.

It was a sure sign that she was recovered.

Jarret's fingers threaded through his hair. The shape of his mouth changed, puffing slightly, as he slowly exhaled. "I don't think any of your family meant to be secretive by design, Rennie; it simply unfolded that way. On your second day here you took a fever, and no one wanted to do or say anything that would impede your recovery."

Rennie put down her fork. She had little interest in her food now. "Such as . . ."

"Such as your mother collapsing when she first saw you being carried in the house." His voice grew grave and quiet. "And again when she saw Jay Mac hovering over her in the entrance hall."

"Poor Mama, seeing Jay Mac like that . . . with no warning. She must have thought she'd died and gone to heaven." Rennie's eyes clouded because what she saw in Jarret's troubled face didn't quite fit her facile explanation. "But she's all right now, isn't she? I mean, she's been flitting in and out of here, caring for me all week. It was just a fainting spell, isn't that right? The shock of everything . . ." She stopped. "What else is it, Jarret?"

"Moira was going to have another child, Rennie. She lost the baby that night." He watched Rennie's face drain of color, her eyes darken and widen. "It's not your fault," he said quickly. "And if you go on believing it for even another minute, you'll be justifying your family's avoidance of telling you. It wasn't the shock of seeing you or Jay Mac, or even the fall. She'd been having pain for some time. Dr. Turner said there was nothing that could have been done, that weeks ago he and your mother discussed that she might not be able to carry the child to term. Your mother's beyond the years when most women can even conceive."

Tears made Rennie's eyes shine. "It doesn't matter," she said softly, sadly. "She loves babies. And Papa . . . he must be grieving. Did he know about Mama's condition before he went west?"

"No. Apparently your mother wasn't certain herself until after you had already left to search for Jay Mac." He could see immediately that Rennie was blaming herself again. "Don't do it, Rennie. Moira had Maggie and Skye here to help her. If you hadn't gone, you couldn't have brought Jay Mac back to her. He hasn't left the house, and he's hardly ever left her side since we returned."

"I thought it was because he was avoiding Nina and the newspaper reporters."

"You know about the reporters?"

She nodded. "If I stand at the window at just the right angle, I can see one or two of them pacing the sidewalk in front of the house. Once in a while a beat cop runs them off. Do you mean he hasn't spoken to anyone about his return?"

"He let Logan Marshall in a few days ago. He gave the story to the *Chronicle* so the other papers would have to make some allowances for the truth in their articles. Your father hasn't been completely forthcoming, either. We've only been through the first ripples of scandal. No one knows that Jay Mac believes, for instance, that it was his wife who tried to kill him and shot you instead. No one save Marshall knows that Jay Mac was probably the intended target. Most people believe you were simply caught in the crossfire of a gun battle between me and one of my bounties."

"Jarret! That isn't what happened. I don't want people believing that somehow you're responsible!"

"You don't have a choice," he said flatly. "Argue about it and I'll rethink my decision to tell you what I haven't before."

Rennie set her mouth in a mutinous line. Only her flashing eyes argued her thoughts.

"Very wise." Jarret leaned back in the armchair and raised his legs, hooking his heels on the walnut bed frame. "The fact that your father hasn't left the house has only been in part because of Moira. I've been insistent that he remain here as well. Moira's condition and your own have made it easier to convince him of the necessity of it, but I've warned him what I would do if he crossed me."

Rennie blinked. "You *threatened* my father?" she asked, incredulous.

"I like to think I *reassured* him that I would do my job." His eyes dropped away from Rennie's face to her shoulder. He could see the bandages through the material of her shift. "There will be no more incidents like the one that almost got you killed."

"That wasn't your fault, Jarret. You saved my father's life."

"It wasn't supposed to be at your expense."

Rennie removed the tray and placed it on the table. She dropped her napkin on top. Without warning she threw back the covers and put her legs over the side of the bed.

Her feet went between Jarret's outstretched ones, and when she stood his were nudged aside. She was trapped in the vee of his legs, exactly where she wanted to be. Leaning forward, she braced her arms on the rounded arms of Jarret's chair. Her face was level with his.

"Get back in bed, Rennie. What do you think you're—"

"I love you," she said. Her voice was tense as pain shot through her injured shoulder. She ignored it. "I know you love me. I heard you . . . at the station. Please tell me I did, that I didn't imagine it."

"Rennie, get back in—"

Her eyes implored him. "Jarret."

He didn't say anything for a long time, searching her face as she searched his soul. His fingers closed around her wrists, and with a gentle tug he pulled her forward and onto his lap. "You didn't imagine it," he said finally, reluctantly.

Rennie's legs curled as she leaned into him. Her slender fingers threaded through his. "Why don't you want to say it?"

He didn't answer. She hadn't thought it all through yet; he knew that. Her legal annulment had already been finalized. Thanks to the influence of Judge Halsey, the decree had been waiting for Rennie when she returned. But in the eyes of the church, Rennie was still very much a married woman. Jarret didn't see things so differently, and neither, in truth, did Rennie. "You should be back in bed," he said.

"I'm where I want to be. Don't chase me away."

He shook his head. As always, she credited him with more strength than he had. He wanted her right where she was. He could mouth a different sentiment, but in his heart he couldn't push her away. "I'm accompanying your father to a meeting at the Worth Building tonight. His intention is to do some . . . spring cleaning, I think he called it. This will be the first time he's met with anyone from Northeast."

"Hollis will be there?"

"He was invited. He'll have the opportunity to answer Jay Mac's accusations. Afterward we're going to see Nina."

"My God," Rennie said softly. "My father doesn't mean to accuse Nina, does he? There's no proof that she was at the platform. You couldn't identify her. I never saw her. Neither did Jay Mac."

"I think I'll know the truth when I see her face to face," Jarret said. "But I don't think it matters one way or the other to your father. Even if I could say with certainty that it was Nina who did the shooting, Jay Mac doesn't mean to accuse her or press charges."

Rennie frowned. "Then, what does he—"

"He hasn't fully confided in me, Rennie, but I think your father intends to demand a divorce."

For a full minute she couldn't say anything. Her head rested against Jarret's shoulder. Both her hands closed around one of his. She held it near her heart. Her closed eyes held back the press of tears. "I can't find it in myself to take any happiness in it," she said at last. "It's so sad . . . all of it." She sniffed and swiped at her eyes. "Do my sisters know?"

"I think so. They've been whispering among themselves lately."

"Mama?"

"I believe she and your father have talked it over. There have been hints. No one's saying anything to me, Rennie. It's not my business. It's not even yours or your sisters'. This is between Jay Mac and Nina and your mother."

"I know," she whispered. "I didn't want to be consulted. Only informed."

"I could be wrong about it," he said.

"No. No, you're not. I've been feeling the tension, the anxiety of the others' unspoken thoughts. If Nina consents, he'll marry my mother—if *she* consents."

"Can you imagine Jay Mac giving either woman a choice?"

385

Rennie's smile was faint, wistful. "He'll steal Mama away."

"It'll be another scandal."

"In light of all the others, a mere peccadillo." Her hands squeezed his. "Did Jay Mac ask you to go with him tonight?"

"No. He wouldn't do that. I volunteered." Jarret felt the full force of her doubting look. "Actually, I insisted."

"Is Nina expecting Jay Mac?"

"No. It would have been a little foolish to inform her."

"To invite Hollis to the board meeting tonight was foolish."

"I doubt it. If he comes, it's because he thinks he can talk himself out of everything we suspect. If he doesn't come, then he's as good as admitted his guilt. More to the point, if he doesn't come, I suspect he's long gone from New York. I don't think he'd wait around to be arrested for fraud and embezzlement against Northeast."

She sighed. "I wish I could be there. I'd like to accuse him of a few things myself."

Jarret could imagine. He helped Rennie to her feet and back into bed. "I have to go to dinner. Your family's probably already wondering what's keeping me."

She sniffed haughtily. "Of course they'd never believe you could prefer my miserable company to theirs."

"God, no," he said, straight-faced. "They'd never believe that. I'll have to think of something else to tell them." He kissed her swiftly on the mouth, pressing hard. It was the first time he had kissed her since leaving Echo Falls, and the sweet taste of her made him want to linger. He just managed to walk away.

He also just managed to duck the pillow she sailed at his head.

Minutes before he was due to leave with Jay Mac, Jarret

poked his head in the doorway of Rennie's room. Except for the firelight, the bedchamber was dark. She was turned on her side away from him, covered by a mound of blankets. He could just make out the top of her head. She had been more active today than on any day since the shooting, and he knew she was tired. Still, he wanted to kiss her. The hurried, teasing kiss he had given her earlier hadn't been nearly enough. He had thought he shouldn't tell her he loved her, now he regretted not saying the words.

Jarret had taken a step inside the room when Maggie appeared in the hallway with a tray of cookies and hot cocoa. Her presence gave him a start. Even carrying china cups and saucers, she could move without making a sound. He stepped out of the doorway and held a finger to his lips. "Your sister's sleeping."

Maggie managed to shrug without unbalancing her load. "I'll just wake her up, then. It's too early for her to sleep through till morning. She'll regret it in the middle of the night." She started to go in, then paused. "Did you want to say something to her?" she asked. "Papa's gone outside to the carriage to wait for you, but you have time."

Jarret was torn. He thought of Rennie's sweet mouth. He thought of Jay Mac outside the house with only Mr. Cavanaugh for an escort. But kissing Rennie in front of her younger sister wasn't the same as kissing Rennie when they were alone. "It can wait," he said. He held the door open, and Maggie ducked past him. "If she's awake when I get back, I'll see her then."

Maggie watched him go, smiling to herself. She placed the tray beside the bed, knocking over some of the chess pieces. They clattered to the floor. Maggie was surprised when her sister didn't stir. "You really are tired," she said, bending to pick up the pieces. She laid them out neatly on the table and spoke to her sister in a sing-song voice. "Rennie. You need to wake up. You'll be restless all night. No one wants you roaming the halls like—" Maggie straightened and leaned over the bed, frowning now. "Rennie. You can stop pretending that you don't hear me." She carefully placed her hand on her sister's uninjured shoulder and gave it a gentle shake. "I want to talk to you about—"

Maggie broke off as the shoulder she thought she was clutching simply dissolved into nothingness. "What in the—" She tore at the covers, stripping away the layers of blankets. Pillows had been laid out lengthwise, plumped just enough to assure there was substance to the mound. On the pillow where Rennie's head was supposed to be, one of her hairpieces had been strategically arranged to give the impression she was most definitely there.

Stepping back from the bed, Maggie's head twisted as her eyes darted around the room. Nothing. She quickly looked in the adjoining dressing and bathing rooms and again found no one.

"Oh, Rennie," she said sadly, leaning against the door jamb. "How could you do this? What do you think you can accomplish?" Shaking her head, Maggie left Rennie's room. Although she ran down the hallway and the main staircase, she missed Jarret's departure. Out of the corner of her eye she saw her mother in the parlor. Moira's interest had been caught by Maggie's pell-mell run to the front door. Maggie took a deep breath, let it out slowly, and forced a smile in her mother's direction. All the while she approached she wondered what she was going to say.

Eleven men gathered in the board room at the Worth Building. John MacKenzie Worth sat at the head of the long walnut table. The ashtray in front of him remained unused while the ones set at regular intervals along the length of the table collected ashes and balanced the glowing tips of thick cigars. Curls of blue-gray smoke rose from ashtrays. A haze of it hung above the men and collected in the gaslight.

Jarret Sullivan did not join the men at the table. He sat by the door, slouched, his hands resting casually on his lap, his legs stretched negligently in the aisle, his head bent slightly forward. Although his lashes shaded his eyes and his posture gave the appearance of uninterest, even boredom, nothing to do with Hollis Banks escaped his attention.

Hollis sat at the far end of the table opposite Jay Mac. His powerful shoulders filled the breadth of his chair. His large hands lay flat on the table surface as he spoke, a bearing that seemed to indicate he had nothing to hide. As he answered questions regarding his role as director in Jay Mac's absence, he neither fidgeted nor gestured.

To Jarret's way of thinking, Hollis's very air of calm was his biggest deceit or conceit.

The Queen's Point project was at issue for everyone at the table, and Hollis handled the questions with great aplomb. "I was assured by the surveying team that the least costly route was also the best," he told the others. "Jay Mac himself relies on the information given to him by his surveyors and engineers. I can't imagine that you think it could be any different for me." He smiled genially, making certain he caught the eyes of every man, including Jay Mac. "When Mary Renee, who was then my fiancée, came to me with another scenario based on her calculations, I listened to what she had to say—in fact, I discussed her conclusions with Jay Mac—and decided, again based on the expertise of men who had been with Northeast much longer than either Rennie or myself, that she had misinterpreted her data.

"The project was begun with the approval of Jay Mac and yourselves—to the accompaniment of some fanfare, I might add—and I was named to oversee it. Jay Mac will recall, of course, that I made several requests to visit Queen's Point myself, and each time some situation here in New York prevented my departure."

Jarret's attention shifted from Hollis to Jay Mac. Although the head of Northeast Rail sat there in stony silence, Jarret could see that Hollis's last statement had taken him by surprise. Not only that, but it was evident Hollis was speaking the truth. Clearly Jay Mac had forgotten that Hollis had asked to look over the project development personally.

' "The last situation, as all of you know," Hollis continued evenly, "was the accident at Juggler's Jump. The Queen's Point project had to take a position of lesser importance in light of our belief that Jay Mac was dead. When I was named to run Northeast, as per Jay Mac's own recommendation, Queen's Point was just one of the developments I had to delegate to someone else."

Jay Mac's voice was hard, his eyes cold. His stare was meant to be intimidating. He wondered that the younger man did not blink. "The Queen's Point project was never developed," he said. "I have requisitions for supplies that were never delivered; payroll receipts for men who never worked a day for Northeast. Tens of thousands of dollars have been spent on lumber, steel, and man hours, and there is nothing in all of Colorado to show for it. You assured me and this board that things were proceeding at the site."

Hollis's broad face was cool and impassive. His dark brown eyes were leveled at Jay Mac. "I take full responsibility for placing confidence in men whom I thought deserved it. I misjudged their character. *That,* gentlemen, is my crime against Northeast, nothing else. And if you believe I am guilty of masterminding a fraud at Queen's Point, then can't the same case be made for Jay Mac? After all, he placed his trust in me.

"I regret that I was unable to supervise the project's growth — and in this case, its start — but I believe my history with this company speaks for itself. During Jay Mac's absence I acted in all ways as a competent president and leader for Northeast, justifying your confidence. With Jay

Mac's return I am quite willing, even anxious, to step down from my post and take up my former position as vice president of operations. I can assure you, my first order of business will be to get to the bottom of the Queen's Point fraud. I will personally lead the investigation, and I will report directly to this board of my progress."

Heads swiveled in Jay Mac's direction. "I already have someone in mind to investigate the fraud," he said. "Someone who doesn't work for the company and generally has no interest in it. I'm afraid, Hollis, that letting you act as overseer of the investigation is kin to letting the fox guard the hen house." Jay Mac ignored the murmurs of surprise that greeted his comment. "You'll understand why I won't tolerate it."

There was the faintest flush to Hollis's face. His reply, however, was smooth. "Not only do I understand it, I applaud it. In your place I would make exactly the same determination." He gestured to Jarret. "Of course, you've named Mr. Sullivan."

"I have."

"A good choice."

It was news to Jarret. He said nothing and merely nodded in the direction of the board members who turned to briefly survey him.

"And Mary Renee will be in charge of the construction at Queen's Point." Board members exchanged wary glances; some cleared their throats at the announcement. The reaction did not give Jay Mac a moment's pause. "I expect the project to get under way this spring. By that time Mr. Sullivan's investigation should be at an end. I will have this matter of culpability cleared, gentlemen, and get on with the business of railroading."

His firm statement of intent was met with agreement. Jay Mac stared levelly at Hollis Banks. "You will, of course, be cooperative with the investigation. You may retain your position as vice president of operations, and should the evidence clear you, I will naturally make a formal apology."

Hollis's smile was cool. His brows lifted fractionally. "The evidence *will* clear me, and at that time, sir, I'll be asking for more than your formal apology." He rose from the table, nodded to Jay Mac, then the board, and took up his hat and coat. His exit was marred only by the fact that he was forced to step over Jarret's outstretched legs.

On the journey from the Worth Building to his home, Jay Mac sat in one corner of the carriage, his face set impassively as he stared out the window. He turned suddenly to Jarret and said, "You're going to take the job, aren't you?"

It was no good telling Jay Mac that the question was more than a bit late, that the time for considering it had long since passed. "Yes," Jarret said. "I'll take the job."

Jay Mac nodded once. He turned away again and said quietly, "There's no pleasure in it. I trusted that man."

"I understand."

"The board's on the fence. He tells a believable story. If you can't prove he's behind the fraud, he's going to ask for my resignation."

"I thought that was his threat."

"I *founded* Northeast. I'm not going to lose it to that bastard."

Jarret said nothing. The carriage pulled up to Jay Mac's palatial first residence. "Do you want me to come inside?" he asked as Jay Mac alighted.

"You can wait in the foyer," he said. "My discussion with Nina is private."

Jarret nodded and followed Jay Mac. Several rooms on the first floor of the mansion were lit. On the second floor, light streamed from French doors that opened onto a stone balcony. They were greeted by a butler whose gaunt face did not show a flicker of surprise at Jay Mac's arrival.

"I want to see my wife," Jay Mac said, handing over his coat and derby. "Mr. Sullivan will wait here. Bring him something to drink, Pinkney, anything he wants."

"As you wish." Mr. Pinkney took Jarret's duster. His lips pursed in disapproval when he saw the gun at Jarret's hip. He started to hold his hand out, thought better of it, and showed Jarret to a padded bench in the entrance hall near the foot of the stairs. "Mrs. Worth is in the study," he told Jay Mac. "May I announce you?"

"That won't be necessary." To Jarret, he said, "This won't take above an hour." He turned back to the butler. "Clear out my wardrobe and chests, Pinkney. Pack it all. Have the trunks taken out to the carriage, and I don't expect Mr. Sullivan to lift a finger in their removal." He strode off in the direction of the study.

"So it's finally come to that," Pinkney said lowly, watching the study door open and close.

"You've been expecting it?" asked Jarret.

For a moment the butler let down his guard. He sighed. "Every day for better than twenty-five years." Hefting the coats and hats in his hands, Pinkney hung them, then went to get help for the packing.

There was no conversation between Jarret and Jay Mac during the journey back to Moira's. The carriage was so full of trunks and baggage that Jarret shared the driver's seat with Mr. Cavanaugh. When they arrived at Broadway and 50th they were greeted at the door with the news that Rennie had disappeared.

Over Jay Mac's head Jarret looked from Moira to Maggie to Skye. Their faces were drawn, their expressions anxious. "How can that be?" he asked. "She was sleeping when I left her."

Maggie shook her head. "I thought she was, too. But

that was only pillows covered with blankets. I have no idea what time she left, perhaps while all of us were dining."

"But why—"

Skye looped her arm through her mother's, taking support as much as giving it. "We hoped she'd have met up with you," she said. "Where else would she go but to Papa's meeting? We all thought she meant to confront Hollis."

"She wasn't there," said Jay Mac. He glanced back at Jarret as if hoping there might be some logical explanation. "Have you sent anyone for the police?" he asked.

Maggie shook her head. "We wanted to make certain she wasn't with you, but Skye and I will go for them now."

"No," Jarret said. "I'll do it. Let me go to her room first and see if there's some indication where she might have gone." He tried to step forward, but no one else moved. He realized they were so stunned by the enormity of Rennie's flight that they couldn't manage the simplest tasks without direction. "Skye, take your mother back to the parlor and see that she has a glass of warm sherry. Jay Mac, ask Mr. Cavanaugh to saddle a horse for me. Maggie, let's go to Rennie's room together. You may notice something that I would miss."

This time the gathering parted. Jarret took the stairs two at a time. Maggie's light step did double-time to match his stride. He threw open the door to Rennie's room and stopped so abruptly on the threshold that Maggie bumped into him.

Apologizing, she looked around his shoulder to see what had brought him up short. Maggie's eyes widened. She blinked hugely. Her mouth parted, but no sound came out.

Rennie was lying on top of the covers, her head propped under one arm. She was snoring softly.

Jarret reached behind him for Maggie and pulled her around, pushing her into the room. "It was a poor joke," he said. "And as far as I can see there was nothing to be gained by it."

"It wasn't a joke," she said. "Rennie *was* gone. I searched for her myself and later Skye helped me."

"You can see for yourself that she's here."

"Of course I can see that." Maggie's expressive mouth pulled to one side as she gave Jarret a look of sheer exasperation. "But as little as twenty minutes ago, she wasn't. Rennie doesn't walk in her sleep."

"I know."

Maggie blinked at that; then she blushed, but she managed not to look away. "Perhaps we should work together to find out what happened," she said. "Instead of arguing."

Jarret nodded. "But first, go tell your parents that she's here and safe." He watched her go. "Spirited little cuss," he said under his breath, approaching the bed. He pushed Rennie's legs to the side as he sat down. He leaned forward, brushing her hair back from her cheek and neck. Her skin was cool. He struck a match and lighted the bedside lamp. Rennie's skin may have been cool, but it was flushed with color, the kind of color that was pressed into the flesh from exposure to the wind or the cold. Rennie's wanderings had taken her outside.

Jarret touched her bare feet. They were no more chilled than her face. He looked around for discarded stockings or shoes. There were none. He checked Rennie's wardrobe and dressing room. There was nothing there.

On his way back to the bed Jarret stopped in front of the French doors. He recalled how easy it had been to scale the balcony, the nearby roof, and drop to the ground. Had it been Rennie's path? Opening the doors, Jarret stepped out. Behind him he heard the approach of Rennie's family.

He stepped back inside. A wet leaf clung to the sole of his boot. He removed it and dropped it on the damp mat of autumn leaves that had never been cleared from the balcony. He had seen enough to know that Rennie had gone that way—and that she hadn't gone on her own.

Rennie was oblivious to the fuss that was being made at

her bedside. She didn't stir as her mother took her hand and patted it gently, repeating Rennie's name in her soft Irish brogue.

"She won't answer you," Jarret said. He pushed a chair toward Moira so that she could sit down. "At least not until she's slept off the effects of the chloroform."

"Chloroform!" Maggie leaned over her sister and smelled her breath. "You're right," she said softly, incredulously. "Rennie's been drugged."

Jay Mac took Moira's hand as her knees seemed to buckle under her. He sat on the curved arm of the chair while Moira leaned against him. "Drugged?" he asked.

Skye came around the other side of the bed and climbed in next to Rennie. She jostled her sister's shoulder. "Rennie? If you're playing some trick on us, it's a poor one."

"It's no trick," said Maggie. "Poking at her isn't going to wake her up."

Skye crossed her arms in front of her and leaned back against the headboard. "I was only trying to help."

"I think what would help," Jarret said, "is for everyone to leave. Rennie's fine. When she wakes we'll be able to get some answers perhaps, but I don't have any for you now."

Jay Mac nodded. "You'll stay with her?"

"You couldn't move me if you wanted. I'll let you know as soon as she's awake. If you want to send Mr. Cavanaugh for the doctor . . ."

"I don't think it's necessary, Papa," Maggie said.

"All right," he said after a long pause. "Moira, come with me. I'm putting you to bed. You've had quite enough for one day."

Moira, assured that her daughter was going to be well *and* protected, recovered a measure of her grit. "Sure and there's no need to be coddlin' me. I'm not in my dotage." She stood, taking his hand now, and led him out of the room. "This is Hollis's work," she said as they stepped out of the room. "He's a cocky bastard. Rennie's church annulment can't happen soon enough to suit me."

Skye and Maggie exchanged wide-eyed glances at their mother's plain speaking. Giggling, they let Jarret shoo them out of Rennie's bedroom.

Jarret shut the door and leaned against it. He watched Rennie sleep her heavy, drugged sleep, but his mind was elsewhere. "He's a dangerous bastard," he said softly. "And an arrogant one."

Rennie's breathing was a series of whispers, of sighs. Jarret got rid of his coat and gunbelt. He pulled off his boots. He locked the doors. Slipping into bed, Jarret's arms circled Rennie. He held her close. The clock on the mantel ticked off the minutes. A light rain spattered in its own metronomic rhythm against the windowpanes, but it was the steady beat of Rennie's heart that lent Jarret the comfort of sleep.

She was groggy when she woke. Stumbling out of bed, Rennie made her way to the bathing room and splashed water on her face at the washstand. A vague sense of nausea lingered. She steadied herself at the basin, uncertain if she was going to be sick or faint. The reflection she saw in the mirror was not encouraging. Rennie did not bother to examine it too closely. She cleaned her teeth, rinsed her mouth, and brushed out the ragged tangles in her hair.

She was on the point of returning to bed when she saw Jarret sprawled across the covers. Instead of climbing back in Rennie dropped into the armchair, stole one of the bed blankets, and nested quite comfortably, drawing the blanket over her bare toes and around her shoulders.

Jarret was sleeping soundly. Rennie dimmed the light from the bedside lamp by turning back the wick. Softening the wash of light on his face did not erase the lines of weariness at the corners of his eyes. Strands of dark blond hair were spiked across his forehead and ruffled against the pillow. There was a certain tautness to his face that should have been absent in sleep but remained nonetheless. Only around his mouth had tension disappeared. Rennie's eyes stayed on the shape of his mouth for a long time, memorizing the curve of it, remembering the texture of it against her own mouth, the damp heat of it touching her skin.

"You're awake."

She blinked, surprised, then looked away guiltily for having been caught staring with such blatant carnal intent. "What are you doing in my bed?" she asked. "I'm not dreaming this, am I? You *are* in my bed and we *are* in my home with my parents down the hall."

"It's a long hall."

Rennie fought back a smile. "You really have to leave, Jarret. Jay Mac and Mama won't stand for this."

"They both know I'm here."

Her eyes grew fractionally larger. "Now I *know* I'm dreaming. This is only slightly more preposterous than what I was dreaming earlier." She yawned and made a half-hearted attempt to cover her mouth. "Excuse me."

Jarret's smile was indulgent. "Tell me about your dream," he said casually.

"It was silly." She stifled a second yawn. "I was at the chapel again. St. Gregory's. Only this time you weren't there to stop the wedding. Hollis's friend Taddy was there, telling me to hurry. So were Hollis's other grooms. I tried to say I didn't want to go with them, but they just ignored me. I was there—and I wasn't there. It was like being a participant *and* a bystander at the same time. We waited somewhere dark, I think, maybe in that little room at the back of the chapel, I'm not certain, and I heard Hollis's name, but I never heard Hollis. That's all I can remember. Oh, and that I had a hard time breathing."

"I see."

"I told you it was silly."

But not unbelievable. Jarret wondered what Hollis's motive was in having Rennie abducted from the house, and just as mystifying, why he had had her returned. He watched Rennie press the back of her hand to her mouth to cover another yawn. Now wasn't the time to tell her. It could wait until morning. He patted the space beside him.

Rennie shook her head. "I couldn't . . . not here."

"I wasn't thinking of anything besides sleeping." He felt the full force of her skeptical look. "Well," he drawled. "I wasn't going to *do* anything besides sleep." He paused a beat and added with solemn intent, "Not, at least, until we're married."

She stilled. "Do you mean it?" she asked softly. "You still want to marry me?"

"I've never changed my mind about that, Rennie. Have you?"

"No!" she said quickly. "Oh, God, no. I . . . I want it more than anything. I just didn't know that loving me meant you were still willing to marry me. I've made such a mess of things, I wouldn't blame you if you just walked away."

"You expected me to do that in Echo Falls, didn't you?" he asked. "When you left the cabin after telling me about Hollis, you thought it was the end."

She nodded reluctantly. "You weren't very encouraging."

"I was —" he searched for the right word — "*staggered*. I needed time to think."

"Jay Mac said that."

"He was right," said Jarret. He was quiet a moment, looking at Rennie consideringly. "Why did you think I accepted work as his bodyguard? And don't say it was because of the money. You know that wasn't a consideration."

"I thought it was because you respect my father . . . and because you wanted to torment me."

He smiled at that. "Those are reasons," he said, "but not my reasons." Jarret propped himself on one elbow. "You

399

were running from me, Rennie. You made up your mind it was all a mistake, and that was the end of it. There's only one reason I considered taking that damnable train ride back east, and that was to be close enough to catch you."

Rennie hugged herself. Her smile was radiant. She felt as if her heart might burst with gladness.

Jarret's laughter was low, slightly wicked and little regretful. "I see that admission isn't going to entice you into this bed."

She blushed, shaking her head. "I'd like it if you'd come to see Father Daniel with me tomorrow."

"Father Daniel?"

"Actually he's Bishop Colden now. It would be about the church's annulment. I think he can help me."

"A bishop? Aren't you reaching awfully high, Rennie?" Then he saw her secret smile, and he realized he had forgotten for a moment that Jay Mac had planned for the protection of each of his daughters. "Your godfather?" he asked, hardly believing it, yet knowing it was true.

Rennie nodded.

"I'll be damned."

"Bishop Colden can help with that, too."

He gave a short bark of laughter. "I'll keep that in mind."

Rennie jumped to her feet, leaned over the bed, and kissed Jarret full on the mouth. She managed to elude the hand that snaked out to grasp her. Slightly breathless, laughing and glowing, Rennie dropped back into the chair. "Tell me what happened at the board meeting."

Jarret sat up. He pushed back the hair that had fallen across his forehead with the heel of his hand. "Your father told everyone what he had seen at Queen's Point—or rather what he hadn't seen—then he allowed Hollis to make his own explanation. Hollis was prepared. He welcomed an investigation. I'll be surprised if anything can be laid at his door. I think he's managed to cover his tracks quite well."

"That depends on who is doing the investigating," she said.

"Jay Mac asked me. Hollis almost dared him to do it."

"Good."

Jarret shook his head. "I'm not so certain, Rennie. This isn't the sort of tracking I've done before. I can follow foot trails, not paper ones. Don't you think Hollis knew that when he suggested it?"

"He probably *thought* he knew it, but you'll prove him wrong." She said it confidently, matter-of-factly, as if the outcome were a foregone conclusion. "Did Jay Mac talk at all about the train wreck?"

"Only to give a small account of what happened to him. He couldn't speak of any of our suspicions, not without implicating Nina and Hollis."

"I suppose it's a mixed blessing that some things are too personal to become public fodder." She sighed. "Did Jay Mac see Nina afterward?"

Jarret nodded. "For less than an hour. I think it must have been a very civil parting. At least there were no raised voices. Mr. Pinkney packed your father's bags and that was that."

"It's hard to believe," she said quietly, staring at the far wall. "I used to dream about Jay Mac leaving her and coming to live with us. Now that we're all grown up it's not quite the same."

Jarret reached out to her with his hand. This time Rennie took it. She let herself be pulled from the chair and onto the bed. She leaned into Jarret, her head resting in the crook of his shoulder, one arm lying across his middle. His fingers brushed her arm, just touching the edge of the bandage, then dropping to her elbow. It was restful to be held by him in just this manner. He seemed to know it. She closed her eyes.

"You'll have to leave soon," she said.

401

He nodded but made no attempt to move.

Rennie was just fine with that.

It was the pounding below stairs that woke them. Jarret was on his feet immediately, reaching for his gunbelt, while Rennie hit the floor a few beats later. She wobbled, trying to get her bearings and still her heart. "What *is* that?" she asked, reaching for her robe.

"Someone's at the door," he said.

Rennie looked pointedly at Jarret's gun. "Is that necessary?"

He didn't bother answering her. He opened the door to the hallway, pausing only when he realized she was following him. "Where do you think you're going?"

This time she didn't bother answering. Ducking under his arm, Rennie hurried down the hallway.

Jarret caught up to her on the stairs. The pounding was louder now and more frantic. The muffled sound of someone shouting could be heard. "You wait right here while I get the door."

Rennie opened her mouth to argue, then thought better of it. Her eyes shifted warily to the large front door, and she held her ground. Above her she could hear doors opening and closing in the hallway as the rest of her family was roused.

Jarret peered out a side window before he twisted the brass knob. When he let the door fly open Mr. Pinkney nearly fell into the entrance hall. Jarret helped steady the man, realizing soon enough that Jay Mac's butler wasn't drunk. His wild-eyed, distraught features had some cause other than drink.

From the top of the stairs Jay Mac demanded, "What is it, Pinkney? What's brought you here in the middle of the night?"

Pinkney caught his breath. His normally pale skin was

ruddy from the exertion of his run. "It's Mrs. Worth, sir," he said.

"What about her?" Jay Mac asked coldly. He felt Moira's hand encircle his. She gave it a light, cautionary squeeze. "Don't be arrogant, darling," she whispered. "Something's wrong."

Jay Mac took a step down from the landing. "Go on, Pinkney, you can say whatever it is here."

Pinkney removed his hat and held it in front of him. "Mrs. Worth's dead," he said. "She threw herself off the balcony."

Chapter Fifteen

Two days after Pinkney's late night arrival, Mrs. John MacKenzie Worth was honored in a stately memorial service that had in attendance nearly every prominent denizen of New York. Jay Mac accepted the condolences of his friends and colleagues as graciously as he was able. From time to time he intercepted the darting looks of the mourners, the secretive glances that seemed to accuse him of Nina's death. It would have been worse had they known of his request for a divorce mere hours before her suicide. His own conscience gave him little respite.

He wished Moira could have been at his side, but, of course, that was impossible. Yet she comforted him and lent her strength when they were alone, beyond the scrutiny of the public eye. His daughters did not desert him or wonder at his grief. They, unlike those who knew him less well, understood that his sorrow was genuine, that there was no hypocrisy in him saying that he would feel Nina's absence for a long time to come, perhaps always. No one thought he loved Moira any less for that admission, least of all Moira.

Two days after Nina Worth had been laid to rest Jay Mac gathered his family in the parlor and announced that he and Moira were going away to the summerhouse in the

Hudson Valley. "It will only be for a few weeks," he told them. "Long enough for me to collect my thoughts."

Maggie, Skye, and Mary Francis were encouraging. Rennie held her comments.

Jay Mac's arm rested around Moira's shoulders. He said to Rennie, "Your silence is speaking to me, Mary Renee. Are you concerned about Northeast while I'm gone?"

Rennie didn't say anything for a moment. Her eyes consulted Jarret, a question in them.

"You tell them," he said. "Or I will. I don't want to wait until your parents return."

Moira looked expectantly at Rennie; then her glance shifted to Jarret. She saw it in their eyes, the subtle exchange of messages without words. Moira patted Jay Mac's hand gently. "This has nothing to do with Northeast," she said. "Not a thing."

Rennie smoothed the material of her dove gray gown over her lap. She folded and unfolded her hands. She knew her uncharacteristic nervousness was giving her family concern, but she couldn't seem to find the words she needed. She looked at Jarret again. Finally she blurted, "Jarret's asked me to marry him."

Mary Francis laughed. "Is that all?" she asked. "We all *knew* that was in the wind, Rennie." Her beautifully serene smile faded when Rennie continued to look anxious. Mary Francis touched her rosary. "Oh, no, you're not going to have a baby, are you?"

Rennie flushed red even as she glared at her sister. "Must you speak *precisely* what comes to your mind?" she demanded. She shot Jarret an annoyed sideways glance as he laughed under his breath. "I am *not* going to have a baby. At least not right now or anytime in the near future. What I'm trying to say is that I'm going to marry Jarret."

There was complete silence; then everyone began speaking at once. Jarret held up his hand and cut them all off. "I think Rennie meant to tell you that we've already spoken to

Bishop Colden. Rennie's annulment was granted this morning. We want to be married right away."

There was another beat of silence; then they all began talking again. This time Jarret leaned back on the sofa beside Rennie and let them go. Rennie was enveloped in her family's good wishes. Jay Mac patted Jarret on the back on his way to pour drinks from the sideboard. He passed sherry and bourbon around and toasted Rennie and Jarret.

"I couldn't be more pleased if I had planned the thing myself," he said, raising his tumbler.

Rennie eyed her father over the rim of her glass. "Papa," she said dryly, "you *did* plan the thing yourself."

Jay Mac thought about that a moment. "So I did," he said. His broad face looked years younger as it was split by a full, proud smile. "Good for me."

They were married three weeks later in the small chapel of St. Gregory's Church. The guests were family and close friends. Mary Michael and Ethan sent their best wishes from Denver by telegraph. That same evening Moira and Jay Mac left for their home in the valley. Mary Francis returned to the convent. Maggie and Skye were delighted to take a suite of rooms at the St. Mark Hotel, enjoying a measure of independence they were rarely allowed to exercise. Contrary to tradition it was the newlyweds who stayed just where they were.

Rennie and Jarret sat on the hearth rug in the study. There was a fire in the grate, and the two long-stemmed glasses that sat between them held a little champagne. A frosty silver pail held the rest. Mr. and Mrs. Cavanaugh had retired to the carriage house for the night. The fire and the champagne sizzled. Everything else was quiet.

Rennie pulled free several of the pins that anchored the upward sweep of her long hair. She shook her head. The unbound curls cascaded over her shoulders and framed her face. The dark red tips lay with feathery lightness against the ivory satin bodice of her wedding gown. She placed the pins on the apron of the fireplace and combed out her hair with her fingers.

"Let me do that," he said. Jarret moved around her so that he could cradle her with his body. She fit between his raised knees and rested her back against his chest. Jarret's fingers toyed with the ends of her hair. The back of his hand brushed her breast.

"What do you think Hollis will do while Jay Mac's away?" she asked.

Jarret gave her hair a tug. "This is our wedding night," he said, growling in her ear. "Let's leave business at the Worth Building."

"All right."

Her capitulation was too quick to suit Jarret. He knew her mind was still wandering. "There's little he can do," he said. "I had all the accounts and records moved from Jay Mac's office to here last night. That way I don't have to worry that Hollis may somehow tamper with things while Jay Mac's out of town."

Rennie frowned. "How didn't I know you'd done that? Where was I?"

"Right here in the study, collaborating with your father over the Queen's Point project."

"I didn't hear a thing." It amazed her. There was a veritable mountain of ledgers that Jarret had been pouring over in Jay Mac's office these last weeks. The task of moving them in the house couldn't have been accomplished quickly or quietly. "You should have said something. I would have helped."

"Maggie and Skye lent assistance." He kissed her on the temple. "You were concentrating on something else anyway. I'm not surprised you didn't hear."

She brought his hands around her middle and laid her own over his. "Do you think it's safe here?"

Jarret heard the thread of anxiety running through her words. For all that Rennie tried to be indifferent about it, she hadn't felt safe in the house since she discovered her odd dreams of almost a month ago had been a drugged reality. She hadn't been alone in a room in all that time.

"No one's going to get in here again," he said. He gave her a small, reassuring squeeze. "I should have confronted him the day after it happened instead of letting you talk me out of it."

She shook her head. "No, it's better my way. In any event, there was no real proof. If you hadn't told me what happened, I would have gone on thinking it was a dream. Nothing good could have come from your meeting with Hollis. Nina had just killed herself, remember? He would have hardly been rational. Anyway, what did he gain by having Taddy and the others take me out of here, even for a little while? You and Jay Mac have gone on with the investigation, and I went through with the annulment. He's succeeded at nothing in all of this."

Jarret wasn't so certain. Rennie was frightened in a way she had never been before. If that had been Hollis's aim all along, then he had succeeded. Jarret didn't mention that. Instead he said, "We still haven't shown that Hollis was the one who authorized all the expenditures. In fact, most of the evidence points to Jay Mac himself. It's as if Hollis, after setting his plan in motion, simply stepped out of the way."

"But Jay Mac signed what Hollis told him to sign. He trusted Hollis."

Jarret sighed. "I know that, but it doesn't change the outward facts that it looks as if Jay Mac was scheming to steal from his own company."

Rennie's back stiffened. "That's outrageous!" She leaned forward and twisted around to look at Jarret. "Have you told Jay Mac this?"

"We talked about it." He picked up a glass of champagne

and sipped it. "He's always known there could be a problem. He's known it since he publicly confronted Hollis. Jay Mac risked a lot to do that. He thinks I'll uncover something."

Rennie relaxed a little. "You will," she said, settling herself against him again. She raised his hand holding the champagne and drank from his glass. "You know that, don't you?"

"I know you believe it," he said. He tipped the glass more and let her drink her fill. When he drew back, her mouth was wet with champagne. Jarret set aside the glass as Rennie turned in his arms. His mouth hovered over hers. His eyes searched her face.

The small space of air that separated them closed. Their lips touched, clung. He tasted champagne and he tasted Rennie, and the blending was a heady one. Jarret's hands slipped around her back. Her satin gown was warm with her body heat and nearly as smooth as the sensitive skin at her nape. He lifted her hair aside and kissed her neck.

His breath was warm, his mouth damp. She felt the gentle draw of his lips on her skin, the tingling suck of his mouth and the rough, moist edge of his tongue. She turned her head, catching his mouth with her own. It seemed that he took her breath.

Rennie's fingers stroked the back of his head, ruffling strands of dark blond hair, then smoothing them back again. She traced a line around his neck, just above his collar, and when she reached the front she broke their kiss and began to remove the studs from his shirt. Her mouth touched his flesh as it was revealed, and he let her take her time, relishing the anticipation as much as the contact.

Jarret shrugged out of his jacket. Rennie followed by removing his shirt. His skin held its bronze cast in the firelight. She looked at him, simply looked at him. Her eyes darkened as they moved over his shoulders, his chest, and when they lowered to the flat plane of his belly, she saw his skin retract as if she'd touched him there. It seemed forever since she had touched him. She was eager; she was shy.

He watched the play of emotion on her face. In his mind he knew the outcome, but the waiting had an erotic power of its own. When she finally leaned forward and touched her mouth to his skin, he nearly came out of it. He looked down at her bent head, at the crown of her beautiful hair, and saw her then in the service of his pleasure and her own. The fragrance of her, the lingering scents of orange blossoms and lavender and soap, became part of his memory of the moment. His fingers sifted through the silken threads of her hair. It curled around his hand, sliding between his fingers and over the back of his hand like rivulets of warm water, leaving a trace of its softness and its scent embedded in his skin.

There were two dozen tiny cloth-covered buttons at the back of her gown. The bodice and long sleeves were tight-fitting, a shadow of lace and satin across her skin. Jarret flicked at one of the buttons tentatively. It held secure. He ran the palm of his hand from her wrist to her elbow to her shoulder. The pattern of lace remained.

He sighed. Rennie looked up. It was the boyish look of frustration on his face that was endearing, the unshielded desire in his eyes that was intriguing.

"You could always toss up my skirts," she whispered. She looped her arms around his neck and pressed small kisses along his jaw and just below his ear. She nuzzled his neck, teasing him with her smile and muffled laughter and the press of her body.

Jarret palmed her buttocks and began inching up her gown with his fingertips. "I think I will," he said huskily.

She pushed at his shoulders. They toppled over on the hearth rug together because he wouldn't let her go. Her hair spilled forward, creating a curtain around their heads. She looked down at him. His hands still held her bottom. His thighs cradled hers. "Don't you dare," she said. She kissed him on the mouth. Their noses bumped as she kissed him again. They laughed, and the last vestige of nervousness was simply washed away in the fading echoes of that sound.

Rennie sat up and presented her back to him, lifting her hair out of the way. His fingers plucked at the tiny buttons. He took his time, placing kisses in the space of parted material. His patience was maddening, perfectly delicious. When he was finished he stood and drew Rennie to her feet. Taking her by the hand, he led her out of the study and up the stairs. Their progress to her room was slow. He kissed her at the foot of the steps and every few steps thereafter. Each one took a bit longer, and the bodice of her gown dipped a little lower. By the time they reached the second-floor landing it was rolled around her waist, and the swell of her breasts rose above her corset and chemise. Jarret's mouth traced the shadowed curves.

Just outside the door to her room he lifted Rennie. Her arms circled his neck. The kiss they shared was long and slow and deep, and then they were at the edge of the bed, stepping out of their clothes with careless regard for their finery. Rennie shimmied out of her ivory gown. She sat on the edge of the bed to remove her shoes and stockings. She cast a sideways glance at Jarret and smiled slowly, with her eyes more than her mouth. He was watching her.

"Siren," he said. His own smile was wicked as his eyes grazed the line of her body. He kicked his trousers out of the way and tugged on the drawstring of his drawers.

Rennie felt her breathing come a little faster. She fumbled with the laces to her corset.

"Need some help with that?" he asked.

He was standing right beside her, and she had no idea how he had got there. She nodded. Speaking just now was difficult.

Jarret's fingers tugged at the laces. He kissed her bare shoulders and the back of her neck. His hands smoothed

411

away the marks on her skin made by the stiff whalebone stays. She twisted around and kissed him full on the mouth. He swept back the covers as she wriggled out of her pantalettes. Out of the corner of his eye Jarret saw them sail in an arc over the side of the bed. His wicked smile was pressed in the valley of her breasts. He could feel her racing heart against his mouth.

Rennie's breasts swelled under Jarret's touch. He traced a spiral with his fingers. Her nipple hardened. He covered it with his mouth, soothed the tingling heat of it with his tongue. The pleasure of it made her gasp. His hand slipped between their naked bodies and stroked her inner thigh. She thought she would never catch her breath. Her skin was all sensation.

Jarret's fingers probed, teased. Her thighs parted. She caressed his back from shoulder to hip and felt the press of his arousal, the heat and hardness of him against her. He whispered in her ear. She barely understood his husky command and responded as much out of her own need as his, raising her hips and guiding him into her. His mouth found the hollow of her throat. She arched her neck, and in the next beat her body followed. Her heels pressed into the mattress. Her fingers made small indentations in his flesh. This time his mouth caught the sound of her desiring and the breathless pitch of her passion.

He thrust into her hard; the rigid length of him filled her. She tightened around him everywhere. Her legs pressed his flanks, and the soles of her feet stroked his calves. Her arms circled him; her hips cradled him.

The liquid heat at Rennie's center spilled over and spread to the tips of her fingers. Her body trembled in the wake of the tension that pulled her flesh taut. Jarret felt her heat, her release, and took it into him as he might his next breath. It felt as necessary.

She watched his face, the features that were hardened by his need. The deep blue of his eyes had all but disappeared.

There was an edge of severity around the line of his mouth. He let her see how much she was wanted, how much she was desired. He was unafraid to let her know, and in Rennie's eyes his naked passion was his strength. She urged him on, entreating him with husky whispers. His thrusts became shallow, quickened. He surged against her as her fingers threaded through his. His knuckles whitened. He was part of her, filling her, his mouth hot on hers when she took his seed.

It was some time later that Jarret pulled a sheet over their perspiring bodies. Their breathing had already slowed. Rennie's eyelids were heavy, her smile sleepy. When he leaned across her to turn back the lamp, she kissed the underside of his elbow. He liked that.

Jarret doubled his pillow under his head so that he could see Rennie better. She turned on her side. Her fingertips lightly stroked his chest. Her skin seemed luminous even in the shadowed room.

"Mrs. Sullivan," he said.

"Yes?"

He laughed. "I was just seeing if you'd answer."

She tweaked him and said primly, "I'll answer when it suits me, Mr. Sullivan."

Jarret leaned toward her. He bent his head so that his mouth was just above hers. "Is that so?" he asked. He managed to make his tone suitably threatening. It was the laughter in his eyes that undid the effect.

"Hmmm."

The flat, serious shape of her mouth intrigued him. She was fighting a smile. He waited her out, nudging her nose with his, kissing her on the corner of her mouth and at her temple. "Mrs. Sullivan," he said.

She smiled brilliantly. "Just now it suits me." Then she opened her mouth under him and kissed him deeply.

Jarret pulled her closer. His hand rested on her hip, and his thumb made a pass across her smooth skin. The kiss became more leisurely, almost lethargic. He drew back, watching her, and laughed lowly as her heavy lids drooped closed. "We've only been married a day," he whispered, "and already lovemaking bores you."

"Not bored," she said, making no effort to open her eyes. "Just tired . . . the champagne does that. You know I have no head for drink." She wrinkled her nose as he kissed the tip and raised a faint smile. "It was a lovely ceremony, wasn't it?" She slipped her feet just under his leg and warmed herself. She placed one hand lightly on his chest. "I think I like being married to you, Mr. Sullivan."

He trapped her hand. "Good. Because I don't care who you know; you're not getting out of it." He noticed that Rennie didn't take offense to his statement. Instead her sleepy smile deepened as she nestled close, secured by his words, not threatened.

It was startling for Rennie to wake and not find Jarret beside her. Outside it was still dark. Where the drapes had been drawn back, moonshine slanted across the floor. Rennie sat up, listening for sounds from the adjoining dressing and bathing rooms. There was nothing. There were no longer any flames in the fireplace, only glowing embers. Shadows on the wall seemed ominous. Rennie felt the first wave of alarm wash over her and tried not to give into rising panic. She consciously steadied her breathing as she sat on the edge of the bed. Her dressing gown was lying on a nearby chair. She put it on and tied the sash securely around her waist.

He wasn't on the balcony or in the adjoining rooms. Rennie lighted the lamp and carried it into the hallway. At the top of the stairs she listened carefully for sounds below. The normal creaks and groans of the house did not seem so reassuring now. Rennie hovered on the first step, then drew back, not able to make herself take the stairs. She leaned against the wall, the lamp trembling in her hand, her heart in her mouth.

"Coward," she said to herself. It was enough to propel her forward along the hallway. She didn't bother searching every room for Jarret; she looked for a crack of light coming from beneath one of the doors. At the foot of the door to his former bedchamber, she finally found it. Blowing out the lamp, Rennie set it aside in the hallway.

She had planned to be furious at him for abandoning her, but when she stepped into the room and saw him, and saw that he was oblivious to her presence, her anger, her fear, simply melted away. Her heart went out to him.

He was sitting in a hard-backed chair, his shoulders hunched over the tiny secretary's desk that had been moved into the room. The chair was too small to contain his sprawling body; the desk was too small to contain the scattering of ledgers and folders. They lay on the floor at his feet and under the desk, piled unevenly in one corner, and stacked haphazardly on the bed. One of them lay open in front of Jarret now. He stared at it for a long time, then sighed. Leaning back in the chair, he stretched his legs and rubbed his eyes.

Rennie approached him from behind. She saw him stiffen as he sensed a presence, then relax just a bit as he sensed *her* presence. She placed her hands on his tightly bunched shoulders and began to massage. A shudder rippled through his muscles, and she absorbed the ache and tension with her fingertips. Rennie leaned forward once and kissed him at the temple. He reached back and laid one of his hands over hers.

"It's the middle of the night," she said softly. "You should come back to bed."

He shook his head. "I wouldn't be able to sleep."

Rennie began massaging his shoulders again, dissolving the knots. "Perhaps I don't want you to."

A weary, but appreciative smile touched Jarret's mouth.

"I wouldn't be able to do anything else, either."

Her fingers tightened on his flesh, pinching a little. She let go when he pretended to wince in great pain. "You don't have to do this tonight," she said more seriously. "These ledgers will be here in the morning."

Jarret twisted around in the chair, dislodging Rennie's soothing hands. "It doesn't matter how long they'll be here—a day, a week, a month—the answer's not going to come to me this way. I'm no good at this sort of thing, Rennie, or at least I'm not as good as Hollis. I can't find anything in all these accounts that points to him. Either the man's completely covered his tracks or there were never any tracks to cover."

Rennie took a step back from his chair. "How can that be?" she said. She walked over to the fireplace and poked at the blistering coals. "There *has* to be something. You're not thinking Hollis is innocent, are you?"

He shrugged. "Perhaps he is—in a way."

Her fingers tightened around the poker. "I don't understand."

"It depends on the accusation. We can't prove anything about the accident at Juggler's Jump from these ledgers. We've always known that if Hollis was responsible for the wreck, he didn't actually pull the pins himself."

"He paid someone," she said. "Maybe even more than one person."

"But not out of Northeast's accounts. That's a dead end." He turned over a page and ran his finger along the entries. "A lot of money went to a contracting outfit in Denver. This company was supposed to be directing the project at Queen's Point and reporting directly to Hollis."

"That's it, then," she said, putting down the poker. "I'll wager when you try to find the contractor you'll discover he doesn't really exist. Hollis has been funneling the money for supplies and wages, and who knows what else, to a company that isn't really there. That money's probably sitting in a bank account in Denver—with Hollis's name on it."

"I've already found the contractor. You're right; it's a front."

Rennie's eyes widened. "But that's wonderful, Jarret! How can you be so discouraged when you've already learned so much? Does Jay Mac know this yet?"

"He knows. I told him as soon as I discovered it. That was several weeks ago."

A faint frown pulled at the corners of Rennie's mouth. She couldn't understand why Jarret hadn't told her before, or why he didn't share her excitement. "It's almost settled, then, isn't it?" she asked. She sank slowly into the large, overstuffed chair and tucked her dressing gown modestly around her legs. "We only have to show that Hollis received the money through the fraudulent contracting company."

Jarret bent down and picked up a file from the floor at his feet. He handed it to Rennie. "In here is the correspondence from the contracting firm to Northeast. Some of it's written, but most of it comes in the form of telegrams. It's all pretty much about the progress of the project. Some of it is a request for release of more funds. You can see that all of it is addressed to Hollis as head of the operation here in New York."

"It all seems legitimate."

He nodded. "I'm sure Hollis's defense will be that he thought it was legitimate, too." He went on patiently when Rennie gave him a puzzled look. "I suspect that Hollis intends to show that *he* was the dupe, Rennie. If he can make others believe that Jay Mac recommended this contracting company, then he has nothing to worry about."

Her frown deepened as she leafed through the correspondence again, this time looking more closely at the name of the contractor and the company.

"I said I found the contractor," Jarret said, "and I even found the account where the money's being held; but I

417

never said that Hollis Banks has his name in any part of it."

Color drained from Rennie's face as she stared at the file in her hands. "Seton Contracting . . . Seton . . ." She looked up at Jarret. "It's an anagram for Stone. The person at the other end of all this money is Ethan, isn't it?"

Jarret nodded and laughed humorlessly. "Not that he knew about it until I sent a telegram informing him. He did indeed discover that Denver's Federal Bank had an account opened for Seton Contracting and that he was named as its owner. There was just over three hundred thousand dollars in it."

"Oh, my God."

"And your father wrote the drafts, Rennie," he said quietly. "Hollis went to your father with the letters in your hands as evidence of how the work was progressing, and your father released the funds for the project. You see how it appears, don't you? It's as if Jay Mac was working with Ethan to defraud Northeast. *That's* what these accounts show."

"No one would believe that," she said. But even to her own ears Rennie did not sound convinced. She dropped the file on the floor so carelessly that its contents scattered. Some drifted dangerously closed to the fire. "We should burn them," she said, starting to rise. "There would be nothing to—"

Jarret stood and blocked her path. He gently pressed her shoulders and encouraged her to sit again. He knelt and gathered the papers. "I'd be very surprised if Hollis doesn't have some record of all this correspondence," he said. "Or at least some witnesses to it. If this suddenly disappeared, it would be more incriminating to Jay Mac." He slid the file on the desk, then sat on the curved arm of Rennie's chair. "We both know there is no conspiracy between Ethan and Jay Mac, yet all the evidence points to one. We're both convinced that Hollis Banks is responsible, yet there's no evidence to support that conviction."

"Hollis knows that, doesn't he?" Rennie said.

"It's the way it was planned."

Rennie was silent, thinking. She rubbed the bridge of her nose with her thumb and forefinger. "Three hundred thousand dollars," she said softly. "All of it in Ethan's name. If Hollis doesn't want the money, then what—"

"Does he want?" Jarret finished for her. "He wants the company. Hollis plans to be the head of Northeast Rail."

"Jay Mac will dissolve the company first," she said fiercely.

Jarret gave her a moment to think about what she'd said before he explained gently. "No, he won't. He can't. Your father's a very wealthy man, Rennie, but Northeast is a company with enormous debt, much more than Jay Mac can pay out of his own pocket. Northeast's creditors, the banks, the private investors, aren't going to let your father simply close his shop when keeping Northeast running means a return on their loans and investments. You know enough about how things operate to realize that."

The eyes that Rennie raised to Jarret were pained. "Jay Mac's thinking of stepping down, isn't he?" she asked quietly. "That's why he's gone to the summerhouse with Mama. It isn't only because of Nina's death that he wants some time away from the city." Jarret didn't have to answer. She saw the truth in his face. "He should have told me . . . *you* should have told me."

"He didn't want it to interfere with our wedding," said Jarret. "And neither did I. Until tonight I suppose I hoped that something would jump out at me, that your faith in me would be justified. But it's not going to happen, Rennie. Hollis has probably won. Jay Mac can still choose to fight it out with him, but the scandal will discredit Northeast, perhaps even start a panic. Loans will be called in. Your father could lose everything. But if the transfer of power is smooth, then Northeast continues to turn a profit; the investors are happy, the banks are happy, and there's public confidence in the company. Jay Mac is also not held up to ridicule."

"He's going to lose shares to Hollis."

Jarret nodded. "More than likely. Hollis is a fool if he doesn't demand a percentage of them in return for taking over the railroad." His tone was dry, resigned. "And I think we've both learned that Hollis is no one's fool."

Rennie rested her head against Jarret's arm. The sleeve of his quilted dressing gown was cool and smooth against her cheek. "If Hollis had all this planned to get control of the company, then why did he try to kill Jay Mac?"

"I could make a guess, but if you want to know the truth, you'd have to ask Hollis."

Rennie drew back, a small crease appearing between her brows as she frowned in deep thought. "Jarret," she said slowly, "if you were tracking someone in the mountains and you lost his trail for a while, what would you do?" She held up her hand, halting his answer a moment. "I mean if you had an idea where he was going in the first place."

Jarret shrugged. It was hardly a trick question. "If I had I good idea where he was going, the trail doesn't really matter. I would get ahead of him and wait. If I couldn't get ahead, I'd corner him and flush him out."

Rennie sat up a bit straighter, her face solemn, her emerald eyes expectant. "Well?" she asked, gesturing at the room full of ledgers and files. "You said it yourself; the answer isn't in the accounts. There's no trail to follow. But you've figured it out without a trail. You know what Hollis's plan is. You know where he's heading with it." She smiled slowly, almost triumphantly. "All we have to do is find a place to corner him."

"Rennie," Jarret said placatingly. "I don't think—"

She wasn't listening to him. "Do you remember when we sought shelter in that abandoned mine? We flushed out that little bear cub easily enough. We were just talking between ourselves, making plans, and he came out because he was curious."

"Hollis isn't a bear cub."

"No, but he's curious. And he's full of pride, Jarret. It's not enough for him to be clever; he has to make certain you *know* he's clever."

Jarret didn't need to be convinced of that. He glanced around the room again, at the stack of ledgers on the bed, the pile in the corner, the mound of them beside the desk. "Flush him out, eh?" he asked thoughtfully. "It could work."

She nodded, making room for him in the chair as he slid off the arm and onto the cushion. They were squeezed comfortably together, both her legs resting across his lap, her bottom pressed tight to his thigh. Her dressing gown opened. Before she could close it Jarret's hand slid under the satin and lay against the curve of her hip.

He bent his head so that their foreheads touched. "You're a very bright lady, Mrs. Sullivan."

She nudged him with her nose. "You inspire me."

His thumb moved back and forth across her hipbone. "I think I like that."

Rennie kissed him softly. "Let's go to bed."

"You *are* full of good ideas tonight."

Hollis Banks stood at the window in his office and stared down on the street below. The traffic seemed to move more quickly when viewed from the height of five stories. It gave him a feeling of power, almost as if he controlled the ebb and flow and changing patterns. He did, in some ways, do just that. Northeast Rail was moving a country, and he was part of it. It was only a matter of time before he controlled it.

That's what made the message on his desk all the more disturbing. Rennie wanted to see him. Turning away from the window, he picked up the note again. It was written in a hasty scrawl, so expansive and sweeping Hollis doubted at first that it was Rennie's hand that had penned it. Close examination did indeed convince him of the genuineness of the letter, if not the content.

"You're bluffing, Rennie," he said softly. He crumpled the paper in his large hand and stuffed it in his jacket pocket. "You don't know the half of it."

He dropped heavily into his chair and swiveled around to face the window again. The early spring sky was clear, bright with sunshine and somehow promising. He let its warmth bathe his features as he leaned back and propped his feet on the windowsill. It couldn't hurt to see her. Jay Mac was out of town. She had to be realizing that control of Northeast was slipping out of her fingers. Her message didn't sound as urgent as it did desperate.

Hollis called to his secretary in the front office. "There's been a change in my plans. Cancel my meeting with Stringer. I'll be leaving early this evening."

Leaving nothing to chance, Hollis arrived at the church a full thirty minutes before his meeting with Rennie. The large oak doors to St. Gregory's opened easily. The vestibule was empty. Hollis's shoes tapped lightly on the polished wooden floors, though he was hardly aware of the sound. He went to the side chapel and poked his head inside. No one was using the room. Satisfied, he closed the door quietly.

A parishioner glanced over her shoulder as he entered the nave of the church. Hollis dipped his fingers in the font, genuflected, and sat down in the last row of pews. It wasn't long before the woman rose from her kneeling bench, lighted some prayer candles at the back of the church, then left altogether. As soon as she was gone Hollis went to the organ loft and investigated. There was no one there. He knelt on the floor and looked under the pews, both in the choir loft and then again in the nave. The rows were clear.

There was no one hiding around the altar or in the nearby robing room. Entering that room made Hollis think of the time Jarret had laid him out on the floor of it. It was not a pleasant memory. He stepped back into the church and glanced around again. He was alone. There was a heavy silence that seemed to lay over everything, as if the air itself absorbed sound rather than conducted it. As it became darker outside, the stained glass windows lost their individual jeweled colors and became nearly as dark as the soldering between the panes.

Hollis adjusted some of the gas lamps. Their light was reflected in the polished wood of the three confessional boxes. He realized there was still a place he hadn't checked. He started walking toward them.

The door in the middle, the priest's box, opened. Hollis stopped in his tracks. The priest stepped out and shut the door. He yawned widely, not bothering to cover his mouth. He noticed Hollis only as he was turning to go to the back of the church.

The priest pushed his glasses up the bridge of his nose and attempted to look alert. Where he had been slumped against the interior wall, sleeping, his hair was rumpled and his cheek was wrinkled. His round and gentle features flushed a ruddy hue. "I've been fairly caught out, haven't I, son?" he asked, smiling a shade guiltily. "I don't usually nap in the confessional."

Hollis smiled broadly and easily. "I believe you, Father."

"Is there something I can do for you?"

"No, I just came in for a moment alone."

The priest looked around the church, nodding, satisfied with that answer. "Then, I'll leave you to it," he said. "My housekeeper's making lemon pie for me this evening." He patted his generous belly and smoothed the twisted fitting of his cassock. "She might hold it back if I'm late." He took a step forward, then paused as the doors to the nave opened. "It doesn't seem like you'll be alone after all, son." His dark eyebrows raised a tad. "Unless you've made plans to meet this one."

Hollis looked over his shoulder and saw Rennie standing on the threshold. She seemed to hesitate when she saw he was not alone. "It's all right, Father. I've never seen her before. We're not using your church as a trysting place."

The priest nodded. "Good evening, then."

Hollis made a polite bow with his head. "Good evening." He sat down on the pew and waited. At the back of the church he could hear Rennie's soft voice as she conversed briefly with the priest. A few minutes passed; then she was sitting beside him.

The church was cold. Rennie kept on her coat. A silk ivory scarf covered most of her hair. She stared straight ahead, and when she spoke her voice barely broke a whisper. "I wasn't sure that you'd come," she said.

Hollis had to bend his head to hear her. "I sent a reply."

"I know. I received it. But I still wasn't sure."

"You'll have to speak up," he said. "I can barely hear you."

Rennie looked around uneasily.

"There's no one else here. I've already checked."

She frowned, turning to him for the first time. "You've checked? What is that supposed to mean?"

"It means I don't trust you, Rennie. I'm not certain why you've asked me here. Oh, I know what your note said, but knowing that you need to talk isn't the same as knowing what you want to talk about." Hollis tried to stretch his long legs under the pew in front of him. It was uncomfortable. He moved closer to the end of the pew and pushed his legs into the aisle. He looked askance at her, almost daring her to slide along the bench toward him. "We were married in this church, Rennie," he said with an ironic smile.

"I don't need to be reminded. If we hadn't had a mass, I

424

wouldn't have required an annulment from the courts *and* the church."

"It didn't seem to prove much of an obstacle," he said, regarding her with a derisive, hooded glance. He laid one hand along the back of the pew. His fingers drummed against the wood, nearly brushing Rennie's shoulder. He waited to see if she would move away. She didn't. "You have some powerful friends. Judge Halsey I've met, of course, but who was the bishop that got you the church decree so quickly?"

"Bishop Colden. My godfather."

Hollis laughed lowly, shaking his head. "I think I made an error choosing Nina over you." His laughter faded, and his dark brown eyes became bleak. "No, that's not true. I wanted Nina. Her death . . ." His voice trailed away. There was a long silence while Hollis stared off into space. He turned to Rennie suddenly and said impatiently, "What do you want, Rennie?"

"The same thing as you," she said. "Northeast Rail."

One of Hollis's heavy brows arched. His fingers stopped their drumming for a beat, then began again. "Is that right? And just how am I supposed to help you achieve your life's ambition?"

"I've seen the writing on the wall, Hollis. You're going to take control away from my father."

"Am I?"

Rennie's features were set gravely, her eyes implacable. She nodded stiffly, watching him closely. "Unless Jarret finds something in the accounts that goes back to you, you've neatly managed to incriminate Jay Mac."

Hollis's broad face was giving nothing away. "That's a serious charge you're making, Rennie. I don't think I like it."

She ignored his subtle denial. "You offered to head the investigation yourself knowing full well that Jay Mac wouldn't stand for it; then you welcomed his naming Jarret to do it in your stead."

"Why shouldn't I?" he asked casually. "I have nothing to hide. I take it your husband's investigation is proving that."

"What I've learned from Jarret is that I've seriously underestimated the depth to which you covet Northeast. I would guess that you've been planning the takeover almost from the moment you arrived at the Worth Building."

"Ambition's not a crime, Rennie." His look was significant. "As you well know. In fact, if you were not so ambitious yourself, I doubt we'd be having this meeting. Isn't that right?"

She didn't flinch from his dark gaze and nodded.

"What is it you expect, then?"

Rennie took a steadying breath and let it out slowly. "I expect to have an equal say in the operation of Northeast," she said baldly.

Hollis didn't blink at her demand. He didn't say anything either. His broad shoulders shook first with the force of his silent laughter. It burst out of him like thunder, reverberating in the hollow interior of the nave. Tears formed at the corners of his eyes, and he eventually pulled out a handkerchief to wipe them away.

She waited him out calmly, and when his laughter faded, she said clearly, "In light of what you've done, Hollis, it's a reasonable request."

He sobered. "What I've done?" he asked. "What *have* I done, Rennie?"

"The night of the confrontation with my father in front of the board, you directed your friends to abduct me from my own home. I recognized Taddy and Hollis, and I heard them talking about you. I know that if things had gone badly for you at the meeting, you would have played me like a trump card, used me to give yourself time to get away."

"I don't know what you're talking about."

His denial was what she expected, and Rennie went on as if he hadn't spoken. "I kept thinking it was the act of a fearful man, and the more I thought about it, the more it surprised me. It appeared you were certain nothing in the ledgers would incriminate you, yet your actions that night would seem to indicate otherwise."

Hollis pulled his legs in from the aisle. He was watching Rennie with a bit of wariness in his dark eyes, but he invited her to go on. "You tell a very good story," he said. "I'm intrigued. What is it that you think you've found?"

She smiled. "Nothing about the Queen's Point project, Hollis. You covered for yourself quite thoroughly there. Quite cleverly, too. Everything points to Jay Mac and Seton Contracting." Rennie chastised Hollis with her expressive green eyes. "Seton Contracting? Seton . . . Stone. That was rather obvious, but then I suppose you meant it to be, isn't that right?"

Hollis shrugged. He folded his arms across his chest. "This is your theory," he said. "You tell me."

"All right, then. It was intentionally obvious. You wanted someone to see the connection. It pointed another finger at Jay Mac by drawing in my sister's husband. You've put Jarret in a bind. The evidence suggests that not only is Jay Mac guilty, but that he was in collusion with Jarret's best friend."

"You should be telling this to the directors, Rennie, not to me. In fact, I would have no way of knowing any of this if you weren't sharing it with me now. Do you think I won't use it?"

"You'd hear it all anyway," she said. "Jarret plans to make a full report. I thought this was a good time to meet with you." She looked around and gestured with her hand to indicate their surroundings. "And a good place."

"Confession?" he asked, chuckling under his breath. "I don't think so. Any confessing I have to do will be done in there." He pointed to the confessionals a few feet from where he sat. He started to rise, finished with his conversation with Rennie. "It's been interesting, but—"

Rennie didn't move. She raised her face to him. "Don't you want to hear about Juggler's Jump?"

Hollis was caught halfway up, halfway down, and completely off guard. He hesitated a moment, then slowly sat down again. "What about Juggler's Jump?"

"Hollis, I've been there. I've seen the wreckage firsthand. I know that what happened wasn't an accident."

"It wasn't?" Both his eyebrows rose as he examined Rennie with new interest. "This is the first I've heard of it."

"How can that be when you were responsible?" She held up her hand, stopping his reply when he would have denied it. "I've always suspected, Hollis, but the difficulty was in proving it. I know you didn't personally pull the coupling pins that derailed No. 412, but you hired the men that did."

Hollis stood now. He towered over Rennie. "I've listened to you this long because what you've had to say has been amusing. That's no longer the case." He started to turn away, but Rennie reached for his coat sleeve and held on. He stopped and stared down at her hand, ready to brush her aside.

"I wondered how you paid them," she said quickly, releasing him before he slapped her away. "I know you're not a wealthy man, Hollis, certainly not in the league where you can pay people to commit crimes for you and then keep paying them to stay quiet about it. At the back of my mind there was always the question of money. I thought you had used Queen's Point to funnel funds to yourself, but the records prove that wasn't the case. Three hundred thousand dollars you let sit in an account in my brother-in-law's name. If Jay Mac had died in the accident, you would have pulled it out, but when he didn't you had to leave it there.

"Juggler's Jump must have cost you something, though. Quite a lot probably." Rennie's smile was sly, her demeanor one of a coconspirator. "And then I remembered something Jarret told me about the afternoon he left New York nearly a year ago. You sent Taddy and Richard and Warren to see him off, and they did it in grand fashion: ruining his gun hand and his livelihood, and taking the draft that Jay Mac had made out to him. The draft was for ten thousand dollars, Hollis. That's enough money to arrange for mass murder and a cover-up."

He backed away from her and stepped into the aisle. "It's a theory unless you have proof."

"You tendered the draft," she said. "I looked through Jay Mac's private accounts. This wasn't a draft drawn on the funds of Northeast, Hollis. He wrote it on his personal account, and when you took it to the bank and forged Jarret's signature it showed up again among my father's receipts. Jay Mac never knew the draft had been stolen and forged. He thought Jarret had collected his money long ago. Only I knew differently."

Hollis shrugged. "So I exchanged the draft for cash. It doesn't prove I used the money to arrange an accident at Juggler's Jump."

"It's a good start, though, don't you think? It's enough for the board to wonder what else you may have done. The draft ties you to Jarret's beating on the platform. It connects you to forgery. I'm afraid it goes to your tactics, Hollis. It gives a person pause when evaluating your character."

He started to walk away. Rennie did not reach for him this time. She had already glimpsed the anger simmering just beneath his rigidly controlled expression. She raised her voice and summoned his attention that way. "Why did you use the draft when you had Nina's money at your disposal?"

Hollis pivoted on the balls of his feet. One of his hands rested heavily on the shoulder of the pew. His fingertips pressed whitely against the wood. "Nina's money?" he asked, one corner of his mouth lifting derisively. "She had no money that your father didn't control. He kept all the house accounts, and he gave her an allowance."

Rennie's mouth parted fractionally. "Oh, just like he did

for my mother. That explains it, then. There wouldn't have been enough to finance a murder." She shied away, retreating a narrow step as Hollis looked as if he wanted to hit her.

He glanced around the church again to make certain they were alone. "You remember what it was like to feel the flat of my hand," he said. "That's good, Rennie. Keep that in mind and stop throwing your groundless accusations at my head."

"I remember your *fists*," she said. "And I'll say what I think. I'm showing you the courtesy of hearing it first. I plan to tell this all to the board." She paused a beat. "Unless . . ."

"Unless?" he asked.

"Unless you give me an equal say in running Northeast."

Hollis's dark eyes narrowed. He thrust his hands in his pockets and rocked backed on his heels. "So we've come back to that."

"It was my purpose in being here," she said calmly.

He was thoughtful. "Who knows about the draft?" he asked.

"Jarret knows it was taken, and he suspects you of arranging its theft, of course; but I haven't told him that I found it in Jay Mac's records." She sighed. "He's been so busy trying to connect you to Queen's Point that I'm quite afraid he overlooked everything else."

"But not you," he said. "You were always clever, Rennie."

Her smile was as insincere as Hollis's compliment.

"Did you tell your husband you're here?" he asked.

"I thought it was better to keep this between us."

"An equal say in running Northeast," he said thoughtfully. "You don't think you're reaching a bit high?"

"On the contrary. I may not be reaching high enough. You *did* try to have my father murdered, Hollis. Sixty people died in that derailment. That's your responsibility."

A muscle worked in Hollis's square jaw. "Let's establish something right now," he said. "Juggler's Jump wasn't my

430

idea. It was Nina's. It was a foolish plan from the beginning, and you're not laying responsibility for it at my feet."

Rennie's mind worked furiously. She wasn't prepared for Hollis to shift the blame to Nina. "You went along with it," she said. "You financed it even though you didn't need to. You had everything already in place for Jay Mac's downfall, yet you agreed to Nina's plan."

"That woman had me tied in knots." As soon as he said the words he wished he could have called them back. He saw Rennie's surprise, and it made him angry and caustic. "You wouldn't know anything about that, would you? How a person can get your thinking all tangled so that you'll do just about anything for them?"

"Is that how it was for you with Nina?" she asked. "I thought you were using her."

"Like I did you?" he asked cuttingly. "No, it wasn't that way with Nina. Well, perhaps at first, but not as time went on. I came to love her . . . or need her . . . I'm not certain anymore what it was. In the beginning I thought our goals were the same, that we both wanted to wrest control of Northeast away from Jay Mac. It was true to a point; then Nina grew impatient and she wanted Jay Mac dead, not merely humiliated."

Rennie was finding it difficult to breathe. "Her method almost succeeded. You nearly gained Northeast after Juggler's Jump. You had control of her interests in the company. You were still married to me, so you had control of mine as well. It almost worked for you."

"It didn't, though. You found your father." His eyes settled hard on Rennie's pale face and bright eyes. "I'm not sorry about that, Rennie. I like Jay Mac. He gave me my first chance. I've always known that someday I wanted to be sitting where he is, but I never wanted him dead in order to do it."

"How am I supposed to believe that?" she asked. "Someone tried to kill him at the train station the moment we re-

431

turned. Are you telling me you didn't have anything to do with that?"

"It was Nina."

"She arranged it."

"She *did* it. Jay Mac knows that. He told her the night he asked her for a divorce."

Rennie frowned. "But how do *you* know that?" she asked softly. "Nina killed herself that night." Rennie's entire body stilled; then her eyes widened a fraction. "You were there, weren't you? She talked to you about what Jay Mac said." She saw it in his face then, the terrible truth that she had never suspected until just this moment. Rennie's knees buckled, and she sat down in the pew again. "Oh, my God, Hollis. You killed her."

"It was an accident!" he said harshly. "We fought about Jay Mac's ultimatum. Nina didn't mind being Jay Mac's widow, but she didn't want to be the former wife. It was all I could do to keep her from going after your father right then. There was no reasoning with her. She went out on the balcony of her room and started ranting there. You can't imagine what it was like. Nina *never* raised her voice. She was suddenly screaming so loud the neighbors could have heard."

"So you pushed her."

"She *fell*."

"You helped her."

"She was going to ruin *everything*." He took his hands out of his pockets and leaned forward, bracing his arms on the back of the pew where Rennie sat. "All my planning. All the intricate work of setting up the Queen's Point project. That was no simpleton's scheme, Rennie. I waited years to find the right project and then had to scramble to make certain you didn't undo it with your maps and your insistence on another route."

"All of it would have been for nothing," she said gently. "You *had* to kill her."

"There was no other way."

"That's right."

He shut his eyes a moment; his shoulders sagged. A breath shuddered through him as he composed himself. "I miss her, Rennie," he said quietly. "I wish things had turned out differently."

"I know you do."

Hollis nodded. His smile was sad, almost regretful. "That makes it easier, then," he said, "to do what I have to do now."

Rennie twisted on the pew to face him better. "What do you—"

Her words were cut off as Hollis's large, powerful hands closed over her throat. Rennie kicked at the pew in front of her and clawed at the wrists that held her neck like a vise. Waves of black clouded her vision. This time she didn't think she was going to faint. She thought she was going to die.

The confessionals on either side of the priest's box swung open simultaneously. Judge Halsey stepped out of one, followed by the uniformed sergeant from the Jones Street Station. Jarret stepped out of the other. His right hand hovered above the handle of his Remington.

"Let her go, Banks," he said. His voice was without inflection and all the colder because of it.

Hollis's eyes darted from Jarret to the judge to the policeman. His fingers loosened on Rennie's throat, but he didn't release her. "Where . . . how . . ." He couldn't believe they had been there all the time. "I *checked,*" he said. He twisted his head as he heard footsteps approaching from the back of the church. The priest who had come out of the confessional earlier was walking toward them.

"A small diversion," the priest called to him. "A necessary one as it turned out. You were very thorough in searching the church for extra ears." His pleasant demeanor faded as he saw Hollis's hands still clutching Ren-

433

nie's neck. "You'd be wise to let my goddaughter go," he said. "Mr. Sullivan looks to be getting a bit anxious about her safety."

Hollis realized the man he was talking to was Bishop Colden. Feeling the trap closing in on him, he released Rennie's neck — and slid his hands under her arms and drew her out of her seat and against him like a shield. In that same instant he saw that Jarret had drawn his gun, but with Rennie's body as his protection, he was unafraid.

"I'm not going to hurt her," he said, "not as long as you let me leave. I have a carriage waiting outside. As soon as we're far enough away, I'll let her go."

"How far is far?" asked Jarret, holding his gun steady. His eyes darted over Rennie, making a quick assessment. She was holding her own, frightened, but not paralyzed by it. "Do you want to leave the city?" he asked. "The state? There isn't any place in this world that's far enough, Hollis. Give it up. Let Rennie go."

"He's right," Judge Halsey said. His gaunt features were stern, his voice compelling. "We've heard everything. Where do you think you can go now?"

Hollis didn't ease his grip. He quickly surveyed the quartet of men. Neither the judge nor the bishop was carrying a weapon. The sergeant only had a nightstick. Hollis's eyes stayed a moment longer on Jarret's gun. It was shaking ever so slightly, just like the hand that held it.

Rennie's attention was also caught by Jarret's gun hand. She saw him attempt to adjust his grip, then roll his shoulder as he tried to get the feeling to return. She realized Hollis had seen it, too, and understood what it meant. Still using her as a shield, he hauled her over the pew and began to back down the side aisle.

"Sorry about the arm, Sullivan," Hollis said. "That must have hurt like hell."

There was no change in Jarret's icy expression, but his shaking gun hand steadied instantly. He raised the Remington confidently and fired off a single shot. It caught Hollis in the shoulder and knocked him backward. His grip on Rennie loosened completely as he fell away.

Hollis was struggling to his knees when Jarret came to stand over him. Jarret put the Remington away and motioned to the sergeant to secure the prisoner. He slipped his hand around Rennie's waist and pulled her close. She was staring at Hollis. "Sorry about the arm," she told him. "It must hurt like hell."

Epilogue

Summer 1877

It was a clear night. The lake surface reflected moonshine. Fish leaped at the stars as though they were glittering bread crumbs. Wrapped in a light shawl, Rennie sat on the grassy bank of the lake and let her feet dangle mere inches from the gently lapping water. A few hundred yards away, separated by a wood of tall pines, was the mining community of Queen's Point. Given the lateness of the hour only a few oil lamps still flickered their smoky yellow light.

Behind Rennie, farther up the mountain, the mining tunnels were marked by lanterns and torches. There was an occasional shout, a tersely barked order, the rattle of machinery as it approached the adit, but most of the sounds of activity in the mines was swallowed in the silver-lined bowels of the mountain.

It did not mean it was a quiet evening. Beyond Rennie's vision, on the downslope of the mountain, a rail gang was laying track along the curve that had been graded only that morning. Hammers slammed against the steel spikes and rails. Heavy timber thudded to the ground. There was a rhythm and a music in the work in progress — at least to

Rennie's ears. Leaning back on her elbows, her eyes closed, Rennie's index fingers wagged to the beat. Her head bobbed slightly in two-quarter time.

She did not hear Jarret's approach. He stopped just behind her, reluctant to invade her favorite sanctuary along the lake. He watched the faint movements of her head and hands. Her dangling feet tapping against the air. When he finally dropped beside her he was smiling. "Conducting?" he asked.

Rennie wasn't startled. These days she no longer needed to hear his steps to sense his presence. Her eyes remained closed. She smiled dreamily and didn't miss a beat. "Hm-mmm. The Queen's Point Symphony."

Jarret listened for a moment. He heard the same steady rhythms and thundering staccatos she did. Tonight she was conducting her own composition. In the morning he would take up the task again. All the men in the rail gang knew who was responsible for deciding what route would be taken, what grades the engines could negotiate, how the tunnels would be structured, and what materials would be used. The men respected Rennie's engineering skills, but as Jay Mac had predicted, they were not keen on taking their orders directly from her. Rennie had written the music; Jarret interpreted it.

It was a good arrangement. Rennie had never aspired to supervise a rail gang, and Jarret was a natural leader. In New York Jay Mac was still taking credit for their success as a team.

Liking the look of her in the moonlight, her skin pale and her lips and hair dark, Jarret leaned toward her and dropped a kiss on her mouth. He meant it to be quick, but Rennie had other ideas. She teased him with parted lips and a hint of peppermint. It took a measure of willpower to pull back.

Rennie gave Jarret a sideways look, her disappointment obvious. "Are you going to be working with the men all through the night?" she asked, suspicious. "They're going to mutiny, Jarret, and then where will I be?"

"I think mutiny can only be properly applied to sailors and their captains," he said dryly. "Anyway, they wanted to lay another quarter mile of track before they quit tonight. We're going to start blasting out the tunnel tomorrow."

"You're three days ahead of schedule."

"I thought you might like that."

She was thoughtful. "I'm not certain I do," she said finally. "I love it here. I'm not so very anxious to leave. Are you?"

"No." There was a lot to recommend Queen's Point, not the least of which was Rennie's own happiness. They had been welcomed by the community from the beginning. The laying of the rails was a much anticipated event, and Rennie's own role in the project was simply accepted. He had never seen her so confident as she was since coming to Queen's Point, and the one thing that had been hanging over her head these last weeks was about to be removed.

Jarret reached in the back pocket of his jeans and pulled out a piece of paper. He waved it in front of her nose.

"What's that?" asked Rennie.

"A telegram from Jay Mac. It just came over the wire. There was a decision this afternoon."

Rennie sat up, took the paper from Jarret, and unfolded it in her lap. She squinted in the darkness to read it.

"Let me help you," he said. "It says, 'Life at hard labor.' The judge finally passed sentence on Hollis, Rennie."

She simply stared at the paper for a long time, saying nothing. It had been six weeks since Rennie and Jarret had finished their testimony against Hollis Banks. The trial had lasted two weeks beyond that. It was sensationalized in newspapers all across the country. Jury deliberations went on for only a few hours before bringing in a guilty verdict. Now the sentencing was done. Rennie had felt as if nothing was settled—until now. "I wondered if it would ever happen." She looked at Jarret, her clear, dark eyes pained. "I'm glad it was this," she said softly. "I never wanted him to hang."

Jarret thought about all the innocent passengers who had died on No. 412. He took back the paper and stuffed it in his pocket. "You're more forgiving than I am."

She shook her head. "I don't believe that. You could have killed him at the church and you didn't."

"I was damn lucky not to have killed you at the church."

Rennie didn't believe that, either. "Your hand was rock steady. You were only shaking to lead Hollis into a misstep—and he took the bait. I was never in the least danger from you."

"You sound awfully certain that's the way it happened," he said, raising his eyebrows and giving her a sideways glance. "Your confidence in me is duly noted, if slightly misplaced."

He had managed to plant a small seed of doubt. She looked at him skeptically, frowning. In return, he grinned. Rennie shook her head, not knowing what to make of him. "You're never going to tell me the truth, are you?" she asked.

"Can't. I'm not certain I know it myself." He remembered his heart pounding, his hand trembling, the shoulder dropping at an odd angle, and for the life of him didn't know what was fear and what was fakery. At the moment Hollis Banks started to leave with Rennie, an absolute sense of calm had settled over him. He acted because it was never a choice *not* to. "I recall they were the longest seconds of my life," he said. "I just don't remember what happened in them."

Rennie laid her hand over his injured shoulder and rubbed his arm gently. "It was bothering you today, wasn't it? I was watching you."

"Were you?" He stretched out, laying his head in her lap. She continued to massage his shoulder, and her touch was as healing as anything a doctor had ever done for him. "That must be it, then."

"What must be it?"

"You'll think I'm crazy," he said, closing his eyes. A small smile came to his lips. "The hair on the back of my neck was standing up most of the afternoon. I thought Dancer Tubbs was around."

Rennie's fingers stilled for a moment, then resumed their gentle kneading. "Jarret, I was watching you this morning while you were handing out assignments . . . not this afternoon."

"It couldn't have been Dancer," he said. "He wouldn't risk showing himself in public during the day."

"He didn't risk it, did he? No one saw him."

Jarret laughed. "Rennie. We don't even know that he was here."

"The hair stood up on the back of your neck. That's good enough for me."

He played along. It was worth it to keep her busy on his shoulder. Occasionally her fingertips would graze his neck just above his collar. That was very good, too. "Perhaps you have some theory as to why he's skulking around Queen's Point."

"Maybe he thinks the railroad is a threat to his peace."

"I don't know. Queen's Point is a good distance from Dancer's bailiwick."

"Maybe he's just curious."

"Dancer Tubbs keeps his privacy simply because he's generally not curious."

"Or maybe," she said slowly, giving his shoulder a slight squeeze, "he's come to take care of a bird with a broken wing."

Jarret's brows came together. "Bird with a . . . ?" He sighed. "You mean me, I suppose."

"Mmmm."

"I hardly think that's likely."

441

"Why? Ever since we got here you've been making certain Dancer's had supplies. I know Jay Mac asked you to look after him, but you would have done it on your own. He's come around to repay you. That's the only way Dancer can accept the gifts." She tapped him on the nose. "And you know what else?"

"Hmmm?"

"I think if Maggie really wants to learn about healing, she should spend time with Dancer Tubbs."

Jarret commented cautiously. "You, Mrs. Sullivan, have a most interesting imagination."

She bent her head. Her mouth hovered just above Jarret's. "You think so?"

He nodded. His lips brushed hers.

"Want to know what I'm imagining now?" she asked slyly.

"No," he whispered. His eyes opened and he looked into hers. He smiled. "I want to do what you're imagining now."

"You're certain?"

"Hmm-mm."

Rennie gave him a nudge and pushed him off her lap. In seconds she was standing up and wriggling out of her gown, stockings, and shoes. Once Jarret got over his shock and realized what she *really* wanted to do, he joined the race, pitching his dusty boots and jeans behind him, flinging his shirt and flannels into the boughs. He dove into the lake water a heartbeat after Rennie.

She came up laughing, shaking her head and spraying water in a circle around her head. He groped, found her legs, and pulled her under. She sputtered until his lips found hers. She blew bubbles against his mouth. They surfaced together this time, exhilarated and out of breath. Rennie's cotton shift clung to her like a second skin. Jarret's fingers slipped under the hem and initiated the molting process. He pitched the shift onto the bank which left Rennie as naked as he. Her body slipped smoothly against him; her breasts brushed his chest. He palmed her hips and caught her mouth with his. She wrapped her legs around him.

Cool water lapped around their heated bodies. Rennie's arms circled his shoulders. Her mouth pressed hard against his as he guided himself into her. He swallowed her gasp and held her still. She kissed the corner of his mouth, his jaw, and buried her face in the curve of his neck. He whispered against her ear, "I love you, Rennie." His teeth caught her lobe and tugged gently. She shivered against him, not from the cold, but from the heat. He absorbed her shudder and said lowly, "The one thing you can't imagine is how much."

She had only the depth of her own emotion as a gauge, and if what he felt for her was only a fraction of what she returned, then she knew she was very well loved indeed. She told him so.

They made love in the silver lake water, ducking the moonshine and skirting the fish. Their laughter skittered across the surface like skipping stones, and they rose up to meet the pleasure in each other's arms.

Afterward they drifted apart, clinging by the merest touch of their fingers as they caught their breath. Rennie was the first to leave the canopy of stars for the darker canopy of pine boughs. By the time Jarret joined her she was dressed in her gown and shoes and carrying her stockings and dripping-wet shift. She held out his jeans to him and went to retrieve his shirt from the branches.

She made two leaps before she managed to pull it down. Something fell out of the breast pocket. Rennie knelt down and searched the dry bed of needles. Her fingers touched something cool and smooth. It fit neatly into the palm of her hand. She backed into the moonlight while Jarret was putting on his shirt and held up the oval object.

For a moment she thought she held a mirror. It was her own reflection staring back at her . . . and yet it wasn't.

443

What she held was a picture frame. She looked up at Jarret and saw that he was watching her, waiting for her reaction.

"This is a photograph of me," she said softly, wonderingly. "It was on the mantel in my bedroom in New York. When did you . . ."

"Stole it, I'm afraid." He stood just behind her and looked down over her shoulder. "That photograph's been a companion of mine for quite a while. I took it before I left New York—the first time."

Startled, Rennie glanced up at him. "You carried this around all those months before I came to Echo Falls?"

"I never thought I was going to see you again." He slipped his arms around her waist and drew her back against him.

She twisted in his arms and tucked the picture frame back into his breast pocket. Her eyes were luminous. "I know you love me," she said softly, "but I've never known until now how very long it's been."

"Almost since the first," he said, touching his forehead to hers. "And that's nothing compared to forever."

Standing in the circle of his arms, one of her hands over the picture, the picture over his heart, Rennie decided forever might, just might, be long enough.

Put a Little Romance in Your Life with
Georgina Gentry

__**Cheyenne Song**   0-8217-5844-6 $5.99US/$7.99CAN

__**Comanche Cowboy**   0-8217-6211-7 $5.99US/$7.99CAN

__**Eternal Outlaw**   0-8217-6212-5 $5.99US/$7.99CAN

__**Apache Tears**   0-8217-6435-7 $5.99US/$7.99CAN

__**Warrior's Honor**   0-8217-6726-7 $5.99US/$7.99CAN

__**Warrior's Heart**   0-8217-7076-4 $5.99US/$7.99CAN

__**To Tame a Savage**   0-8217-7077-2 $5.99US/$7.99CAN

Available Wherever Books Are Sold!

Visit our website at **www.kensingtonbooks.com.**

BOOK YOUR PLACE ON OUR WEBSITE AND MAKE THE READING CONNECTION!

We've created a customized website just for our very special readers, where you can get the inside scoop on everything that's going on with Zebra, Pinnacle and Kensington books.

When you come online, you'll have the exciting opportunity to:

- View covers of upcoming books

- Read sample chapters

- Learn about our future publishing schedule (listed by publication month *and author*)

- Find out when your favorite authors will be visiting a city near you

- Search for and order backlist books from our online catalog

- Check out author bios and background information

- Send e-mail to your favorite authors

- Meet the Kensington staff online

- Join us in weekly chats with authors, readers and other guests

- Get writing guidelines

- AND MUCH MORE!

Visit our website at
http://www.kensingtonbooks.com